Red Rose Academy

Thomas Brant

Published by T Brant Publishing

Printed in Great Britain

Print ISBN 978-1-0683772-1-1

eBook ISBN 978-1-0683772-9-7

This is a novel which is pure fiction. All characters are of the age of consent in the United Kingdom (age 18+) and feature scenes of a sexual nature. There are no relationships between students and lecturers, however some student tutors and their peers may have relations in this novel.

If you are under the age of adulthood in your local jurisdiction, please stop reading immediately and hand this novel to an adult for them to return it to the retailer who sold it.

Consent is key in healthy relationships, and, although this does not show consent being given in the novel, the characters, off screen, do give consent. If you have any concerns about a relationship, you may be in and need more advice about consent, go to https://www.areyouok.co.uk/sexual-violence-and-abuse/a-z-of-consent/. Other resources are available in your local jurisdiction.

CHAPTER 1 – What Happens In The Ballet Studio...

Monday 28th October 2024

If anyone ever asked Maria Kovacs what she'd think, being a Third Year at the Red Rose Academy of Performing Arts, a university in all but name, where drama, ballet, music, and the finest threads of theatrical tradition wound through every corridor and hidden stairwell, she would have rolled her eyes and said something sarcastic, something dismissive—because she had learned, quickly, that to show you cared was to invite disaster. But inside, she cared so much it hurt. The Academy had become the pulse of her life, a place where ambitions, rivalries, and fragile, electric hope sparked and fizzed from dawn until the small hours.

The Academy, a Mancunian institution which, in its formative years in the 1960s and 1970s, when Manchester was part of the county of Lancashire, its name had first been whispered with a mixture of awe and scepticism, now sat in the heart of a city reborn. Old brickwork met glassy modernity, the traffic's constant hum interrupted by laughter or, sometimes, the faintest echo of a piano etude escaping open windows.

In its heyday, graduates from the esteemed Academy would go on to Pinewood, Granada, Central or even Elstree film and television productions, West End theatre, the Royal Ballet and, in rare cases, further afield to New York or the stages of continental Europe. Nowadays, post-pandemic, it was a hotbed of sweat, sex and performances, as the lecturers and tutors, a mix of former

BBC day players, radio hosts, failed West End stars and a Chancellor who was more interested in running for elected office than running the place, tried to steer a new generation through an old, stubborn world. To Maria, all this was simply the air she breathed. If the walls of Red Rose were spattered with the ghosts of genius, so too were they saturated with anxiety and desire, with the clatter of tap shoes down corridors and the muffled sobs of students who'd crashed and burned—sometimes on stage, sometimes just behind it.

This Monday, the clocks had gone back, and the city felt both sharper and greyer for it. The day was brittle. The trees along Oxford Road wore their last, battered leaves like a costume that might drop at any moment, and Maria pulled her battered North Face jacket close as she darted across the traffic, ignoring the shout of a Deliveroo cyclist who barely missed her at the lights. She was late—again. There had been a night out, a bottle of red, and an orgy that, Maria knew, was not an exception to the rule for Red Rose students who danced, sang, acted, and ached their way through their early twenties with the unrepentant, romantic hedonism of those who believed, with every cell, that they might just be special. There'd been laughter and music and bodies pressed together in someone's poky flat above a vegan curry house in Chorlton, her best friend, Aisha, an Omani Muslim who was the daughter of an Oman Air executive, taking 10 cocks in her mouth and two in her pussy like a seasoned libertine while reciting a Shakespearean sonnet between thrusts while her Israeli boyfriend, an IDF soldier who was stuck in the West Bank, was forced to watch on Facetime, Aisha warning him that if he "even considered wanking, she'd fly straight to Israel and cut his balls off with a rusty kitchen knife."

Maria, for her part, had ended up being anally drilled by a Hungarian cellist who was a First Year at Red Rose, his erection miniscule and his ego unbearably inflated, as he was the eldest son of the Hungarian Minister for Transport, and so had no intention of being anything other than entirely, obscenely entitled. It had been a night of collisions: flesh against flesh, egos against egos, whispered promises and drunken boasts that faded in the grey morning light. By the time Maria had stumbled out of the flat, shoes in hand, jacket askew, hair slicked to her cheekbones with sweat, the trams had already begun their Monday shuffle, and the world had lost its forgiving, nocturnal softness.

Now, as she pushed through the battered green doors of the Academy's main entrance, Maria could smell the institution itself—sweat, floor polish, something slightly fungal beneath the radiators' metallic heat. The receptionist, an ancient drag queen named Lorraine who claimed to have once been up for a role in Coronation Street but lost out "on account of being too beautiful for telly, darling," raised a pencilled eyebrow.

"You're late, Kovacs. Again." Lorraine's voice slid between threat and affection, never quite one or the other.

Maria grinned, but it was the kind of grin that didn't reach her eyes. "Wouldn't want to break tradition."

"Miss Yelena's gone sick, and you're to act as tutor for the First Year Ballet Class today."

Maria sighed, as Miss Yelena, a Russian born ballet mistress whose temper was legendary and whose classes were only slightly less terrifying than death itself, never took sick days. The idea that Yelena, who once danced lead in Novosibirsk with a broken ankle, would submit to something as mortal as a 'sick day' was unthinkable. It stank of a cover-up, of politics, or—worse—some kind of power play that Maria had stumbled into without warning.

As a Third Year, she and her fellow Thirds were often required to cover as student tutors for lecturers who had been sacked, gone AWOL, or simply vanished between terms—a hazard at the Academy, where no contract was sacred and every day felt like a test you didn't remember agreeing to. Being 21, and so capable enough to command a room, but not yet so accomplished as to be immune to humiliation, Maria found herself frequently balanced on the knife-edge between awe and resentment. Especially with the First Years—those wide-eyed, freshly scrubbed hopefuls whose every movement seemed to announce I belong here (and yet, secretly, Do I belong here?).

She took the marble steps two at a time, long legs burning from too little sleep, and pushed through the fire doors that led to the staff changing room adjacent to Studio 3— the so-called "ballet crypt," named for its basement setting and draughty chill. Her trainers squeaked on the parquet, the echoes ricocheting off the mirrors like mocking laughter. For a split second, she caught her reflection—dark eyes smudged with kohl, black hair twisted back, mouth set in a line that could have been determination or exhaustion.

From her rucksack, Maria pulled her battered ballet kit: soft shoes, spare tights, the 10th pair she'd brought this term, as, when the lecturers were absent or just plain zoned out, as they were underpaid, understaffed, and despite being a degree granting university in all but name, unprepared, the students like herself would fuck, be it in the ballet studios, the changing rooms, the theatre, or even in the dining hall. One time they had had an orgy in the ballet studio itself, the mirrors steamed and fogged, every pirouette and plié echoing with the memory of sweat-slicked skin and urgent, half-choked laughter. That was the unspoken legacy of Red Rose: genius, debauchery, the endless, desperate need to carve out a story in the stonework, to matter, even if only for a night.

Maria's mind was already drifting back to those shadowed hours as she peeled off her jeans and hoodie, shivering in the staff changing room as the heating clanged and coughed like a dying beast. Her phone buzzed: Aisha, a string of exclamation marks and a selfie, pouting with a coffee and last night's eyeliner. Maria ignored it. She didn't need more reminders of everything waiting for her outside this day's duty.

She fastened her hair in a messy knot, snapped the elastic tight. Her muscles twinged—telltale reminders of her own over-indulgence—but discipline forced her movements into ritual: tights, leotard, ballet shoes laced, back straight, chin high. She was Maria Kovacs, Third Year, and today she would rule the crypt.

Through the small window in the staff door, she could see the First Years waiting. Some perched nervously on the benches, others stretching, while one of the male ballet students was giving a female one oral, as she was on her hands, him holding her steady while her ripped tights revealed pale thighs, his tongue flicking with the casual obscenity of someone entirely at home in this world.

The fact that she was used to it, as, when she was a first year, barely the day after Freshers week, she had lost her own virginity on these very benches—against the cool mirror, bruised by the parquet, watched in lazy amusement by two drama students and a pianist—no longer shocked Maria. The fact that the duo were being filmed, no doubt for the Red Rose Noticeboard, a social media app that the Academy used as a sort of unofficial blackmail board, barely raised her eyebrow. If you survived a year at Red Rose, you learned to ignore the click of cameras and the thrum of exhibitionism—unless you were the one with leverage, or the one being leveraged.

Watching, she felt a kind of perversion, watching 18 year olds doing what, in a way, she herself had done merely 3 years earlier when she was a First Year herself—eager, uncertain, hungry for the thrill of breaking every rule that Red Rose pretended to care about. A pang of nostalgia, as sharp as a bruise, struck her as she remembered the icy burn of the floor, the press of someone else's skin, the music of whispered encouragements and mocking laughter. Nothing here was truly private; secrets at Red Rose were just currency—bargained, traded, spent, and spent again until nothing remained but memory and reputation.

As she walked in, she felt someone rush in behind her, and fall into her, and she instantly knew it was a male with the way his cock rubbed against her arse as they fell forwards.

"What you doing here?" she heard, and she instantly knew it was Justin Harrison, a fellow Third Year ballet student, the son of a co-op checkout worker, and constantly erect who never seemed to take anything seriously—except, perhaps, ballet, and even that he approached with the irreverence of someone who had always been told "no" and decided that, instead, he would make "yes" an art form. Justin's laughter was always just on the edge of mockery, and right now, his grip on Maria's waist was more possessive than apologetic, fingers digging into her hipbone with the easy entitlement of someone who, for all his working-class origins, had mastered the social choreography of the Academy's relentless, pleasure-hungry society.

She felt him lift her up, and, turning, noticed he was mere millimetres from her pussy with his cock, his erection pressed against the thin fabric of her leotard, the heat of him seeping through like a brand. The studio's mirrors caught every angle: the spill of her dark hair, the flush creeping up her neck, Justin's grin—crooked, unrepentant, eyes glittering with the kind of mischief that had got him suspended twice last term and yet somehow never expelled. The First Years had frozen mid-act; the girl on the bench let out a small, involuntary gasp, her partner's head still buried between her thighs, though his rhythm had faltered, tongue stilled by the sudden shift in the room's gravity.

"Justin, get off me, you absolute prick," Maria hissed, but there was no real venom in it—only the reflex of someone who had learned that outrage was a luxury she couldn't always afford. She twisted in his grip, elbow jabbing sharply into his ribs, and he released her with a theatrical stagger, hands raised in mock surrender.

"Easy, Kovacs. Just making sure you're awake. Heard Yelena's croaked it—flu, they're saying. Or maybe she's finally defected back to Putin. Either way, you're the boss now." His voice carried, loud enough for the First Years to hear, and a ripple of nervous laughter spread through the room like spilled water. Justin's erection hadn't flagged; if anything, it strained harder against his leggings, a blatant advertisement of his priorities. He was twenty-one, same as her, but carried himself like a man who'd never been told no and never would be.

Maria shoved Justin away with a force that sent him stumbling back a step, his bare feet slapping against the parquet like an off-beat castanet. The First Years were still gawping, the girl on the bench—blonde, freckled, legs akimbo—clamping her thighs shut as if modesty had suddenly remembered her address. Her partner, a lanky lad with a mop of curls and a tongue that had been mid-flick, wiped his mouth with the back of his hand, eyes wide as saucers. The phone propped against a water bottle on the floor kept recording, its red light blinking like a voyeuristic heartbeat.

"You know we've got no tutorial material," Justin said, wrapping his arms around her like a cloak, breath warm against her ear. "Might as well let them shag, and us two go into the Governess's Office and fuck ourselves."

Maria snorted, not so much in amusement as in a kind of weary acknowledgment. This was Red Rose, after all; the rules were more like suggestions, and the only true sin was to be forgettable. But even as Justin's hands lingered, his thumb tracing idle circles along the curve of her hip, Maria kept her eyes on the room—a room that had, in the last three years, become both confessional and execution chamber, a place where secrets were currency and desire was simply another form of communication.

And then she felt it, her 10th pair of tights rip, obviously because they were the cheapest ASDA ones that she had brought due to the fact she was a student and so money was always tight, and suddenly the cold air was prickling not just her skin but her pride. The rip was nothing, just a thin line up her thigh, but she knew from experience it wouldn't last long before it tore wider, a ladder unspooling, an invitation for anyone with a predatory instinct. Maria cursed softly under her breath, feeling the hot pulse of embarrassment—ridiculous, considering everything else that had happened in this room.

"Your fault, Jus. I'm going to have to spend this session commando now," she said, even though, in a way, she did want Justin to fuck her like a dog in heat, and even more so because the ballet studio was both stage and sanctuary, witness and accomplice. But Maria, with a small shrug, kicked away the torn tights, the motion practiced, almost balletic in its resignation. The room, thick with the scent of bodies and anticipation, seemed to lean closer.

Justin grinned, eyes following the pale line of her thigh with open approval. "No one's going to complain,

Kovacs." His hand hovered at her waist again, thumb pressing just above her hipbone, a silent claim.

But Maria shook her head, already pushing him off with the barest pressure. "Later, Jus. First Years need wrangling, or they'll end up eating each other alive—literally and otherwise." Her words were half joke, half warning.

It was then that she noticed the Russian student, Darya, had already pulled her leotard off and her tights, and was on her knees, sucking Tobias, a tall, gaunt boy from Norfolk whose only remarkable feature, so the joke went, was his cock—rumoured to be the only thing in Norfolk worth the train fare to Manchester. Darya, with her pale, inscrutable eyes and knife-sharp jawline, looked up at Maria, her lips stretched around Tobias, eyes blazing with a mixture of challenge and worship. The mirrors, ever vigilant, threw the image back from every angle, multiplying the act until the room itself seemed a maze of limbs and open mouths.

"Fuck it, might as well," Maria said, sighing as Justin's gentle fingers reached the hole in her tights, the gentle pressure making her knees tremble, the anticipation vibrating through her as if she were about to take the stage for a solo.

The ballet studio had always been a paradox—sterile, disciplined, a shrine to control—yet here, control was only ever skin-deep. Power, Maria thought, was a game best played without rules.

She walked to the barre, the old wood warm from the radiators, the metal brackets scarred by years of hands and feet and, more recently, by acts for which the timetable made no allowance. Around her, the First Years moved in the electric, expectant chaos that came whenever authority was absent. Maria didn't bother to check the register; she'd know soon enough who was here and who wasn't by the stories that would circulate on the Noticeboard by lunchtime.

The rip in her tights laddered higher as Justin's fingers slid along the seam. She caught his eye in the mirror, the silent dare passing between them: how far? How much? The ballet studio was never empty, never truly private, and that was the point. Performance and exposure, shame and pride, were just steps in the same dance.

Maria's hand tightened on the barre, the wood slick beneath her palm from generations of rosin and sweat. Justin's fingers had found the tear in her tights and were tracing it upwards, slow, deliberate, like a conductor marking time. The First Years were no longer pretending to stretch; they watched openly now, the blonde girl's thighs still parted, her partner's chin glistening. Darya's head bobbed with mechanical precision, Tobias's hands fisted in her platinum hair, his hips jerking in tiny, involuntary thrusts. The mirrors caught it all—every angle, every flicker of eyelid, every bead of sweat sliding down a temple. Maria felt the room's pulse sync with her own, a low thrum that started between her legs and radiated outwards.

She gritted her teeth, keeping her gaze cool, detached, as she addressed the room. "If you lot are going to fuck, at least do it with proper extension. We are ballet dancers, not rutting pigs."

There was laughter—nervous, mocking, and delighted all at once. A boy in the corner was kneeling between two girls, each of them with a leg over his shoulder, and he gave Maria a cocky grin, thrusting his tongue out with exaggerated flourish. Someone else, a drama student who always found his way into ballet for the orgies, clapped sarcastically.

But the laughter was just another part of the Academy's discipline. Shame was currency here, too, and you only survived if you learned to spend it with style.

Justin, taking her words as permission, peeled Maria's leotard down until her breasts spilled free, her nipples already stiff from the chill and the anticipation. He pressed her against the barre, pushing her hips forward so her arse jutted out, exposed to the room and the mirrors.

"You want everyone to watch, Kovacs?" he whispered, the words half threat, half promise.

Maria bit back a moan, forced herself to laugh. "This is Red Rose. If you're not being watched, you don't exist."

Her words echoed, mirrored in the glass, even as Justin slid a hand between her thighs, fingers gliding over slick, heated skin. The sounds in the room—panting, giggling, moans—rose in volume, the rhythm of bodies finding each other in the cold morning light.

Justin's fingers pressed inside her, a deliberate invasion—unhurried, unashamed, making a spectacle of her as much as himself. Maria caught her own eyes in the glass, seeing the flush rise along her cheekbones, the bite-marked line of her lips. There was nothing to hide, not here: only to perform, to let shame curl into a kind of feral pleasure. The room was a kaleidoscope of tangled limbs and reflected faces, gasps rebounding between panes.

She knew that she'd no doubt be on the Noticeboard within the hour, and was, in a way, grateful that only present students could see posts that she was tagged in, not past students, not lecturers, even though some of the past students had made their profiles public, meaning that any of the current students could still trawl through years of debauchery, humiliation, and minor triumphs at their leisure, constructing a private history out of public shame. It didn't matter. Maria's shame was already spent—burned out in the first year, currency she'd traded away for acceptance and a fleeting sense of power. She could feel the eyes on her now—Justin's, yes, hungry and mocking, but also the First Years', all their stares blending into one hot, humming chorus of anticipation.

Justin's hands roamed, unhurried, as if he was kneading dough rather than flesh. He knew how to keep her hovering—never quite giving in, never quite pulling away. His cock, still encased in his leotard, was pressed so insistently between her thighs that Maria half wondered if the thin fabric would give way from sheer force of will. She could feel the wetness slicking her skin, a flush of heat and humiliation and pride all tangled together.

"You remember our first time?" Justin muttered as he fingered her, his cock pressed hard against her inner thigh, voice a low thrum that vibrated in her ear as if he were reciting some forbidden catechism. "Freshers Week. You'd just fucked Harry and Kelv, and you had their cum in your hair, and there I was, nervous as fuck, wanking over the cum on your tits, and then I blasted my load into your mouth."

Maria chuckled, the memory of having had her first threesome, mere hours after losing her virginity, drunk on WKD and vodka shots, stumbling through the corridors of the dorms, Maria only wearing a smile as she was, at the time, 18 and horny as fuck, having been a virgin and having spent the past nearly two years in COVID lockdowns, her only real company a Bluetooth wand and a parade of internet strangers on Telegram. The world had reopened, and Maria had been determined to taste every forbidden thing, to carve her mark into the walls of Red Rose with sweat, spit, and laughter. Justin, for all his laddish banter and crooked smile, had been the first to understand her hunger.

Now, as his fingers curled inside her, coaxing a shudder from deep in her core, Maria's eyes locked with his in the mirror. She could see the challenge there, the invitation to break—just a little—for the crowd, for the institution, for herself.

"Don't stop," she murmured, but Justin was already grinning, teeth flashing as he pressed harder, working her with a lazy, practiced confidence. The room had dissolved into a riot of movement behind them—Darya, still on her knees, had switched to another boy, and two girls in the corner were giggling as they took selfies with one hand, the other tangled between each other's legs. It was chaos, it was theatre, it was a kind of brutal communion that only Red Rose seemed capable of sustaining.

"I never thought that I would find a way out..." the smart speaker in the corner of the room started blaring out, and Maria knew that someone had asked it to play Bee Manic, a Mancunian radio station based at Piccadilly Gardens. She knew that the breakfast show was finishing, as it was nearly half 9, and that the playlist would, like Hits Radio, turn from the biggest hits at 10am to an hour of throwback songs—something absurd, some relic from the 2000s that would bounce off the ballet studio's mirrored walls and turn everything from debauchery to parody. Justin's laughter was hot on her neck, his rhythm never faltering as the pounding bass line shuddered through the cheap speakers. "You hear that?" he whispered, tongue flicking her earlobe. "Perfect soundtrack. Maybe we'll go viral."

Maria only rolled her eyes, half lost in the movement of his hand, in the convergence of memory and sensation. She was aware, always, of every set of eyes on her, of every First Year whose initiation into the Academy's hidden curriculum was happening right now—not in the pages of a student handbook, but in the sweat-slicked, gasping lessons of bodies tangled together before the morning sun had even cleared the city's towers.

She could hear the moans, the slap of skin on skin, the sharp laughter, the music swelling as if the speakers themselves were desperate to drown out the noise. Justin's fingers drove deeper, faster, and she clenched around him, hips bucking, her own voice caught somewhere between gasp and snarl. "Harder," she demanded, and he obeyed, because in this moment, in this room, Maria was queen and supplicant all at once.

And then he stopped, fingers curling wickedly as he withdrew, and she nearly cried out at the sudden emptiness.

"Don't be greedy, Kovacs," Justin whispered. "Let the Firsties fuck you too."

Maria sucked in a large gulp of breath, as she knew that, yes, she would happily give some of the First Years their first real taste of the Red Rose rites; there was a cruel satisfaction in watching the nerves, the hunger, the desperate need to belong. And why not? If you were going to be a legend here, better to be the sort that left an impression carved into flesh as much as memory.

"Ok, then, Jus. If you want me to do that, then... you're going to date me again," she said with a grin that meant that she grasped the reins, if only for a heartbeat. Justin's smirk didn't fade, but there was something in his eyes—surprise, perhaps, or something closer to pride. The power, like everything in Red Rose, was slippery, mercurial; she would give it, take it, spin it between her fingers like ribbon.

"You want a relationship now, Kovacs?" he taunted, but there was a tremor beneath the tease. "Or you just want to make it official for the Noticeboard?"

"Does it matter?" Maria asked, voice low, eyes glinting. "It's all a performance. Singh's still a virgin, isn't he?"

"Yep, he's still got his cherry," Justin replied, his tone dipping from mockery into a strange sort of reverence, as if even here, among the tangled limbs and half-spilled secrets, something as unspoiled as Arjan Singh's innocence was a relic from a different world. The son of a British-Indian shop owner, Arjan was one of the more reserved students—a scholarship boy with perfect pirouettes and hands that trembled whenever anyone looked at him for too long. He'd survived Freshers' Week on sheer invisibility, sliding between the cracks, quietly taking notes and, so the rumour went, praying under his breath before class. He had become, almost unintentionally, the running joke of the year: "You'll never make it at Red Rose until someone's fucked you in the studio, mate." It was said with laughter, with mock-threats, but beneath it lay the truth: Red Rose didn't allow innocence. It chewed it up and spat it out, glittering and changed.

Maria's gaze swept the room, finding Arjan stretched in the far corner, his eyes flicking back and forth between his phone and the floor, as if the device might offer sanctuary from the cacophony of the ballet crypt. His skin shone with the faintest sheen of nerves. Maria smiled, sharp and bright as a razor's edge, and sauntered over, every step a deliberate performance. She could feel Justin's eyes tracking her, the whole room holding its breath, some of the First Years pausing mid-thrust or mid-giggle, curiosity blooming across their faces. The music throbbed in the background—a 2010s pop hit now, absurd and sweet in its nostalgia.

She crouched down beside Arjan, close enough that her bare thigh brushed his, close enough that he could smell the mixture of sweat and perfume, arousal and old floor polish that clung to her skin.

"You alright?" she asked, voice pitched low, gentle but edged with challenge. "You don't have to do anything you don't want, you know. But you can't hide in the corners forever. Not here."

Arjan looked up, eyes huge, dark and shining with a blend of hope and terror. "I'm not hiding. Just… waiting."

"For what?" Maria prompted. The room, sensing a drama unfolding, stilled—a few thrusts slowed, laughter fading to a hum.

Arjan licked his lips, fingers twisting the drawstring of his leggings. "For… the right moment, I suppose. Or the right person." His voice was soft, almost swallowed by the music, but Maria caught every word, felt the tremor in it like a plucked string.

She placed a hand on his knee, feeling the tension coiled there, the way his muscles jumped at the contact. "This is Red Rose, Arjan. There's no 'right moment.' Only now." Her fingers traced upwards, slow, deliberate, mirroring what Justin had done to her moments ago. The mirrors threw the image back: her crouched form, breasts still exposed, nipples peaked; Arjan's flushed face, the bulge in his leggings betraying him despite his best efforts at composure.

Behind her, Justin chuckled, the sound rich with approval. "Go on, Singh. Kovacs doesn't bite—unless you ask nicely."

Arjan's breath hitched. He glanced around the room, taking in the tableau: Darya now straddling Tobias, her hips rolling in slow, hypnotic circles; the blonde girl from earlier being passed between two boys like a shared secret; the drama student in the corner filming everything on his phone, his free hand stroking himself lazily. The air was thick with the scent of sex—musky, sharp, mingled with the faint tang of rosin and sweat. The Bee Manic playlist had shifted to some forgotten 2000s banger, the kind with a beat that pulsed like a heartbeat, urging bodies into motion.

Maria leaned in closer, her lips brushing the shell of Arjan's ear. "You've been watching, haven't you? All term. Taking it in. Wondering what it feels like to be part of it." Her hand slid higher, cupping the unmistakable hardness through the fabric. He was impressively endowed, she noted with a flicker of surprise—rumours had undersold him. "Let me show you. No strings. Just… initiation."

Arjan swallowed hard, his Adam's apple bobbing. "I… I don't know if I can. In front of everyone."

"That's the point," Maria whispered, her thumb circling the head of his cock through the leggings, feeling the damp spot where pre-cum had already seeped through. "Red Rose isn't about hiding. It's about owning it. Owning yourself." She tugged at the waistband, pulling it down just enough to free him. His cock sprang out, thick and veined, the tip glistening. A collective murmur rippled through the room—appreciation, envy, excitement.

Justin sauntered over, his own erection still straining, and clapped Arjan on the shoulder. "Mate, you're hung like a horse. No wonder you've been keeping it under wraps. Afraid you'd scare the girls off?" He laughed, but there was no malice in it—only the easy camaraderie of shared debauchery.

Maria didn't wait for Arjan's consent to solidify; she could feel it in the way his hips twitched towards her touch. She wrapped her fingers around him, stroking slowly, firmly, her grip practiced from countless encounters. Arjan's head fell back against the mirror, a low groan escaping his lips. The glass was cool against his skin, a stark contrast to the heat building in his core.

"See?" Maria murmured, leaning down to flick her tongue over the tip, tasting the salt of him. "Nothing to fear." She took him deeper, her mouth hot and wet, lips sealing around his shaft as she bobbed her head. Arjan's hands fisted at his sides, knuckles white, as if he were afraid to touch her, afraid this was all a dream that might shatter.

The room erupted into cheers and whoops, the First Years egging them on like it was the climax of a particularly raucous pantomime. Someone cranked the volume on the smart speaker, the bass thumping harder, syncing with Maria's rhythm. Darya paused her ride on Tobias to watch, her eyes gleaming with vicarious thrill. "Da, take him all," she called in her thick accent, before resuming her grind, her own moans blending with the music.

Justin knelt behind Maria, his hands sliding under her leotard to cup her arse, spreading her cheeks as he positioned himself. "My turn to join the fun," he growled, and without preamble, he thrust into her from behind, filling her pussy in one smooth motion. Maria gasped around Arjan's cock, the vibration sending shocks through him. Justin set a punishing pace, his hips slapping against her, each thrust pushing her mouth further down Arjan's length.

Arjan's innocence cracked like an eggshell. His hands finally moved, tangling in Maria's hair, guiding her—not roughly, but with a tentative exploration that quickly turned eager. "Fuck… oh God," he panted, his voice breaking. Maria hummed in approval, hollowing her cheeks, sucking harder as Justin pounded into her, his balls slapping against her clit with every drive.

The mirrors captured it all in infinite regression: Maria on her knees, impaled from both ends; Arjan's face contorted in ecstasy; Justin's grin feral and triumphant. The other First Years, inspired, redoubled their efforts. The blonde girl was now on all fours, taking one boy in her mouth while another fucked her from behind, her cries muffled. Darya had pulled Tobias into a standing position, her legs wrapped around his waist as he lifted her, bouncing her on his cock against the barre.

Maria pulled off Arjan with a wet pop, strings of saliva connecting her lips to his glistening shaft. "Your turn to lead," she said breathlessly, standing and pushing him gently towards the centre of the room. The parquet floor was cool under her bare feet, sticky in places from previous spills. She lay down on her back, spreading her legs wide, her pussy swollen and slick from Justin's attentions. "Come here, virgin boy. Claim your place."

Arjan hesitated for only a second before crawling over her, his cock bobbing with each movement. Justin stepped back, stroking himself as he watched, his eyes dark with lust. "Go on, Singh. Fuck her like you mean it."

Arjan positioned himself between Maria's thighs, the head of his cock nudging her entrance. He looked down at her, searching her face for any sign of mockery, but found only encouragement. "Are you sure?" he whispered.

"More than sure," Maria replied, reaching down to guide him in. He slid home in one thrust, burying himself to the hilt. The stretch was delicious, filling her completely. Arjan groaned, his eyes fluttering shut as he savoured the tight, wet heat enveloping him.

"Move," Maria urged, bucking her hips. "Fuck me, Arjan. Hard."

He did. Tentative at first, then with growing confidence, his thrusts deep and powerful. Maria wrapped her legs around his waist, her heels digging into his back, urging him on. The room spun around them—moans, laughter, the wet sounds of flesh meeting flesh, the relentless beat of the music. Justin knelt beside them, feeding his cock into Maria's mouth, and she sucked him greedily, tasting herself on him.

Arjan's rhythm faltered as he neared his peak, his breaths coming in ragged gasps. "I'm… I'm going to…"

"Do it," Maria mumbled around Justin. "Cum inside me."

With a cry that echoed off the mirrors, Arjan exploded, his cock pulsing as he filled her with hot spurts. The sensation tipped Maria over the edge; she clenched around him, her own orgasm crashing through her, waves of pleasure radiating from her core. Justin followed seconds later, pulling out to paint her breasts with his release, the warm liquid splattering across her skin.

The room applauded, a smattering of claps and cheers that dissolved into more frenzied activity. Arjan collapsed beside Maria, panting, a dazed smile on his face. "That was… incredible."

"Welcome to Red Rose," Maria said, ruffling his hair. She sat up, cum trickling down her thighs, and surveyed her kingdom. The class was in full swing now—not ballet, but something far more primal.

But the morning was young, and Maria had a class to "teach." She stood, legs shaky, and clapped her hands sharply. "Alright, you lot. Enough foreplay. Pair up. We're doing pas de deux—but with a twist. No clothes. And make it count."

The First Years scrambled to obey, shedding leotards and tights with eager abandon. Maria paired them off herself, her voice cutting through the chaos like a conductor's baton. "You—blondie—with the curly-haired lad. Lift her properly, or I'll make you do it again." She demonstrated with Justin, who hoisted her effortlessly into an arabesque, his cock nestled against her arse as she extended her leg high.

Arjan, still flushed and spent, was paired with Darya. The Russian girl eyed him appreciatively, licking her lips. "Come, virgin no more. Show me what British-Indian boys can do."

As the pairs formed, the studio transformed into a living sculpture garden of erotic ballet. Lifts became opportunities for penetration; turns allowed fingers to explore hidden places. Maria circulated, correcting form with a touch here, a slap there. "Extension, darling—push those hips forward." She pressed against a girl's back, guiding her into a deeper penché while the boy behind her thrust in time.

Justin, ever the instigator, had claimed two girls for himself, sandwiching one between him and the other, their bodies moving in a tangled trio. "See, Kovacs? This is proper tutoring."

Maria laughed, pulling Arjan aside for a private moment. "How's it feel, losing it in front of an audience?"

"Terrifying. Exhilarating." He glanced at Darya, who was beckoning him with a crooked finger. "Think I'm ready for round two."

"Go get her, tiger." Maria watched him go, a strange pride swelling in her chest. This was mentorship, Red Rose style.

****

CHAPTER 2 – Sound Check...
Monday 28th October 2024

Irene Walsh knew that, as a Second Year technology student, an irony in itself as the majority of courses at Red Rose Academy were performing arts degrees, with only a handful devoted to the technical crafts, she was always going to be something of an outsider. Not that she minded. In fact, she rather relished it. There was a thrill in knowing things others didn't, a satisfaction in mastering the arcane arts of soundboards and lighting grids while the rest of them twirled and emoted on stage. If she'd wanted to be among the crowd, she would have chosen Drama or Dance, would have painted her face and practised her plosives and pirouettes. Instead, Irene found her domain in the wings, in the control booths, the labyrinthine basements beneath the auditorium, and the strange, silent intimacy that came before a show.

The official technician at Red Rose, a Polish man named Marcin Kaczmarek, was already legendary in the whispered lore of the Academy. It was said he could coax clarity from the muddiest of feedback, that he could rewire a mixing desk blindfolded and drunk (not that he ever was—Marcin was sober to the point of asceticism), and that he had a sixth sense for when someone had left a plug loose or a cable trailing. He had the bearing of a medieval monk and the vocabulary of a dockhand, but he'd taken Irene under his wing, recognising a kindred spirit in her precise hands and methodical mind.

Today, however, he was at his "other job", working for a call centre selling double glazing in Oldham—a fact which both amused and vaguely disconcerted Irene. Instead, she and Mario, an Italian Third Year, were in the cramped booth, testing lighting rigs for the auditions the following day for West Side Story, as, in the first term every year, the Mancunian Academy insisted on a large-scale musical to "foster cross-discipline collaboration".

The irony that the booth was literally that tight that, if she moved two inches to the left, Mario would be dry humping her arse with his knee, was not lost on Irene. Outside the booth, she knew, were some of the other technology students, either shagging, or actually preparing the rigging for the microphones, or even testing the lapel microphones with a level of seriousness that would have made Marcin proud. But inside here, the air was thick with the whirring of ancient fans, the scent of solder and the acrid residue of burned-out gels, and the slightly sour sweat of Mario—who, being Italian and apparently born for opera, had a way of turning even technical failures into melodrama.

'Turn channel six up a bit,' Mario said, leaning dangerously close. His long, spidery fingers hovered over the main fader, coming behind her, and Irene felt his erection stiffen against her arse, the micro dress she was wearing raising as she leant over the control board.

"Fuck, are you on Viagra or something, Mario? That stiffy is a workplace hazard," Irene muttered, not bothering to move. Her voice was low, sardonic—a note of challenge threaded through it. She pushed the fader up with calculated precision, keeping her eyes strictly on the LED levels, not Mario's face.

Mario only grinned, unembarrassed. "Don't blame me, bella. Blame the dress. If you wanted me to act like a monk, you'd have come in overalls, no?" His accent thickened in private, the edges of his words curling around her, part joke, part invitation.

Suddenly she felt her knee buckle and, falling forwards, felt Mario's hands on her breasts, and, suddenly, over her braless nipples, the rough heat of his palms was both a shock and a confirmation of the unsaid tension that had crackled between them all term. For a moment, Irene simply let herself lean into it, the sensation of being gripped and steadied mingling with the sharp, bright panic that flared when she remembered just how exposed they really were.

"Fuck, your nipples are so stiff," Mario grunted with a hungry urgency, not bothering to disguise the predatory gleam in his eyes. His voice was low, vibrating with that deep Mediterranean masculinity that so many of the Drama girls swooned over, though none would have admitted it if pressed. Irene gripped the edge of the desk, back arching reflexively, her dress lifting over her pantieless derriere. "And no panties either? Brave as a lion, or just an exhibitionist?" he whispered, one hand tracing the curve of her hip with slow, unhurried precision. There was a flicker of a challenge in his tone, the sort of dare endemic to Red Rose—a place where boundary-testing wasn't merely tolerated, but cultivated as a mark of creative courage.

Irene, still staring at the LED array as if it were the most absorbing thing in the world, curled a slow, sardonic smile. "You're the one who came in skinny jeans, Mario.

If we both get electrocuted in here, the post-mortem report
will be rated X."

Mario's reply was lost as a burst of feedback yelped from
one of the on-stage monitors, snapping both of them back
into the immediate, practical present. With a shared
reflex, Irene darted a hand to the master mute, killing the
circuit with a thump. A moment's silence fell, filled only
by the faint hum of the theatre's ancient ventilation.
Beneath it, the thrumming pulse of desire was still there,
but, for a heartbeat, professional instinct trumped lust.

"Fuck, it's hot in here," Mario suddenly said with the
restless, abrupt energy of a man half-choked by both heat
and his own hormones. He shoved back from Irene,
exhaling through his teeth, trying to compose himself.
"Your fault, you know. I blame you, always." He offered
her a wolfish grin, but she could see the flicker of
admiration underneath—recognition that she hadn't
missed a beat on the desk, even when his hands had
threatened to derail her composure entirely.

Irene rolled her eyes and stepped aside, tugging the hem
of her micro dress down as if it might restore some
semblance of decency. She doubted it. "My fault? I'm not
the one who set the air con to *sauna* and then started
humping the faders like a Labrador."

She turned her attention to the desk, fingers gliding over
the rows of sliders, dials, and illuminated buttons. The
console was a battered Allen & Heath model, old even by
Red Rose standards, with notes of gaffer tape over certain
sliders, and a soft throb of warmth where its circuit boards
fought the dying chill of a Manchester October. The

familiar landscape of faders was more intimate to her than any lover; she could navigate it blindfolded, the way a pianist plays scales in the dark.

Behind the glass, the stage was a faint suggestion in blue: masking flats, a ballet barre, a few upended chairs from the earlier rehearsal, and in the distant wings, the shadows of other techies moving methodically—rigging, testing, sometimes laughing too loud. Through the half-open door to the booth, Irene could just hear the distant voices of the Dance students rehearsing for something impromptu, their lines and pirouettes marked more by bravado than accuracy. Somewhere beneath it all, the building's ancient bones creaked and hummed.

Mario took a ragged breath and nudged his hip against her, his tone lowering as if confiding some grand conspiracy. "You know, in Italy, there's a tradition. Tech booth is holy ground. No sex, no drinking. Only work."

Irene snorted. "That's bollocks. I've seen your group chats, Mario. I know exactly what you lot get up to during scene changes." She tweaked the gain on Channel 10, watching the red LEDs flicker. "Anyway, it's Red Rose. You could have a drug-fuelled orgy in the orchestra pit and as long as you reset the lights for Act Two, nobody would bat an eyelid."

Mario considered this, then grinned. "That's why I stay. English girls, and English rules—none at all." He leaned closer, eyes lingering on the sharp profile of her jaw as she scanned the desk. "Except with you. You're the only one who makes me nervous."

That admission, raw and unexpected, hung in the air for a beat too long. Irene didn't answer, but she didn't move away either. Instead, she flicked the comms switch, listening as one of the First Year sound students muttered about a dodgy XLR cable, the static echoing in her earpiece like a heartbeat.

Suddenly the sound of a lock being closed made Irene jump, as, because the door to their booth was closed, she had a feeling that someone was about to intrude on their fragile truce of professionalism and lust. Feeling Mario's cock against her hip once more—hot, insistent, neither accidental nor entirely deliberate—she let her focus split in two: half on the ancient, temperamental console, half on the swirling eddies of energy that defined every inch of Red Rose.

But the worry of if their booth was locked or if someone might burst in was just another layer of the game here. At Red Rose, the boundaries between public and private, work and pleasure, were as fluid as the ghost lights that flickered in the rafters after midnight. Irene glanced over her shoulder, hoping it was an unreliable latch, and not someone deliberately locking the door until Mario and her fucked like their lives depended on it. She wouldn't put it past half the cohort to engineer such a scenario just for the story. At Red Rose, every day was a rehearsal for something more scandalous.

She gave the handle a perfunctory jiggle—locked, her fears confirmed.

"Looks like one of the First Years has locked us in, or the latch's buggered again," Irene muttered, the corners of her mouth quirking in resignation rather than alarm. She gave the door another gentle shove, the muffled thud lost amid the drone of the ventilation. "Brilliant. Well, at least there's air. Shame it's mostly Mario's aftershave and the ghost of burnt tungsten."

Mario shrugged, utterly unbothered. "We'll just call for rescue when we're done. Or wait until Marcin appears, yes?" He leaned in, his voice dropping low and dangerous, "Unless you want to give them a show."

But the prospect of being watched—even just the threat of it—had always given Irene a dark thrill. At Red Rose, everything was a performance; the only question was how many people would remember it in the morning, and whether your legend grew or your reputation merely warped into something new and awkward. She grabbed Mario's hands and placed them on her breasts, the hint of a dare in her eyes.

"Might as well give the fuckers what they want," she murmured, voice pitched low so only Mario could hear, though she was keenly aware of the theatre's peculiar acoustics, how sound could creep along the rafters and find new ears. "But after the bloody feedback's sorted. I've got some standards left, you know."

Mario's laugh rumbled against her spine, his hands lingering, squeezing just hard enough to remind her that here, boundaries were the thinnest of membranes, always ready to tear. He took a step back, and the absence of his touch was suddenly louder than the static fizzing through the desk. But Irene was used to holding her own. She ran through the checklist in her head, recalibrated the levels, then shot him a look over her shoulder.

"Right," she said crisply, flicking the comms toggle to OFF, "Channel Six, gain down a hair, Channel Ten, monitor to stage left. Try not to drool on the submaster, Mario, or we'll blow the amps."

"Si, signorina," Mario replied, giving her a mocking little salute that was half flirtation, half genuine respect. "But you know, it's much easier to focus when I don't have to think about your arse."

"Then try harder. That's what the bursary's for." Irene grinned and, satisfied the board was running clean, pressed the button to open the booth intercom.

"All clear. We're running patch test. Tell the dance lot if they want more foldback, they can move their bloody feet. Not my problem."

There was a pause—then the familiar cackle of Tamsin, one of the First Years, came through, thick with bravado: "Aye, boss! We'll keep it down, promise." Background noise filtered through—footsteps, laughter, a squeal of sneakers on varnished wood. A typical Red Rose afternoon, saturated with the anticipation of scandal, sweat, and the faint scent of hot resin and old velvet.

And then she felt it again, Mario's erection, dry humping her through his jeans and her dress, the stiffness of his cock insistent as the tension—thick and dangerous as stage fog—hung between them. The whirring fans and humming wires, the muffled shouts from the auditorium beyond, seemed only to sharpen the sense that the booth was now a world apart, a bubble on the edge of bursting.

"It's fucking hot in here," Irene said with a grin, her hands behind her back as she started to undo her zip, the metallic teeth parting with a sound barely audible above the persistent hum of the booth. Her fingers, deft and unapologetic, paused just long enough to ensure Mario's eyes—dark, hungry, always watching—were on her. It was a silent, wordless agreement, the kind made a hundred times in corners, wings, and storage cupboards across the academy, a reckless challenge thrown out into the stale air of the theatre.

She pulled the dress down, first off her shoulders, then sliding it over her breasts, the fabric grazing nipples already taut and eager. The booth's half-light, filtered through scratched Perspex and the battered control desk, caught the pale sweep of her back as she slipped the dress to her waist, leaving her bare above the hips, skin marked only by the faint pressure lines of fabric and Mario's lingering fingerprints.

Mario's breath hitched, rough and eager. "Dio mio, Irene," he managed, the Italian vowels slipping between them like a prayer, or perhaps a curse. He pressed closer, his jeans now tight and uncomfortable, but he didn't care. One hand, trembling slightly—though not from nerves— cupped her breast, thumb stroking the edge of her areola, while his mouth found the side of her neck, kissing along her pulse.

"You know, you're making my cock want to say its prayers and then commit mortal sins," Mario growled, his lips pressed hot against the hollow of her throat. The accent deepened, more animal than human, the vowels round and stretched with want. "I'd have to go to Confession again because of you, Irene. You make me believe in original sin."

Irene couldn't help the brief, husky laugh that bubbled up. "You lot are obsessed with guilt. English girls just want the job done right."

She didn't wait for his reply. Her hand found his waistband, quick fingers undoing the button, dragging the zipper down until she could feel the hard, hot length of him through his boxers, the fabric damp with need. Mario groaned, low and desperate, and pressed forward until she was braced against the battered sound desk, the LEDs casting staccato shadows over her bare skin. The sensation was electric—her nipples tight, the air prickling cold over her exposed breasts, the heat of Mario's body a welcome contrast.

She watched as Mario's lips connected with one of her nipples, and the sensation was sharp, almost shocking—a flash of pure, animal pleasure through the veil of professionalism she'd always worn like a second skin. Her breath caught. Irene's hands curled over the battered edge of the soundboard, knuckles whitening with the effort of maintaining the last vestiges of composure. All the while, the whirr of the booth's fans and the distant thrum of activity outside seemed to fade to a backdrop, irrelevant compared to the molten urgency in Mario's touch.

He kissed lower, tracing the path of a stray copper wire across her ribs, his other hand ghosting down her spine, pausing at her hip. For all the hungry bravado in his words, Mario's fingers were surprisingly deft, lingering, almost reverent as they mapped her body. There was a tenderness here, a slow savouring that belied the raw heat between them. Irene's body arched, not in surrender but in challenge, her head tipping back so the arc of her throat caught what little light there was in the booth.

Outside, a distant crash—laughter, someone dropping a mic stand—reminded her, distantly, that they were not alone. They were never truly alone at Red Rose. The thought added a delicious shiver to the tension, the ever-present threat that a First Year might press their face to the dusty booth window and see her, half-naked and pinned against the ancient Allen & Heath, a living myth in the making.

Mario, sensing her brief distraction, nipped at her nipple, drawing a hiss, then met her gaze—eyes dark with anticipation, pupils wide. "You like the risk, don't you?" he whispered, his accent roughening every syllable. "You want them to see how the sound gets made. Maybe hear it, too."

She swallowed, throat tight, her laughter shaky but real. "Don't flatter yourself. I like efficiency. Two birds, one soundcheck."

But the game was a familiar one: work and want, the friction between them a kind of energy, a current that ran through every socket and plug of the Academy. She shifted, forcing Mario to step back so she could slide her dress down fully, pooling it at her feet, leaving her in nothing but her battered Doc Martens and a look of unwavering, ironic composure. If anyone did burst in now, she would not cower or scramble for cover. At Red Rose, shame was a luxury few could afford.

"Y'know, in the Church, they say a condom is a sin," Mario said suddenly, and Irene just raised an eyebrow, entirely unbothered by the invocation of Vatican disapproval. "However, I say its optional. Do you want me to grab one from my wallet, or are we going to hell by the express route?" His smile was wicked, but there was a flash of gentleness in his question, the genuine kind beneath the bravado.

Irene chuckled. "I'm clean, and I presume you've not had the clap?"

Mario shook his head, eyes glinting in the half-light, his cock twitching in his hand. "Not since Milan, and that was a misunderstanding. Besides, I got my NHS text, si?" The words came out half-mocking, but the intent was real, that small sliver of truth beneath the dirty banter. Irene appreciated it. She was used to risk calculations— decibels, voltage, disease.

"Good," she said, and took him in her hand, her grip firm and businesslike, as if calibrating a piece of equipment. "Then just fuck me. I'm nowhere near my fucking fertile window and if anyone comes in, well, let them take notes." Her voice was crisp, more technician than seductress, though her eyes flashed with a wild spark that belonged nowhere but here, in the murky, liminal space between rehearsal and revelation.

Mario grinned—a wide, wolfish flash of teeth—and pressed himself against her, the battered control desk digging into her hips. With practised efficiency, she guided him between her legs, bracing herself on the soundboard. The first thrust was a shock: sharp, urgent, utterly physical. Irene gasped, her fingers scrambling for purchase among the maze of faders and buttons, her body arching back into him as the electric crackle of risk merged with raw pleasure.

"Quiet," she hissed, though she was smiling, voice pitched low for the intimacy of the moment and the thin walls of the booth. Outside, she could hear footsteps— maybe someone running lines, maybe a stray dancer rehearsing their way through a haze of nerves—but it only heightened her sense of power, of being right at the centre of the Red Rose mythos. She was the keeper of the sound, the maker of the moment, and now—just for this brief interval—the absolute architect of Mario's need.

His hands were everywhere at once: gripping her hips, sliding up her sides, kneading her breasts as he drove into her with mounting urgency. Each movement was accompanied by the familiar symphony of backstage life: the squeak of sneakers on the stage, the clatter of a distant lighting rig, the low hum of a distant PA amp. But in the booth, it was all narrowed to sensation, to the throb of Mario inside her and the wet heat slicking her thighs.

Irene, half-laughing, half-breathless, twisted to bite his shoulder. "If you knock the sub out of phase," she muttered, "I'll staple your bollocks to the... well, I'll staple them."

Her fingers found the edge of the desk, nails scraping over the battered wood. For a moment, her mind flickered to the legend of Marcin and the old story about a first-year tech who'd once managed to short-circuit the entire lighting rig by having an ill-timed shag in the bio box. At least, Irene thought with a private smirk, if she broke anything, she'd know exactly how to fix it.

"Fuck, I need you harder," she muttered as Mario obeyed—without words, without even a breath between, the animal urgency overriding all preamble. He adjusted his grip, anchoring her hips against the scarred edge of the console, and thrust deeper, harder, until the world contracted into nothing but the heat and friction between their bodies. Irene's cheek pressed into the desk, LEDs swimming before her eyes in constellations, the comforting thrum of electronics drowned beneath the slap of skin and the ragged staccato of their breath.

She felt the vibrations through the soles of her boots: the bass pulse from a sub still humming somewhere under the stalls, the footsteps of dancers crossing the stage, the echo of a distant laugh—life in the theatre carried on around their private cyclone. She knew, abstractly, that any second a fellow student could glance up to the booth window and glimpse the shadowed outlines of their entanglement: Irene, naked except for her boots, Mario, jeans around his knees, hips moving with the desperate rhythm of someone fucking both for pleasure and posterity.

"Just let me have my fun tonight..." the sound of P!nk's U + Ur Hand came through as Irene accidentally caught the play button on the CD player beneath her thigh, the track blaring suddenly through the ancient speakers hung over the stage like battered sentinels. The unmistakable stomp and snarl of early-2000s pop-punk filled the theatre, the lyrics leaping from the shadows and ricocheting around the empty seats. It was a Red Rose moment in every sense—half farce, half defiance, the sort of chaos that could only arise here, in this strange cathedral to ambition, excess, and raw creative need.

For an instant, both Irene and Mario froze. It was as if the song itself—raunchy, defiant, unapologetic—had called time on their private show. Then Mario, grinning wide, fucked her harder, his thrusts falling perfectly in time with the thumping bassline, the rhythm rolling over them like a dare. Irene bit down on her own wrist, stifling laughter and pleasure in one ragged, helpless gasp.

'Careful,' she whispered, voice all teeth and adrenaline, 'if we knock the power out, Marcin will crucify us both.'

'Then we'd better finish before the chorus,' Mario muttered, and there was something almost sweet in the way he bent to kiss the nape of her neck, even as he fucked her like a man possessed.

He didn't slow, not even when the song's chorus came around, the old battered speakers hissing with every syllable. On stage, footsteps paused, uncertain; then the rhythm of someone clapping along, thinking perhaps it was a rehearsal cue or some in-joke. At Red Rose, chaos rarely meant an emergency—it meant art, or at least the promise of some new story for the myth-hungry halls.

Irene pressed her forehead to the desk, eyes squeezed shut as Mario's thrusts matched the beat, the mesh of pleasure and peril making her body shudder. Her hands flailed for a moment, trying to find mute or stop—anything to kill the track and keep their secret at least half theirs—but Mario's hips pinned her, his weight a physical yes to every unspoken risk. It was so utterly Red Rose—work and want, professionalism and filth, layered together until the only true sin was boredom.

The speakers rattled. Someone in the auditorium below wolf-whistled, and Irene thought she heard the unmistakable cackle of Tamsin again, probably thinking one of the Drama girls had hijacked the booth for a prank. Irene twisted, hair falling across her cheek in a dark curtain, meeting Mario's eyes over her shoulder—a dare, a challenge, a promise. He grinned, sweat streaking his brow, his voice ragged with laughter and lust.

"Nearly there, bella," he gasped, fingers bruising her hips. "Unless you want to make it a duet for the gallery?"

She laughed, short and sharp, her body arching to meet him, the pleasure cresting like a cymbal crash. "Just don't—ah—hit the comms or the house lights or—oh fuck—Mario—"

But the warning died in her throat as Mario's hand, sticky and shaking, found her clit. He worked her with a technician's confidence, two fingers rolling in deft, circling flicks that sent shock after shock through her nerves. It was always like this with him—chaotic but careful, every wire mapped, every button pressed with intent.

The music cut out. For a second, she thought Mario had finally managed to short something with his arse, but then she realised someone below had killed the main feed, the sudden silence broken only by their ragged breathing and the hum of the ancient fluorescent light above the desk.

For a moment, the hush was total, intimate and infinite, broken only by Mario's murmured Italian—soft, dark, devotional as prayer.

Irene came first, the pleasure sharp and sudden as a cracked solder joint, her body shuddering around him. She bit down on her fist, swallowing her cry, but knew that at Red Rose there were always ears—always a story. Mario followed with a gasp, clutching her to him, his hips jerking in a last, desperate rhythm, filling her with heat that felt like triumph.

They froze there for a second: two students tangled over the battered altar of the soundboard, the ghosts of a thousand rehearsals pressing in around them. Irene, naked and unashamed, let Mario fold her into his arms, her laughter echoing off the perspex. She would have been content to linger, body humming with the afterglow and adrenaline, but Mario was already on his feet, hunting for tissues or a scrap of something to clean up.

"Oi, we heard that, gallery," one of the Drama girls yelled from the wings, the amplified sound of the microphone that was being tested making Irene jump with a start. The voice—lilting, half-mocking—rang out through the theatre, carried on the very PA system Irene had just calibrated with such care. Mario, half-naked and sheepish but still grinning, shot her a look of pure mischief as he yanked his jeans back into place, zipper hissing up over his spent cock. "10 out of 10 for the sounds of shagging!"

Irene looked at Mario, surprised, as she realised that, during their tryst, either she or Mario had caught a fader which made the booth mic sound out across the entire theatre—broadcasting, for a brief, shattering eternity, the living, panting proof of Red Rose Academy's culture of spectacle and abandon. It was the ultimate techie's nightmare and a performer's fantasy, all in one: not only had they been heard, but their symphony of flesh and breath and profanity had become a part of the official soundcheck, immortalised in the memories—and possibly the social media feeds—of anyone within earshot.

For a moment, the booth was filled with nothing but stunned, mortified silence. Irene stared at her hands, at the battered sound desk, her nakedness suddenly rendered absurd by the fact that everyone in the stalls and wings now knew precisely what she and Mario had been doing. Her first instinct was to cringe, to scrabble for her fallen dress, to shrink into the corner like any ordinary, half-shamed twenty-year-old.

But she wasn't ordinary. She was Red Rose. And Red Rose, in all its ungovernable, anarchic energy, never apologised for its excesses. It wore its chaos as a badge of pride.

Mario, to his credit, recovered first. He barked out a laugh—loud, free, a kind of brazen triumph in the face of certain infamy. He hoisted his jeans, smoothing his T-shirt over his lean chest, and winked at Irene. "If we're going to be famous, we might as well take a bow."

The truth of it struck her, and slowly, the humiliation bled away, replaced by the madcap joy that always came in the wake of a disaster so total that nothing could be done to repair it. Irene stood up straight, shrugged her dress back over her shoulders—though she didn't bother with the zip—and leaned into the intercom, voice composed, tone crisp as ever.

"Technical note, everyone: That was the new, immersive audio test. Audience participation optional. Now, could someone unlock the booth? I'm not missing lunch for a repeat performance."

Laughter exploded from the stage and the gallery, a riot of jeers, wolf-whistles, and the kind of applause reserved for scandalous triumphs. Even the First Years in the wings—kids still learning the ropes, their wide eyes taking in every sin and legend—were swept up in the chaos, their own boundaries shifting with every new outrage witnessed.

For all the theatre's battered grandeur, the rules of Red Rose were absolute: what happened in the building— every fuck, every fight, every humiliation—became the stuff of legend by the time the next show opened. And in that moment, Irene knew that she'd just secured herself a new chapter in the Academy's unofficial history.

But as the buzz faded, practicalities crept back in. Mario, still grinning, bent to retrieve a battered toolkit from beneath the desk, brandishing it like a magician about to perform his next trick. "Let's fix this latch and make sure we don't get locked in again, eh? Or next time we'll have to charge tickets."

Irene laughed, more from relief than anything else, and began running her post-mortem check over the console—searching for any sign that their romp had shorted a relay or knocked a fader out of alignment. But all seemed well; the Allen & Heath, as battered and ancient as it was, had survived worse than two horny students using it as a sex bench.

She thumbed the comms open again, careful to check the fader positions this time, and called down to the tech crew: "Right, boys and girls, let's see some hustle on the lapel mics. Channel seven is giving me static, so whoever's got the dodgy Sennheiser, bring it up for a look."

One of the techs below—a First Year with a nervous stammer and a mop of unruly blond hair—poked his head through the curtain, grinning. "You want the mic, or should I just join you up there for the afterparty?"

"Just the mic, Josh. We're running a theatre, not a brothel. Not until tonight, anyway." Her tone was dry, measured, but she couldn't keep the laughter out of her voice.

As Josh bounded up the narrow steps to the booth, Mario unlocked the door, and the cramped little space was suddenly filled with the smells and sounds of the wider theatre. Sweat, resin, coffee, and anticipation; the slap and shuffle of dance shoes on the floor below; the distant, melodic warm-up scales from a soprano warming her voice for auditions.

Josh arrived, thrusting the battered lapel mic into Irene's hand. "Heard you on the monitors, by the way," he said, eyes wide and voice low. "Legendary. That's going on the Noticeboard, for sure."

The Noticeboard: Red Rose's infamous, student-run app, where every scandal, rumour, and minor catastrophe was immortalised for posterity, with photos, ratings, and a savage comments section that could make or break a career. Irene felt her cheeks flush with something between pride and mortification.

She fixed the mic with a deft twist of her screwdriver, talking as she worked. "You know, in some universities, students spend all day revising and worrying about their CVs. Here, if you haven't shagged someone in the booth by Second Year, they send you back to Salford Tech."

Mario, now fully composed and leaning against the doorway, chimed in, "And if you haven't blown a channel with your orgasm, you're not trying hard enough."

Josh laughed, his awe for the older students clear. "You lot are insane. No wonder the Drama lot are scared of the techies."

Irene finished her repair and passed the mic back. "We're not insane. We're just committed to a full-spectrum education. Now get down there and tell the cast we'll run the number again, but if anyone else tries to lock me in here, they're sorting the rats in the basement next term."

Josh scampered away, still giggling, and Irene, with a last check of her faders, let herself exhale. Mario slipped his arm around her waist, his lips brushing her ear.

"You know, you're going to have to top that next time," he murmured. "The booth is famous now. We're going to have to find somewhere new."

She elbowed him, laughing, and together they stepped out into the wider world of the theatre, blinking as the cool air from the corridor rushed in to meet the muggy warmth of the booth. The world outside was unchanged: students in various states of undress and rehearsal attire, props scattered over every available surface, the chaos of a musical in tech week ramping up toward mania.

****

CHAPTER 3 – ASDA is an Early Morning Shag Site…
Tuesday 29th October 2024

"Oi, Kovacs," Anton Parsons, one of the Third Year BMus Composition for Screen students at Red Rose, said, as he strolled past the hosiery aisle of the ASDA superstore in Salford. His voice had the ragged cheerfulness of someone who'd been up too long, smoked too much, and survived entirely on meal deals and caffeine. He wore a fraying trench coat over his pyjama bottoms and slippers, as if the concept of getting dressed had become a negotiable suggestion. "I see you're on the Noticeboard shagging that Indian ballet lad who finally lost his virginity."

Maria didn't even flinch. She reached up to grab another cheap pack of 60 denier black tights—her fourth this month—and threw a sidelong glance at him. Her hair was scraped into a messy knot, no make-up, an old hoodie hanging off her shoulder. She looked like what she was: hungover, sexed-out, and clinging to the last rags of functional adulthood.

"Morning to you too, Anton," she said flatly. "Are you stalking me, or are you just here to shoplift a Twix and tell the self-checkout it's a carrot?"

Anton raised his arms in mock surrender, the long sleeves of his coat flopping like a bedraggled bat. "You wound me, darling. I'm here for essentials. Coffee, condoms, inspiration."

Maria snorted, and dropped the tights into her basket next to a bottle of ASDA own-brand energy drink and a multipack of cheese and onion crisps. "You write scores, Anton. Not fucking dubstep pornos."

"Speak for yourself. I did the music for last year's 'Fanny in the Façade', remember? That got streamed ten thousand times and a cease-and-desist from the Royal Academy of Music." He waggled his eyebrows. "Also, your tits look great in that mirror shot. The studio one? Fucking cinematic."

She gave him a cool look. "I'm flattered. I'll be sure to frame it for the Chancellor's Christmas card."

Anton grinned. "That'd be an improvement on last year's. Remember when he sent everyone one of Starmer, Rayner and Reeves when he was trying to get the nomination for the Metro Mayor, which Burnham got?"

Maria gave a weary half-laugh as she trailed down the aisle, the pack of tights bouncing lightly in her basket as she nudged it against her hip. "Yeah, nothing says festive cheer like receiving a Labour Party PR shot with a note that said, 'The future is ours—believe in policy!' I pinned it to the fridge next to my eviction notice and a used condom wrapper."

Anton laughed, the sound more cough than joy. "Peak Red Rose. They should've printed the slogan on the ballet studio wall. Right under 'Ad astra per aspera' and 'to the stars through sweat and fingering.'"

"I thought it was 'through difficulty'?" Maria raised an eyebrow as she reached for a family-sized bottle of ibuprofen.

"Same difference," Anton said breezily. "You do know I've got a RADAR key in my pocket, and, as it's just gone 1am, they've just cleaned the bogs... and the changing rooms."

Maria looked at him over the rim of the energy drink bottle she'd just cracked open. Her lips pressed to the mouthpiece, her stare unblinking. "You mean to tell me you're about to proposition me for bog sex in ASDA, at 1am, while I'm wearing yesterday's knickers and smelling like yesterday's sins?"

Anton held her gaze, deadpan. "Not propositioning. Merely observing that opportunity knocks in unexpected crappers."

She took a long swig. The bitter-sour fizz bit at her tongue. "And when was the last time you went to the GUM clinic for more than a free pack of condoms and a sympathy biscuit?"

Anton placed a hand dramatically to his chest. "I go regularly, thank you very much. I'm practically a brand ambassador. I even get the student loyalty card stamped. Five check-ups and you get a voucher for a Costa."

Maria snorted again, shoulders relaxing just slightly as the early-hours absurdity settled over them like a well-worn coat. She eyed him as he examined a display of budget air fresheners—Summer Meadow, Citrus Shock, Rainstorm Euphoria.

"Why are you actually here?" she asked, voice lower now, the tiredness creeping into her tone. "No bollocks."

Anton selected a Citrus Shock, sniffed it, grimaced, and threw it into his basket alongside a packet of prawn cocktail crisps and a bottle of Lucozade. "Couldn't sleep. My flatmate's shagging his girlfriend, and, well, y'know Helena... we're on an off period."

Mike, Anton's flatmate, was dating a Manchester School of Music girl who sang like Joni Mitchell possessed by a demon and moaned louder than a soprano doing a bad death aria. Maria had heard her through the wall once while visiting Anton's flat, and thought someone was dying until the sound resolved into wet, rhythmic slaps and an off-key whimper of "God, yes, ruin me like Brexit did the arts."

"Right," Maria muttered. "So it's insomnia by sex soundtrack."

"More like post-traumatic lust disorder." Anton grabbed a multipack of 'Jammy Dodgers' and gave her a look. "It was either come here, or wank in a bus stop in Picc Gardens."

Maria arched an eyebrow. "You're the reason those benches are always sticky."

Anton cackled, wheezing a bit as he followed her into the self-checkout zone, which, at this hour, was only haunted by a lone security guard half-watching the CCTV while scrolling on his phone. Maria scanned her tights, the beep far too loud in the hollow, fluorescent-lit silence. Anton's groceries followed, a graceless cascade, each item thudding with comic pathos. The fact that she was wearing a crop top and shorts, no panties, no bra, no tights, not even a single sock, barely registered until she caught her own reflection in the dead-eyed blackness of the ASDA self-checkout screen. Her jacket hung open, hair still damp from a midnight shower that had failed to wash away the day. She scanned the tights, the ibuprofen, the crisps, the bottle of energy drink, the kind of dreary, British haul that marked the aftermath of a night—no, a lifestyle—lived at the far edge of care.

Anton, meanwhile, was digging in his coat pockets for his Red Rose student card, half for the discount, half as a kind of tribal badge. The scanner rejected his battered plastic, beeping in rebuke. He thumped it again, louder.

"Mate, it's not a contactless shag," Maria muttered, punching her code into the card machine, fingers stiff with fatigue. "Just scan it. It's not going to come."

"Speak for yourself," Anton retorted. "I've seen you work a card slot."

The security guard's gaze drifted lazily their way, then right past them, bored. At this hour, it would take an armed robbery to muster more than a yawn.

They bagged their shopping in silence, the plastic crinkle sharp in the cavernous, empty store. The air tasted of disinfectant and lost hope. Outside, the car park glowed under the sodium haze of streetlights, slick with rain. Maria felt the edge of the bottle in her palm, the cold sting of November pressing through the thin skin of her clothes.

Salford was never beautiful, but at 1:24 a.m. on a Tuesday, it was at least honest.

"So," Anton said, as they lingered under the flickering strip of awning outside the main doors, "I noticed you updated your status on Facebook and Noticeboard. Justin, eh?"

Maria's laugh was a ghost of what it had been back in the ballet studio—softer, roughened by the early morning, and layered with the brittle armour of fatigue. "Not exactly updated. More like… tagged. The algorithm at Red Rose has more dirt on me than MI5. I get notifications for things I haven't even done yet."

Anton snorted, jamming his hands deeper into his pockets as the wind whipped down the empty car park. "He's a prick, you know. There again he's also a bottom too."

"Yeah, I know," Maria said with a grin. "He filmed you two rutting last week and showed me this afternoon while fucking me in Yelena's office. His arse is a right cock sleeve, just right for you."

Maria then kissed Anton, her hand tracing his erection through the shorts that, despite it being October, he was still shamelessly wearing, bare legs prickled by the cold and already blotched with rain. Anton's breath hitched, but his response was immediate, greedy—Red Rose had conditioned all of them to respond to heat with heat, hunger with hunger, no matter the setting.

"You know there's an alley the other end of the car park, Kovacs," Anton said with a grin, and Maria knew that she was grinning back before she'd even decided to, the smile crooked, ugly-beautiful in the neon wash of the ASDA sign. There was something about this time of night—when the world's mechanisms wound down to the barest thrum, when the only people left outside were those too restless, too lost, or too unwilling to go home—that felt like a dare. Maria loved a dare, even when it was the sort that would read, in the cold light of day, like a catalogue of self-inflicted wounds.

Maria knew that the Chancellor, Rowan Hardcastle, would probably not even notice that his desk had acquired a few new stains so long as no one knocked over his commemorative mug of Angela Rayner doing shots at conference. The thought flickered through her mind—a glancing amusement—before the cold brought her focus back to the present, to Anton, to the charged, secretive thrill that always hovered between them.

The awning was little shelter, the wind a petty tyrant battering their exposed legs. Maria pressed closer, feeling the warmth of Anton's body through his thin coat and pyjama bottoms, his pulse a jitter under her palm. Their laughter mingled, quick and ragged, before Maria caught his mouth with hers again. The kiss was sharp, all teeth and hunger, the taste of energy drink and cigarettes and something like despair. She pulled back just enough to look at him, to see the question in his eyes—Are you sure?—and the answer in her own—Of course I am, don't be boring.

She tugged him towards the shadowed corner at the edge of the awning, barely out of sight of the drifting security guard. They were exposed, yes, but at this hour, in this city, shame was another word for boredom. Anton's hands found her hips, fumbling, urgent. Maria laughed, half in challenge, half in exhaustion, as he hitched her up against the cold brick. Her shorts bunched around her thighs; her skin goose fleshed and burning at once.

"Fucking hell, Kovacs," Anton breathed, his voice rough with anticipation and nerves, "you really do have no sense of self-preservation, do you?"

She grinned, biting at his jaw, her hand slipping beneath his waistband. "None at all. You going to make this worth the criminal record?"

He shuddered as her fingers curled around him. "If we get caught—"

"—if we get caught, I'll compose the soundtrack for the police cell, live," Anton whispered, his breath coming in short, misty bursts that vanished instantly into the damp air. The laughter in his eyes flickered, edged by genuine danger, but Maria could see—could feel—the wild momentum that had always driven them both through the back alleys of Red Rose's nights, the sense that nothing mattered except the next moment of sensation, of risk, of claiming some piece of a world that never felt like it truly belonged to them.

She pushed him harder against the wall, the brick scraping her exposed thighs. Rain glittered in Anton's hair. The car park, for all its blaring lights and sprawling emptiness, might as well have been a stage built only for them. She hooked her foot around his calf, dragging him closer, her mouth hot against his neck as she whispered, "Shut up and get on with it, Parsons. Unless you want the coppers to catch you mid-chorus."

He fumbled at her waistband with hands that shook—not with nervousness, but with cold, adrenaline, and the kind of anticipation that had nothing to do with romance and everything to do with the glorious, fleeting violence of their need.

She could see, in the faint reflection in the glass doors behind them, the ghosts of other students: the ones who would wander through ASDA's aisles at 3am, clutching Red Bull and Super Noodles, making choices that would seem absurd in daylight but were the only kind that made sense in the acid-bright clarity of insomnia. The glass blurred their forms, made them spectral, unmoored. She knew that they wasn't just Red Rose students either, but Manchester University, as well as the more elite Manchester School of Music.

Anton slid his hand up beneath her hoodie, fingertips skating along the bare skin of her stomach. "You're fucking freezing," he whispered, but there was reverence in it, as if her chill were a relic to worship, proof of her presence, her survival. Maria grinned, teeth chattering a little, and pressed closer, her own hand still working him with the careless expertise of someone who'd long ago given up on decorum.

"To be fair, Kovacs, I've already got a banning order from every Sainsbury's, so what's another supermarket on the pile?" Anton smirked, eyes glittering half-mad with the freedom of exhaustion and the promise of reckless oblivion. His breath curled in the air like smoke, mingling with the steam of Maria's own, their exhalations the only evidence of heat in the glacial early hours.

Maria could feel his pulse under her palm, wild and erratic, more alive than anything she'd touched all week. The familiar shudder of rain and adrenaline sang through her skin. "Let's make it count, then. Something for the Red Rose scrapbook," she murmured, catching his mouth in a bite of a kiss, raw and laughing and edged with the possibility of being caught. Her hand never left his body, just shifted—skimming up his chest, nails raking through the thin fabric of his pyjama top, leaving red trails of promise for later discovery.

Anton's hips bucked involuntarily, but he stilled himself with effort. "You know, I was saving my criminal record for a more impressive debut," he muttered, glancing over her shoulder, past the paltry shelter of the awning, at the silent car park stretched under the sodium wash. "Arson, maybe. Or pissing on the Chancellor's car. Something with legacy."

"Your legacy's already immortalised on the Noticeboard," Maria reminded him, lips ghosting over his jaw. "Under 'musicians who'll shag anything with a pulse and a tune.'"

He laughed, and the sound was real this time—hoarse but unguarded. "Takes one to know one."

Her hand slid down, bold as ever, pulling him in, her grip expert, not hurried now but slow, commanding, making him work for it. His fingers tightened on her hips, grounding himself, trying not to lose what little control he still had. A gust of wind made them both shiver, and she pressed closer, warmth leeching through their mismatched clothes.

"Shit," he muttered, "I think I actually might die of exposure before we get arrested. You do know it's minus two, right?"

"Shut up and focus, Parsons. Or do you need sheet music?"

He snorted. "Give me the tempo, maestro."

Maria's laugh was a ragged exhale as she ground her body into his, guiding him with a confidence born of hundreds of nights spent straddling the knife-edge between want and consequence. The threat of discovery only added to the atmosphere—a single cough from the security guard, a car turning into the lot, a CCTV lens shifting fractionally, and the whole thing would collapse in farce and scandal. But she trusted the hour, the anonymity of the late-night city, the fact that nobody in Salford wanted to pay enough attention to interrupt.

Anton's hands—so deft on keys and fretboard, less so now in his haste—found the waistband of her shorts, tugging them down clumsily until her thighs were bared to the slicing wind. Maria shuddered but didn't retreat, biting her lip as her back met the cold brick, a grounding pain that kept her tethered to the moment.

His mouth found hers, desperate now, tasting of nicotine, stale Red Bull and the irrepressible tang of lust. His voice was just a ragged whisper in her ear: "You're an absolute menace, Kovacs."

She grinned, baring her teeth. "And you love it. You're still flaccid."

Anton's hands fumbled in earnest, shaking with laughter and the uncertain bravado that came with knowing exactly how far he could push and how much further Maria would drag him. The cold was a bite, but the adrenaline made it negligible, almost a joke—this kind of chill felt more like a dare than a deterrent. He pressed closer, body heavy against hers, and Maria felt the brick scrape the skin of her lower back as he pinned her there, their faces barely inches apart, breath tangling in clouds between them.

"Maybe I just need the right soundtrack," Anton shot back, his voice a little steadier now, picking up that familiar note of defiance that always slipped into his tone just before he gave in. "Or maybe the ASDA tannoy's killed my vibe. Next time I want to hear 'Blue Monday' or I'm staging a walk-out."

Maria snorted, her laughter rough and bright, head falling back against the wall. "You stage a walk-out every time you forget your keys, Parsons. Or when the Chancellor puts on another performative diversity panel and serves sausage rolls from Greggs."

"Hey, those sausage rolls are the only thing keeping me on campus," Anton replied, and the hand on her thigh squeezed, his thumb tracing the seam of her shorts before slipping inside. His other hand gripped her hip, holding her in place with the determined tenderness of someone who understood exactly how far to push before she'd bite. "Besides, you know I love a bit of performative diversity.

Remember the time I joined the Red Rose folk ensemble just so I could score with that harpist from Birmingham?"

"You lasted two rehearsals and got thrown out for turning 'Scarborough Fair' into a trap remix."

"I call it creative license." Anton's grin was crooked, all mischief and hunger now, the previous weariness burned away by proximity and the sharp, kinetic spark of the hour.

Maria's head lolled back, exposing her throat to the yellowed light spilling from the awning. She felt every nerve ending come awake, every ache and fatigue and leftover buzz from the night before converging in the cold space where his hands roamed. For a moment, neither of them said anything, just the wet slap of rain on plastic, the faint electric hum of the lights above, and their tangled, urgent breathing.

"Look at us," she murmured, voice nearly lost in the wind. "Ballet drop-out and failed composer, fucking in the shadows of Salford's best value retailer. It's practically a Jane Austen plot."

The next thing Maria knew, Anton's member became fully erect, and, poking into her, he lifted her up, and then dropped her straight onto his member, her pussy filling with the speed and pain of the moment—pain edged with adrenaline, cold and want layered and indivisible. The shock of contact, the bruising bluntness, made her hiss through her teeth, laughter and violence tangled up in the same breath.

"Fuck, that hurt," she gasped, teeth clenched and eyes squeezed shut against the sharpness of it. The cold air seemed to press harder against her skin, the sting of the night amplified by the sudden shock of pain that spread through her like wildfire. But even as the ache flared, it morphed into something fierce and consuming—a reminder that she was alive, raw and untamed, even if only for these few reckless moments.

The fact that it hurt was almost beside the point—maybe even the point itself. Maria's body welcomed the sensation like an old friend, her arms locking around Anton's neck to steady herself as her back scraped the rain-slicked brick. The world outside their cocoon of feral heat was silent, hollowed by night, the only witnesses the indifferent city lights and the odd flicker of movement from within the supermarket's shell.

Anton's breath caught in his throat, a hiss and a whimper tangled together. He pressed his mouth to her shoulder, biting back both laughter and the instinct to apologise. Red Rose had made them both creatures of spectacle, where pain and pleasure were just two sides of the same dare. "Sorry—fuck—just, you know, gravity," he managed, hands clutching her thighs with a reverence that was almost comic in context.

She ground herself down onto him, shifting to claim all of him, the friction a balm against the numbness that sometimes threatened to swallow her whole. There was a glory to being reduced to need, to sensation, to something as elemental and shameless as rutting in a public car park at half past one on a Tuesday morning. Her thighs trembled, her hoodie riding up to expose the bare flesh of her hips, and Anton's hands skated up her ribs, anchoring her as though she might vanish altogether.

"Don't stop," she muttered into his ear, her voice low and urgent, the old ballet discipline reimagined in the staccato rhythm of their bodies slamming against cheap brick. "If you apologise again I'll tell everyone you came in your pants."

Anton snorted with laughter, the sound muffled by Maria's hoodie, his breath hot against her collarbone as he adjusted his grip. "Yeah, but if I don't last longer than the security guard's tea break, you'll ruin me on Noticeboard anyway."

Maria just squeezed him harder with her thighs, smirking through the chill that bit every inch of her exposed skin. The lights from the car park shimmered, rain beading on their faces, on the plastic bags discarded by their feet. Anton's fingers dug into her thighs, half for leverage, half because there was nothing else anchoring him in this world except the undeniable, aching gravity of Maria's body against his.

"God, fuck me harder," she groaned, as she noticed, out of the corner of her eye, a couple of UCEN Manchester students—one in a pink hoodie, the other in a long, rain-stained puffer jacket—ducking under the ASDA awning at the far end, sheltering from the wind and rain, utterly oblivious, or perhaps merely pretending to be. The anonymity of the hour was both shield and invitation, the city's indifference a balm against every exposed nerve. Maria's grip on Anton's shoulders tightened as the sounds of the world retreated behind the ragged thrum of their bodies—just rain, wind, the distant clatter of a shopping trolley being wrangled by some unseen hand.

Neither of the students spared more than a flickering glance. They were deep in their own argument about bus times and vape cartridges, voices drifting on the wet wind. It didn't matter. The risk didn't fade, only deepened, lent the moment a knife's edge—Maria felt it in every scrape of brick on her back, every hot, desperate thrust of Anton's hips, every cold burst of rain against her thighs.

She pressed her lips to his ear, half-whisper, half-growl. "You ever think we're wasting our lives here?"

Anton laughed, the sound tumbling from him like a breaking string, wild and on the verge of hysteria. "All the fucking time, Kovacs. But right now? I don't care."

"Good answer," she breathed, arching against him, finding a rhythm that banished everything but sensation. She could taste blood in her mouth—her lip, bitten in the dark. The pain mingled with pleasure until they became indistinguishable, each feeding the other, each stoking the heat that kept her alive when everything else felt numb.

He braced himself with one arm against the wall, the other splayed on her hip, guiding her movements with the subtle control of a composer coaxing chaos into song. "God, Maria," he gasped, "you're going to be the death of me."

"Promises, promises," she spat back, but there was laughter there too, the kind that only came at the end of something—be it hope, or night, or self-control. "If you die, make it loud. I want headlines."

The UCEN students finally drifted off, their retreat marked by the slap of trainers on wet tarmac and a cloud of sweet, artificial fruit as they passed. Anton's grip on her tightened, a silent exclamation, his pace growing rougher, more desperate, as if the absence of witnesses somehow made their obscenity more real, more urgent.

Maria let herself be carried by the violence of it, lost in the rough cadence of skin on skin, the sharp ache blooming in her thighs, the obscene slap of flesh punctuating the silence. Her own voice surprised her—a gasp, then a string of expletives muffled against Anton's shoulder as she rode the crest of sensation. It was not gentle, was not tender, but it was real—alive in a way that nothing else seemed to be anymore.

She felt Anton start to lose his rhythm, the telltale tightening of his jaw, the staccato breaths that meant he was near the edge. She locked her ankles behind his back, driving him deeper, faster, her own release clawing its way up her spine like a live wire. For a moment, the world narrowed to this point, this heat, this shared violence—no past, no future, only the bright, animal certainty of pleasure.

He came with a choked cry, biting down on her shoulder to muffle the sound, his hips stuttering in a final, ragged crescendo. Maria followed a heartbeat later, the aftershocks shuddering through her, sharp and sweet, painting every inch of her with proof of her own survival.

For a moment, neither of them moved, bodies slack against the brick, breathing in ragged counterpoint. The rain pattered on, a gentle metronome to mark the end of their fugue. The car park was empty again, save for the distant orange glow of the streetlights and the spectral presence of the security guard inside, now deep in a game of Candy Crush and blessedly oblivious.

Maria slid down from Anton's grasp, her bare thighs smarting from the roughness, her shorts bunched around her knees. She fumbled to pull them back up, not caring about the damp or the grit or the faint stickiness on her skin. It was a badge of honour, a wound, a proof. Anton tucked himself away with all the delicacy of a man who has just realised how exposed he really is.

"Jesus," he muttered, "You know, I could go another round in an Uber if you book it quick. I'm not even joking, Kovacs. I've got a tenner left on my app, and the back seat's cleaner than the ASDA bogs."

Maria, still panting, pressed her forehead to his, the chill of the night forgotten for a moment, overridden by the wild, throbbing pulse in her blood. Her laughter was breathless, all smoke and mockery. "You are an absolute animal, Parsons. And a fucking idiot."

Anton grinned, his teeth flashing white in the sodium wash. "I take that as a compliment, coming from the girl who just risked public indecency charges for a cheap shag outside the George Street ASDA."

She drew back just enough to watch him properly—his cheeks flushed, the hollows under his eyes deeper than ever, his hair wild and damp. He looked feral and alive, a creature of the small hours, and for a moment, Maria felt a pang—a half-forgotten, impossible ache for something softer. But softness was a luxury for another life.

Instead, she just grinned, the cruel curve of her mouth matching his. "Get your shit together, Anton. My legs are freezing and my arse is numb. If we're not arrested, I'm at least getting a Greggs on the way back. And you're paying."

Anton made a show of gallantry, scooping up their bags and swinging them over one arm. "Your wish is my command, o dark queen of Red Rose." He straightened his trench coat, tucked his pyjama waistband in, and did his best to look like anything other than a dishevelled music student who'd just fucked his classmate against a supermarket wall.

Maria pulled her hoodie down over her exposed midriff, giving her thighs a brisk rub to chase away the sting, and together they made their way to the edge of the car park, stepping carefully around puddles that gleamed like oil slicks in the streetlights. The world was so quiet, so profoundly empty at this hour, that even their laughter sounded like a threat—a promise of mischief still to come.

They cut across the deserted bus lane, Anton pausing to scrawl something rude on the steamed-up window of the only parked car they passed. Maria glanced over her shoulder at the ASDA, still glowing, impersonal, indifferent, and felt a pang of grim satisfaction at the mark they'd left, invisible but irrevocable.

The Uber arrived within minutes, its headlights slicing through the rain, the driver—a middle-aged man in a

Christmas jumper, despite it being late October—barely sparing them a glance as they clambered into the back. Maria sprawled across the seat, legs stretched out, daring the world to care. Anton slid in after her, dropping their plastic bags between them, and gave the driver the address of the Red Rose Halls without meeting his eyes.

The drive through Salford was silent, except for the soft burble of some bland pop song on the radio. Maria watched the rain streak the windows, neon blurring into rivers of pink and blue and gold, the city flattened into an impressionist painting, all edges lost.

Anton, quieter now, glanced over at her, something softer flickering in his gaze before he masked it with a joke. "You know, I could probably work this into my portfolio. 'The ASDA Suite: Variations on a Theme of Shame'."

She snorted. "Make sure you include the sound of wet trainers and the faint whiff of Red Bull. Realism, Parsons. Nobody at Red Rose ever buys into the fantasy."

He grinned, but there was a tiredness underneath, a shared knowledge that the laughter was armour, and the only thing thinner was the clothes clinging to their damp skin.

They were dropped at the gates of the Halls, the driver not even pausing to wish them a good night—just eager, perhaps, to be done with another two students who looked like the punchline to every joke about Salford after dark. The air was even colder here, the blocky outline of the halls looming up, their windows dark, except for a single strip-lit kitchen glowing on the third floor.

They climbed the steps, Anton fishing for his card key, swearing as it slipped from his frozen fingers. Maria watched the puddles swirl around their feet, the reflected city lights like fragments of lost dreams, and felt the ache in her thighs with every step—a soreness she relished.

Inside, the warmth was jarring, almost unpleasant after the chill outside. The corridor stank of disinfectant, cheap aftershave, and something vaguely chemical that might once have been food. Maria padded barefoot to Anton's flat, letting herself in, barely glancing at the pile of junk mail stuffed under the door—club flyers, eviction threats, the endless bureaucracy of student life.

Anton's flatmate, Mike, was nowhere to be seen—no doubt collapsed into a post-coital coma with his soprano girlfriend, leaving the living room scattered with takeaway boxes and battered sheet music. Maria and Anton moved in automatic concert, shucking off their outer layers, finding solace in the little rituals of familiarity: kettle on, mugs found, instant noodles unearthed from the depths of a battered cupboard.

Maria perched on the edge of the grimy sofa, watching as Anton fiddled with the Bluetooth speaker, queuing up some obscure synth-pop track that bounced off the yellowing walls. For a moment, they were just two exhausted students, adrift in the ragged hours between night and morning, clinging to each other out of habit, hunger, and the bone-deep loneliness that gnawed at everyone in Red Rose.

Anton joined her on the sofa, his knee pressed to hers, warmth blooming in the space between their bodies. He handed her a mug—lukewarm, oversweet, but welcome all the same. "So," he said, voice softer now, "are you going to actually tell me what happened with Justin, or do I have to check Noticeboard like everyone else?"

"Well… if you must know, we're back together again," she said with a grin as she stared into the swirl of grey liquid in her mug, weighing her answer.

She traced a slow circle with her finger around the rim, the ceramic warm against the chill that lingered on her skin. "It's as shit as you'd imagine. He's got new choreography, new traumas, new ways of making me feel like I'm both the prize and the consolation prize. I don't know, Anton—he's fun, but he's also like drinking bleach out of a champagne glass."

Anton barked a laugh, his eyes crinkling with exhaustion. "Romantic as ever, Kovacs. Do you actually like him, or is it just that you're both too stubborn to stay broken up for long?"

Maria considered that, leaning back, letting the music fill the space between her words. The synths were bright and brittle, synthetic cheeriness cutting through the staleness of the flat. "You ever get that thing where you know something's bad for you, but the alternative is… what? Nothing? I think I'd rather be scraped raw than empty. At least with Justin, it's never dull. Or safe."

****

CHAPTER 4 – Facetiming with the Israeli Boyfriend...

Wednesday 30th October 2024

"You know why I play the Muslim big titted stereotype?" Aisha Al-Siyabiya said to her latest First Year Music student that she was deflowering as a coy distraction from the fact that she still had her iPhone angled so that the screen, glowing bright in the otherwise muted lamplight of her college rooms, could catch the boyish face of her Israeli boyfriend as he watched, eyes wide and jaw slack, from his own bed in Tel Aviv.

Aisha let the question hang in the thick air, punctuated only by the soft, rhythmic sounds of the bed's protest beneath them. Her latest conquest, a curly-haired, pale-skinned Music student named Henry, looked up at her, blinking, as if realising only now that there were more layers to this seduction than just his own initiation.

"Because I'm the only one who'll own it," she said, shifting her hips deliberately, her hand splayed over his mouth to muffle the gasp that threatened to rise. "The professors love a trope. The students love a rebel. And my boyfriend—" she threw a pointed look at the screen, a lazy smile curling her lips as she rolled her hips again, "— knows that if he so much as even wanks while watching your cock in my tits or pussy, I'll use a pair of rusty scissors and cut his bollocks off."

The boy on the screen, Aisha's boyfriend, Yair, didn't laugh at her threat. Dressed in the uniform of the Israel Defence Forces, he was sat there at attention, his body as if she were his property as much as the battered bed beneath her. Yair's eyes flicked from Aisha's smirking lips to the trembling frame of Henry, whose fingers now knotted unconsciously in the bedsheet, confusion and lust tumbling through his expression. Yair was silent—only his breathing, slightly ragged, betrayed any emotion.

There was a reason the Omani was always in control when it came to Yair, and that was because she was serious. She knew his IDF unit was responsible for killing some of her second cousins who, like fellow Muslims, had been aiding by way of the Red Crescent, Palestinian residents who had been under daily bombardment due to Israel and Hamas. She had found out that he, specifically, had been the one to fire on Saddam and Abdullah, when, a few months earlier, he had been granted a weeks leave, and they had gone to Ibiza, which, for an Omani who was born the youngest of 12, the only girl in a family of male offspring, the father of who was an executive at Oman Air, was as unusual as the story itself—a Gulf girl bedding an Israeli soldier, an impossible paradox so perverse that even Aisha sometimes felt a sick delight at the secret she carried.

The fact that she had travelled first to Tel Aviv on Sprint Air Oman, the Omani branch of the British ultra-low cost airline, to meet him, and then on a Sprinter Europe flight to Madrid, and then on to the party island. She had been prepared to give herself to him that night, but had got him drunk, and, 4 drinks in, he had confessed that he had deliberately killed 5 Red Crescent workers, "because they were probably Hamas, or helping them, and because nobody would ever know. And if they did, what could they do?" Yair's words had been cold, precise, sobering.

He hadn't begged her for forgiveness, nor pretended regret. Instead, he'd wrapped his arms around her, let her decide what came next. She'd spent the rest of that holiday riding a knife edge between hatred and desire, love and loathing, dominance and submission.

The fact that, unbeknownst to Yair and her family, who all expected her originally to be pure, her family still of the opinion that she had never been touched by any man, had been ironic, as she had lost her virginity on her first day at Red Rose, two years earlier, to a then returning third year Drama student named Hans, a German, who was into BDSM and rough discipline, and who had left her with a small scar under her chin as a trophy. That wound had long healed, but the lesson remained: the only power worth holding was that which others never suspected you possessed.

"You know, habbibi," she said to the camera. "Henry's cock is bigger than your micropenis, and he's lasted longer than you did in that Tel Aviv hotel room with the blackout curtains. Should I be proud of my English boys? Or should I just call you the next time I want someone to watch me finish?"

The words, sharp as lemon juice in a wound, hit Yair with surgical precision. She saw it in the way his throat worked, his Adam's apple bobbing, his military composure straining at the edges. In the close, digital intimacy of her lamp-lit student room, the only sound beyond the wet friction of flesh and the creak of bedsprings was the gentle static hum of his connection, barely a breath of latency between them—a line stretched between Manchester and Tel Aviv, taut as a violin string and just as liable to snap.

Henry, underneath her, shivered at the mention of his own cock, confusion and pride warring for purchase. He was a scholarship boy, one of those who'd grown up with a piano for a best friend, parents who'd been suspicious of Red Rose until the offer came—half out of snobbery, half out of fear of what the place did to children. He'd heard stories about the Academy, and about Aisha, the glamorous Third Year with her predatory smile and her disregard for boundaries. None of them had prepared him for this: her body pressed tight to his, her hand muffling his every word, and the cold, impossibly intimate eye of her iPhone recording it all, the blue light turning her wild brown eyes to midnight.

Aisha kept her hand tight across Henry's lips, not to silence his pleasure, but to remind him—gently, inexorably—of his place in this tableau. She had always been a master of context, of myth, of making the moment a story that no one else could tell. She leaned forward, her thick, dark hair tickling Henry's cheeks as she arched her spine and pressed her breasts together, knowing the camera's lens would catch every bead of sweat and every cruel flicker of mischief in her eyes.

"Look at you," she whispered, letting her accent lilt just for Yair's benefit. "So eager. I could let you come, you know. But then what would you have to brag about?"

Henry's breath was frantic against her palm, his eyes wide with the bewilderment of first passion, of the moment when fantasy collides with the thundering, messy fact of another person's body. Aisha enjoyed the power—relishing it even more because she knew Yair, thousands of miles away, could only watch, could do nothing but feel the burn of it in his chest, helpless.

She eased her grip, just enough for Henry to breathe properly. "Relax," she murmured, as if she were speaking to a shy animal. "This is all part of the curriculum. Didn't they warn you? Music at Red Rose is about improvisation. You know my besties want to join? Do you think you can take on 5 Third Years?"

Aisha let the words hang in the air with all the weight of a dare, her tongue flicking over her teeth as she watched the flicker of shame and excitement shift across Henry's face. He didn't reply—he couldn't, not with her hand pressed so close to his lips, not with the iPhone glinting beside her left hip, Yair's gaze swallowing every detail from afar. Instead, he simply stared up at her, his breathing harsh and shallow, as if the air itself was laced with something narcotic.

She could almost taste his uncertainty—could feel it humming beneath his skin as she rolled her hips, drawing out a tremor from deep within his chest. He was shaking, but not with fear. Red Rose had already started to do its work on him, that intoxicating mix of humiliation and ambition, the sense of spectacle that clung to the walls and to every waking hour. Here, nakedness wasn't shameful, it was currency; a girl like Aisha could spend it as she pleased, could transform it into power.

"Don't worry," she whispered in a voice too sweet for the venom laced within it, letting her words spill towards the glowing iPhone as much as towards Henry, "I'll be gentle. With you, anyway. Yair, on the other hand…"

She knew exactly what she was hinting at when she said that with a pointed look at the screen, as if letting Yair feel the threat, the promise, the pleasure—all at once. The lamp on the battered desk threw uneven shadows over the three-way tableau: Aisha's poised authority, Henry's rapt surrender, and Yair's remote, helpless fascination.

The night was muffled beyond the sash window, the rain on the quad cobbles barely audible, but inside her tiny, lived-in set of rooms, the air was dense with the sticky perfume of sex, anxiety, and the cheap vanilla candle Aisha always burned when she wanted to toy with nostalgia. She kept Henry's face pressed into her palm until he whimpered, not from discomfort but because he was struggling to catch every syllable, every flicker of dominance she offered.

She let him go at last, sitting back to give him air. His eyes swam with adrenaline and something like awe, and for a second she almost pitied him—almost. But pity was not what had drawn her to Manchester, or to Red Rose, or to Yair. Power, contradiction, spectacle: those were the currency of her adulthood, and tonight she had all three clutched in her painted fingers.

Aisha reached down, teasing a fingernail along Henry's jaw as she leaned in close, her lips brushing the shell of his ear. "Are you going to be a good student for me, Henry?" she purred, pitching her voice low so the words seemed meant for him alone. "Are you going to show Yair how your cock satisfies me more than his tiny little IDF dick ever could? Or are you going to cry because a Muslim girl rides you better than any white girl you ever brought home to your mum?"

"I... I've never brought a girl home to my mum... she's a Reform supporter, you see, and—"

Aisha burst out laughing, the sound slicing through the tension like a shard of glass. It was loud, undignified, wicked—exactly what the moment needed. Even Yair on the phone, his posture military-stiff, couldn't help but crack a faint smile, as if the English boy's confession—offered up in the most vulnerable of moments—was proof that the whole world, even in its moments of transgression, ran on the same insecurities and awkwardness.

"Of course she is," Aisha grinned, her accent curling luxuriously over every consonant. "She's terrified you'll bring home someone who'll make her question the world outside The Times editorial page." She let herself relax atop Henry, folding forward so her hair tumbled around his face, draping them both in a curtain of silk. Her phone, still angled to give Yair a perfect view, captured the intimacy as well as the spectacle—a private universe shared between three people, none of whom would ever truly meet as equals.

She kissed Henry's jaw, then his cheek, and finally brushed her lips along the soft whorl of his ear. "I think your mum would like me, you know. I could tell her I don't pray. I drink. I have sex. I vote Labour, most years, but only when I'm not blackmailed into the Green Party by my lesbian aunt in Hove. She'd still think I'm trying to recruit you for Isis or steal your family silver. That's the beauty of it. It's the not-knowing that keeps the English up at night."

Yair's face flickered as he listened, something ancient and hard crossing his features. For a moment, Aisha wondered if he would finally say something—some brittle defence of his own people, his own tribe. But he only watched, a witness to a ritual whose logic made sense only to the exiles and border-dwellers of their generation.

When she broke off, Aisha swung her head back so her hair tumbled across her shoulders, sweat-slick and untamed. She reached for her iPhone, shifting her hips just enough to make Henry squirm beneath her, and pointed the camera downward so Yair could see exactly how thoroughly she was using her English boy. The tiny blue LED reflected in her eyes as she stared, unblinking, at her lover across the digital void.

"Do you remember the day you shot them?" she asked, her voice calm, almost offhand, as if making polite conversation. "The Red Crescent van, outside Rafah. Did you use the M16 or was it a drone this time?"

Yair's expression, framed by the flicker of his own lamp—IDF-issue, of course—twisted, the tension rising in the set of his jaw. He said nothing. Aisha didn't care. She wanted him to feel this: her power, her control, her utter disregard for the old rules of shame.

Yair's voice, when it came, was small and uncertain. "You think I care?" he said, in English, his accent thick, the edge of tears making his voice brittle. "You think this means anything, Aisha? You can fuck your English boys. You're still mine."

Aisha's laughter cut through the static of the connection, light and vicious, her contempt wrapping itself around Yair's insistence as if she could coil it back down the fibre cables of the internet to Tel Aviv and choke him with it. She didn't bother dignifying his possessiveness with a reply, not at first. She just let the silence grow—comfortable for her, raw for him, the pressure in Henry's body rising in time with Yair's futile longing on the screen. Only when she sensed both of them close to some edge—different edges, but equally sharp—did she speak.

"Mine?" she repeated softly, letting the word hang in the air as she raked her nails down Henry's chest, leaving faint, reddening lines across his pale skin. "You don't even own your own secrets, Yair. You think because you've seen me like this, because you've fucked me, because you've killed my blood, that makes me yours? I'm not even mine, half the time. But at least I don't lie about it."

She leaned into the camera, her face momentarily so close that Yair could see the flecks of mascara smudged under her eyes, the gloss wearing off her lips. "You only own what you can hold, ya habbibi. And I'm holding Henry now. Maybe tomorrow I'll let someone else hold me. Or maybe I'll hold myself. Maybe you should try it."

Henry gave a shuddering gasp beneath her. Whether from her words or the relentless, grinding pressure of her hips, she didn't care. She liked the confusion: the mingling of pride, submission, awkwardness, lust and bewilderment that seemed to animate every inch of his inexperienced body. She relished how it made Yair's jaw clench, his eyes hard and bright, as if this was the war he truly wanted to fight one fought not with rifles or checkpoints, but with flesh and power and humiliation. He was a soldier who had never been truly vulnerable; she was a civilian who'd made herself into the world's most unpredictable battlefield.

Aisha slid her hand up to Henry's throat, feeling his pulse race wild beneath her fingers. Her lips brushed his ear again. "I want you to tell him how good it feels," she murmured, her breath hot. "Go on. Tell the nice Israeli soldier how much you love being used. Tell him how much you love making me come, knowing he's got nothing but his fists and his uniform and his little green WhatsApp ticks to keep him company. Tell him how you're going to knock me and my friends up, make nice Muslim-Christian babies who worship Allah and God, who throw Molotovs at each other in the playground and then shag in the girls' toilets because at Red Rose we don't believe in original sin, just original choreography. Go on, Henry. Use your words. You're a musician, aren't you?"

For a long moment, Henry just stared at the iPhone, wide-eyed, unable to process the weight of Aisha's dare. His Adam's apple bobbed. A faint, stammering sound—half laughter, half panic—escaped him, but Aisha, merciless, rolled her hips again and squeezed her hand gently on his throat, just enough to make the world narrow, his vision swimming with adrenaline and want.

"I—" he managed, voice trembling, "I… I want to make you come, Aisha. I want to make you come so hard you forget about him—about everyone. I want to… I want to make you forget your own name—"

She silenced him with a kiss, brutal and sweet, and for a moment it was just her mouth against his, the taste of sweat and saliva and the faintest hint of vanilla. Then she pulled back and laughed, glancing at the phone, at Yair, whose expression had soured to a mixture of pain and fury.

"You hear that, habbibi?" she called, triumphant. "He wants to make me forget you. He wants to make me forget Tel Aviv, forget Gaza, forget everything except his English cock and the fact that, for tonight at least, he's the one inside me."

She leaned forward again, moving the phone so the camera caught the flushed, desperate look on Henry's face. "What do you think, soldier? Still convinced I'm yours?"

Yair's voice, when it came, was low and tight. "You can play your games, Aisha. But in the end, you'll come back to me. You'll always come back. Because nobody else will ever understand you."

Aisha snorted. "Understand me? You barely understand yourself. You think killing makes you strong? It makes you boring. It makes you predictable. I want more than that. I want risk. I want someone who's not afraid to look foolish. Someone who can still blush."

She looked down at Henry, who was indeed blushing furiously, but who met her gaze now with a mix of awe and hunger, his hands tentative at her hips. "That's the thing about English boys," she murmured, almost to herself. "They're so earnest. They're so hungry to please. Even when they don't know what the fuck they're doing."

"You're going to finish for me," she told him, her words a command, her voice unyielding. "But you'll wait until I say so. If you finish before I let you, you'll have to tell everyone in first-year seminar how Aisha Al-Siyabiya made you come like a desperate little schoolboy. Understood?"

Henry's answer was lost in a moan, his eyes fluttering closed as he tried to hold back, his entire body trembling with the effort. Aisha reached for her glass of water on the bedside, took a long, deliberate sip, and then poured the last dribble over his chest, letting it trickle down between his nipples, over his belly, making him gasp at the sudden cold.

"Everything is performance," she said to the room, as if she were onstage, and for her, she always was. "Even this. Especially this. Do you know how many boys I've broken here, Henry? Do you know what they say about the girls from Muscat?"

He shook his head, desperate for any answer that might win her favour.

"They say we're all virgins until we're married," she said, and the irony in her voice was so thick you could taste it. "They say our brothers would kill for our purity. My brothers would, too—if they had any idea. But I'm not here to die for a flag or a faith. I'm here to make you remember me."

Yair's voice, when it came, was small and uncertain. "You think I care?" he said, in English, his accent thick, the edge of tears making his voice brittle. "You think this means anything, Aisha? You can fuck your English boys. You're still mine."

Aisha rolled her eyes so hard she could feel the strain at the back of her head. The beauty of the distance—miles, time zones, half a world between Tel Aviv and this ramshackle dorm in Manchester—was that it let her amplify her contempt without worrying about the consequences. What was Yair going to do? March into England with his little Tavor rifle and a vendetta? She thought not. He couldn't even leave his base without six forms and the approval of a colonel.

She moved her iPhone, angling it for a better view of Henry's face, sweat-streaked and a little dazed, already deep in the fog of desire and confusion that was Red Rose's signature gift to the uninitiated. The lamp behind her flickered, accentuating the sharp lines of her cheeks, her collarbones, the faint golden shimmer of the necklace she never took off, the one her mother gave her before she left for university—an heirloom she'd weaponised into something less sentimental, more totemic. She was reminded, just then, that her mother still thought she prayed five times a day.

There was a knock on the door, and Aisha knew that it was her friends, Maria Kovacs, the Mancunian who's paternal grandfather was Hungarian, then there was fellow Third Years, Ariana Butera, Sarah Smith and Lucy Grand, all gathered in the corridor, as always—unapologetically loud and on the hunt for post-rehearsal drama, or perhaps sensing the low thrumming pulse of spectacle from within Aisha's room. The door rattled as Maria's unmistakable accent filtered through, as Mancunian as Old Trafford, Sarah, the Scouse drawl following a split-second later, the two voices overlapping in a cheerful cacophony of student chaos.

"Oi! Aisha! You finished breaking the First Year yet, or do you need reinforcements?" Maria shouted through the fire door, laughter in her voice, no doubt already clutching a bottle of cheap rosé pinched from the faculty fridge. Behind her, Ariana chimed in with mock outrage, "If you're going to use up all the freshers, at least leave us some for the afterparty!"—her Brooklyn vowels slicing the northern gloom, and Lucy, deadpan as always, offered, "Don't mind us, we'll just wait out here with our dignity. Not that any of us have that left."

Aisha rolled her eyes, grinning at Henry, whose entire body seemed to tense at the prospect of more witnesses, his embarrassment deepening the blush high on his cheeks. "You see what I mean?" she murmured, leaning forward to whisper just for him, though Yair could no doubt pick it up as well. "At Red Rose, privacy's a myth. Everything's a performance. You don't get to be anonymous here, not even with your trousers round your ankles."

With a flourish, she flicked her wrist, grabbed a pillow from the floor and tossed it at the door. "Five minutes, girls!" she called, voice clear and ringing. "If I'm not done by then, you can break the lock and join in—but no stealing my moment, or my boy!" She shot a wicked glance at her iPhone, making sure Yair had a clear view of her mischief, her smirk, her absolute control over every element of the scene. "And if any of you start live-streaming, I'll post those photos of Ariana's disastrous Romeo audition on the Noticeboard."

That drew a chorus of fake groans and laughter from the corridor, footsteps shuffling as the girls retreated, plotting god only knew what mischief in the shadowy hallway. For a brief, liminal moment, Aisha felt the full weight of her strange, precarious adulthood: both adored and feared by her peers, always the ringmaster, never quite the mark.

Henry, beneath her, whimpered softly, his nerves and arousal mingling with a dizzy kind of disbelief. Aisha softened, just for a second, brushing sweaty curls from his forehead. "You're alright, Henry. You're not the first, and you won't be the last. But you might be the first who didn't ask me for a selfie after. That's something."

On the screen, Yair watched silently, the mask of military indifference restored, though his eyes were glassy with the sharp, bitter edge of longing. Aisha lifted her chin, holding his gaze. "Is this what you wanted, ya habbibi? To see me take someone else? To see what it's like when I have power, not you?"

Yair's response was a long, loaded pause. "I want you to be safe," he said at last, in a voice more vulnerable than he'd shown before. "I want you to come back to me, when you're ready. Not because you hate me, or because I make you angry. Just—because."

Aisha's expression softened, a flicker of genuine emotion slipping through her usual wall of irony and performance. "You know I'll always come back, one way or another," she replied, the words laced with both promise and threat. "But only if you remember you're not the only one who's lost people, Yair. You're not the only one with scars."

She glanced down at Henry, who was watching her with something like awe. "You know what the difference is between you and him, Yair? He still believes love is possible. You believe in war. Maybe that's why I can't quit either of you."

Henry blinked at that—too innocent to quite parse the layers, but sensitive enough to feel the change in atmosphere, the way the energy shifted from raw carnality to something deeper, older, almost sacred. He reached for Aisha's hand, squeezing it with unexpected strength. "You're not alone, Aisha," he said, his voice trembling but clear. "Not here. Not ever."

She let the words settle between them, heavy and real, a momentary balm against the ache of old wounds. Then, with a final glance at the iPhone—at Yair, whose eyes now shone with the shock of unshed tears—she leaned down and kissed Henry, slow and unhurried, her body moving with deliberate tenderness.

After a long, breathless moment, she broke the kiss, smiling crookedly. "That's enough for now. You can tell your mum whatever you like—but remember, if she ever meets me, I'll be the one bringing the wine, not the bombs."

With a theatrical sigh, she rolled off Henry, landing with a thump on the tangled bedspread. She snatched up her phone, holding it so Yair could see her face clearly, her cheeks flushed with triumph and exertion. "Goodnight, soldier," she murmured, the words equal parts mockery and affection. "Don't do anything I wouldn't do. And try not to shoot any more aid workers, yeah?"

Yair managed a sad, crooked smile, then hung up. The screen went black, the severed digital tether leaving Aisha oddly lighter, as if some invisible burden had been temporarily set aside.

She lay there, breathing heavily, letting the silence seep into her bones. Henry, curled on his side beside her, stared at the ceiling as if seeing it for the first time. In the corridor, her friends were already growing impatient— she could hear the tell-tale clink of glass, the shuffle of feet, the high, excited voices that meant the night was far from over.

Aisha sat up, raking her fingers through her hair, and regarded Henry with a gentle, mischievous smile. "You alright, love?"

He nodded, wide-eyed and awed. "I… I think so. I mean, I've never… Not like that. I thought you'd be… I don't know. Cruel, maybe. But you weren't."

She shrugged, tossing him a fresh towel from the radiator. "I'm cruel when I need to be. But mostly I'm just bored. And bored girls do dangerous things."

He watched as she slipped from the bed and padded naked to the window, peering out onto the sodden quad below. The lights of Red Rose flickered in the drizzle, casting odd, broken shadows across the flagstones. The world outside was grey, wet, and relentlessly ordinary—so far from the fever-dream that throbbed within these four walls.

"Why do you do it?" Henry asked, wrapping the towel awkwardly around his waist, suddenly self-conscious. "Why… all of this?"

Aisha considered him for a long moment, silhouetted against the city's glow. "Because I can. Because it makes the world pay attention. Because sometimes, when I look at myself in the mirror after nights like this, I almost believe I exist. And because I like knowing that somewhere, someone will remember me."

****

CHAPTER 5 – Halloween In The Drama Classroom…

Thursday 31st October 2024

Ashley Ketchum had to admit, as a Second Year drama student at Red Rose, being predicted a Third in his Batchelor of Arts for Drama degree was, if he'd have been at any other university, probably a mark of disgrace. At Red Rose Academy, however, the threshold for humiliation was always shifting, and so long as you kept yourself afloat—barely, sometimes gasping and spluttering—it was counted as a minor victory. The place rewarded survival over brilliance, persistence over genius.

Lounging on the stage that was in one of the drama studios, cock in hand while waiting for Dr Peterson, a former Oxford lecturer who had resigned from the famed faculty with little explanation a decade ago, Ashley was aware he was pushing boundaries, but the entire institution seemed to exist to prod at boundaries and then cackle when they tumbled down.

The fact that it was well known Peterson was a drunk, and that he'd spend more time at the pub on campus than in his office, made the drama department a place of swirling chaos and shifting hierarchies. Ashley looked around the half-dark drama studio—one of the three that Red Rose managed to keep funded, more by sheer belligerence than budgeting—and grinned to himself. The old wood floor still bore the scars of a thousand staged murders, betrayals, and agonies. The lights overhead flickered faintly as if afraid to fully illuminate what students got up to on this stage after hours.

Tonight, Halloween, the students were expected to produce something memorable for Peterson—a scene, a piece, or even just an improvisation that would linger in the air like the cheap dry-ice that sometimes billowed from the wings. Everyone suspected the real task was to see who could scandalise him, or at least make him laugh. Peterson had said as much, last Tuesday, after draining his mug of tea (rum, everyone presumed):

"I want to see something raw, something true. Not Shakespeare's bones dug up yet again. Make me regret leaving Oxford."

He'd laughed, but his eyes—red-rimmed, twitchy—had dared them all to try.

He and Maya Leverne, one of the other Second Years, had planned to do the most scandalous performance ever, him dressed as Puck from A Midsummer's Night Dream, and her as a "sweet, innocent, virgin princess", and shag for the entire 8 minute slot that they had been allocated.

Maya had been the mastermind—her mother, a porn actress in her heyday, had coached her on the mechanics of shocking an audience, but Maya was more interested in the reaction of her peers and the challenge of pushing Peterson's boundaries.

Ashley admired her audacity almost as much as he admired her ability to memorise and recite Shakespeare with the sweetness of a lamb and the venom of a viper.

The irony that the audience would be literally the Second Years, Peterson and the Chancellor, and that was only if Hardcastle hadn't decided to go to yet another Labour Constituency meeting to try and get the nod to run for elected office, wasn't lost on Ashley.

Red Rose always felt on the verge of collapse or eruption—nobody could ever tell which, and the administration seemed to thrive in that perpetual state of suspended disaster. The students had learned to do the same, and tonight, on Halloween, chaos felt like a kind of worship.

The irony that the theatre itself had been blocked from being used by Peterson, who was the Head of the Drama Department, added to the general feeling of siege. The official reason was "repairs to the lighting rig," but everyone knew Peterson simply preferred the intimacy, the sweat-soaked confessional quality, of the old drama studios. No grand stage tonight—just a splintered floor, moth-eaten curtains, and the nervous pulse of anticipation.

"What a tiny faggot!" Carl Stevenson, a fellow Second Year in the drama programme, snarled from in front of him. Ashley noticed that the 19 year old's cock was out as well, erect, and larger than his 3 inch appendage, a detail that Carl flaunted with the brash, unthinking cruelty of someone who had never truly suffered for anything in his life. He sauntered across the scuffed stage boards with the swagger of a minor tyrant, grinning at Ashley with teeth that gleamed slightly, as if freshly bared for a fight. "Bet you can't take all of mine like Maya did!"

Ashley licked his lips, as, despite being straight, he, like most of the Red Rose students, would happily shag anyone, be they male, woman, trans or nonbinary. That was the true Red Rose spirit: chaos, lust, and the collapse of old borders, all mixed together like gin and regret. He knew that Carl's 6 inch erection could be deep throated by him, as he had had a 10 inch appendage before from Kiera, a trans Third Year the previous school year, when he was a First Year, and she had taught him how to deepthroat with the skill of a drag queen raised on Soho backrooms and Covent Garden afterparties.

"And if I can't?" Ashley said with a lopsided grin, his voice a blend of bravado and self-mockery, because that was the only way to survive in a room with people like Carl Stevenson—meet the jab with another, sharper one, and pretend you'd never flinch. That was the unspoken game at Red Rose: the first rule of humiliation was to wear it like a badge.

"If you can't, you owe me a pack of Camels and a bottle of Smirnoff for the afters," Carl leered, his cock bobbing slightly as he leaned in, stage-lights sketching brutal planes across his face. He was dressed—if one could call it that—as a demonic faun: latex horns, red suspenders, nothing else. Every Halloween the Red Rose drama cohort outdid themselves with costumes that hovered between burlesque and full-on pornographic. "If you can, then you'll let me fuck your arse, no lube."

Ashley had to admit, the offer of his rival for the few actual passes that his cohort were predicted in their Bachelor of Arts, as the majority, Maya included, were predicted a Fourth or even an outright failure, was oddly enticing in its cruelty. At Red Rose, stakes were always measured in currency of shame, bravado, and transgression. He shrugged, the stage chill pricking goosebumps along his arms.

"Deal," Ashley said, and his grin was sharp as a razor's edge. He spat in his palm for show, as if to lubricate, but it was all theatre—always theatre, even when the lines between role and reality dissolved. Carl's laugh was rough, savage, and echoed off the high black ceiling as if mocking the world beyond these battered walls.

Laying down on the wooden stage, the lacquer of the boards sticky against his skin, Carl got down on his knees in front of him, his erection stiffening as if it could do it any further, the eye of the snake coming ever closer as Carl made his way up Ashley's torso, which was topless as he was going to put on the Puck wings shortly, and he was going to oil himself with oil mixed with glitter, as Maya had demanded for their debauched fairy duet. But that could wait—the performance had already started, after all, and in Red Rose, every moment could be a scene, and every act, an audition.

Carl's breath was hot on Ashley's bare stomach, the faint tang of vodka lingering from pre-show swigs in the corridor. The hush in the room grew deeper, the anticipation thickening as students filtered in, half-naked, costumed, draped in fishnets, sequins, latex, or simply the arrogance of youth. Some jeered, some whistled, but none looked away; nothing so compelling as the prospect of humiliation, especially when it wasn't your own.

Ashley glanced at Maya, who had one of her besties, Nya Kingston, between her knees, and he knew that Nya was eating Maya out with the gusto of someone who hadn't been fed. Before he knew it, he could feel Carl's cock on his chin, it being slapped across it like a performance of both cruelty and invitation, a wordless demand to open up, to submit, and yet to do so as if the outcome had already been scripted. The room, cloaked in the half-light of cheap stage gels and the blue-white flicker from a battered portable LED bar, seemed to draw in on itself: the audience of peers and competitors, the shadows of a thousand earlier nights echoing along the wooden walls. The floor, rough and unyielding, dug into Ashley's spine as he tilted his head back, letting his tongue loll, throat relaxing in anticipation.

Licking the shaft with an almost ceremonial flourish, Ashley could taste the mingling flavours of sweat, anxiety, and some aftershave that Carl had probably borrowed from one of the dance students. The act itself was so public, so ruthlessly exposed, that for a split second the world narrowed to the heat and pulse of Carl's body above him and the tension in the room, a collective intake of breath. The Red Rose drama studio, with its battered curtains and flickering lights, had borne witness to many unspeakable things, but even so, Ashley could feel the charge in the air—a challenge not just to Peterson, but to the very institution itself.

He let his tongue swirl around the head, lips pressing in a parody of gentleness, eyes flickering up to meet Carl's for the briefest moment—a dare exchanged, a game with neither shame nor mercy. The audience—such as it was— was rapt, frozen between anticipation and the sick thrill of seeing how far the boundary would be pushed tonight. Out of the corner of his eye, Ashley could see Maya, now naked from the waist down, writhing against Nya's mouth, her painted nails scraping the girl's braids as if conducting her own symphony of destruction. Other students had gathered by now, drawn by the rumour of chaos, the chance to see the two most arrogant boys in Second Year go head-to-head (or mouth-to-cock, as the case may be).

Carl thrust forward, not ungently but with a competitive edge, as if the entire performance was still for points on a scoreboard only they understood. Ashley, for his part, relaxed his throat in the way Kiera had taught him last year, eyes fluttering for a second as Carl's length pressed deeper.

"You're a natural, Ketchum," Carl grunted as Ashley felt his legs and arse being lifted and his jeans being yanked down to his knees. There was no real privacy left, only the shell of modesty that the Red Rose crowd—drama students most of all—wore as costume. The audience's attention, bright and unflinching, bore down on Ashley as Carl's cock filled his mouth, his jaw aching with the stretch and the raw physicality of it. The humiliation was a living thing in the room, a haze almost thicker than the reek of sweat and alcohol, but Ashley swallowed it down, letting the motion become a rhythm, something nearly transcendent—performance and penance wrapped in one.

It was then that he found lips were being applied around his own erection, a warmth and pressure that made his breath catch in his throat, sending a ripple of raw, immediate sensation up his spine. He barely registered whose mouth it was, as his vision was Carls cock, ball sack and crotch, the back and forth as he sucked the shaft like an icicle, but he knew that there was also another mouth on his ball sack which was drawing his attention slightly.

"You know, you look gorgeous like that," Carl said with the grin of someone who was enjoying being swallowed whole. "Just think, once I've painted your mouth and arse, you'll be the damned masterpiece of this grim little theatre."

Ashley barely registered the words; they mingled with the hot flood of sensation swirling through him, the pressure of lips and tongue and teeth just gentle enough to tease but firm enough to assert dominance. The fingers digging into his thighs, the slight pinch of nails, the whispered laughter from the corners of the room—all melded into a chaotic symphony that could only exist at Red Rose on a night like this.

His vision blurred for a second as Carl's cock brushed the back of his throat, his gag reflex dancing on the edge but held at bay by practice, by need, by a strange kind of pride. Ashley's hands found purchase on Carl's hips, squeezing just enough to claim, just enough to urge him deeper. Somewhere behind his eyelids, the sharp scrape of Maya's laughter cut through the thick haze, mixing with the low moans and gasps of the watching crowd.

"Go on, Nikki, suck that little cocktail sausage," Ashley heard Barty Young shout, and then felt the speeding up of who he presumed was Nikki Swanson, Carl's regular fuck buddy, giving his 3 inch cock the kind of urgent, teasing attention that set his nerves alight and made his body hum with a dissonant mix of pleasure and humiliation. Nikki's warm mouth moved over his balls with a teasing persistence, her tongue flicking sharply, each motion rippling through Ashley's core like a current.

The crowd's murmurs swelled into a cacophony of encouragement and ribald laughter. It was a ritualistic scene, one part theatre, one part raw chaos—exposure stripped to its barest, most electric essentials. Ashley could feel the tension rising inside him like a tidal wave, swelling with every breath, every touch, every whispered command. The flickering LED bar cast intermittent shadows, exaggerating the gleam of sweat and glitter on skin, making every detail vivid and immediate.

Carl's hands gripped his hips tightly, pressing him down as if to anchor Ashley to this moment, this performance. His breathing was ragged, punctuated by rough grunts that echoed against the worn wood. The contrast between Carl's fierce intensity and Nikki's teasing softness created a dissonant harmony that left Ashley dizzy.

His throat tightened as Carl pressed his length deeper, the sharp edge of sensation brushing the back of his mouth. It was a dangerous dance with his gag reflex, and Ashley let himself teeter on the brink, holding steady through the burning sting, propelled by the adrenaline of the crowd's watchful eyes.

"Fuck, you're brilliant at this," Carl growled, his voice thick with something that bordered on affection and possession. "You're gonna make the bastard proud, Ketchum."

Ashley wanted to laugh, but his voice caught somewhere between a gasp and a moan. He felt Nikki's lips slide away from his balls to plant a trail of kisses along the inside of his thigh, her nails raking gently, just enough to mark him, to claim him.

The world narrowed. The weight of all those watching, the sharp taste of Carl's skin, the slick heat of Nikki's mouth—all condensed into a single point of awareness, an epicentre of sensation and power. Here, on this battered stage with flickering lights and moth-eaten curtains, the boundaries between audience and performer, pain and pleasure, control and surrender dissolved.

"Fuck, I'm gonna cum," Carl grunted, and Ashley felt his classmate spill into his mouth like a hose, the liquid filling his mouth with its salty taste.

The next thing Ashley knew, Carl was removing his cock from Ashley's mouth and, raising himself, spreading the remains over Ashley's chin, nose and hair, the mixture of the recent oral sex that he had given Carl, and the oral that he was receiving from the redhead second year that was taking on his 3 inch member.

Looking to the left, he saw Maya and Nya had concluded their first act and were now sitting next to each other, their fingers busy petting each other while their tongues were locked in a dual for dominance.

"God, Nikki, I'm nearly cumming," Ashley gasped, hardly believing how the pleasure—tinged as always with the ever-present threat of ridicule—spiked in him under the combined ministrations of tongue and teeth, the rustle of whispered commentary, the electric thrum of being watched, judged, envied, or despised. "Carl still has to fuck my arse."

The irony, Ashley knew, about Nikki servicing him was that she was a cousin of one of Manic Radio's drive time hosts, Callie Hall, 21 years old and who had recently run for Mayor of London on a platform of banning Capital FM, nationalising Chicken Cottage and Spoons, and free WKD for all over 18s. After finishing a campaign tour that was half music festival, half political stunt, she'd gone to Clacton to stand as an MP candidate against Reform UK's Nigel Farage. Nikki, meanwhile, wore her cousin's notoriety like a badge—a sort of unspoken dare to anyone at Red Rose to one-up the wildness she carried in her blood.

Tonight, Nikki's laugh carried across the room—mocking, brittle, as if the whole university's latent madness was distilled into that single, glitter-dusted sound. The crowd in the studio thickened, all eyes locked on the spectacle: bodies sprawled, knickers round ankles, faces flushed with vodka or the thrill of something irredeemable. In the far corner, someone had climbed onto a battered table and started reciting lines from The Duchess of Malfi in a northern accent, pelting stray wine gums at anyone who dared to heckle.

Ashley's thoughts swirled as he came with only a minute amount, barely enough to coat Nikki's tongue. She swallowed with exaggerated flourish, sitting up and wiping her mouth with the back of her hand—her eyes never leaving his, glitter swirling at her cheekbones as she flashed him a shark's smile. Around them, the half-dark of the studio vibrated with an energy that was half arousal, half the feverish excitement of a riot about to break out. Every surface was sticky with spilled drinks and anticipation.

As Carl rose, licking his lips, there was no time wasted in the choreography of humiliation. He strutted a circle around Ashley, arms wide as if absorbing applause, his faun horns askew, sweat glistening in the hollows of his collarbones. "Right then, Ash. You know the bet." His voice was a low growl—there was triumph in it, but not malice, just the merciless, ritual camaraderie that passed for friendship at Red Rose.

Ashley, wiping Carl's seed from his chin with a careless swipe, looked out into the crowd, whose expressions ranged from rapt horror to naked glee. He knew Dr Thomas Peterson wouldn't be arriving for another 12 minutes, if at all, and as for Chancellor Hardcastle, it was as likely as a naked Morris dance breaking out in the staffroom. The rules were clear—if you lost, you paid. If you won, you surrendered, and sometimes, at Red Rose, the surrender was the victory.

Getting to his knees, Ashley remembered his first anal experience, Kiera's breasts against his back while her erection had softly and tenderly penetrated him.

Ashley knew that the Noticeboard would be full of pictures and videos, but he didn't care, as he knew the faculty wouldn't access it, even the ones who had barely finished postgraduate studies at other universities and were barely old enough to teach.

As he got on all fours, he saw Nikki was getting on the floor, her toned body covered by a bloodied nun's outfit, the performance that she and Nya were slated for being a satirical Halloween sketch where a nun had slayed a vampire and Nya, playing God, was about to raise the nun to sainthood with an elaborate mock-baptism—half comedy, half heresy, and all Red Rose.

"You know, Ashley," she said sitting, her legs under his chest, "You're lucky. I've tried to get Carl to that to me for a month, but he only ever gives in for a crowd." Her grin was feral, wicked, bright as the blade of a knife in a music video. Ashley just smirked, the world a haze of sweat, old wood, and hormones, and tried not to flinch as Carl's hands gripped his hips, showman's rough, ready for a spectacle.

"On three, then," Carl said, his voice carrying through the low thrum of the room, daring anyone to look away now. The whole of Red Rose was a ring—no true privacy, no pause for reflection, only the raw, grinding, perpetual now.

Ashley closed his eyes, not out of shame but anticipation, and let himself drift on memory: Kiera's gentle encouragement, her laughter in his ear, the slow, insistent rhythm that had first taught him what real submission, and trust, could feel like. Tonight would not be gentle. That was the point.

He then noticed Nikki had hitched up the 'penguin' suit up, and notice that she wasn't wearing any underwear at all, that her hairless legs, obviously waxed, were much unlike Maya's, who shaved them weekly, not waxed.

"You like?" Nikki said with a grin that Ashley could only describe as predatory, the kind that promised mischief wrapped in anarchy. Her bare legs gleamed under the flickering studio lights, stark against the blood-splattered white of her nun's habit. "You know, you can eat me out while Carl fucks you like the animal you are. Or you can just bite down on my thigh, see if I scream louder than Maya." Her laughter, sharp and edged, spiked through the room, setting off a ripple of wolfish grins and hissing laughter from the half-drunk audience slouched along the studio walls. There was always a gamble at Red Rose, and tonight, Ashley was the table everyone was betting on.

Carl, behind him, spat theatrically on his palm, the gesture as much for the audience as for any practical purpose. He ran a slick hand down Ashley's back, pressing a palm between his shoulder blades as if to remind him—yes, you're here, yes, everyone's watching, yes, this is happening. Ashley gripped Nikki's thighs and pressed his face to the soft, bare skin, the faint scent of sweat and faded perfume mixing with the tang of vodka in his nostrils.

The first push was a shock, blunt and invasive, and he grunted, teeth scraping Nikki's thigh just to anchor himself, just to have something to bite, something to taste other than Carl's salt and spit. Around them, the energy ratcheted up—a dozen mobile phone screens winked on, some faces hungry for scandal, others just glazed with the bored entitlement of those who'd seen it all before. But this—this was different. This was the boundary, and as the friction built and Carl's hips pressed forward, Ashley realised he was crossing it and didn't want to stop.

Nikki, ever the mistress of chaos, slid a hand to his head, guiding his mouth between her legs. "Be a good boy," she hissed, voice pitched for the audience as much as for him. "Show Carl how grateful you are." Ashley complied, tongue darting out, tasting her, finding her slick and already trembling with anticipation. He could feel Carl's breath hot on the back of his neck, the guttural growl as he thrust, the rough slam of pelvis against arse, and the laughter and shouts of the crowd—some shocked, some cheering, some simply hungry for more.

Ashley's world condensed to the taut throb of the moment: flesh, humiliation, performance, the edge between agony and bliss. Every fibre of the old Red Rose studio seemed to pulse with the rhythms of their bodies, of the crowd's savage delight, of a culture where shame was just another part of the dance. Each thrust from Carl sent a sharp electric jolt through his core; each scrape of Nikki's thigh against his teeth, the taste of her on his tongue, grounded him in the animal heat of now.

He heard a voice—Maya's, unmistakably wicked, from her perch beside Nya. "Don't let him make you cry, Ash!" she called, and the room erupted in a volley of whoops and cackles, the derision tinged with envy, a recognition that for a fleeting instant, he was the centre of the universe. Maya, already half-naked and tangled with Nya in a symphony of limbs and laughter, looked every inch the vengeful goddess she had styled herself for tonight: crown askew, lipstick smeared, body shining with a film of sweat and triumph.

"We can get down like there's no one around..." Britney's warble bled through the battered Bluetooth speaker in the corner—probably Maya's, though who could tell with the detritus of half a dozen half-dressed students strewn across the studio floor. The lyric, accidentally apt, sliced through the chaos as if to mock the very idea of privacy. But Red Rose was never private, not truly. That was its curse and its liberation, the constant performance, the ceaseless audience—every act, every groan, every shudder destined to live in the collective, glitter-soaked memory of the academy.

Ashley's face pressed harder into Nikki's thigh, the bloodied nun's habit bunched around his ears, her thighs clamped around his head as her fingers tugged at his hair. The taste of her—sweat, vodka, and cum from where she had fingered at herself with the vigour of a woman possessed, no doubt when she had been making Ashley's erection, the small swell of flesh that passed for his cock, ache with a kind of giddy anticipation—was intoxicating. Nikki's thighs, steely and slick, pressed either side of his face, forcing his tongue deeper into her folds, every flick and swirl of it drawn from muscle memory and a primal hunger to please, to survive, to perform. The taste was sharp, electric, a living testament to the chaos they were all so addicted to. Somewhere in the back of his mind, Ashley was aware that this scene would haunt the Red Rose grapevine by morning—edited, posted, memed, immortalised and dissected until its every shameful beat was a shared legend.

Behind him, Carl's rhythm grew faster, more insistent. The pain—a burning, tearing shock—mingled now with a dark, swirling pleasure that left Ashley gasping into Nikki's heat. He bit down on her thigh, not hard enough to break skin but enough to make her jolt and moan—a sound that, in the context of the carnage around them, seemed almost delicate, almost a secret shared between them in the midst of the spectacle. Carl's hands, rough and certain, gripped his hips like a steering wheel, steering Ashley through the rapids of pain and submission, a journey with no destination except surrender.

A hand—Nya's, presumably, slick with Maya's juices and glitter—reached down to grip Ashley's shoulder, steadying him as the force of Carl's thrusts threatened to knock him off balance. The laughter and jeers, the slap of skin on skin, the shrill electric wail of Britney Spears in the background: all of it merged into a delirious fever dream that, for a moment, made the world outside the battered studio recede until there was only this, this moment, this communion of pain and pleasure and unashamed spectacle.

Nikki came with a sudden, sharp shudder, her nails digging twin crescents into Ashley's scalp, thighs tightening like a vice as she ground herself against his face. He rode out the wave, swallowing her cries, the salt and heat of her release flooding his mouth. Her head fell back, crimson hair tumbling over her face, as she gasped out a prayer—or a curse—at the cracked plaster ceiling.

"Fuck me, Ketchum, you're good for a drama boy," she laughed, voice hoarse, her body trembling still. Around them, the crowd cheered and hooted, some beating on the floor with their shoes, others pelting sweets and scraps of costume in a manic, spontaneous ovation. "Give the lad a degree in eating out," Barty called out, and the laughter rolled through the studio in waves, breaking against the walls and returning, amplified and fractured.

Carl, close to his own climax, slammed into Ashley with a final, brutal thrust. He came with a guttural shout, using Ashley's hips as anchor, marking the conclusion of their wager with a savage, almost tender finality. The sense of being claimed, used, and displayed—raw and unfiltered—was like nothing Ashley had felt before. There was no room for shame, only a weird, dizzy sense of pride. Here he was, in front of half the year, bent over and fucked, but still present, still himself, still unbroken.

He collapsed forward, cheek pressed to the sticky grain of the stage floor, vision tunnelling and pulse a staccato drum in his ears. Nikki slid away, the taste of her still sharp on his tongue, the imprint of her thighs hot on his cheeks, and for a moment the world was nothing but a blur of flickering lights and thunderous applause—the savage glee of an audience that had tasted blood and wanted more.

Carl pulled out with a slap, the motion punctuated by a howl from the assembled crowd. Someone threw a crumpled plastic cup at Ashley's feet. "Encore!" came the shout, echoing from the shadows where students pressed shoulder to shoulder, their eyes shining with a mix of hunger and disbelief. Red Rose, for all its posturing, still found ways to shock itself.

Ashley rose on shaking arms, feeling the sweat trickle down his back, mingling with the lingering ache that radiated from his arse, a dull throb offset by the wild, heady rush of endorphins. He could smell himself, Carl, and Nikki all over his skin—evidence of the night's spectacle, impossible to wash away. He reached for his jeans, tugging them halfway up his hips, but thought better of it. Why bother, here?

Carl strutted, cock glistening, a gladiator post-victory. He gave a mock bow, then fell sprawling beside Ashley, laughing so hard tears shone in his eyes. "Never let it be said you didn't pay your debts, Ketchum," he crowed, then pressed a sloppy, laughing kiss to Ashley's temple, a parody of affection. "You'll get your vodka later, mate."

Nikki sat cross-legged, straightening her habit and fixing her hair with a comb she produced, impossibly, from the chaos of her costume. "Next time you owe me dinner first," she said, flicking a wink at Ashley. "Or at least a bag of chips." Her voice was steady, but her eyes were glassy, wide, and wild—an edge of something raw and real beneath the bravado.

Around them, the studio had become a riot of sound and colour: Maya and Nya had collapsed in a tangle of limbs, their laughter ringing out like bells over the drone of Britney's relentless chorus; Barty was draping himself in a moth-eaten curtain, declaiming something in cod-Elizabethan; others traded costumes, drinks, and kisses, the air thick with the stink of sweat, arousal, and cheap vodka.

The old drama studio was more confessional than classroom, more den than theatre. By now, even those who'd only come to watch were swept up in the festival of bodies and defiance.

The floor was a chaos of spilled drinks, costume fragments, and sweet wrappers, trampled beneath the careless urgency of a night that would live in memory and rumour for months.

****

CHAPTER 6 – Not A Porcelain Doll...
Saturday 2nd November 2024

The irony was not lost on Darya Ivanova that, despite having lost her virginity nearly a month ago, that, being Russian born and a ballet student, she was treated as if she was a porcelain doll—fragile, enigmatic, a symbol of some old-world, frostbitten purity that only existed in the fevered imaginations of others. Born in Moscow, Darya's family moved to London in 2013, when she was 7, not out of fear or love for Britain, but for her father's lucrative appointment at an oil conglomerate headquartered in Mayfair, and for her mother's restless craving for new shops, new gossips, new scandals. She had gone to prep schools with the children of oligarchs and hedge funders, developed a perfect, lilting English that only showed its accent when she drank, and, by seventeen, had already danced in Vienna and Paris on summer residencies, always as "the Russian"—never quite allowed to be just a girl in a leotard, sweat on her brow, calluses on her toes.

She wasn't the first Ivanova to be involved in ballet, as her paternal aunt, Anistasia, was a member of the prestigious Bolshoi Ballet in Russia, a certain legacy that hovered over Darya like a spectral chaperone. Family dinners always brought up Anistasia's triumphs, the standing ovations in Moscow, the endless flowers, the photo on the grand staircase. For Darya, that ghost weighed heavier than any pas de deux. It was a mantle she both craved and resented, one stitched not of tulle but of stories, expectation, and the distinct loneliness that came from always being the exception, never the rule.

Red Rose, for all its chaos, hadn't been her first choice of university, as, due to the 2022 sanctions when the Motherland invaded the Ukraine and the resulting collapse in East-West cultural exchange, her Bolshoi option vanished, Royal Ballet had "paused" all Russian scholarships, and, even in Paris, the competition for one spot had become a war of surnames and allegiances. Manchester, in all its rain-slicked Northern gothic, was a compromise—one her parents disapproved of, but could not prevent. Red Rose had its own strange prestige, less imperial, more infamous; it offered freedom, or at least the appearance of it, and, most importantly, anonymity. Here, Darya was not just an Ivanova. Here, she could be rewritten, if only she dared.

Looking at her iPhone, she looked at the Red Rose Noticeboard app, and saw a video of her from Monday, being anally fucked by Justin, her tiny whimpers as his cock sawed her in half, the room alive with laughter and panting, the mirrors fogged, the chaos so absolute that, for a brief second, she almost mistook her own cries for someone else's. She watched herself on the little screen: back arched, mouth open, eyes fluttering shut as Justin gripped her hips, his knuckles white, the room behind them a blur of limbs and bodies, half in motion, half in silhouette. For a moment, she could almost smell the studio again—sweat, rosin, floor polish, and the faint metallic tang of blood where someone's toenail had split open.

@HarryMcKenzie: *Bet the doll can't take on all us Third Years on Saturday #whimperqueen*

Darya stared at the screen a moment longer, the dopamine twang of shame and adrenaline sparking up her spine. She could see the number of views: 438. It would crest five hundred by nightfall, she knew. It had become a game at Red Rose: how many would watch, who would comment, whose voice would tip the scales from mockery to worship, or back again. She was not the only one featured this week, not the only one tagged. But today, she was the one trending.

She knew every Saturday, The Rose Petal, the club that the Red Rose Student Union ran, would host a night of cheap drinks, debauchery and lots of music, and there were rumours that Manic Radio might be sending a host down from their Liverpool studios to do a DJ set. That, however, was only a rumour, Darya knew, but she knew one thing.

She was going to fuck every Third Year male, either orally, anally or vaginally, before the sun came up on Sunday—just to prove the so-called "porcelain doll" was neither fragile nor for display. She wanted to see their faces when they realised that she was as relentless, as hungry, as any of them. She wanted them to speak about her in the corridors and on the Noticeboard, but with something other than patronising awe or sleazy lust; she wanted the taste of power, the sharp cut of it, the chance to rewrite the story of Darya Ivanova with her own hands, her own body.

As the grey November afternoon melted towards dusk, the anticipation in Darya grew restless, jittering under her skin like a trapped moth. She danced alone in Studio 2 as the sun set, her legs straining against the chill, the mirrors reflecting every flicker of uncertainty and resolve. Her playlist, all Russian synth-pop and sharp-edged house, echoed off the battered floorboards. Her hair, loose from its bun, whipped her cheeks as she spun, turning until the room blurred and all that was left was her heartbeat thudding through the quiet.

"Menya polnostyu net..." the sound of the music filled the studio, the words—I am nothing—reverberating in her chest, only half-understood, but perfectly resonant. She knew that the English version of the t.A.T.u song Ya Soshla s Uma—"All The Things She Said"—was more inaccurate compared to the literal translation, "I'm in serious shit, I feel totally lost", being the English produced version, but tonight, she craved the original, the jagged vowels of her mother tongue.

Suddenly the door opened, and a Second Year BA Dance (Street Dancing) student, Daniel Parkinson, walked in, his outfit all trackies and tight vest, the sort of half-hearted attempt at athleisure that passed for both club and studio attire at Red Rose. His hair, buzzed at the sides and left wild on top, framed a face as pale as Darya's own, though Daniel's pallor came from too many all-nighters and a strict diet of Greggs sausage rolls and protein shakes. He hovered in the doorway, watching her spin, not bothering to announce himself. At Red Rose, privacy was more performance than reality.

"U nas yest' 3 chasa do otkrytiya Petal. Khotite kofe?" he asked, and Darya narrowed her eyes, surprised by his Russian—thickly accented, clumsy, but recognisable. She slowed her spin, toes squeaking to a halt on the battered floorboards, breath fogging in the unheated chill of Studio 2.

"I'm fine," she replied in English, not quite able to keep the suspicion from her voice. "And your accent is shit."

Daniel grinned, sheepish, hands shoved in his pockets. "My mum's from St. Petersburg. She left when Yeltsin was still chucking vodka at the White House. I've heard her curse in Russian since I could crawl. But, yeah, it's bollocks. Anyway, didn't mean to startle you." He watched her catch her balance, the ghost of her spin still echoing in the air, and his eyes flickered to the mirror, as if checking to see whether she was real, or just a reflection conjured by the half-light.

Darya shrugged, the old prickling anxiety of being watched shifting under her skin, but she kept her chin high. "Everyone comes here before The Petal. What do you want, Daniel?"

He considered her for a moment, and she saw—just for a second—the flicker of nerves, the faint uncertainty in his posture. "You. I know you're not some porcelain doll, to be preserved like a museum piece or perched on a plinth, right?" Daniel's grin was just crooked enough to suggest both nerves and bravado. "I want to fuck you. Or more precisely tie you up on the barre and make you beg me to breed you like the whore you really want to be. Make you pregnant and needy."

Darya knew Daniel had a pregnancy kink, and that he had been winding up half the year with his shameless, half-ironic boasts about knocking someone up before graduation—a running joke, except that, at Red Rose, no kink was really off-limits, and everyone's threats were half promises, half rehearsals for the next performance, sexual or otherwise.

She smirked, letting the tension stretch, relishing the cold, buzzing spike of his desire. "You'd have to last longer than two minutes for that, Daniil," she shot back in Russian, the diminutive lilt both mocking and intimate. She dropped into a deep plié, stretching the ache from her calves, eyes locked with his in the mirror. "Besides, I don't think you could handle me."

"Yeah?" He said, approaching her like a hunter does its prey, his movements languid, predatory, every step a deliberate performance. The air in the studio felt charged, as if the dust motes themselves were humming to the tension between them. Daniel lingered at the edge of the old Marley flooring, the battered ballet barre separating them like a line in the sand.

"I could handle you, Darya," he said, dropping his voice to a husky challenge. "But could you handle what everyone's going to see when the Noticeboard gets my footage up?"

She rolled her eyes, masking the flicker of nerves that always came when the threat of exposure, the endless camera's gaze, pressed in around her. At Red Rose, shame was public property, and secrets were just another kind of social credit. "If you're going to make a show of it," she replied, stretching a foot onto the barre, "at least make it worth the audience's time. Nobody needs another video of you dry-humping the furniture, Daniel."

He grinned, flashing crooked teeth, swaggering forward to hook an arm around her waist, spinning her to face him in a single, practiced motion. For a moment, Darya's muscles tensed, the old instinct to fight or flee sparking at her spine, but she held her ground, letting herself lean into the provocation.

Daniel's hand drifted to the small of her back, fingers splaying, thumb pressing the sharp knobs of her spine. "Say the word," he murmured, lips brushing her hair, "and I'll tie you to this barre right now. Let the whole of Red Rose see you're no fucking doll."

Darya's breath caught, half with anticipation, half with the cool clarity of decision. She met his eyes in the mirror, the ghostly overlay of their bodies fracturing in the failing afternoon light.

"You think I care?" she said, her Russian accent thickening, the words curling like smoke in the air. "You think I'm afraid of your little games?"

His hand tightened, possessive. "No, I think you're waiting for someone to treat you like you're breakable, and I'm not that bloke. Let's give them something to talk about, Darya. Or are you all talk and no action?"

She didn't answer with words. Instead, she caught his wrist and spun, letting the momentum drag her closer to the barre, her grip firm, confident. She raised her other leg in an arabesque, hips tipped just so, the stretch pulling through her thigh and glute. "If you want to tie me, you'd better do it before someone else claims me first. I've got a queue tonight, you know. All the Third Years are waiting. It's an open invitation."

Daniel barked a laugh, half surprise, half delight. "All of them, yeah? That's ambitious, Ivanova. You want to be legend or a warning?"

"Why not both?" she replied, a shadow-smile curving her lips. She dropped her leg, pressed back against the barre, and arched her back, displaying herself not just for Daniel, but for her own pleasure—defiance in every line of her body. "I'm done being the girl who's too precious to fuck. Tonight, I'm the one everyone's going to remember."

Daniel watched her, eyes narrowed, hunger and calculation battling in his gaze. "Then you'd better get started. Because I'm not the only one watching." He gestured with his chin to the high window at the side of the studio. There, silhouetted by the last glow of evening, two First Year girls—likely drama or musical theatre, their faces half-familiar—pressed their noses to the glass, phones already out, eager for the next rumour to leak through the digital grapevine.

Darya turned to them, gave a little wave, then blew a kiss, her laughter sharp, challenging. "Enjoy the show," she called, her accent melting the words into a soft threat.

Daniel pulled a length of elastic from his pocket—a habit, for dancers, to always have one spare—looped it round her wrist, then the barre, knotting it with a deftness that spoke to hours spent improvising makeshift restraints in dressing rooms and wings.

"You sure?" he murmured, low, as the elastic pulled tight, leaving her arms stretched above her head, her chest thrust forward, vulnerable, exposed.

She looked him dead in the eye, voice as cold as the Volga in January. "Make me beg, Daniil. If you can."

He grinned, grabbing her arms, his lips by her ears, and Darya felt his erection stiffen as he grinded against her from behind, the friction sudden and brazen, grinding the last of her shyness to dust. The studio was chilled, and the glass at the window now vibrated with the delighted gasps of their unexpected audience. Daniel's hands slipped beneath the hem of her sweatshirt, callused palms skating up the hard curve of her abdomen, cupping her breast, fingers squeezing with a carelessness that was entirely deliberate.

"You know what you are? A little slut. All you Russians think you're so mysterious, so untouchable. You think that just because Putin is your leader that you're made of stone, but you're not. You're just flesh and need, same as the rest of us."

The slap that he administered as he slid his palm against her face made Darya feel dizzy—not from pain, but from the sharp clarity of its sting, the rupture of decorum, the smashing of every glass slipper ever forced onto her feet. The sound echoed around Studio 2, brittle as cracked ice, and for a moment, Darya saw herself as the others did: stretched out and bound, hair wild, cheeks flushed from the blow, a single tear streaking down her cheek—not from humiliation, but from the shock of being seen, truly seen, in a way the stage and the mirror had never allowed.

Daniel laughed quietly, low and triumphant. "You know, Monday, I'm going to tie you to the bookshelves in the library, naked, and let everyone, male or female, fuck you like the whore you are. And if one of them gets you pregnant, then good, because your tits will no longer be like pancakes, but swollen and heavy, leaking for everyone to see. You'll walk the corridors of Red Rose with a belly full of someone's bastard, and every student will know you were just a vessel for their amusement. And if you don't get preggers Monday, I'll tie you up in the library every day until you're knocked up, and I'll move into your dorm and fuck you each day until you're bred and ruined, until your whole reputation is just a memory, a footnote on some gossip chain, a story girls tell in whispers when they think no one is listening." Daniel's breath was hot against her neck, voice velvet-dark, laced with mockery, with desire. "That's what you want, isn't it? Not to be anyone's princess, but to be everyone's plaything."

Darya knew it was his kink talking, and that, in reality, she'd love to be knocked up and used, ruined, celebrated only as a shared trophy. But she knew that it was only, in part, talk, that he wanted to push her, to test the limits not just of her body, but of her sense of self, her story, her legacy. And in the crucible of that desire, her own heart hammered out a rhythm not of fear, but of anticipation— hungry, sharp, so acute it almost made her dizzy.

The elastic bit into her wrists as Daniel's hand left her breast and slid lower, his other hand firm on her shoulder, pressing her into the barre until the wooden rail was an iron band across her chest. His fingers found the waistband of her dance shorts, yanking them down with rough impatience, exposing the pale, muscular curve of her hips and the ballet-cut line of her knickers—black, silk, with a deliberate cut in the crotch so she could finger herself whenever she wanted, Ann Summers having thought she was 16 when she walked into the Manchester branch of the infamous adult shop. The salesgirl hadn't blinked twice—girls like Darya, ethereal, too serious, and dressed in the battered glamour of the city's dancers, came in often, their secrets tucked behind pale, impassive faces and heavy, oversized coats.

Manchester, Darya knew, was full of girls who grew up too fast, the city itself a grinding wheel of hunger and want, all of it reflected now in the sharp ache at the core of her body as Daniel's hands made her a spectacle.

The chill air kissed her exposed skin. Daniel's hand slid between her thighs, and Darya let out a small, involuntary gasp—not from shyness, but from the nakedness of being watched, from the thrill of her own body's need. The laughter from outside the window, sharper now, punctuated by the flutter of phones pressed to glass, only sharpened her focus. Every nerve sang with anticipation, every movement a performance with no audience but those who would tell the story later—always exaggerated, always whispered.

"You know, they've got one of your warmongering Ukrainian killers in WARS next season, and apparently he's got a cock that would tear your pussy apart. Maybe I'll get him to take a turn after me, just to see if you can still walk after tonight," Daniel whispered, tongue flicking over the shell of Darya's ear as his fingers hooked her knickers aside, exposing her to the cold, prying air of the studio.

Darya knew what WARS was, a racing series that was set to compete against Formula 1 and Formula 2 called World Apex Racing Series, and that Viktor Sidorov, a Russian born Brit, was singing onto the inaugural World Apex Racing Series Juniors championship, a second tier series to the main WARS series. She had seen photos of him on Instagram, and had often fingered herself over his chiselled body, the soon to be DreamJet Racing driver having a six pack that she knew would bruise her with every thrust. She had even commented anonymously on one of his private posts, a thirsty "those hands could break me in half" under a photo of him wrenching his helmet off after a rain-drenched lap at the Goodwood Festival of Speed earlier in the year.

He hadn't replied, but she sometimes fantasised that he'd seen it—that he'd clicked on her profile, that he'd see that she was a ballerina, that she was, like him, from Russia, that she would—

"You'd like that, wouldn't you?" he murmured again, lips brushing the nape of her neck as his hand slid deeper between her legs. "That little WARS fuckboy dragging you into the paddock, grease on your thighs, his pit crew watching while he bends you over the nose of his race car."

His words painted lurid, impossible images behind her eyelids—smoke, burning rubber, the metallic reek of petrol; Viktor's hands slick with oil, his fingers gripping her waist as if she were nothing but a tool, a mechanism to be used and discarded. The vision sent a sharp tremor of want through her, so vivid it almost hurt. Darya's fingers curled against the barre, wrists chafing against the elastic, her hips twitching in involuntary anticipation. She could feel the scrutiny of the girls at the window, the certainty that everything—every gasp, every half-whispered plea—would become rumour by midnight. The thought did not scare her. It exhilarated her.

Daniel's hand was relentless now, two fingers probing her, knuckles grinding as he worked her open, rough and unhurried. He knew his audience as well as she did. Each movement was exaggerated, deliberate—a performance as much for those outside the glass as for Darya herself. His other hand gripped her shoulder, pinning her in place, ensuring the curve of her back was displayed for all to see.

"Maybe that's all you need," he sneered, hips grinding against her bare arse, the hard line of his cock straining against his joggers. "A real man. Not these little northern boys with their shite music and shitter football. Someone to break you open for good. You want to be ruined, don't you? That's the real reason you came here—so far from your precious Bolshoi. You wanted to be anonymous, but you can't help yourself. You want to be seen."

She arched against him, not quite able to stifle her moan, her words slurred by the rush of blood in her ears. "Maybe I do. Maybe I want them all to see me. Not just as a doll, but as—"

"A fucktoy?" Daniel supplied, smacking her again. "Because that's what you are. A little commie fucktoy who better obey her masters, yeah?"

The irony, Darya knew, that even though she didn't agree with Putin, or the Soviet method of Communism, the fact that he was commanding her with abuse and power turned her on, it turned her into something raw, a creature of the moment, stripped of ideology and history and name. She let the sensation wash through her—the pain and humiliation, the wild thrill of relinquishing control, the knowledge that she was not porcelain at all but flesh and nerves, hunger and will.

Her body responded before her mind did, arching beneath Daniel's grip, legs trembling as his fingers worked her faster, deeper, her hips pushing back against him with each brutal thrust. The elastic binding her wrists bit deep, leaving pale crescents that would mark her as surely as a tattoo. Her face burned with more than cold: it was the heat of being watched, of knowing the window's two faces had multiplied into many—more First Years pressed to the glass, phones capturing every detail, every moan and gasp, a slow-burning scandal already brewing.

But she didn't care. In that moment, she wanted it. All of it.

"Say it," Daniel hissed, breath hot against her ear. "Say what you are."

"I'm—" Her voice broke, the words catching in her throat. The Russian tried to rise, but English came out, thick and ugly with need. "I'm your fucktoy. Your whore. Do what you want with me."

"Louder."

She raised her voice, the words ringing off the battered walls. "I'm your fucktoy. I'm a whore. Use me…master."

Daniel grinned, his hands gripping her hips so hard she knew she'd bruise, his breath hot and savage against her neck. The performance was no longer just for the crowd at the window; it was for herself, a ritual of self-destruction and revelation that felt, paradoxically, like the only true act of agency she had left. The brittle image of the "porcelain doll" had shattered long ago, its shards ground underfoot in the rehearsal studios, in the beds of boys who wanted her only for the ghost of someone else's legend. Now she was nothing so delicate, nothing so pure.

She felt Daniel's cock press against the wet seam of her cunt through the slit in her knickers, the head forcing past the silk, the intrusion sharp, stretching. He didn't ease in, but pushed, slow and relentless, hips grinding until the resistance gave way and she was filled, the barre beneath her chest now the only thing keeping her upright. Darya bit her lip hard, forcing herself not to cry out, but the audience outside the glass—now four, six, more—caught every micro-expression, the flutter of her eyelids, the quiver in her jaw.

He fucked her with the merciless rhythm of someone trying to prove a point. Every thrust was measured, deliberate, calculated to display her to the window, to the mirrors, to herself. Darya felt herself splitting—not in body, but in spirit, the demure, haunted ballerina sundered from the girl who revelled in her own destruction. She felt the split and embraced it, hips bucking back into Daniel's every thrust, her moans now loud, ragged, ricocheting off the walls.

The girls at the window giggled, pointed, filmed. One of them licked her lips and mimed a lewd gesture, their eyes wide and hungry with the power that came from seeing someone else's fall from grace. Darya looked at them through the sweat-tangled strands of her hair, and for a moment she felt something close to love—no, not love, but kinship, the recognition of mutual need. They wanted to see her ruined because they wanted to know it could happen, that the legend was a lie, that even a Russian doll could crack and spill its secrets.

"Harder," she gasped, not even sure if she meant it for Daniel or for herself. "Show them what you do to me."

He obliged, his hands tightening on her waist, each thrust now a piston, a blunt proof of her own appetites. He leaned over her, lips pressing against her ear. "You'll remember this when you're sucking them all off later," he hissed. "When every Third Year is lined up for their turn, when you're gagging and sobbing and begging for another cock. You'll remember this and know you wanted it."

Darya's world narrowed to the savage thud of Daniel's hips against her arse and the heat of his breath against her sweat-slicked neck. She tasted salt and iron in the air— her own exertion, the sterile reek of the studio, the ghostly tang of old blood and varnish—and the chatter from the window was no longer distant; it pulsed in time with the rhythm of her body, each thrust another shattering of boundaries she had always pretended were hers to draw.

The ballet barre creaked under the violence of their coupling, the mirrors echoing every movement, every humiliation, in triplicate. Her legs trembled with exhaustion and arousal, a dancer's stamina battered into something more desperate, more animal. For a moment, she caught her own reflection: eyes glazed, mouth slack, hair plastered to her cheek in tangled, sweat-damp locks. She was beautiful, but not in any way that her mother or the Bolshoi would have recognised. This beauty was ugly, raw, profane—a living challenge to everything she had ever been told about virtue, legacy, womanhood.

Daniel's voice was a low, relentless drone at her ear, a soundtrack to her own undoing. "You're going to walk into The Petal tonight with my cum running down your legs," he spat, a threat and a promise. "Every Third Year will smell it. They'll know you're already broken in, already marked. The queue's going to start the moment you step off this floor. And you're going to love every second, aren't you?"

Darya didn't answer with words. She bucked her hips, grinding back against him, making herself an accomplice in her own degradation. Her breath was a staccato, gasping rhythm, the heat in her belly blooming outward until it threatened to consume her entirely. The elastic bit deeper into her wrists with every thrust, a bright, slicing pain that grounded her even as her body threatened to float away on the dizzying tide of sensation.

Behind the glass, the crowd had doubled. Boys now, as well as girls, their faces slack with awe and hunger, phones aloft, the red pinprick of a recording light reflected in the window. Darya met their eyes, her own expression a wordless challenge. Watch me. Judge me. Need me.

It was an act of war, in its own way—a declaration that she would no longer be the porcelain doll, the ice princess, the untouchable. If they wanted a show, she would give them one they would never forget.

Daniel came with a snarl, hips stuttering as he emptied himself inside her, his grip bruising on her hips. Darya felt the wet heat flood her, a visceral proof of her own ruin, and shuddered, half in pain, half in triumph. He pulled out and then, lifted her up, inserting his spent cock into her arse.

"You ok?" he whispered, inaudible to the cameras that had been filming her, his tone softening for just a heartbeat. There was no tenderness in his touch as he smoothed her hair, only the weary triumph of someone who has taken exactly what he wanted, and would take more if given the chance.

Darya didn't answer right away. The sting in her wrists, the ache in her hips and arse, the humiliation—the complete, raw spectacle of her body used and displayed—coursed through her like a fever, leaving her breathless, trembling, and alive. There was pain, but it was sharp, clarifying; a signal that she was still here, still choosing.

"Yeah," she suddenly said, as she knew that her own voice, though raw and ragged, did not waver. "I'm more than ok," Darya replied in Russian, the syllables a private benediction. "Thanks for helping me stop doubting myself."

The aftermath was silence—heavy, prickling, threaded with the echoes of Daniel's breath and the stifled giggles from outside the window. For a long moment, Darya simply leaned into the barre, wrists stinging, thighs sticky with evidence, and let herself feel every atom of the ruin she had demanded. The room's smell had changed: the familiar tang of sweat and resin now layered over with sex and something sharp and metallic from her abraded skin. Daniel zipped his joggers and lingered, as if debating whether to say more or to reclaim the old, brittle boundaries that governed the rest of their student lives.

He did not apologise. There was no need—everything had been negotiation, transaction, performance, desire made manifest. At Red Rose, that was the only currency that mattered.

The faces at the window had begun to drift away, replaced by others; the grapevine, already quivering with the fresh meat of a scandal, would see to it that the story was not merely told, but sculpted, polished, honed to razor sharpness by breakfast. Darya straightened, hands trembling as she pulled her shorts back up and wiped the wetness from between her thighs with the edge of her sweatshirt, careless of the stains. She turned, met Daniel's eyes with a gaze that was neither gratitude nor resentment, only something defiant and unrepentant.

"Want to come to mine to clean up and... well, have some... calmer, more intimate fun before the real party starts?" Daniel asked, his tone somewhere between an invitation and a challenge, the traces of adrenaline and pride still shaping his smile.

Darya kissed him on the cheek, and she knew that, yes, she needed to, maybe, have a more tender moment with Daniel—maybe to reclaim some softness, maybe to reinforce the knowledge that she could choose, not just be chosen.

****

CHAPTER 7 – When You Go To Study and Shag...

Monday 4th November 2024

Tammy Knight had to admit, seeing Darya Ivanova tied to a bookshelf, with Ashley Ketchum pounding the Russian's pussy with the speed of a jackhammer while she was studying her notes from the morning lecture about screenwriting was, in some ways, making her horny, while at the same time distracting the Third Year from the intricate nuances of Joseph Campbell's monomyth. The autumn light slanted through the tall, half-frosted windows of the Red Rose Academy's Reading Room, catching in motes the faintest tang of musk and the pages of her battered exercise book. Every now and then, Tammy found her eyes drifting up from the arc about "Refusal of the Call" to Darya's wide, helpless eyes, half-defiant and half-pleading, her wrists bound with school regulation ties to the heavy oak shelves stacked with literary criticism and gothic novels.

Like everyone else, she knew that Daniel Parkinson was making her the Free Use girl, obviously to show that the slut wasn't a porcelain doll that couldn't be handled or dirtied. He wanted the academy to see Darya broken in, her ice-queen hauteur melted away, her compliance a message as clear as her parted legs. The deal was infamous already—rumour had spread by Sunday night, and by Monday morning, most of the girls were pretending to ignore it, while the boys hung back, watching, smirking, evaluating.

Watching Ashley's cock fill the quim of Darya, Tammy couldn't help but compare her own fantasies to the ruthless spectacle on display between the book stacks. It was impossible to concentrate fully on Joseph Campbell with the syncopated rhythm of bodies, the slap of skin and damp gasps overlaying her attempts to focus on the "Call to Adventure." Darya's pale thighs shivered against the library's ancient floorboards, and Ashley grunted, sweat shining on his collarbones, eyes flicking to see if anyone else was watching—if he was being marked, judged, envied, or all three.

In the way of Red Rose, the Reading Room was never empty. Even in the lulls between classes, someone was always drifting through: an earnest first-year leafing through Brecht, a costumed Musical Theatre student making a TikTok on the window ledge, a lost philosophy major seeking either sex or a cigarette. Today, though, the room's current was dominated by the fraying tableau at the back, where Darya was learning obedience by degrees and Ashley was proving, yet again, that at Red Rose, shame was only ever a passing costume.

Tammy tried—she really tried—to keep her biro steady as she annotated the mythic arc, but the ambient groans and slaps at the back of the Reading Room kept derailing her inner voice. She would scrawl "Separation: The Hero leaves their familiar world behind" and find her gaze pulled to Darya's parted lips, her jaw slack and brows drawn together in concentration and pain. The Russian's long, pale feet scrabbled uselessly at the bookshelves, toes flexing with every fresh thrust from Ashley. The shelf behind her rattled, threatening to send a rain of battered paperbacks onto their heads, but neither of them flinched.

Tammy tried to focus on her own script notes—her handwriting had already started sloping off at angles, the pages gradually invaded by stray lines about "inciting incidents" and "the belly of the whale." But the only mythic journey being undertaken today was Darya's, and hers had more to do with humiliation, hunger, and the fleeting power of spectacle than any quest for wisdom or justice. If Joseph Campbell had walked into Red Rose's Reading Room today, he'd have thrown away his typology and picked up a bottle of vodka, if only to dull the edge of what passed for ritual here.

The rest of the Reading Room was a picture of almost parodic academic calm: students hunched over laptops, battered Penguin Classics and spiral-bound scores, the quiet punctuated by the click of nails on keyboards and the occasional sneeze. A faint trace of weed drifted in from the quad outside, mingling with the scent of old wood polish and printer toner. It was, in short, a perfectly ordinary Monday—except for the fact that, at the far end, a Russian ballerina was being methodically fucked against the reference section, and nobody, not even the librarian on duty, seemed remotely inclined to intervene.

Tammy's own libido had been humming all morning, fuelled in part by gossip—she'd heard the plan through the grapevine, as everyone had. Darya had announced it herself in the girls' toilets after ballet class, standing barefoot at the sinks, hair twisted into a loose knot, make-up smudged, her eyes glittering with a manic dare. "I want to know what it's like," she'd said, voice just loud enough to carry over the noise of the hand dryers, "to belong to everyone. Or at least to everyone who wants me. I'm not a fucking ornament. If they think I'm fragile, they can prove it." Her accent, a hybrid of Moscow and Chelsea, was both charming and chilling.

By eleven, the story was already legend: Daniel Parkinson, grinning with the predatory satisfaction of a lad who'd managed to turn kink into campus folklore, had tied her wrists with two navy-and-silver Red Rose ties, looping the ends through the bookcase slats. Darya's skirt, uniform regulation black, was bunched at her waist, her shirt unbuttoned to the sternum. Her knickers—silk, expensive, with a subtle Russian monogram—hung from one ankle like a flag of surrender.

Now, as Ashley pounded her with a mixture of concentration and competitiveness—determined, perhaps, to best Justin's performance from the viral video—Tammy found herself shifting in her chair, crossing and uncrossing her legs. She glanced down at her notes, tried to force herself back to the "threshold guardian," but the threshold she was most aware of was the one being trampled at the back of the Reading Room, and she found her mind wandering back and forth between the monomyth and the raw, living myth before her.

Darya was making noises now—tiny, broken gasps, punctuated by the choked-off syllables of Russian curses and English pleas. Her hair, usually immaculate, had come loose, strands sticking to her cheek and neck with sweat. There was something operatic about her suffering, something calculated and ancient. Tammy wondered, not for the first time, whether all true performance wasn't at root a form of exposure, an offer of the self for sacrifice.

130

At Red Rose, the line between humiliation and transcendence was thinner than anywhere else.

Tammy shifted in her chair again, aware that her biro had stopped moving and that the words on the page—"Refusal of the Call"—blurred into irrelevance against the steady, obscene rhythm playing out behind her. She knew she should look away, should pretend to be as studious as the girl across from her who was typing furiously on her MacBook with headphones jammed in. But the temptation was irresistible. Every time Ashley drove forward, the shelves shuddered, and with them the books seemed to moan in sympathy: Derrida, Barthes, Foucault, their spines trembling like reluctant witnesses.

She let her eyes flick up once more, taking in the picture: Darya's wrists bound tightly enough that the tendons in her arms stood out pale and taut; Ashley's jaw clenched with effort, sweat dripping down to the hollow of his collarbone; Daniel lounging nearby with his arms folded, smirk broad, as though the whole enterprise were his stage-managed production. Around them, the scattered audience had grown—quiet, half-hidden observers leaning over laptops, feigning concentration, but their glances gave them away. Some first-years were whispering, pretending to scroll Instagram but clearly filming, their phone cameras angled low.

Tammy wondered what the Noticeboard caption would be this time. *Free Use: Ivanova's Library Tour*? Or perhaps something more brutal, like *Russian Doll Cracked at Last*. She found herself both appalled and drawn in, scribbling a line in the margin of her notes without meaning to: "The

Call is always sexual." She stared at it a moment, then underlined it twice.

Ashley groaned, hips slamming forward, and Darya let out a guttural, almost bestial sound that carried through the hush of the Reading Room. Heads turned. A philosophy student two tables over closed his copy of *Being and Time* with exaggerated slowness, as though Heidegger had just been outdone by this live display of ontology.

"You're doing this for them, not for you," Daniel said lazily from the armchair by the radiator. His voice carried, low and amused. "Every cunt in this room is getting off watching you burn. How's it feel, Darya?"

Her reply was a half-sobbed curse in Russian, her voice cracked, and Tammy, despite herself, felt the sound reverberate in her chest. There was pain there, yes, but also an edge of triumph, a challenge that made every onlooker complicit.

Tammy tapped her biro against the page, the rhythm matching the cadence of Ashley's thrusts. She tried again to focus on Campbell. *Crossing the Threshold*, she read, then glanced up to see Darya's body crossing far more intimate thresholds. She bit her lip, hard.

No, this can't do, she thought, her hand streaking down to the waistband of her knickers beneath the library table, her pulse racing in time with the obscene ballet at the shelves. She hesitated, fingers pressed against the elastic, acutely aware of the precarious choreography between propriety and the raw, aching need that had been building in her since she'd first walked into Red Rose. Outside this building, Tammy Knight was a quiet Third Year screenwriting student—high marks, well-behaved, proud of her place at a university known for scandal but demanding of brilliance. But here, in the Academy's gothic heart, every student was, sooner or later, drafted into the ongoing theatre of flesh and confession.

"Fuck me, Ketchum", the voice of third year Joanna Taylor said, and Tammy looked to see her fellow classmate curled up in an armchair, dildo in hand, a Robert Galbraith novel in her lap. "Your cock's that small, the commie bitch needs a microscope to find it!"

Ashley shot Joanna a lopsided grin, not pausing in his rhythm, sweat flicking from his fringe. "Jealous, Jo? You've had it. Twice."

Joanna snorted, flicking her tongue over the tip of the pink dildo before sinking back into her reading, thighs spread with the lazy arrogance of someone utterly at home in the wild fringes of Red Rose. "Yeah, and I finished myself both times. Come back when you've got stamina, darling."

A snicker rolled through the Reading Room, tension curling around the students like steam in a Turkish bath. Daniel, half-hidden behind a stack of battered Loeb Classics, let out a wolf whistle. "Careful, Ketchum, you'll need more than speed if you want a legacy. Try keeping her quiet for a full minute."

Ashley responded with a thrust that made Darya gasp, her voice ringing against the old oak. Tammy, cheeks burning, closed her eyes for a moment, willing herself to concentrate—Campbell, not cock, Campbell, not cock—but the sticky hum of the Reading Room overpowered her, every sense tuned to the raw performance at the back.

But she knew her fingers were otherwise busy with starting to tease her own clit, the biro falling from her hand and rolling off the edge of the table with a faint clatter that nobody noticed. The faint buzz of her phone—another Red Rose group chat, no doubt documenting the minute-by-minute escalation—went ignored. She pressed her thighs together and let her fingers slip beneath the waistband, tracing slow circles, her breath shallow as she kept her gaze fixed on her notes, though her mind and body were anywhere but.

Looking at the notes she had written, Tammy noticed that she had made a mistake, that she had written "The Call is always sexual" three times in a row along the page margin, the handwriting slanting and wild, betraying the way her pulse had accelerated. She shook her head, cheeks hot with the mortifying knowledge that anyone walking past might see the scrawl, but she couldn't stop. The scene at the back of the Reading Room had her hooked; she was as much a part of the audience as the grinning first-years, as the casual voyeurs in battered jumpers pretending to be lost in their Penguin Classics.

The wooden chair beneath her felt impossibly hard, the grain pressing into her thighs through her tights. She shifted, her skirt riding up, and let her gaze travel up the spines of battered library books—Nabokov, Carter, Woolf—each name a silent witness to the performance unfolding under their dust. She wondered how many

134

others, over the decades, had succumbed to the same tangled urges here: lust, envy, curiosity, the slow burn of shame.

A faint chorus of gasps rose from the cluster of students by the window as Ashley, hands splayed wide over Darya's hips, changed his rhythm, slamming her harder against the shelf. The ties binding her wrists creaked, the silk cutting into her skin, a detail that made Tammy's own wrists ache in sympathy. Darya's pale arms were trembling now, fingers clawed, her head tipped back against the ancient wood.

Daniel, never content to be just a bystander, got to his feet and wandered closer, his trainers silent on the worn carpet. "You want to take bets on who's next?" he said, raising his voice so that more of the room could hear. "I'm thinking—Smith, then Parsons, then maybe a couple of the music lads. Let's see if the ballerina can hit a new record before tea break."

A ripple of laughter ran around the Reading Room. A fresher—a girl Tammy recognised from scriptwriting class, who had never looked up from her laptop before— flushed bright red and pretended to type, but Tammy saw the way her eyes flicked over the top of her screen, wide and hungry.

Ashley grinned over Darya's shoulder, still moving, sweat running down his chest. "You keep the queue coming, mate, and I'll keep the standard up."

Darya, in her own haze of pain and pleasure, barely seemed to register the banter. She was making a low, keening sound now, her legs shaking, eyes glazed. The power dynamic had shifted, Tammy noticed—this was no longer just about breaking her, but about something more complex. Surrender, yes, but also a kind of claiming: not just by Ashley, but by the whole room, every gaze a brand, every laugh a lash.

Tammy felt her own fingers pressing more insistently now, lost in the pulse beating between her thighs. The autumn light shifted on the pages of her notebook, turning the ink silver. The noise from the window—a group of second years, passing a bottle of Sainsbury's rosé between them—rose and fell with the rhythm at the shelves, their laughter sharp and edged with excitement.

Tammy's pulse thundered in her ears as the Reading Room's temperature seemed to climb, sweat prickling at the nape of her neck, dampening the collar of her blouse. For a fleeting moment, she tried to will herself to stand, to collect her books and notes and retreat to the safety of her boxy, impersonal flat. But Red Rose was a vortex; it didn't just seduce or scandalise—it consumed, and she, like everyone else, was moth to its perpetual bonfire.

Darya's body moved in waves against the bookshelf, the ties biting harder as her wrists flexed. Ashley, breathing hard now, cheeks flushed pink, pressed his face between her shoulder blades for a moment—seeking privacy where there was none, seeking meaning in the midst of performance. His hips stuttered. A low, broken groan escaped his lips, and for a moment, the whole room seemed to hold its breath.

It was Daniel who broke the spell, striding forward and clapping Ashley on the shoulder with a grin as wide as the Irwell in flood. "You look like you've run a marathon, mate. Want me to tag in?" His voice was pitched deliberately loud, a challenge as much to Ashley as to anyone else watching.

Ashley looked up, sweat running in rivulets from his hairline, and with a flourish, withdrew, making a show of patting Darya's hip. "She's all yours, Parkinson. Try not to break her—she's got ballet tomorrow."

A ripple of laughter swept through the scattered onlookers—sharp, electric, tinged with something halfway between awe and hunger. Ashley stepped aside, still breathing hard, and Daniel, with a laziness that bordered on insolence, loosened his joggers, revealing the faint line of a tan and a cock already swelling in anticipation. He didn't even glance at Darya's face; instead, he positioned himself behind her, hands on her hips, and with a swift, practised thrust, entered her with a grunt.

The first push drew a ragged sound from Darya—pain or pleasure, nobody could tell. The bookshelf rattled. Above her head, a copy of *Sexuality in Victorian Literature* shivered precariously, the dust jacket creased from years of neglect. Tammy, unable to help herself, caught the title and almost laughed. Even the books were complicit in this theatre.

Daniel moved with a different rhythm to Ashley—slower, more deliberate, as if savouring the sensation of eyes on him, of Darya's shudders, of the sheer spectacle of conquest. He leaned forward, lips pressed to her ear, whispering something that made her arch her back and gasp, her hair falling forward to hide her face.

At the nearby tables, the audience had multiplied. Some students affected boredom—heads down, eyes averted, AirPods in—but their posture betrayed them. Others were blatant, iPhones raised just above the level of their textbooks, screens blinking in silent testimony. The Noticeboard app would be flooded by nightfall, the mythology of Red Rose written in pixels and pixels and a hundred frantic, half-jealous messages.

Tammy watched the shadows flicker across Darya's face, a kaleidoscope of agony, ecstasy, humiliation, and pride. She pressed two fingers deeper, circling her clit with increasing urgency, breath coming shallow and fast. Across the room, Joanna Taylor was sprawled, head tipped back, pink dildo disappearing between her thighs with every lazy stroke, her eyes half-lidded with satisfaction and amusement.

"Do you reckon they'll let her go to the bar after this, or just keep her chained up for open mic?" Joanna muttered, voice husky with arousal and scorn.

Tammy's only reply was a half-muffled whimper. She'd forgotten her self-consciousness; the Reading Room was transformed, not a place of study, but an amphitheatre of sex and shame. Outside, the wind rattled the windows, carrying the scent of dying leaves and rain. Inside, the air was humid, thick with musk and anticipation.

It was then that Tammy felt the pleasure of her first orgasm spread internally, the sensation blooming up through her belly and spine like the first fire after winter, hot and forbidden. Tammy held her breath, thighs pressed tight together under the table, the faintest tremor shaking her fingertips as she rode out the shudder, careful not to gasp, not to draw eyes. No one noticed: the centre of gravity in the Reading Room was all at the shelves.

The epicentre was Darya: hair wild, body trembling with every deliberate stroke Daniel gave her, wrists straining in their bonds, hips bruised against old English oak. The shelf rattled each time Daniel drove forward, threatening a domino fall of battered books and half-read essays, but the bindings held—both the ones around Darya's wrists, and the ones that kept the Reading Room's voyeurs in their chairs, each more captive to the spectacle than the girl herself.

Tammy let her head drop onto her folded arms, still hidden behind her copy of *Hero with a Thousand Faces*, heart hammering as the aftershocks of orgasm pulsed through her body. She risked a glance sideways, only to catch the eye of Tomás, a first-year composition student, who gave her a sly wink

"Enjoying fingering yourself, Knight?" Tomás asked, a grin on his face. "You know, my cock's stiff if you want to slide under the table and get a taste of something different than Campbell for once."

Tammy felt her face flush, but she gave Tomás a crooked, knowing smile—the kind you only learn at Red Rose, where boundaries were drawn in chalk and wiped away before nightfall. "Only if you read me something from your essay afterwards," she replied, voice low, letting the innuendo hang between them like incense.

"Deal," he said, and Tammy decided to abandon her studious persona for the moment—a persona that, in this swirling, feverish den of creative chaos, felt less like a shield and more like a denial of something essential. The tension of the morning—the gnawing itch of distraction and envy and curiosity—had grown into a low, insistent ache. Now, with the Reading Room transformed from a cathedral of learning into a stage of exhibition and confession, Tammy found herself ready to step through her own threshold, to surrender to the moment and become, even if only for an hour, another story in the unending saga of Red Rose.

She tucked her biro and notebook into her bag, nudging it beneath the table with her foot. The carpet muffled the motion; nobody in the immediate vicinity seemed to care, their gazes fixed on the drama by the shelves. With a quick, conspiratorial glance at Tomás, she slipped under the table, knees brushing the cool wood, her skirt riding higher with every inch she shuffled forward.

The world shrank to the dark, humming space beneath the desk—her breathing, Tomás's shifting hips, the gentle thud of her own heartbeat in her ears. She reached out, feeling for the hard outline of his cock beneath his jeans, her hand steady despite the flush that burned up her cheeks. Tomás let out a shaky laugh, the sound muffled by the pages of his essay. She grinned in the darkness, her fingers finding the zipper, working it down with the deliberate care of someone determined to savour every moment of her own rebellion.

Above her, the sounds of the Reading Room continued unabated—the slap of Daniel's hips against Darya, the chorus of gasps and murmurs from the impromptu audience, the rustle of Joanna's pages as she flicked idly through her Galbraith novel while the dildo worked between her thighs. Tammy let the sounds wash over her, an illicit soundtrack that only heightened her own hunger.

Tomás's cock sprang free, stiff and hot against her palm, the head already slick with pre-cum. Tammy leaned in, her lips parting, tongue flicking out to taste the salt and musk. She took him into her mouth, slow at first, her own arousal a steady thrum as she found a rhythm that matched, perversely, the tempo at the bookshelves behind her. Tomás's hand slid beneath the table, fingers threading through her hair, guiding her movements with a gentle insistence that left her light-headed and eager.

Each stroke, each swallow, each wet glide of her mouth along Tomás's cock, was a tiny act of surrender—and an act of taking, too. Tammy felt the power that pulsed in the space between them: his pleasure, her control, the risk of exposure, the absolute certainty that everyone in the Reading Room was, in their own way, playing a part in the ongoing orgy of performance.

She came up for air, lips slick, eyes bright, and shot Tomás a wicked smile. "Well? Where's my reading?"

He laughed, voice shaking, and fumbled for his essay. "Right, right... 'Music as Narrative: Subverting

Expectation in Postmodern Composition.' You sure you want to hear this? It's mostly me waffling about Ligeti and glass harmonicas."

Tammy giggled, licking the head of his cock. "Surprise me. Make it dirty."

He cleared his throat, but the pretence of academic gravity was lost. Still, he began to read, voice trembling as she took him back into her mouth, words tumbling out in a heady mix of theory and lust: "The use of dissonance as a means of destabilising auditory expectation can be read as an erotic gesture, a form of teasing, the delay of resolution becoming, in itself, a kind of foreplay…"

She moaned around him, the vibrations making him shudder. Beneath the table, time stretched and warped: the relentless rhythm at the shelves, the susurrus of pages and whispers, the quickening beat of Tammy's heart as she felt herself slipping deeper into the Red Rose mythos.

It was then that she felt a pair of hands on her buttocks, and the sound of someone—she couldn't yet tell who—easing her skirt up with the slow, bold confidence of a Red Rose veteran. Tammy froze only a second, then relaxed, letting her cheek rest against Tomás's thigh, mouth still wrapped around his cock.

"Mind if I join in?" Luke Roberts, a third year student in the Actor-Musician course, whispered into the half-shadow under the desk, his voice honeyed with mischief and the lazy confidence of someone who'd already lost count of his own public scandals. The scent of cheap aftershave and last night's rolling tobacco drifted towards

Tammy as Luke, unhurried, slipped a palm along the curve of her arse, then slid two fingers beneath the gusset of her tights.

Tammy's first instinct was a fleeting twinge of embarrassment—she was, after all, under a library table with a cock in her mouth and another boy's fingers working their way between her thighs. But at Red Rose, embarrassment was as fleeting as the morning's drizzle: swept away in the shared current of risk, hunger, and the silent dare to outdo the stories already echoing through the building's bones.

She made a small sound, half protest, half invitation, never breaking rhythm on Tomás's cock. Luke took it as permission, his fingers finding the slick heat of her arousal. He stroked, slow and deliberate, matching the undulating pace of her bobbing head above, every movement deliberate, theatrical, as though he were playing to an invisible audience—which, in a sense, he was.

Overhead, Tomás's hand tightened in her hair, hips lifting involuntarily as he tried—and failed—to keep his composure. "Fuck, Tammy," he whispered, so low only she could hear, his essay sliding from his lap to the carpet with a soft thud.

Tammy let herself be filled with sensation: the hard heat of Tomás in her mouth, the insistent press of Luke's fingers as they found her clit and teased slow circles, the smothered gasps and unsteady breath from both boys above and behind her. She pressed her hips back against Luke's hand, desperate for more friction, more sensation, more proof that she wasn't just watching the Red Rose myth unfold—she was living it, writing her own chapter in flesh and sweat.

She heard, distantly, the low rumble of Daniel's voice from the far end of the Reading Room, boasting about Darya's stamina, betting on how many cocks she'd take before the hour was out. The audience had grown: a pair of dance students draped across the radiator, a trio of Music Tech lads perched on beanbags, even Lorraine from Reception lingering by the door with the kind of world-weary amusement that only staff at Red Rose could muster.

Ashley had joined the knot of spectators, trousers loose on his hips, hair a tangled mess of sweat and bravado. Darya, hips bruised red where Daniel gripped her, had all but surrendered to the rhythm, her voice ragged, torn between English and Russian, pleasure and pain, submission and defiance. Each new thrust drew fresh murmurs from the audience, a communion of need and spectacle, ritual and ruin.

Beneath the table, Luke shifted, tugging at Tammy's tights and knickers, pushing them down to her knees. He dropped to his own, his lips warm against the flesh of her inner thigh, tongue tracing the salt-and-copper tang of her skin before finding her clit and lapping with slow, measured strokes. Tammy moaned around Tomás, the vibrations making him shudder and curse, his free hand bracing against the edge of the table.

The illicitness of the act only fuelled her arousal—here she was, a diligent Third Year, known for her wit and precision, reduced to a squirming, gasping tangle of need beneath the same desk where she'd once scrawled careful notes on narrative structure and three-act arcs. There was a freedom in surrender, she realised; a permission to step outside herself, to be rewritten by the fever of the moment.

Luke's tongue worked in lazy circles, each pass sending a fresh wave of pleasure spiralling up her spine. She ground back against him, greedy for sensation, her own moans muffled by the thickness of Tomás in her mouth. Above her, Tomás's voice grew strained, the half-formed words of his essay dissolving into incoherent groans.

When he came, it was sudden, a hot rush of salt and musk filling her mouth. Tammy swallowed, the taste earthy and immediate, feeling the tremors in his thighs as he gasped and shook, his hand gentle in her hair. She let him slip free, licking her lips, grinning as she surfaced from beneath the table.

"Hero's journey, yeah?" Tomás managed, still a little breathless. "You're bloody Odysseus, Knight."

She snorted, a warm flush creeping up her cheeks. "More like Persephone," she shot back, glancing over her shoulder at Luke, who was still kneeling behind her, his face slick with her arousal. "Dragged to the underworld and loving it."

Luke laughed, rising to his feet, adjusting himself in his jeans. He leaned in, mouth close to her ear. "I've got a rehearsal in ten, but if you want a round two—music practice rooms, after lunch?"

Tammy smirked. "Only if you promise to play piano with your tongue."

He winked, sauntering away with the careless gait of a boy who knew he'd made an impression. Tomás pulled up his jeans, tucking in his shirt, a sheepish smile tugging at his lips.

The air beneath the table was thick with heat and the ghost of forbidden things, but above it, the Reading Room had returned—briefly—to something like normalcy. Tammy climbed back into her chair, her skirt rumpled, cheeks pink, but her eyes alive with the energy that only Red Rose could conjure.

****

CHAPTER 8 – Communism in Sex Does Not Go...

Tuesday 5th November 2024

Sarah Johnson was, if she was honest, completely like her father, Ian, in that she didn't agree with the capitalist system that Great Britain held itself in. In fact, she had been one of 500 people in her home town of Kingswinford who had voted for her father, Ian, a member of the new Communist Party of Great Britain, in the General Election. The seat, won by the Conservative Party's Mike Wood, had been a new seat following the boundary changes and the endless waves of demographic churn, but Sarah—Sarah with her copper hair cropped boyishly short, her battered Doc Martens and her collection of Gramsci essays in an oilskin rucksack—hadn't just voted for her father out of filial loyalty. She genuinely, ardently believed that the system was rigged, the media corrupt, and that history's great locomotive was due another stoking of the fires. Even if her father's campaign had managed only a distant sixth behind Labour, Tory, Reform, Lib Dems and even an independent Green, Sarah had worn the red star on her lapel like a badge of stubborn hope.

Now, perched in a Red Rose Academy library carrel, Sarah found herself in a place where no ideology— certainly not one as earnest as hers—ever survived contact with the local environment for long. The Academy, despite the best efforts of its embattled Student Union, was not a site of proletarian consciousness-raising. Instead, its hallowed halls were a fever swamp of ambition, narcissism and sexual exhibitionism, where the only redistribution was of bedsheets and STIs, and the only thing commonly owned was shame, quickly shed and seldom missed.

Walking out of the GUM clinic, where she had, being a Fresher, a First Year, done a quick chlamydia test and listened to a brusque nurse explain the virtues of latex and regular check-ups, Sarah had caught her own gaze in the streaky mirror of the student toilets. Her reflection was not the picture of a utopian revolutionary; she looked, instead, like what she was: a nervous, clever, slightly anxious nineteen-year-old with an indelible scuff of mascara under one eye and a rucksack weighed down by unread Penguin Classics. Outside, the campus thrummed in that way only November evenings could summon, all sodium-orange light on puddles, soggy leaf-drifts and the chemical tang of hot food and cold vape clouds. And as she'd pressed through the bustling quad, boots squelching, Sarah found herself feeling—against her better judgement—lonely.

As one of the BA Sound and Music for Games and Media students, Sarah was used to being surrounded by a particular breed of person: the quietly intense, the headphone-wearing, the laptop-clutching, the ones who could pass unnoticed for hours at a time beneath the relentless blitzkrieg of the Dance and Drama kids. While ballet and musical theatre ruled the upper echelons of Red Rose's social order, her course existed in the margins— half-technical, half-artistic, and wholly overlooked by the majority of the school's scandal-driven noticeboard ecosystem. Her only claim to notoriety so far was an ill-advised attempt to pass off a Kate Tempest sample as original composition, an error quickly exposed by a sharp-eyed second year and the subsequent flurry of Discord mockery.

It was not, Sarah reflected, the best start to a university career. But then, she mused as she hunched deeper into her jumper, perhaps that was exactly the point: no one at Red Rose expected anyone to be anything but themselves, so long as themselves was interesting enough to watch, fuck, or ridicule. The old joke went that Red Rose didn't do "cliques"—it did "fucking, and lots of it", and if you couldn't handle the heat, you stayed well away from the drama studio or, for that matter, the communal showers in Dance. In Sarah's first fortnight she'd seen more bare flesh—glittering, tattooed, pierced, indifferent—than in her entire Midlands childhood, and while this had initially left her hot-cheeked and mortified, by November she had learned to walk on by, pretending nothing phased her, even as the latest couple (or triple, or sometimes quadruple) stumbled out of a rehearsal room, shirts half-done and eyeliner streaked.

Still, tonight, she was alone, and there was nothing particularly glamorous about it. Her stomach rumbled—a consequence of spending her last £4.90 on an oat milk flat white and a bus fare from the front entrance of Red Rose to the GUM clinic in Hulme, where a world of weary Manchester medics processed students by the dozen. She checked her phone—no messages, as usual. Her group chat, 'Comrades in Arms (And Each Other)', had gone quiet since last week's protest fizzled out in the drizzle, and her only real friend on the course, Jonas, was at some surrealist film night with his new boyfriend. A fine night, then, for sitting in a chilly library carrel and trying to write a three-minute composition on "The Politics of Sound in Non-Linear Narrative Spaces".

But the walls here were thin. Even in the library, Red Rose life oozed through the cracks: snatches of laughter from the stacks, a furtive giggle behind the periodicals, the distant, unmistakable clunk of someone getting fingered under a table. Communism in sex, Sarah thought, does not go. Not when everyone was so hopelessly, fiercely individual, their passions less about sharing than about spectacle, and self-conquest.

Her mind drifted, fingers tracing lazy arcs on her battered trackpad. It wasn't that Sarah disliked sex—she was. In fact, she had lost her virginity to one of the young Labour activists in Kingswinford who had only joined the party as his father was a long time Labour voter, and, even though Kier Starmer was the leader, Rolf, the 23 year old, had said, was, in Rolf's opinion, "too far right for the Labour Party, while Corbyn was a fucking legend—just too nice for this bastard country," as Rolf had muttered with bitter fondness while fumbling off his Sex Pistol's God Save the Queen T-shirt, their first time together in his dad's freezing conservatory after a local Momentum meeting. Sarah had thought, at the time, that sex was supposed to feel like a revolutionary act, some fusion of bodies and purpose, but it was just as awkward and anticlimactic as the party branch's annual general meeting: over too soon, slightly damp, and followed by a joint and an earnest post-coital chat about the NHS.

The irony, she knew, about that specific T-shirt, celebrating a monarch's Silver Jubilee while also being weaponised by the Sex Pistols and their ilk, wasn't lost on her; neither was the irony of Rolf's passionate disdain for everything, except, it seemed, being the only person in Kingswinford capable of growing a credible moustache at twenty-three. It summed up her sense that her generation, and this country, were forever caught between detesting the systems they lived in and half-heartedly mimicking them at every turn—mocking, ironic, desperate for authenticity but unable to give up the shallow pleasures of spectacle. If anything, Red Rose was that contradiction in its purest, most vulgar form: a school that declared itself a sanctuary for the artistically radical, yet managed to turn even the most utopian ideals into grist for its rumour mill and, inevitably, its next Friday night orgy.

"You look like a million people have fucked you," the voice of Daniel Parkinson from the other end of the library interrupted her reverie, echoing against the half-empty stacks, and Sarah knew why, as Darya Ivanova, who it turned out that, during the weekend, had decided to shag and date Parkinson, was being used this week as a free use doll, someone who, when lectures and practicals had finished, would be tied up in the library and used for the pleasure—or, as the actors insisted, "artistic exploration"—of the Red Rose student body. Daniel's words were not an insult at Red Rose, merely an offhand observation that, in any other context, would have resulted in a slap or at least a trip to the principal's office. Here, it was a conversation opener.

Sarah looked up, forcing her eyes to focus as Daniel forced his erection into Darya's mouth, and, sawing it between her lips with the practised disregard of someone who had spent the last forty-eight hours as both exhibitionist and connoisseur, offered Sarah a half-grin that seemed almost kind, in its own feral way.

Sarah could have been disgusted. She could have walked out, righteously, or at least turned back to her laptop. But the truth was, as she set her chin in her hand, that she was as much a creature of Red Rose as any of them. She watched, not in approval, but with a weary sort of fascination. Darya's fingers tightened around the arms of the chair she'd been lashed to; Daniel, never gentle, muttered something about "method acting" and the tension between desire and domination. There was, Sarah realised, a rawness to it—nothing about pleasure, everything about being seen, being witnessed, as if shame itself were being communally recycled.

All around them, the academy moved in its many small, perverse orbits: pairs snogging in the stacks, a first-year girl sobbing softly into her phone, a chorus of tech students hunched over their laptops dissecting the acoustics of last night's gig at The Rose Petal. In a far corner, someone strummed an out-of-tune guitar. The security guard, no doubt paid far too little for what he witnessed nightly, strolled by with a bored "evening all", then vanished toward the stairwell, a knowing smirk on his face. In another time, another place, this might have been a scandal. At Red Rose, it was merely a Tuesday.

She knew that Daniel had a pregnancy kink, that he wanted to breed Darya—words he used shamelessly, like the filthiest confession or a badge of some new, primal order. That morning, Sarah had overheard him in the café telling Nikki Swanson, "It's not about power, not really. It's about seeing if you can make someone more than they were before you touched them." Nikki, dressed as some kind of neo-Victorian domme for a drama exercise, had just rolled her eyes and replied, "You boys are all the same. You want to see your name on someone's skin, but you'd scream if a girl wrote hers on yours with a knife." At Red Rose, even the kinks had subtext, layered with the kind of politics Sarah pretended she didn't care about anymore.

Sarah watched as Daniel came, choking a grunt into Darya's hair. Darya, cheeks slick and breathless, turned her gaze toward Sarah, defiant and not at all humiliated. If anything, she looked bored. When Daniel withdrew, Darya flashed Sarah a conspiratorial wink as if to say, "This is just what happens now. Don't make it poetry." That, too, was part of the unspoken contract of Red Rose: nothing was sacred, not even your own suffering, and certainly not the meanings people assigned to your body.

After Daniel zipped himself up and sauntered off toward the media suite—probably to brag, or perhaps just to refill his vape—Sarah stared at Darya, now left to her own devices, lashed to the chair. There was a quiet between them. Sarah bit her lip, unsure whether to speak or simply go. Instead, she found herself rising, almost against her will, and approached.

"You all right?" she said, softly.

Darya grinned, the cum in her mouth showing. "Yeah, I'm alright. You know, back home in Russia, I'd be earning more than my tuition fees for this kind of show. But here I get something else—legend status, and nobody's mother comes looking for revenge," she replied, tongue tracing the inside of her teeth before she swallowed and fixed Sarah with a dazzling, vodka-proofed smile. "You look like you need something to do that isn't just watching."

Sarah hesitated, but only for a moment. At Red Rose, lines were invitations, not boundaries. "I think I'm more observer than participant," she said, tugging her sleeves lower. "I'm not really into…" She glanced at the ropes, the rawness of Darya's wrists, the bruised tenderness with which the other girl flexed her fingers. "Well. All that."

Darya snorted. "You're a Red Rose student. You'll be into anything if you're bored enough." Her accent twisted each syllable with sardonic intimacy. "Go on. Taste me. You know you want to, little commie girl. You know, in Russia, you'd be sent to the gulag for some of your pro Stalin politics. Here, the only gulag is the one in your head. And maybe the one between my legs, if you're brave enough."

Sarah had to laugh at that. It was the kind of exchange you could only have here, in this madhouse, where everyone was performing—sometimes for an audience, sometimes for themselves, sometimes because it was the only way they knew how to be real. Her cheeks flushed with something that wasn't embarrassment, exactly. Curiosity, maybe. Defiance, perhaps.

But Darya, for all her bravado, had the same flicker of need behind her eyes that Sarah had seen in the cracked mirrors of a hundred Midlands pubs, a need to be acknowledged, to be wanted, to be significant—even for a moment. Sarah crouched beside the chair, lowering her voice so only the two of them could hear.

"Are you serious?" she asked, lips twisting into a lopsided smirk, half-mocking, half-earnest.

Darya leaned in as far as her bonds would allow, her breath tickling Sarah's cheek. "You have two choices, Sarah Johnson. You can go back to your little carrel and write a Marxist analysis of audio in open-world games that no one will ever read, or you can stay here and eat my pussy out like the whore you want to be. You know, its not a crime to want to be desired," she finished, the edge in her voice sharpening into something closer to challenge than seduction.

For a moment, Sarah just knelt there, letting the words settle between them. The rational, self-policing part of her brain—the voice of Ian Johnson in a threadbare suit, telling her to respect herself, to stand for something greater—sputtered in the background. But here, in the library of Red Rose Academy, that voice was barely a whisper against the riot of everything else: the heat radiating off Darya, the absurd, electric sense of being invited—commanded, even—to step beyond herself.

Sarah found herself laughing again, more from disbelief than anything else. "You know," she said, "in every pamphlet my dad ever wrote, there was never a section about this sort of mutual aid." The joke earned her a peal of laughter from Darya, which dissolved into a sharp exhale as Sarah, with all the deliberate awkwardness she could muster, brushed her fingers along the inside of Darya's thigh.

It wasn't graceful. It wasn't artful. But as she leaned forward, tasting the salt and musk of another girl's skin for the first time, Sarah understood—on some deep, irrepressible level—that this, too, was a kind of politics. Not the grand, historical sort that her father preached or the utopian nonsense of student societies, but a micro-politics of want and consent and spectacle: who chose, who performed, who dared to cross a line.

Darya sighed, head tipping back, eyes fluttering half-closed. "There you go, little commie," she whispered. "Share the wealth." The phrase, so ludicrous in the moment, broke the tension for both of them. Sarah snorted, which sent both of them giggling, bodies shaking as Sarah's fingers lost their tentative hesitance and began to move with the kind of rough, impatient honesty that was the signature of every Red Rose encounter.

All around them, life in the library flowed on: books thumbed, laptops clicked, distant shouts and gasps from a group of drama students improvising a murder scene between the reference shelves. None of it seemed to matter. Sarah, who had always imagined sex as a kind of performance she was unsuited for, suddenly found herself centre stage—not because she was the star, but because she was willing to try, to risk the embarrassment of being seen.

Darya was a generous audience. Her thighs parted without self-consciousness, her hips rolling forward as much as the ropes would allow, her moans carrying just enough to be overheard by the next table. If anyone cared, they didn't show it. This was Red Rose, after all—a place where privacy was a fiction, shame a currency nobody bothered to trade in anymore.

Sarah felt the heat bloom in her cheeks, a tide rising somewhere between nerves and exhilaration. Her hand trembled a little as she slid her palm higher, feeling the sticky, cooling traces Daniel had left, the sweat and tang of hours of use, the marks of rope on bare thighs. For one floating instant, Sarah thought she should be disgusted, recoiling from the crude communal theatre of it all. But instead, as she pressed her lips to Darya, tasting salt and latex and something sweeter underneath, she only felt a fierce, animal curiosity. What would it be like, she wondered, to be as unashamed as Darya? To make a spectacle of oneself, to be wanted, to surrender and to demand at the same time?

Darya's laughter was replaced by a low, throaty moan, her body tensing against the ropes. Sarah's hands were awkward at first, clumsy, uncertain, but Darya's encouragement—sharp exhales, whispered Russian curses, murmured instructions in a half-mocking, half-tender voice—brought her quickly up to speed. It was nothing like the hurried, fumbling sex she'd had in Kingswinford; it was nothing like the abstract, disembodied politics she'd spent so much time theorising. It was immediate, greedy, performed and yet, for a fleeting second, honest. Darya writhed in her chair, making no effort to muffle her pleasure, eyes fixed on Sarah's face as if daring her to look away.

Sarah didn't look away.

She tasted Darya—her come, her sweat, even the lingering musk of Daniel—and instead of revulsion she felt a sudden, dizzying kinship. This was not a secret; this was the public, pulsing body of Red Rose made flesh. You belong to this now, a voice in her mind whispered. You're not outside, you're not immune. You're part of the story.

"Don't stop," Darya hissed, her accent harsh, her hips bucking. "Don't you fucking dare stop." Her legs strained against the ropes, feet drumming against the polished floor, and Sarah, swept up by the absurdity and intensity of it, found herself laughing into Darya's cunt. It was, she realised, liberating. She could have her theories and her politics, her shame and her desire, all at once. She could be seen and still be herself.

It was then that she heard the giggles, the sound of her fellow students all talking about how it was about time the "commie girl" finally joined in. But Sarah didn't care. Let them talk, let them watch, let them roll their eyes and text their friends or upload a snap to the notorious Red Rose Noticeboard app. At this moment, she was not audience or commentator, but utterly, defiantly participant—her hands steady now, her mouth growing confident as Darya's encouragement lost all irony and became a simple, raw gasp for more.

And that was the rhythm of Red Rose: observation turned participation, shame transformed into spectacle, each encounter both a performance and a subversion of whatever rules might once have existed. Sarah's tongue found its pace, moving in slow, deliberate circles at first, then faster, as Darya strained against the ropes and muttered encouragements in a feverish mix of Russian and English. It was, Sarah realised, an act at once intimate and outrageously public. She knew they were watched— she could feel the prickle of a dozen gazes from students "revising" or pretending not to look, their attention split between their laptops and the living theatre unfolding amongst the stacks.

For a long moment, time lost its shape. Darya's body arched in the chair, her pleasure spilling over, ragged, unashamed, and Sarah felt a kind of victory—not just over her own hesitance, but over the world of closed doors and silences she'd grown up in. Here, desire could be a commons, and even pleasure might be, for a minute, shared property.

Eventually, as Darya's shudders subsided and her head lolled back in the chair, Sarah lifted her mouth, lips slick, cheeks red. She glanced up into Darya's eyes and found not mockery, not even pride, but a kind of warm, grateful recognition. "See?" Darya whispered, voice rough and fond. "Even a Marxist can be decadent."

Sarah giggled, wiping her mouth with the sleeve of her jumper, the nervousness receding to a pleasant hum. "Only for the sake of international solidarity," she whispered back, and both girls burst into laughter—a true, shared moment, even as the sounds of the library reasserted themselves around them.

"Hey, ladies," Andy Warhol, a First Year Composition for Screen student, said, walking past, and Sarah knew that— no matter what had just transpired—Red Rose Academy was always an open stage. Andy shot them a lopsided grin, headphones draped around his neck like a priest's stole, and nodded as if the whole library tableau was just another part of the curriculum. "Don't forget, the AV suite's closed after midnight, but I can let you in if you want to record this for posterity."

Sarah snorted, unable to suppress the giggle that rippled up her chest and out her throat. Darya, equally unbothered by the intrusion, shot Andy a wicked grin. "Only if you want to be the boom operator, darling," she replied, accent thickening, legs still parted, ropes digging pink and angry into her pale thighs.

Andy chuckled, unzipping his jeans with the swift nonchalance of a boy who had grown up with TikTok, OnlyFans and the omnipresence of performative sex, to reveal a 7 inch erection which was already throbbing with adolescent eagerness. He didn't even pause to check if anyone was looking—of course people were looking; at Red Rose, someone was always watching, and half the point was being worth the attention. He sauntered up to Sarah, and, kissing her neck with the affection of someone who had rehearsed the move in a hundred mirrored selfies, started undoing her blouse, and, noticing the clasps of her bra were at the front of it rather than the back, grinned at her with the delighted surprise of someone discovering an unexpected loophole in a game. "You know, you wear this like a revolutionary," Andy murmured, sliding the cups apart, revealing her small, sharp-nippled breasts to the cool air and the library's indifferent glow.

Sarah felt the self-consciousness threaten to flare—her instinct, always, to cover, to retreat. But Darya's laughter, raw and appreciative, cut through it, along with the background noise of the library's living theatre: someone in the far stacks singing Bowie badly, the crackle of a crisp packet, the squeak of trainers on laminate. Andy's hands were gentle, unexpectedly so, as he bent to suckle at Sarah's nipple, his lips cool and careful, his hand finding hers and guiding it to his cock. He pressed her

160

palm against its heat and throb, his eyes flicking up for permission, but not pausing long enough for protest.

Sarah tightened her grip, feeling the pulse, the weight, the sheer fact of another body, and thought of all those times she'd sneered at "sexual economics" in Gramsci. Here, there was nothing transactional—no shame, just appetite, just the messy, uncontainable collision of bodies wanting.

Darya watched, a lazy, satisfied smile on her lips, as Sarah let Andy tip her back against a free desk, her boots scraping at the legs. He knelt, trousers halfway down, still wearing his T-shirt, headphones dangling, and nuzzled her stomach, kissing the soft, pale skin below her navel, as if offering an absurd benediction. Sarah's thighs trembled, her breath coming sharp and uneven, and she let herself laugh at the absurdity of it, at the way her body responded so easily, so helplessly.

Andy's mouth was hot, almost too hot, as he tongued her, working with a slick, unhurried greediness that was almost studious. Darya, still bound, watched with an expression Sarah could only read as pride. "See? I told you. Communism in sex is just a question of how much you're willing to give away."

Sarah could have paused—she could have retreated into herself, into her father's words, the dozens of lectures about dignity and solidarity, or the political purity that made her roll her eyes at the sexual economies of Red Rose. Instead, she felt the charge of the moment course through her, a reckless energy that was half shame, half liberation. Andy's mouth at her cunt was deliberate, almost ceremonial, as if he had some unspoken respect for the occasion; each flick of his tongue seemed to echo off the library walls. The line between the vulgar and the sacred blurred to nothing.

"First, I'll let you have the pleasure of my cock," Andy whispered, "then our porcelain friend will have my baby batter."

Sarah didn't answer, not right away. In her head, a dozen retorts jostled for space—ironic, sharp, Marxist, flippant—but all died on her tongue, replaced by a gasp as Andy's fingers found her, deft and gentle, coaxing her thighs apart. There was no choreography, no elaborate negotiation; it was simply understood, as it always was here, that you surrendered or took, played your part, then rewrote it as you pleased. She reached down, circling her hand around the base of Andy's cock, feeling its weight, the heat of living flesh, not theory. Andy grinned, almost bashful for a second, then guided himself between her legs, pressing just enough to tease, his breath sweet with coffee and weed.

Darya, watching with lazy satisfaction, flexed her bound arms and muttered, "In Soviet Russia, cock fucks you! But here, in Red Rose, you get to choose." Her laughter was warm, echoing in the makeshift cathedral of the library, as Andy entered Sarah with the careful, teasing rhythm of someone who understood—perhaps for the first time—that spectacle and sincerity weren't mutually exclusive. There was a hush, an unsteady truce between performance and intimacy. Sarah bit her lip, willing herself not to flinch at the first push—Andy was bigger than Rolf, certainly more confident, but his movements were gentle, exploratory, as though he was cataloguing her every sigh and shiver, learning the language of her body with every stroke.

Sarah's back arched, the desk biting into her shoulders. For a moment she shut her eyes, wanting to be anywhere but here, wanting to be everywhere but here, her mind pinging between the Midlands, her father's lectures, the pounding pulse of Red Rose's endless dance studios. But then Andy shifted, the angle changing, and the pleasure was immediate, liquid and sharp, chasing away embarrassment and theory alike. She gripped his forearm, feeling muscle and intention, and realised with an incredulous little gasp that she wanted this—not in some abstract, revolutionary way, but as herself: Sarah Johnson, nineteen, alive, being fucked by a boy she'd barely spoken to in a library full of half-watching, half-bored artists.

Darya, watching, offered a running commentary. "Yes, like that. You see, Sarah, you can learn more from a night here than in all the books in Manchester. This is what your philosophers forget: the body is the first property you own, and the last thing you share." She licked her lips, still tasting the aftermath of her earlier conquest, and added, "If you want to be radical, be shameless. Only the shameless get remembered."

Sarah would have retorted, but Andy's thrusts were picking up, steady and deliberate, his hands braced on either side of her ribcage as if he were holding her open to the world. She gave in, letting the swirl of sensation and humiliation and something dangerously close to joy carry her past shame. The desk rattled beneath them. A book tumbled to the floor, splaying its pages like wings. There was laughter—someone in the next carrel applauding mockingly, a far-off voice yelling "Go on, Johnson, show us what the workers can do!"—but Sarah heard none of it, her world shrinking to the insistent rhythm of Andy's hips, the hot slick between her thighs, the wild, grateful ache gathering inside her.

It didn't last forever—Red Rose sex never did, always more about momentum than endurance, heat than tenderness—but it was enough. Andy came with a soft, surprised grunt, his face buried in the crook of Sarah's neck, and for a moment they were just two bodies tangled together in the ruins of theory and practice. Sarah held him close, her arms loose and uncertain, not sure if she should laugh or cry. Instead, she did neither, just breathing him in, aware of the way Darya's eyes lingered on them both—hungry, amused, approving.

Andy pulled out, standing and fastening his jeans with the unhurried confidence of someone who'd never been shamed for anything in his life. "Not bad for a commie," he quipped, winking at Sarah before giving Darya a mock-salute. "Now, as promised, let's give our Russian queen her tribute."

He crossed to Darya, her limbs still bound, her cunt flushed and gleaming in the low light. Sarah watched, breath returning in ragged, uneven bursts, as Andy positioned himself between Darya's legs. He didn't ask for permission; he didn't need to. At Red Rose, boundaries were a game, rewritten on the fly, and everyone played knowing the risks, the rewards. Andy pushed into Darya, who arched and laughed, biting her own wrist to muffle her moans. He fucked her with a careless, joyous abandon—quick, showy, his eyes

164

flicking from her face to Sarah's, hungry for the approval of both.

Sarah found herself moving closer, curiosity edging out jealousy or fear. She knelt beside the chair, one hand on Darya's thigh, feeling the tremble of muscle, the taut shiver of a body so thoroughly used, so extravagantly desired. Andy was rougher now, his movements less considerate, more urgent—he wanted to finish, to claim his share of the legend, to mark Darya as his, if only for a moment. Darya, for her part, seemed to relish the spectacle, her moans rising in pitch, her hips bucking despite her restraints.

Andy climaxed with a loud, unselfconscious groan, pulling out and painting Darya's belly with a wet, glistening spatter. He stepped back, panting, his chest heaving with exertion and pride. "There you go, my darling collectivist," he said, grinning down at Sarah. "Now you've both had your fill."

For a moment, no one spoke. The library was a cacophony of distant voices, the clatter of keyboards, the hum of fluorescent lights. Sarah stared at the mess they'd made— her own body still tingling, Darya's skin marked and sticky, Andy already slipping away, the world resuming its ceaseless motion.

But then Darya spoke, voice raw and quiet. "Untie me, Sarah. Please." The word surprised Sarah, that flicker of vulnerability, the simple, human plea beneath all the bravado. She nodded, her fingers clumsy as she worked at the knots, freeing Darya's wrists, helping her stand. Darya shook out her arms, wincing at the red marks, then leaned in to kiss Sarah softly on the mouth—a kiss that was neither performative nor mocking, but tender, grateful, real.

"Thank you," she murmured. "You did good, little commie. Now let's get out of here before someone calls security."

They gathered their things, the spell of the moment already breaking as the realities of Red Rose life reasserted themselves. Andy had vanished into the stacks, whistling Bowie's "Heroes" off-key. Sarah and Darya slipped out into the corridor, the air cooler, cleaner, the thrum of adrenaline fading into something quieter, almost companionable.

"Where to now?" Sarah asked, half-joking, half-hopeful.

Darya shrugged, looping her arm through Sarah's. "Wherever the night takes us. There's always another party, another stage. This place never sleeps."

As they walked together through the emptying halls, Sarah felt the strange, fragile warmth of connection—a sense that, for all her cynicism, she belonged here, that she was part of the living, heaving story of Red Rose. It wasn't the utopia her father had dreamed of, nor the revolution she'd imagined as a girl. But it was real, messy, and utterly her own.

****

CHAPTER 9 – Why Not Take A Crazy Chance...

Wednesday 6th November 2024

Marnie Taylor knew she was the opposite of her older sister Jess, a radio presenter at Manic Radio's Newcastle station. In fact, the way that she dressed, the way she looked, even her hairstyle, was much different than older sister and the fact that Manic was what Jess described as a den of sin, all because 99% of the staff treated the place more like a shag pad and less of a professional workplace, was all the more reason Marnie had applied to Red Rose. After all, it was her sisters alma mater, but her sister had graduated prior to the pandemic, when the place was strait laced, when sex wasn't a selling point, nor a power. Jess, having a 2:1 in Music, had graduated back in 2020, at the height of the pandemic, but the institution she'd left behind was nothing like the one Marnie entered in 2023. There were no warning stories in her sister's tales about secret parties or whispered alliances in the corridors, nothing about the casual, transactional way desire and popularity ruled the social order now. Marnie sometimes wondered if it had changed overnight, or if Jess had just never looked behind the right doors.

Looking at her iPhone, Marnie knew it was nearly 4pm, her sister's drive time programme about to start any minute. Loading the Manic Prime app, she changed it from Bee Manic, the local Manic network station, to Manic Radio North East, the Tyneside station. She pressed play, and the final few minutes of the Kyle and Sue mid-afternoon show burbled through the tinny speakers. The hosts were laughing at some in-joke about Greggs' festive bakes, their accents warm and familiar, filling her room with the clatter and chatter of home. Marnie let herself drift for a moment, recalling the Newcastle streets—the golden stone, the wind off the Tyne, the weird comfort of drizzle on a November evening. She was a hundred and fifty miles away, but the sound made the walls of her modest single dorm seem less oppressive, less like a holding cell for her anxieties and more like a place she'd chosen.

While the adverts were on, she felt the cock that was in her arse, that of Justin Harrison's, press into her like a physical reminder of where she was and what she was doing. In her pussy, however, was a strap on that her fellow Second Year Drama student, Nya Kingston, was on the other end of, the two cocks, a real and a fake one, in deep rhythm as they were locked in their wild, urgent dance. The tension in the room was electric, thick with sweat and the low hum of shared heat. Marnie's breath caught in her throat as Nya whispered something sharp and teasing into her ear, her voice like silk and fire combined.

"Feeling brave today, aren't we?" Nya purred, her fingers trailing down Marnie's spine, sending shivers through every nerve ending. "You always talk about taking chances… maybe it's time to really live that."

Marnie smiled, eyes half-lidded, heart hammering as she surrendered to the moment. Taking chances was the whole point of being here at Red Rose Academy now, wasn't it? To break free of the chains of past selves, old expectations, and the suffocating predictability of the life she'd left behind.

Here, in this cluttered dorm filled with the tang of sweat, leather, and the faint metallic hint of polish from the ballet barre by the window, the old Marnie—quiet, self-conscious, afraid—was shedding like a snake's skin. The new Marnie, bold and untethered, was rising.

The small speakers in the corner of her room crackled with the opening beats of Manic Radio North East's drive-time jingle, and Marnie caught the familiar voice of her sister cutting through the haze.

"Good afternoon, North East! It's Jess Taylor here, coming to you live on Manic Radio, with the best tunes to get you through the last stretch of your day…" Jess's voice was smooth, confident, and a little sharper than the day's usual banter. Marnie felt a pang of both pride and wistfulness. Jess had carved out a niche for herself, no doubt by playing the game her way—always impeccably polished, rarely caught slipping, the consummate professional. Marnie envied that. But she also loved how wild her own world had become, how it wasn't just about fitting in but standing out. "We've got some Basement Jaxx coming up, but first, how would you like to win half a million quid with the £500k Money Drop?"

Marnie knew the promo off by heart—she'd heard it a hundred times over the past year, mainly on the JJ and Hallie Drive show on Bee Manic, but also on the litany of regional and national Manic Radio channels that blanketed the country's airwaves. Still, Jess delivered it with a freshness that sounded as if this was the first time she'd ever read it, and not the thousandth.

"All you need to need to do is text DROP to 87106 or hop onto our website at manicradioplays.co.uk and click through to enter online. Entries cost £3, but there's also a free entry route, by calling 0330 880 3601, which is included in most phone plans. So, there's your chance, folks—£500,000 up for grabs, and with just a few taps or clicks, you could be in with a shot. It's a network competition across all Manic Radio stations, as well as all Manic Dance, Manic Metal, Manic Goldies, Manic Rock, and Manic Soul shows—so the competition is definitely heating up! Lines close Friday at 7pm, straight after Drive, where Dr Manic from Manic Dance will be calling one lucky listener live. Imagine that, eh? Don't say I never gave you anything. Anyway, later, I want your voice notes as Greggs have announced that their Christmas menu is coming back, with the return of Festive Bakes, Christmas baguettes, and—controversially—pigs in blankets with cranberry ketchup. Are you queueing already, or is it all marketing hype? Drop me a WhatsApp on 0191 498 0120 and I'll read your messages out after half 4. Up now we've got Romeo and TayTay's Love Story, as I'm feeling soppy and in need of a little musical romance to see us through this grey Newcastle Wednesday."

Marnie knew that the tracks being played wasn't her sister's choice, as she had been in the Manic studios in Huddersfield, where the Tyneside feed came from, and learned that Manic's Speke network centre dictated the network playlist, with presenters doing the links between the scheduled songs and sponsored content, all carefully coordinated from hundreds of miles away. Jess, for all her natural on-air charisma, was simply one voice in a seamless corporate machine, each show stitched together from a dozen cities, every link pre-approved and every song slotted in like clockwork. It was funny, really, how spontaneous radio was now just another illusion, even as it comforted homesick students in their shoebox rooms.

But Marnie had no time for homesickness. Not with Justin's hands locked tight on her hips, his rough grunts muffled by the duvet clutched between his teeth, and Nya's fierce grip pulling her back, driving the rhythm between them into a fever pitch. Her phone, perched on the windowsill, throbbed with Jess's voice, splicing familiar sounds of home into the tangled, alien heat of her new life.

A knock—hard, deliberate—struck the door. The three froze, the sudden tension slicing through their shared haze. For a moment, no one moved, the only sound the insistent thump of Jess's radio voice and the gasps still hanging in the air.

"Shit," hissed Justin, withdrawing, the condom dragging as he moved. "You expecting someone?"

Nya grinned, defiant. "Let them knock. It's your room, Marnie."

It was her room, and as the knock came again—this time sharper, a warning—Marnie felt something shift inside her. Old Marnie would have panicked, scrambled to hide, to straighten her hair and shirt, to act innocent. But new Marnie was hungry, half-naked, and burning with adrenaline. She wrapped the sheet around her hips, ignoring the stickiness of sweat and lube on her thighs, and padded over to the door.

She opened it a crack, just enough to reveal a wedge of corridor, and found herself face to face with Ella Forbes, wearing nothing but a robe and a strap on, and her brother Tim, a Third Year, wearing the tightest of Y fronts he could, his erection spewing out from under the elastic in a way that was not quite accidental. Ella's blonde hair was up in a messy bun, her blue eyes sharp as she looked past Marnie's shoulder, surveying the aftermath with a glance that saw everything and missed nothing.

"Room service?" Ella deadpanned, twirling the rubber cock at her hip like a set of keys. She smirked, the confidence of someone who never asked permission.

Tim, taller, darker, but with the same irrepressible glint, raised a single eyebrow, lips curling. "You started without us?" His accent was Red Rose through and through, vowels stretched by arrogance and too many late nights.

Marnie didn't flinch. The old her would have. She simply stepped aside, the sheet falling a little as she did. "We're just warming up," she said, and heard her own voice, how steady it was, how unafraid. "If you're joining, shut the door. Or are you here to complain about the noise?"

"Complaining? No, I just want to fuck Justin," she said with the grin of someone who had no use for decorum. "Tim wants to too, so…"

Marnie grinned with the same hungry boldness, letting the last threads of her old shyness dissolve into the steamy air of the room. "Then get in. There's plenty of him to go around."

Ella's smirk sharpened, and she slid past Marnie with practiced ease, the open robe exposing the glint of her strap on in the slanting late afternoon light. Tim followed, his presence large and unashamed, shutting the door behind him with a soft thud that seemed to seal them off from the rest of Red Rose—one room, one set of rules, their own.

Justin, half-off the bed, chest still heaving, caught Ella's eye and grinned. "You're late."

"Fashionably, darling," she drawled, her gaze sweeping up and down his naked form. "And you're leaking."

"Well, I was close to cumming when you knocked on the door, so I had to wank myself to distraction," Justin shot back, not bothering to hide his arousal, nor the faint flush that crept up his neck. He didn't move from his place, sprawled and open, as if inviting the chaos that was always, inevitably, Ella's entrance.

Marnie knew that having both Ella and Tim want to double penetrate Justin was as close to a taboo as you could get at Red Rose, and that was saying something. But boundaries here were like cobwebs—delicate, beautiful, and torn away by the lightest touch of want. It was why Marnie had chosen this place, why she'd bled herself into new shapes, forged from the heat and friction of shared desire and the electric knowledge that nothing was forbidden except boredom.

The next thing Marnie knew, Ella slipped behind Justin and, a bottle of lube in hand, started slicking up her strap on, the movement practised, unhurried, her fingers deft and businesslike. She gave Justin a knowing smirk, the sort that promised both torment and delight. Tim, meanwhile, perched at the edge of the mattress, stripping off his y-fronts with theatrical nonchalance, his cock springing free with a certain pride, as if announcing itself to the room.

"Need steadying, sis?" he asked, and Marnie watched Ella nod as Tim slipped behind him, intent on double teaming Justin, whose body was already taut with anticipation. Nya had moved aside, propped up on the pillows at the head of the bed, her eyes glittering with both amusement and competitive hunger as she watched the Forbes siblings move in on their prey. The dorm was a tangle of limbs and heat, a mess of clothes flung in every direction, the musky, electric scent of sex heavy in the air.

"Please, little bro," Ella obliged, patting Tim's arm in a gesture that might have seemed almost sweet if not for the wicked edge in her grin. "Just don't slip, yeah? Or you'll be in your hot sister's pussy quicker than you can say family counselling." The words hung in the charged air, edged with mockery, almost daring someone to blush or back out. But here, in this room, no-one had anything to prove. At Red Rose, there were no boundaries left—just appetite and bravado, and an audience that knew the rules had all been torn up and tossed out with last term's coursework.

Marnie felt turned on by the potential incest angle that she knew Ella and Tim acted out, as, even though they were siblings, they were careful not to even let anything "real" happen—at least, that's what everyone said. It was all for effect, part of their brand of dangerous, dazzling mockery, a play within a play that thrilled and horrified the more straitlaced students. But Marnie saw the flicker of real hunger in their eyes, the way Ella bit her lip as she guided her brother's hips, the way Tim's hand lingered on Ella's thigh just a moment too long.

She wondered, as she watched, where the act ended and the truth began, if it mattered at all in a place where every performance was both mask and confession. Nya seemed to sense her thoughts, because she caught Marnie's gaze and gave a little smirk, as if to say: Welcome to the real Red Rose.

Justin, for his part, was already pushing back against Ella's strap on with a kind of desperate greed, his body open, needy, shameless. Tim leaned in, spit slicking his cock, lining up beside his sister, the two of them working in a rough, perfect tandem. Justin groaned, fingers clawing at the bedsheet, caught between pleasure and the exquisite ache of too much, too soon.

"Romeo, save me, I've been feeling so alone…" the speaker from Marnie's phone spilled the chorus of "Love Story" into the overheated air, Taylor Swift's yearning voice at total odds with the obscene ballet playing out in the centre of the tiny dorm room. Marnie's mind flickered with surreal humour—if her mother or Jess could see her now, wrapped in a crumpled sheet, watching two siblings tag-team her classmate while the pop soundtrack of her teenage years chirped in the background. It was a world away from the careful, curated life she'd left behind in the North East.

But Marnie felt alive—her pulse wild, skin tingling, the boundaries between observer and participant rapidly blurring. She knelt on the far side of the bed, hands resting on her knees, watching the dance of bodies—Nya sprawled back, legs splayed, one hand idly stroking herself, the other playing with the remote for the toy still lodged inside Marnie, teasing her with unpredictable jolts of vibration. The threat of pleasure kept Marnie's muscles taut, every nerve ending on edge.

Ella was in her element, mocking and merciless. She leaned over Justin, teeth glinting as she whispered filth into his ear—words Marnie couldn't quite catch but which made Justin whimper, his body arching against the double intrusion. Tim's face was flushed with effort and delight, sweat slicking his forehead, the muscles in his jaw tight with focus. He looked, in that moment, exactly like a boy who'd always been given what he wanted—and knew he would have it again.

"Come on then, little man," Ella cooed, voice syrupy with cruel affection, "let's see who can make him come first. Bet you five quid you won't last as long as me."

Tim shot her a scornful look, grinding his hips forward, fingers digging into Justin's waist. "Put your money where your mouth is, sis. Or maybe in my mouth, yeah?"

"…Through this material, today's youth can be stimulated to sexual activity to which he has no legitimate outlet. He is even enticed to enter the world of homosexuals, lesbians, sadists, masochists and other sex deviants," the speaker then intoned—a sudden, jarring shift as the drive-time show's playlist abruptly cut out, replaced for a split second by what sounded like a snatch of a decades-old public service announcement, the audio warped and faintly tinny as though played from an ancient cassette. For an instant, the room paused: even in the thick of their orgy, every ear pricked at the incongruous sound. But just as quickly, Jess's familiar voice snapped back in, a cheekiness in it.

"Seems Producer Johnny's been watching Clubland TV again and has decided to play the same break bumpers that they air as a gag. You see, back in 1965, a video was released by George Putnam which was one of those moral crusader clips—the kind of thing they used to frighten your nan with. Yes, I admit, I watch Clubland TV when I've finished here at Manic Radio—don't judge me! But, honestly, imagine thinking you could 'protect' anyone from a bit of Taylor Swift or a disco ball. Anyway, coming up, we've got two Tyneside legends, PJ and Duncan, yes, Ant and Dec in their earliest, cheesiest form, but I reckon you can't call yourself a true Geordie unless you can sing along to 'Let's Get Ready To Rhumble'. But first, we've got some news about House of Manic, and yes, there's 4 events of House of Manic, and for the first time, the Utilita Arena, powered by Manic Radio... yes, the old Metro Radio Arena, will be hosting one of the biggest dance nights in the North East! And we've got our own headliner, not the same one as our Brummie, London or Scouse cousins... as Mr Slim Shady himself is headlining on Friday the 26th, live at the Utilita Arena, with Manic Radio North East broadcasting the whole thing live, plus there'll be pop-up Greggs, free Manic ponchos, and more chaos than a Bigg Market Friday. I'll be there, backstage, presenting live and exclusive, but the week before, we've got the first edition, live from Brum, and hosting it will be Manic Dance Breakfast's Ali Hussain and Tom Lode with a line-up that'll blow your mind. Details are on the app, so make sure you grab your tickets and start the countdown. But for now, I want you to send in your Greggs …memories, your best Festive Bake stories, and, as ever, your song requests and shout-outs. The WhatsApp is open, and I'll read the best ones after five. Now, back to the tunes—you're listening to Manic Radio North East, with me, Jess Taylor, keeping you company all the way to seven…"

As the music returned—"Let's Get Ready To Rhumble," absurdly bouncy—Marnie looked at the writhing knot of bodies on her bed, the absurdity of her old and new worlds colliding making her want to laugh out loud. But there was no room for self-consciousness here, only for heat, desire, and the delicious sense that, for once in her life, she was exactly where she needed to be.

Ella and Tim were hitting their stride, both deep into Justin's arse like a pair of competitive dancers, bodies moving in perfect, relentless counterpoint. Sweat beaded and rolled down Tim's chest, his dark hair plastered to his brow, while Ella's face gleamed with the effort, her jaw set in a grin that seemed part challenge, part triumph. Justin whimpered, caught between pain and pleasure, his hips rocking to meet each thrust, his knuckles white on the sheets.

Nya's laughter rippled from the head of the bed, breathless and sharp. "Keep going, Justin—let's see if you can handle two more Taylors next time," she teased, her hand never still as she edged herself closer, the remote for Marnie's plug still clutched in her palm. With each jolt she delivered, Marnie's knees threatened to give, her own body trembling with a mixture of anticipation and envy.

Ella twisted, rolling her hips, and pressed her lips to Justin's ear, her voice a vicious caress. "You ever had two siblings in you at once? Does it make you feel filthy, or special?"

"Both," Justin gasped, voice wrecked with need. "Don't stop."

Tim grinned, teeth flashing. "Who said we would?"

Marnie, unable to help herself, crawled forward and pressed a lingering kiss to Justin's shoulder, tasting salt and the edge of something wild. His body arched into hers, helpless, his moans muffled by her hair. The world outside—the radio, the November chill, even Jess's familiar voice—was nothing but a distant hum, the only reality the tangle of bodies, sweat, and reckless, shared need.

"Mind if I fuck you?" Marnie said to Nya with an impish smile, her voice as light as the question was obscene. Nya looked up, eyes glinting with a challenge that matched Marnie's own.

"Take your shot, Taylor," Nya replied, tossing the remote aside, the plug inside Marnie buzzing one last time before it stilled. "If you can focus, with all this chaos going on."

She sprawled back, thighs splaying wider, the harness she wore glistening with lube. Marnie took the harness off Nya, her lips connecting with the pussy like a pulse of heat, tongue flicking with hungry purpose. The taste of Nya—salty, slick, a mingling of sweat and arousal—filled her mouth, grounding her in sensation even as the room spun with noise, music, and the endless push-pull of bodies around her.

Nya gasped, the sound jagged, clawing at the thick air. "Oh, fuck—" She dug her fingers into Marnie's hair, arching her hips up, her thighs trembling with anticipation. Marnie pressed in deeper, her tongue working in slow, languid circles before teasing the edge, drawing out a whine that turned quickly into a rough, almost desperate plea.

"Is this what you meant by taking chances?" Marnie murmured, her breath hot against Nya's slick skin. "Because I could get used to it."

Nya didn't answer with words—her answer was a buck of her hips, a pull on Marnie's head, and the low, broken sound that escaped her throat. Around them, the bed creaked, the duvet twisted under their knees, and somewhere behind Marnie, Justin let out a ragged moan as the Forbes siblings pushed him to a new crescendo.

"Harder," Nya hissed, her voice sharp, almost feral. "Don't stop, don't you fucking stop—"

Marnie obliged, shifting to press two fingers inside, curling them with practised, insistent rhythm, her mouth never leaving Nya's clit. It was messy, it was wild, and it was everything old Marnie would have run from, but now it was like a fire she couldn't stop feeding.

Behind her, Ella's laughter rang out, low and triumphant. "Look at you, Taylor—never thought you had it in you."

Tim, flushed and grinning, leaned in to bite at Justin's shoulder, his free hand twisting his sister's nipple with the sort of casual brutality that bespoke long practice. Justin, lost to the world, groaned—a sound muffled into the mattress, desperate and animal, his body the battleground for the siblings' unyielding, ruthless pace. Sweat painted everyone: bodies glistening, muscles trembling, skin flushed with the effort and abandon of it all.

"Fuck, Timmy, you love your sister's nipples," Ella said with a taunting lilt, her eyes dancing with mockery and triumph as Tim squeezed and twisted with deft, merciless fingers. "You play them better than you ever played the piano, and you always did like to show off for an audience."

Tim just laughed, the sound rich and shameless, his teeth grazing Ella's earlobe as his thrusts grew rougher, timed perfectly with hers. "It's a duet, isn't it?" he murmured, not caring who heard. "Besides, you always said you liked it when I stole your solos."

The incestuous banter, half a performance, half a secret thrill, cut through the air like a wire—taut, sharp, ready to slice any pretence to pieces. Marnie watched, transfixed, the scene before her at once theatrical and raw: Ella, straddling Justin with her strap on, hips rolling in relentless rhythm; Tim, pressed flush against Justin's side, fucking him with a greedy, desperate energy, both of them sharing their prize, their eyes locked in a battle of wills.

Nya moaned, her thighs clamping tight around Marnie's head, the scent of her arousal thick and dizzying. "God, don't stop—" she gasped, her words barely intelligible. "Just like that, Marnie, don't you dare stop…"

Marnie's tongue never faltered, fingers pressing deeper, curling to find the spot that made Nya's voice break in a stuttering, breathless whine. She lost herself in the work—each flick, each suck, each slow, deliberate movement of her hand an act of reclamation, proof that she belonged here in this wild, untameable place.

Marnie let herself be pulled further into the vortex of sensation, as if every muscle in her body had been attuned to the riotous music of pleasure and risk that hummed through the room. Her mind had splintered into fragments of the present: the taste of Nya's slickness on her tongue, the muffled slaps and gasps from the knot of bodies behind her, the low throb of music and radio chatter bleeding out from her phone on the windowsill. It was as though she'd been torn in two—half a watcher, half a participant, her old sense of self now a distant echo.

She didn't know how long she stayed there, working her mouth and fingers with a feverish, precise rhythm. Nya's thighs clamped tight around her, shuddering and desperate, her words dissolving into a series of strangled moans and staccato breaths. There was something fiercely honest about the way Nya surrendered, her façade of control crumbling, her hips jerking up against Marnie's mouth with wild, helpless hunger.

Marnie only dimly registered the crescendo behind her—a rising, ragged chorus of breathless cries and animal grunts as the Forbes siblings pushed Justin towards the edge. The bed rocked and groaned, springs protesting beneath the combined weight and ferocity of their bodies. Marnie could hear Ella's laughter, edged with mockery and satisfaction, and the sharp hiss of Tim's voice as he spurred Justin on with obscene encouragement.

It was then that Marnie felt her pussy being filled, not by a fake cock, but by Justin's, obviously him trying to fuck her while he was being double penetrated, his hips twisting around so that, with effort and an almost acrobatic desperation, he could thrust up into her from behind. Marnie arched with a cry of surprise and delight, the angle awkward, the sensation overwhelming—two cocks still inside Justin, Justin's cock inside her, the whole tangle of bodies a testament to how thoroughly boundaries had dissolved in this cramped, overheated room.

She felt Justin's hands grip her hips, his movements jerky and urgent as he tried to keep pace with Ella and Tim's brutal rhythm. It was like being caught in a riptide—each thrust sending aftershocks through the tangled mass of limbs and slick skin, every moan and gasp adding to the rising storm of sensation.

"Fuck, Justin," she breathed, not sure whether it was plea or command. Her body trembled, torn between the insistent demand of Nya's orgasm cresting beneath her tongue and the dizzying pulse of Justin's cock inside her.

Behind her, Ella caught her eye and grinned wickedly, sweat running down her temple. "You didn't think you'd just get to watch, did you, Taylor?"

Tim only laughed, one hand reaching out to squeeze Marnie's thigh as he shifted his weight, grinding deeper into Justin with a grunt. "You're in the thick of it now," he said, voice rough with exertion. "No way out but through."

Marnie shivered, her nerves on fire. The room was a mess of sound—Nya's desperate, whimpering pleas, Justin's strangled groans, Ella's goading laughter, the wet slap of bodies meeting and the persistent, absurd background of Manic Radio's playlist, which had moved on now to the giddy pulse of another club anthem, its thumping bassline echoing the relentless drive of bodies in motion.

Then Nya's back arched, her hands knotting in Marnie's hair as she finally broke apart, her orgasm racking through her in helpless, shuddering waves. She cried out, her hips bucking up into Marnie's mouth, her whole body quivering as the release tore through her composure.

Marnie rode it out, fingers and tongue working Nya through the aftershocks, only surfacing when the other girl collapsed back against the pillows, panting and flushed. Nya's eyes met hers—dark, wild, and fiercely alive.

"That," Nya managed, her voice hoarse and thick with satisfaction, "was fucking ridiculous."

Marnie just grinned, her lips and chin slick, the taste of Nya still on her tongue. She looked over her shoulder to see Justin's face twisted in concentration and abandon, Ella and Tim flanking him, the three of them locked in an obscene, beautiful tableau of sweat, spit, and sex.

"You know, it's weird, that Maria and I are back on our on stage, yet I'm fucking you, while Ella and Tim are pounding my slutty arse," Justin said with a reckless, breathless laugh, his words tumbling out in a mixture of bravado and disbelief. "Who'd have thought second year would be like this, eh, Taylor? Back when I was getting bollocked by Yelena for missing pliés, I never dreamed I'd be the filling in a Forbes sandwich with your mouth around my cock and Nya's legs round your head."

Marnie felt her laughter bubble up, giddy and wild, echoing off the thin plaster walls. "You never know where the ballet barre will lead you, mate," she fired back, voice hoarse from effort, "Red Rose is full of surprises." The sweat-slicked tangle of bodies vibrated with aftershocks of pleasure and the unspoken thrill of boundary-pushing. It was raw, hungry, glorious, and for a dizzying moment, Marnie felt the universe contract to just this room, just these friends, just this impossible, beautiful chaos.

Justin, still half-seated in Marnie, thrust erratically as his own body began to betray him. "Ella... Tim... I'm gonna—" He barely got the words out before his body spasmed, buried between the siblings and inside Marnie, his orgasm tearing through him in shuddering, helpless pulses. The siblings didn't let up, milking him for every last wave of sensation, their own movements relentless, working towards their own crescendos.

Tim grinned, sweat dripping from his nose. "Go on, mate. We'll see you through it." He glanced at his sister, the banter barbed and affectionate. "Shall we finish him off, El?"

Ella, never one to back down, braced her hands on Justin's back and ground in deep, her strap on moving in perfect counterpoint to Tim's thrusts. "I always finish what I start," she purred, biting Justin's shoulder lightly for emphasis. Her eyes met Marnie's over Justin's trembling body—a look of challenge, complicity, and the fierce joy of being alive.

Marnie, still quivering from the intensity of it all, pulled herself up to kneel beside Nya, pressing a grateful kiss to her slick thigh before crawling up to curl beside her, both of them watching as Ella and Tim chased their own highs. The air in the room was thick, heavy with the scent of sex, sweat, and something like victory.

Nya, her voice softer now, murmured, "You've changed, Taylor. This place... it suits you." There was no judgement, just quiet admiration and maybe a trace of envy. "You were always the good girl in first year, weren't you? Look at you now. You're the fucking heartbeat of the room."

Marnie felt the words settle deep inside her, a warmth that had nothing to do with the tangled sheets or the heat of their bodies. "I guess I just needed permission," she whispered, nuzzling into Nya's shoulder. "Red Rose gave it to me. Or maybe I just stopped asking."

****

CHAPTER 10 – The Islamic Council of Red Rose...

Thursday 7th November 2024

Amir Hussain was sat in the Islamic Council of Red Rose Academy's office, a small building a few minutes' walk off the Oxford Road to the south of the campus proper, just past the battered blue fence that marked the Red Rose car park from the wild overgrowth of an abandoned pub. It was one of those cold, utterly grey Manchester mornings that soaked into your bones, as though the world itself had lost the will to shine. The clatter and bass thump of student life—buses, mopeds, distant laughter—bled through the thin window. Inside, everything was beige and brown: cheap flat-pack furniture, a kettled corner where old teabags congregated, the persistent scent of carpet cleaner and cumin.

Amir watched the steam coil from his tea, aware of the low-level anxiety that had settled in his chest since Fajr. The Council was supposed to be a home, a safehouse, a place where the city's chaos and the Academy's excesses melted away. Today it felt like a waiting room for an exam he hadn't revised for, where the examiner might at any moment decide to test him on all the things he'd rather leave forgotten.

Unlike some of the other students on the Council, he was a strict Sharia adherent, his father, an Iman, who was on the Muslim Council of Britain and a firm believer in Sharia Law, meaning that he knew that the excesses of Red Rose were haram, that they were an affront not just to his upbringing, but to the idea of a disciplined, dignified life. He tried, every day, to draw a neat boundary between the world inside—the quiet, the prayer mat, the Qur'an by the window—and the world outside, where flesh and laughter and ambition pressed up against the glass.

The Council, formed of men only, although they represented the female members of the student body, was a hotbed of debate as even though Amir was a firm and strict adherent, the group's makeup was anything but uniform. Red Rose Academy's Muslim cohort included everything from devout Sunnis and Shias to progressive Sufis, casual cultural Muslims, and those who rarely attended prayer at all but turned up for the food and fellowship. Arguments flared over the smallest things: who had washed up, whose turn it was to refill the tea caddy, whether the local takeaway's "halal" chicken could really be trusted. And, of course, about how to handle the relentless tide of the Academy's complete lack of sexual boundaries.

Amir knew that half of his fellow students, as it was only students, not faculty, as they were the body that policed itself, had committed Zina, the act of fornication, or at least boasted about it, their bravado drifting through the kitchen with the same easy bravado as the smell of frying onions. He tried not to listen, not to judge, but it was hard not to notice how the boundaries they debated so fiercely here dissolved the moment any of them set foot outside the battered door. The discipline, the clean lines, the sense of purity—gone, replaced by sweat, jokes, hunger, and the desperate need not to be left out of Red Rose's epic, endless party.

This was the paradox of the Islamic Council of Red Rose: it existed both as a retreat and as a battleground. Even the flat's design spoke to its compromises—worn prayer rugs lined up by the window, battered sofas dragged from skips or donated by parents, posters of Mecca alongside gig flyers and flyers for campus parties no one here would ever admit to attending. Aisha's battered copy of The Butterfly Mosque lay dog-eared beside the Qur'an, half-hidden beneath a stack of energy drink cans and lecture notes. The council was a space where you could, if you wished, shed the Red Rose identity and put on, for an hour, a version of yourself you remembered from before university, or perhaps only ever dreamed of being.

But that identity was under siege. Always. Amir looked at the clock: nearly nine. Soon, the others would arrive for the weekly Council session, their bags laden with pastries from the Turkish bakery and the familiar, shy hope that this week, someone would bring good news. He took another sip of his tea, then moved to tidy the living room, folding the tartan blanket over the back of the sofa and straightening the stack of prayer books. He knew what was coming, and dreaded it.

It was, inevitably, about sex. It was always about sex.

After all, there had been rumours that last night, on the Noticeboard app, something that Amir refused to even use due to Hayaa, or the principals of modesty, had erupted again. A viral post, posted by a white Liverpudlian student, Sarah Smith, a third year drama student notorious for both her on-stage brashness and her tendency to use the Noticeboard as a confessional booth, had detailed in graphic, taunting prose, that tomorrow, she wanted every single male student in one of the drama rooms, as she was going to filming a 6 hour live stream on her OnlyFans platform, one which she would "fuck the cum out of all of the male student body, all 3 years' worth of students, all nearly 190 students, within the 6 hours, no matter who is watching, no matter if it's the morning or the last call before security kick us out, and if you're Muslim, Sikh, Christian, Jewish, or whatever, you better turn up or else everyone will know you're a coward, or worse, a bore." She'd posted a list—half-joking, half-sinister—of names from every year, including several known to come regularly to Council meetings.

Amir watched the steam coil from his tea, aware of the low-level anxiety that had settled in his chest since Fajr. The Council was supposed to be a home, a safehouse, a place where the city's chaos and the Academy's excesses melted away. Today it felt like a waiting room for an exam he hadn't revised for, where the examiner might at any moment decide to test him on all the things he'd rather leave forgotten.

"...had me fuck her while Yusuf was also deep in her," a voice coming up behind him broke the stillness, and Amir nearly flinched, the tea sloshing dangerously in his cup. He turned, managing to compose himself just as Musa Khan—final-year Technical Theatre student and one of the more permissive members of the Council, on the phone, no doubt to one of his Leicester based siblings. "For an Omani whore, she's tight as a drum, innit."

Amir instantly knew who Musa was talking about, Aisha Al-Siyabiya, daughter of an Oman Air executive, someone who the Iranian born student knew was, if it came out in the wider Islamic community, destined for instant disgrace.

"Yeah, bruv, innit, she looked great with our sperm on her face while she her massive tits were just flopping everywhere, wallahi, the girl is built for sin. She had her Zionist boyfriend on Facetime, and bruv, he's a cuck. She makes him watch every second she's getting railed by the brothers, y'know what I'm saying?" Musa's voice was low and gleeful, the kind of brag that sounded like a joke until you realised that he meant every word. His trainers squeaked on the laminate as he collapsed into one of the battered chairs, tapping away on his phone with the restless, hyperactive confidence of someone who'd never known a day of genuine guilt. "She had some white first year fuck her last week, and her boyfriend was forced to watch before he killed more of our Palestinian cousins, yeah? Anyway, tomorrow, I'm going to be fucking this white bitch who wants every lad here at Red Rose to fuck her in a 6 hour livestream, and, honestly, I'm not gonna say no if they put my name on the list. It's all just banter, innit? If we don't, the drama lot'll just put it on the Noticeboard and clown us for being 'frigid'—or worse, they'll start saying we're all closeted or something. Bruv, it's Red Rose, not Al-Azhar, yeah?"

Amir noticed that Musa was still on the phone and so he kept his tone deliberately neutral, refusing to meet Musa's eyes as he moved past, quietly setting out a plate of plain hobnobs by the kettle. He didn't want to get drawn in. To engage would mean to judge, and to judge would only widen the gulf between him and the rest of the Council. He knew that in these halls, righteousness became arrogance all too easily, and arrogance was a poison that drove everyone away. Amir's job—he reminded himself—was to hold space, to offer somewhere for even the most lost or corrupted of his brothers to find some brief peace.

But the words clung to the damp air, just as the filth from the outside world always seeped through the thin council walls. *Built for sin... the girl is built for sin...* It was that casual tone, the way they all treated Red Rose as a world apart, a kind of theme park of lust and bravado, that always undid him most. He'd heard it before: from fresher-week speeches, from drunken mates, even from his own cousin, who'd failed out of the first year because the temptations of the Academy proved greater than any loyalty to mosque or family.

"Yeah bruv, I'm gonna knock that whore up and raise the baby on Red Bull and trauma, wallahi!" Musa cackled at his own joke, still half on the phone, and half trying to catch Amir's eye, daring him to bite back. "Me and the lads are gonna fuck her hard after the show, 6 of us and her, and she's gonna be bred like the white slag she wants to be. Bro, I told you, this place is haram central, but it's the best three years of my life. Half the girls back in Bradford would be down on their knees, sucking our cocks, if they knew what it was like here, but none of them would ever believe it, innit? There's one white lad here with a cock that's as small as a biro, wallahi, and even he's managed to get balls-deep in half the Asian girls on the first floor. Red Rose is mad, bruv." Musa's laughter trailed into a series of beeps as whoever was on the line hung up, or maybe just faded out, unbothered by the relentless disclosures of the morning.

Amir let the silence return, broken only by the creak of the old radiator, and the faint, persistent pulse of traffic. It was a kind of quiet that felt, to him, like holding his breath underwater: sooner or later, you'd have to surface. He glanced at the window. Rain, again. He pressed his palm flat to the glass and felt the chill, grounding himself with the cold. He closed his eyes for a moment, silently mouthing a du'a for patience and restraint.

Behind him, Musa was already scrolling through his phone, thumbs flicking with the compulsive energy of someone always searching for the next distraction, the next crumb of validation. Amir wondered, sometimes, what it would take for men like Musa to really be present. What would it take to make them stop, look up, and see each other—see themselves—as they truly were, stripped of banter and bravado, just men, tired and hopeful and broken, like anyone else?

The door opened with a clunk and in shuffled Haris, tall and stoop-shouldered, hood pulled up against the rain, a plastic bag bulging with simit from the Turkish bakery in one hand and an umbrella in the other. His beard was patchy, but he wore it with a sort of stubborn pride, as if compensating for everything else about him that didn't quite fit the ideal. "As-salaamu alaikum," he said, voice low and cautious.

Amir returned the greeting. "Wa alaikum as-salaam." He forced a smile and gestured to the table. "You're early."

Haris shrugged, setting down the simit, his face tight with fatigue. "Didn't sleep. My housemate was up all night, listening to grime and trying to chat up some Zionist drama girl. He wasn't lucky, but damn, she opened her legs when I showed her my Weapon of Mass Pussy Destruction."

Amir looked at the London born First Year Music student, and noticed that he was still grinning. The fact, he knew, that the younger male had slept with a Jew, which was forbidden according to both his family and tradition, seemed only to amuse him more—part trophy, part rebellion, part cry for someone to notice how lost he really felt beneath the laughter.

Musa snorted, "You lads need to stop chasing the haram, bruv. You'll end up with drama you don't need—and a trip to the GUM clinic."

Haris grinned, but Amir saw the flicker of discomfort cross his face. For a moment, the bravado dropped, and Haris just looked like a tired student, shoulders hunched beneath his sodden hoodie, eyes rimmed red from a sleepless night. "It's just a joke, bro. No one's getting married in Manchester."

"Still, the choices we make," Amir began, careful with his words, "they don't disappear just because we laugh about them."

"Come on, bruv, Allah probably shagged your mum to get you here," Musa interjected with a smirk, puncturing the moment with crude irreverence. The others snorted, some with genuine amusement, others with that brittle laughter people muster in groups when they don't want to stand out for being the killjoy. Amir gave a tight, weary smile, letting it roll past him. There was always a line to be walked, a balance between letting the ribaldry pass without rebuke, and standing up for the dignity he wished the Council would embody. He reached for the stack of prayer books, more to steady himself than to prepare for prayer.

He turned instead to practicalities, "Did you both see what was posted last night?" He meant the Noticeboard disaster. The question was aimed at Musa and Haris, but also for himself—to name the thing that threatened to pull the Council apart, if not in public, then quietly, within each member's heart.

"Who didn't see it, bruv?" Musa scoffed. "I mean, you could see her fingering that hole while she read out the list of names, yeah? My little brother at Manchester School of Music says his mates are all making side bets on how many 'proper Muslim lads' are actually going to turn up. He's subscribed to her OnlyFans."

Amir felt the muscles in his jaw tense, his tongue searching for the words that would both calm and guide, but all that came to mind was the ache of embarrassment. He knew this, too—the private humiliation, the sense of being watched by invisible crowds, measured against a scale he hadn't chosen. Even the mention of OnlyFans stung; it was a platform he'd only encountered in the abstract, a place whispered about in mosque car parks and shamed from minbars, now the main stage for the academy's latest scandal. He took a measured breath, seeking the patience that so often eluded him, especially on mornings like this.

"You talking about that slag Smith?" a new voice cut in—deep, flat, and just tired enough to betray he'd barely slept. Sadiq, a thickset second-year ballet student, dropped his battered rucksack by the heater and wiped his hands on his jeans. He barely looked up as he moved past the others, already fishing out his phone to check the notifications that never seemed to stop. "I'm in two minds. I mean, the teachings say that zina is haram, obviously, but we're blokes, and obviously sex is what we constantly think about. Plus, to be honest, my dad's trying to arrange a marriage for me and she looks like she's fell off the ugly tree, so shagging the slags here is the only way I'll ever get some sex before I'm forced to marry someone I can't even look at." He threw himself down on the sagging settee, the springs giving a protesting groan, and fixed the room with a look that dared anyone to challenge his logic. "Honestly, if we was in Saudi, we'd be stoned for just talking about this. Anyway, y'know what makes me laugh is all that 72 virgins stuff the morons who go to blow themselves up talk about—like bruv, if you really wanted virgins, just do first year at Red Rose."

"Like that Russian bird, Darya? She was a virgin until that Justin Harrison split her open in the studio, yeah?" Musa fired back, voice rising, eyes flicking around the room for someone to challenge him, to turn the heat of the banter into something more serious. "Banged her the other night after that commie whore Sarah Johnson had her in the library, apparently. Mate, half the first-year lads reckon they've had a go now. No point pretending it's all pure when it's open season on everyone. Why do you think the Noticeboard's full of it? That's what people want. No rules, no shame."

For a moment, the conversation hovered on that precipice between bravado and something darker—envy, perhaps, or the desperate need to believe that everyone else was as lost as you. Sadiq, leaning back, gave a one-shouldered shrug. "The world's haram, bruv. Might as well enjoy it before you get locked down, innit."

Amir closed his eyes and tried not to sigh too audibly. He was outnumbered and, on mornings like this, he felt it keenly: not just by the men in the room, but by the very air in Red Rose, thick with the expectation that nothing was off-limits except boringness. He wondered if the other societies—the Christians, the Jewish chaplaincy, even the Hindus in the back rooms above the union—felt this same exhaustion, this sense of trying to keep water in a sieve.

But there was no time to wallow. Others were arriving now, one by one, the familiar shuffles and clatters announcing each entrance as the Islamic Council slowly filled. Tariq, the self-appointed 'media officer', dropped his bag with a thud and immediately began tapping out an angry message on his battered Samsung. Bilal, the resident Sufi, drifted in after him, already humming something under his breath, eyes half-shut and blissful, as if to shield himself from the sharp edges of everyone else's stress. In the kitchen, Hasan and Naveed squabbled over the teabags—PG Tips or Yorkshire?—in the half-playful, half-desperate way of people who need the world to be simple, if only for five minutes.

Amir, sensing the gathering, gave up on the hobnobs and stood by the window, watching the drizzle carve tiny rivers down the glass. He let the voices rise and fall—

snatches of gossip, football scores, a heated debate about the best kebab in Rusholme. They sounded, for a moment, like any other group of lads at any other university. But beneath it all was the hum of tension that never quite left this place: the uneasy truce between faith and the city, desire and discipline, shame and survival.

He only truly came back to himself when Tariq, finished with his phone, snapped, "Right, lads, let's actually do Council before everyone buggers off to lecture. Amir, you're chair today?"

Amir nodded, feeling the weight settle on his shoulders. He stepped forward, cleared his throat, and the room, reluctantly, began to hush.

"Bismillah-ir-Rahman-ir-Raheem," Amir began, invoking the name of God, and felt at once both comforted and exposed. He always hated this bit—the moment when everyone pretended, for five minutes, that they were better, more unified, than the sum of their secrets.

"Welcome, everyone," he said, "to this week's Council. First, a reminder that we have Jumu'ah prayers tomorrow, and Dr Parvez will be giving the khutbah at the union. Now, before we move on, I need to bring up...the Noticeboard post."

A ripple of unease moved through the group, like the first tremor before a storm.

"Look," Amir continued, steady but firm, "I know some of you think this is just banter, or that it doesn't matter what people say online. But it's our reputation. People are watching us—our families, our communities, the wider

Muslim student network. What we do here, what we get associated with, matters. Especially when it's public, and especially when it's about something as serious as zina and public sexual behaviour."

"Come on bruv, you're just a virgin who never had the chance to taste real life," Musa muttered, too loudly for it to be a private aside. His words caught on the edges of laughter and derision around the room, the kind of ripple that was both challenge and shield. "You think the rest of us aren't aware? Bruv, this isn't some Sunday madrasa, this is Red Rose. Nobody outside this campus gives a toss what we get up to, and if they do, they're just jealous 'cause their uni's dead."

Amir, for a split second, nearly flinched at the phrase. He took a measured breath instead. "You're right—this isn't a madrasa. And none of us are angels. I'm not pretending. But we do represent something, even here. Not for the university, not for the city—for each other, and for what comes after. If we let them write the story of who we are, if we let them turn us into a joke, what's the point of the Council? Or do you just want to be the punchline?"

There was a sullen, shifting silence. Sadiq, sprawled like a cat on the sofa, looked up with half-lidded eyes. "Bruv, if you're so worried about reputation, maybe tell that to Al-Siyabiya. She's dating a Jew and making him watch her shag any random lad who passes through the door, and nobody's stopping her from calling herself a good Muslim. The rest of us are just living in the same world." A couple of the others muttered in agreement, their words muffled by bites of simit, but the tension was thickening. Musa drummed his fingers on the arm of his chair, tongue poking his cheek with the effort of not exploding into another rant.

For a moment Amir thought about responding directly, defending Aisha, but he stopped himself. It would only descend into more name-calling and 'whataboutism'. The council always came perilously close to that—a swirl of accusations, jokes, and grievance, until it was hard to tell whether you were fighting to preserve dignity or just to avoid humiliation.

Instead, Amir let the silence linger, the kind of silence that shamed people more than shouting. Eventually, Bilal, the Sufi, spoke up, his tone as soft as ever but with a steel core underneath. "We all have our weaknesses, brothers. But sometimes, I wonder if we spend so much time pointing at others, or mocking them, because it's easier than facing up to our own choices. If you've fallen into zina, if you've made mistakes—own it, and try to return. Allah is the Most Merciful. Don't make someone else's shame your armour. It won't protect you on Yawm al-Qiyamah."

Nobody responded for a long moment, but some of the eyes in the room softened. Musa rolled his head to one side, affecting boredom, but Haris seemed to shrink a little, his bravado ebbing in the stillness.

Amir seized the moment. "Look, I'm not here to judge anyone's past. I'm here to say, we need to be there for each other. Not just when it's easy, not just when it means joining in the jokes or pretending nothing matters. If someone's struggling, we help. If someone's going too far, we try to guide them back—not with shaming, but with friendship. We can't force the rest of the Academy to change. But we can set an example, even if it's just for ourselves."

He paused, letting his words hang, hoping they would sink in. "And as for tomorrow—this, whatever Smith is planning—nobody here is under any obligation to join in. Not for banter, not for clout, not for fear of what others will say. You don't have to prove anything by being there. You do have to live with the consequences, though, whatever you choose."

"Well, I'm going," Musa said with a shit eating grin. "Any pussy is a chance to lose yourself, bruv. That's the only thing anyone will remember at the end of this degree— how many you fucked, and how loud you laughed while you did it. Anyway, what's Allah gonna do? Smite us and send us to the fires for not being as boring as the Salafis want? He's got bigger business with those infidels in Israel who are killing our cousins in Gaza."

But Amir pressed on, his voice calm but iron-clad. "Don't use our pain as a shield for your own choices, Musa. The people dying in Gaza—they don't get to choose. We do. That's the point. Don't make a mockery of them by turning it into an excuse for your own pleasure."

"Come on man, we both know that at the end of the day, the better way to die is with a massive pair of tits round your cock than in some shitty jihad or some war nobody cares about, bruv," Musa sneered, the flippant, smirking edge in his voice attempting to mask something rawer beneath. "Look, don't start acting like your dad's Friday sermons now. No one here's going to become an Imam, yeah?"

But Musa's words didn't quite land with the conviction they might have done a year ago, Amir noticed. The bravado felt tired, hollow, like the last shout of a comic long after the crowd had stopped laughing. Perhaps the relentless party of Red Rose, the carnival of boundary-breaking and shame-annihilating 'banter', was wearing even its most devout hedonists thin.

Still, Amir pressed on, determined not to let this become just another round of who-could-shock-the-room-the-most. "We're not here to hand out punishments. Nobody's getting stoned, nobody's getting excommunicated. But we do have to decide: do we stand for something, or do we just take whatever the world throws at us and call it freedom?"

A hush fell. Even Musa, it seemed, was momentarily out of wisecracks. In that quiet, with the drizzle whispering at the window, Amir felt the smallest kernel of hope kindle within him: maybe—just maybe—today wouldn't be another loss.

The tension broke when Bilal, smiling gently, reached into his bag and pulled out a battered box of Turkish delight. "Who wants one?" he murmured, holding the box out to the group. The offer, as innocent as it was incongruous, acted as a balm; the younger lads reached for the sweets, Tariq groaning that he was "off sugar for the sake of Allah, and his BMI," laughter trickling around the room.

"Let's move on," Amir said quietly, and this time nobody challenged him. He ran through the Council's practicals: reminders about prayer times, charity collections for

Gaza, upcoming interfaith events, the need for volunteers to help clean the prayer space. The rhythms of council life, comforting in their regularity, began to assert themselves.

Yet even as he read out the announcements, Amir felt the undercurrent in the room. He saw it in the sidelong glances between Musa and Sadiq, the way Haris gnawed his lip, the way even Bilal, the kindest of them, looked as though he carried a sadness he wouldn't name.

"And to any other business," Amir said finally, after the last of the Turkish delight had been claimed and the kitchen's battered clock had ticked its way well past half nine. There was a shuffling of papers, an expectant pause. These final minutes of Council were always the hardest: where the regularity of faith and habit was abandoned, and the raw edge of Red Rose life returned, flickering in every glance, every joke, every silence.

Hasan spoke first, a wiry, baby-faced second-year whose tone always wobbled between earnestness and exasperation. "Yeah—just a quick one. Circling back to tomorrows... thing... I've texted my uncle who's on the Sharia Council, and he's come back with some advice."

"Go on then, Hasan," Amir said, willing his voice to stay even. If nothing else, this was what the Council was for— guidance, clarity, or at least the attempt. The whole room shifted, a subtle realigning of postures, bodies leaning in. Even Musa's phone stilled for a moment.

Hasan thumbed open his phone, squinting at the WhatsApp screen. "'He says,'"—Hasan adopted a self-conscious formality, reading directly—"'the Prophet, peace be upon him, taught us to avoid not only that which is haram, but also that which leads to haram. Our dignity is not just in abstaining, but in not being associated with open shame or foolishness. If you're pressured, you stand firm, but without arrogance or insult. Allah knows the hearts. If someone mocks you for not taking part in indecency, let them. Their words can't harm you with Allah, and in the end, your restraint will be your honour.'"

A murmur of reflection, not quite agreement but not dissent either, passed through the room. Amir felt the words settle, as if someone had finally thrown open a window and let in cleaner air. Hasan added, more quietly, "But he's also said that so long as we use protection, then personally, even though officially he's against it, the Council would see it as 'teaching the Western whores their place and not allowing them to humiliate the Muslim brothers in public' and that it's in the end up to the individual interpretation of Allah's teachings."

Amir looked at him with a steady, searching gaze, his mind trying to process the words, the weight of them settling heavily in the space between them. Hasan's words, though from an uncle whose position was authoritative, seemed like an attempt to justify something none of them could truly reconcile within their hearts. For a moment, the room hung in that liminal space—the crossroads of what was taught, what was lived, and what was quietly whispered in the shadows of Red Rose's corridors.

He exhaled slowly, trying to keep his voice measured, "It's about balance, Hasan. You know that. We walk a line here, every day, in this place. And we can't let it break us, break our dignity. Not for the sake of some temporary pleasure, not for the sake of fitting in with what's becoming the norm here." His eyes flickered to Musa, then Haris, then back to Hasan, his tone insistent yet calm, "Not even for the sake of being able to say, 'we did what everyone else is doing.' We can't be defined by their standards."

The silence that followed was deep, like the moment before a storm hits the coast. For a brief instant, Amir thought that maybe, just maybe, the Council could return to the purpose it was intended for. But before anyone could speak, Tariq, the self-appointed 'media officer,' broke the silence, his voice flat and final. "Whatever anyone does tomorrow, or the day after, it won't change a thing about who we are—inside or out. Just remember, no matter how much we try to protect our image, it's the actions that count."

Amir nodded slowly, unwilling to contradict him but also unwilling to entirely concede. The battle between their faith and Red Rose's chaos was never going to be solved here and now. Not in a room like this, not with voices so fractured, so full of conflicting stories and desires.

And yet, despite the heavy air that surrounded them, the session came to its natural end. Everyone shuffled their feet, eyes briefly glancing down at the floor as if to dismiss the weight of the conversation. Even the bravado in the room seemed to dull, retreating into the corners, hiding from the reality of what was laid bare.

Amir sighed, feeling the tension ease only marginally. He stood for a moment, staring at the empty cup of tea on the table before glancing out the window. The rain had picked up, now pounding heavily against the glass, streaking down like the wash of his thoughts. In that moment, he knew: no matter how hard they tried to impose order, Red Rose would always be a crucible—a place where faith, lust, and youthful rebellion collided in an unforgiving alchemy. The question remained: could they survive it, or would it break them, one by one?

As the Council began to disperse, Amir caught sight of Haris still chewing on his simit, his phone back in his hand, the dull thrum of the Academy's party-saturated culture already creeping back into the room. Aisha, too, had left early, her absence only further emphasising the silence that clung to the space. The questions lingered, unanswered. Could the Council still act as a refuge? Could it shield them from what Red Rose threatened to do to them all?

The answer, as always, was uncertain.

****

CHAPTER 11 – A Stage of Bodies...
Friday 8th November 2024

The camera, Sarah Smith, knew, was set up ready, with it being set to stream onto OnlyFans as well as the Red Rose Noticeboard her course mates worshipped with the same religious intensity as first-years did Adderall. Surrounding her was every male student at Red Rose, all furiously masturbating with the intensity of a dying man down to his last cigarette—except it wasn't just dying. It was ritual, spectacle, the culmination of a dare, a test, a punishment, and a performance all at once.

Sarah knew that she wanted it, however, standing in one of the drama studios, dressed like the 'girl next door' stereotype, looking as if she had just come in from a Friday evening shift behind the bar at Wetherspoons, her make-up artfully casual, hair up in a loose ponytail, wearing denim shorts and a yellow top, her hair in a pony tail, sans underwear as she knew that this challenge that she had set herself would be controversial, yet also define her. There was a sickening thrill to the whole enterprise, a shimmer of anticipation that danced beneath the overhead fluorescents and made her skin itch with nerves and power.

The challenge that she had set herself was simple. She was going to shag every male student at Red Rose, all 180 of them, in 6 hours, the time limit being so she couldn't back out, couldn't slack, couldn't hide in the slow rhythm of ordinary, private sex. She wanted, needed, the boundary—something so audacious, so unrepeatable, that it would be written into the academy's mythology. The lads had agreed that it wouldn't just be for the Noticeboard, however, but also for her OnlyFans subscribers, for those who willingly paid to see the kind of spectacle that could only happen at Red Rose, where shame and bravado were currency and every body was both actor and audience.

Being 21, she knew, meant that she could legally drink, screw, and broadcast her being ridden by every single student, no condoms, nothing, as they had all willingly signed a contract hastily written by a law student from one of Manchester's other universities, spelling mistakes and all. The contract, which Sarah had insisted upon, was a wry kind of shield—a relic of the bureaucracy she'd learned to wield since her second year, even as she had abandoned every other social rule at Red Rose. It was a thin document, more symbolic than enforceable, but everyone had signed.

The reason why she had insisted on the contract? Because she knew that she was monetising the risk, the chaos, the spectacle, and even her own body—not just for a night but as the very material of her legend. Sarah wasn't naïve about what Red Rose Academy was: a crucible for future West End stars and lost hopefuls alike, a playground where reputation was as valuable as skill and as disposable as yesterday's pantomime script. She knew she'd be dissected, envied, hated, desired, and imitated. That was the point. She wasn't simply submitting to the gaze; she was orchestrating it, taking hold of the narrative and turning herself into a myth even as she trembled with adrenaline and a flicker of fear.

"Fuck, this is insane," Ashley Ketchum said, his three inch cock being sucked by a first year as the chaos around him erupted into something approaching a religious rite. Sarah had to chuckle at how even the gay students at Red Rose had signed up, gleefully, competitively—some for the notoriety, some for solidarity, some for the game of upstaging masculinity itself. There were boys here who had never so much as kissed a girl sober, others who'd already become campus legends for their stamina or depravity. Now, the challenge was as much about their performance as it was hers. The thrill in the room was thick and hot, woven with nervous banter, laughter, bravado, the slap of flesh and the click of iPhone cameras.

Sarah's hands trembled as she stood in the centre, not from nerves alone but from the knowledge that this was no longer just a dare, or a stunt, or an act of rebellion— though it was all of those things, deliciously so. This was history. She knew how the Noticeboard would light up, how her OnlyFans would explode with subscriptions, how her DM inbox would fill with propositions and threats, praise and outrage. She felt herself vibrating between terror and glory.

She stepped up onto the makeshift dais—an upended storage crate, wobbly beneath her trainers—and let her gaze drift around the studio. It looked like a casting call from hell, bodies packed shoulder to shoulder, every face expectant. She grinned, feeling the heat on her cheeks and the sweat prickle down her spine.

"Rules are simple," she declared, her voice carrying over the fidget and laughter. "Six hours, 180 of you, no breaks except for water and a piss if you really can't hold it, and

I'm not fucking any of you if you can't keep it hard. You all get one go, that's it—unless you're quick enough for another round before time's up. No condoms, no out, no exceptions. If you can't manage it, move aside for the next lad. Fair?"

A chorus of yells and catcalls—"Yes, Miss Smith!" "Fair, boss!"—echoed back at her, some in voices already strained with anticipation.

She heard the steady throb of the music, the pulsing beat from the Bluetooth speaker set on top of a battered old prop trunk, and felt it in her bones: the sound was like a second heartbeat, driving her forward.

There was no grand announcement, no countdown. The challenge began as soon as she knelt, opening herself with one hand, pulling the first boy forward with the other. He was shaking, whether from nerves or excitement she couldn't tell, but it didn't matter. The camera caught every angle, every gasp, every thrust. She performed for the lens as much as for the room, making sure every moan, every shudder, every clutch at her hips was on display.

She was the centre of a storm, and the world narrowed to skin, breath, rhythm.

Looking at the first erect cock, belonging to Justin Harrison, who had his on/off girlfriend Maria Kovacs being his personal fluffer for the event, her tits wrapped around the cock like a pair of velvet gloves,

"So, Justin, you get the honour of undressing me," she said with a grin, the fact that she looked exactly like a girl next door who had stumbled into the world's filthiest audition not lost on her or the crowd. Justin, ever the showman, slid his hands up Sarah's bare thighs with exaggerated delicacy, making a pantomime out of unhooking her shorts, exposing her in full, beaming towards the camera as though the world would never forget this frame. Maria, ever the agent provocateur, paused to spit on his cock, glancing up at Sarah with a look equal parts challenge and solidarity—a brief, wordless moment of female camaraderie amidst the testosterone haze.

Justin's erection twitched, guided by Maria's hands, as he stepped forward. There was a tension between all three—Justin, Maria, and Sarah—fuelled by memory, rivalry, and the knowledge that tonight nothing would be off the record. Sarah braced herself, welcoming Justin with a gasp that was half-played for the camera, half-genuine. The crowd hooted, someone whistled, and the first thrust felt like the starting pistol for an obscene marathon.

Time became elastic, measured in moans and claps, the slap of hips, the half-shy, half-brash comments shouted from the ring of onlookers. Justin finished quickly, as expected—his legendary stamina, it turned out, was mostly myth when faced with the full weight of an audience and the Noticeboard's omnipresent gaze. He withdrew, spent and grinning, and Maria high-fived Sarah before darting off to fetch water for the next in line.

The challenge had begun.

Sarah knew that she was going to become more than just a campus rumour or a half-whispered legend. She was carving herself into the stone of Red Rose Academy's mythology with everybody, every wordless gasp, every ragged breath that filled the room. She barely had time to steady herself before the next boy stepped forward, trousers already around his ankles, face flushed with a cocktail of fear and hunger. She looked up and met his eyes—a fresher, thin, ginger, sweating with the kind of terrified excitement only Red Rose could summon in a first-year.

He hesitated. Sarah smiled, reached out, drew him in with a hand on his thigh. "Come on, love. Let's not keep the queue waiting," she teased, her voice pitched to both reassure and provoke, aware of the camera, aware of the massed audience who needed her to lead, to keep the performance spinning so nobody would have time to wonder if any of this was madness.

The fresher fumbled, stammering a thank you as if she were handing out grace rather than her body. He slid inside, trembling, the crowd roaring encouragement and mockery—"Go on, ginger! Show her how it's done!"— and Sarah arched her back, meeting him with practised, performative relish. When he came, far too soon, she let the applause cover his shame, whispering a soft, "Well done, pet," before sending him off, red-faced but grinning.

And then another, and another. The line at the door stretched out of sight—boys from drama and dance, music and tech, known faces and strangers, each carrying his own reasons for being there. Some were already legends—Musa Khan, who swaggered up with a condom dangling from his ear like an earring, before Sarah snatched it away and tossed it to the side with a theatrical flourish: "Not tonight, Musa. Rules are rules." Musa just grinned, stuck his tongue between his teeth, and set about performing with the same bombast he brought to every stage.

Others were more hesitant: Tariq Siddiqi, ever the diplomat, apologised to the camera for his "lack of stamina," blaming a late-night essay and the "weight of expectation." He lasted longer than most, buoyed by the ribald encouragement of his mates, but eventually succumbed to the inevitable, gasping Sarah's name as though it were a prayer.

The studio was hot now, thick with the smells of sex, sweat, Lynx Africa, and anticipation. Sarah felt herself detaching, floating above her own body, noting the movements—the way her skin gleamed under the harsh lights, the glistening slickness between her thighs, the ache already building deep inside. But she did not falter. She kept smiling, kept making eye contact, kept drawing every new participant into the world she was conjuring: a place where shame and ambition melted into one and the same thing, where being watched was both punishment and reward.

Occasionally, the line slowed. A boy couldn't get hard, or stumbled over his own nerves, or needed a word of encouragement. Sarah was patient, gently teasing, coaxing, making it clear that here, tonight, failure wasn't the real humiliation—giving up was. One lad, a bearded second-year from the music department, blurted, "I'm sorry, I've never—" and she hushed him with a finger to his lips, a slow stroke of her hand, a whispered, "You will now. That's all that matters." He left the dais starry-eyed, barely able to walk straight, to the cheers of his mates.

Behind the cameras, the stream chat exploded: emojis and exclamations, crass jokes and staccato praise, subscriptions pouring in faster than the next lad could unbuckle his jeans. The Noticeboard app was melting down—posts, screenshots, memes, all chronicling Sarah's marathon, her myth-making in real time.

An hour passed. Then two. Sarah drank water between partners, snatched brief moments to towel herself down, to wink at the camera, to flash a grin at the crowd. There were brief lulls—when boys lingered to talk, to pose, to relive their moment on the dais—but she kept the pace, her mind ablaze with adrenaline and endorphins, her body a live wire of sensation and exhaustion.

There were highlights—moments that would live forever in the annals of Red Rose. The three dance boys who insisted on choreographing their entrance, pirouetting naked onto the stage and taking turns as if auditioning for a pornographic version of Swan Lake. The technical theatre lad who produced a strobe light and a bottle of lube from the props cupboard, transforming his two minutes into a feverish rave. The drama boy who, in the throes of climax, declaimed Hamlet's "To be or not to be," collapsing onto Sarah in peals of laughter and spunk.

For a brief while, the room's edge frayed; bodies pressed in, hands found hips and backs, tongues sought lips, and for a moment the orgy threatened to spill into chaos. But Sarah, now slick with sweat and come, held court— calling for order, rallying her "cast" back into the procession, determined to keep the challenge within the bounds she'd set. It wasn't about chaos, not really. It was about performance. It was about her.

By the fourth hour, Sarah was hoarse, her muscles shaking, her pussy raw and tender from use. But she refused to let the pain show. She chugged more water, forced herself to keep moving, to keep taking every lad as though he were the first. She let herself moan for the camera, to ride the pleasure when it flickered through her, to let the world see her as both victim and queen, slut and star.

"You alright babes?" Maria asked her, and Sarah flashed a crooked, sweat-soaked smile.

"I'm living the dream," she rasped, voice nearly gone but eyes shining with an animal brightness. Maria, more a stage manager now than fluffer, offered her a cold Red Bull and a wet towel. The brief, gentle gesture was enough to remind Sarah that—tonight, for better or worse—she was both the show and the scaffolding, the ritual object and its high priestess.

The crowd had shifted as the hours wore on. The mood oscillated between uproarious banter—someone scrawling "SMITH 180 CLUB" on a whiteboard, the room erupting as another boy "graduated"—and something more awed, almost reverent. Even the cockiest, most cynical lads found themselves, when finally standing in front of Sarah, subdued by the scale of what was happening, by the simple, exhausting, glorious audacity of it.

Before Sarah could say anything, she noticed, in the doorway, one of the "Muslim Council" looking at her, disapproving. She knew from the way Amir Hussain stood, arms folded, shoulders taut, eyes grave beneath the low fluorescent light, that this was not the first boundary he had watched fall since his arrival at Red Rose.

He was not the only one to hover there, either—Bilal, the soft-eyed Sufi, drifted in behind, hands in his pockets, jaw set. Next came Musa Khan, who—having long since taken his own turn, shameless as always—had doubled back, trailing a gaggle of mates, all eager to see what became of the "Smith Challenge." Their presence was a kind of shadow cast across the raw glare of spectacle, a whisper of another world at the edge of this one. But Sarah refused to let herself shrink beneath it.

Amir did not move closer. Instead, he took in the scene with a long, cold gaze that settled over Sarah and each of the assembled boys in turn. For a moment, the banter softened, the studio's raucousness muted as word spread: "The Council's here." Whispers tumbled through the crowd—some taunting, some defensive, some simply curious.

Sarah steadied herself, rolling her shoulders, refusing to drop the performance even for this. The cameras rolled; the chat on OnlyFans, on the Noticeboard, pulsed with speculation, expectation, delight and condemnation tangled in a single, ever-refreshing feed. The Red Rose myth machine was already working overtime.

Musa swaggered forwards, grinning as he met Amir's stare, "Bruv, you here to join or judge? Might as well get in line—there's still half an hour left, innit."

Amir's response was a quiet, unamused shake of the head. "We all have to live with ourselves in the morning, Musa. That's all." He looked at Sarah, meeting her gaze. "And some things don't wash off. Not with all the water in the world."

But Sarah had spent the last four hours turning shame to currency. She smiled at Amir, voice cracked but clear. "You don't get to write my story, Amir. I do." She let the words hang in the air, as much for the camera as for the man. She felt the charge in the room, the sudden uncertainty, as if the crowd themselves were waiting for some judgement to be handed down. "Anyway, doesn't Islam allow multiple wives? Or are you waiting for the 72 virgins?"

"She's got you there, bruv," Musa said, and Sarah notice he was wearing shorts with his bulge showing quite well through the cotton, a sight that brought a ripple of laughter from the cluster of lads closest to the dais. "Might as well fuck her, Amir, or you'll be the biggest bore Red Rose has ever seen. Besides, you can always ask Allah for forgiveness after, innit?"

A murmur ran through the crowd, part nervous, part entertained, some glancing to the door as if worried the wind itself might carry rumours down to their parents' ears in Rusholme, Bury, Bradford, or Salford. Amir didn't move. If anything, his stillness became the moral axis of the room—a fixed point around which the chaos spun. For a moment, Sarah felt her own defiance tremble against that refusal. She saw, in his set jaw, a refusal to let her or anyone else claim the last word. Not from shame, but from dignity: the kind that was heavier, she realised, than any banter or bravado.

"Bial'iidafat 'iilaa dhalika, fahi eahiratun, wanahn naelam 'ana aleahirat mufidat liqadibina aljihadii," Musa then said, and Sarah knew that she didn't know a word of Arabic. "Ariha kayf yasheur alrajul almuslim alhaqiqiu biqadibiha fi thuqub tilk aleahirat al'iinjiliziati"

The words hung in the air, alien and sharp, slicing through the din like a knife through silk. Sarah caught the ripple of confusion and curiosity that flickered across the faces near her. Musa, with his usual cocky grin, looked at Amir and then at the crowd, clearly relishing his cryptic, half-serious jab. The room, thick with sweat and expectation, seemed to hold its breath—some waiting for a translation, others just sensing the weight of the moment.

And then she noticed Amir stalk towards her, a look in his eye that was both resolute and burning with quiet fire, like a man who had carried the weight of worlds on his shoulders long before tonight's spectacle had begun. The room shifted around them, the noise dimming to a murmur, the anticipation folding into something raw and more profound than any of the ribald jokes or lewd cheers.

Sarah's breath hitched as he stopped just a few feet from the dais, the scent of his cologne—something earthy, almost medicinal—cutting through the heady perfume of sweat and sex. The camera remained trained on her, but even its sterile eye couldn't quite capture the gravity of this moment. Amir looked at her not as a contestant or a performer, but as a woman laying her soul bare on the altar of her own choosing.

"You think this makes you powerful?" His voice was low, measured, but heavy with challenge. "That turning your body into a stage, your shame into currency, is freedom?"

Sarah's grin faltered for a split second, her heart pounding in her ears. "I'm not asking for your permission, Amir. I'm rewriting the rules."

That was when she felt him slap her.

The slap echoed through the studio louder than the bassline, louder than the catcalls. It was not the playful smack of lovers, nor the drunken lashing of a frat boy—it was sharp, precise, deliberate, delivered with the quiet authority of a man who had measured the cost of his actions before letting them fall. The air itself seemed to split in two, the shockwave rolling across the packed room like the aftershock of a bomb.

Sarah's head snapped to the side, the sting flaring across her cheek, a rush of tears springing instinctively to her eyes—not from hurt, but from the sheer violence of the moment, the spectacle turning in on itself. For a single beat, the entire audience froze, caught between outrage, awe, and the gleeful hunger of those who lived only for escalation.

The camera caught it all, merciless and unblinking: Sarah with her lip curled, Amir with his hand still raised, the silence of 180 lads who'd spent the last hours laughing, jeering, moaning, all suddenly stripped of voice.

And then—

A roar, half in shock, half in exhilaration.

"Oi oi! He's fuckin' done it!" someone bellowed.

"Bruv went full alpha on her!" another shouted.

"Jesus Christ, did he just—?!"

The noise returned, now jagged and wild. The Noticeboard live feed exploded with messages, screenshots of the slap going viral within seconds: #SmithSlapped already trending. Some wrote legend, others abuser, the discourse fracturing before Sarah herself had even moved.

She touched her cheek with trembling fingers, feeling the heat blooming beneath the skin. She turned her head back slowly, ponytail swishing, eyes narrowing into something that was neither defeat nor humiliation. It was theatre. She knew it. He knew it. They all did.

"Fine," she rasped, her voice cracked and sharp. "Show me, then. Show me what a man who doesn't bend to the crowd actually does."

The studio quivered under the weight of that provocation. The boys shifted, muttering, the air thick with the scent of sweat, cum, adrenaline, and now—violence. A violence that wasn't the crude thrust of cock into cunt, but something heavier, older, ritualistic in its sudden appearance. Sarah's cheek still burned, the mark red as a brand, while Amir's hand hovered in the crowd's collective memory like a shadow puppet caught on the stage wall.

For one jagged heartbeat, no one moved.

Then Amir stepped up onto the dais. He didn't swagger, didn't smirk like Musa had, didn't stumble like the freshers or boast like the theatre lads. He climbed with the steady inevitability of a tide swallowing the shore, shoulders squared, eyes set on Sarah with an intensity that shredded the braying humour of the boys into silence once again. He was still clothed—hoodie, joggers, trainers laced tight—and in that moment, his refusal to bare himself only made him more naked, more exposed, than the lot of them.

Sarah's chest rose and fell in ragged rhythm, her body vibrating with exhaustion and defiance. She was drenched—skin gleaming with a patina of lust and sweat, thighs tacky with semen, hair slick to her forehead. She was already half-mad with fatigue and sensation, but she was not going to let him rewrite the challenge. This was her show.

"Take your clothes off," she commanded, her voice sharper than it had been in hours, slicing through the wall of noise like a whip crack. "If you're here, you play by my rules. I don't care if you slap me, sneer at me, judge me—you still strip like everyone else."

A ripple of laughter broke through the tension, lads elbowing each other, emboldened again by Sarah's defiance.

Amir didn't move. He stared at her, his jaw working, a muscle flickering at the side of his temple. Then, slowly, deliberately, he peeled off his hoodie and tossed it aside. The T-shirt followed, revealing a lean, wiry body, more sinew than bulk, his chest dusted lightly with hair. His joggers came down last, leaving him in nothing but briefs that did nothing to hide his hardness, the fabric straining at the edge of decency.

The roar that followed was deafening.

"Go on, Amir!"

"Finally, lad's in the club!"

"Smith'll tame him yet!"

The chant began, crude and relentless: "Take her down! Take her down! Take her down!"

Sarah's smirk was shaky, more fragile than she wanted it to be, but she kept it plastered on. She motioned him closer with a crook of her finger, eyes never leaving his.

Amir stepped forward, every stride slow, deliberate, until he stood directly in front of her, his cock outlined like a weapon through the thin cotton. Sarah spread her legs wider on the crate, her cunt raw and swollen, glistening in the harsh fluorescence.

"You wanted to show me," she whispered, pitched low so only he could hear, though the cameras would pick up every syllable. "Then do it. Do it in front of them. Prove you're not just words and slaps."

His response was to strip the last barrier away, briefs sliding down his thighs, his cock springing free—dark, thick, heavier than she'd expected. The crowd roared again, and somewhere in the back Musa whistled like a referee.

Sarah reached out, wrapping her hand around him before he could make the first move. The heat of him pulsed against her palm, a solid reality cutting through the surreal haze of the last hours. She gave him one slow stroke, eyes locked on his, daring him to flinch, to falter, to lose the intensity he wore like armour.

But Amir didn't falter. He grabbed her wrist, forced her hand away, and pushed her back onto the crate. The sharp edge dug into her spine, her legs falling open, and for the first time that night she wasn't the one dictating the pace. Gasps and catcalls echoed through the studio, the spectacle transforming before their eyes into something they hadn't seen yet: Sarah Smith, the untouchable, the orchestrator, losing control.

When Amir pushed into her, the room erupted.

It wasn't like the others. Not fumbling, not frantic, not performed for the crowd, though the crowd devoured it with hungry eyes. His thrusts were deep, deliberate, punishing, each one driving into her as if staking a claim. Sarah cried out, the sound raw, less a moan than a ragged scream pulled from her throat. She clawed at his back, nails digging into his skin, leaving trails of red.

"Jesus fuck," someone shouted. "He's killing her!"

"Go on, Amir! Wreck her!"

But Sarah's mind was far from wrecked. Even in the haze of pain and ecstasy, she knew what this was: the climax not of her body, but of her myth. She had set the challenge, drawn the line, orchestrated the madness—but here, in this moment, Amir was rewriting it, adding his own chapter whether she wanted it or not. And the crowd was eating it up. The Noticeboard feed, visible on a screen in the corner, was a blur of messages, hearts, fire emojis, the slap already immortalised, now this—the reversal, the spectacle of Sarah Smith undone.

Her orgasm hit her like a knife through silk, sudden, violent, tearing a scream from her throat that silenced even the rowdiest boys. She convulsed beneath him, body spasming, tears streaking down her cheeks, and still Amir moved, still he drove into her, relentless, merciless, until he finally spilled inside her with a guttural groan, his face twisted with something between agony and release.

But he didn't pull out.

He didn't yield.

Instead he pressed his weight against her, pinning her to the crate with the unyielding finality of a man who wasn't here for applause, wasn't here for the Noticeboard or OnlyFans, wasn't here to become another notch in the long, sweaty chain of bodies. He was here for something else—something harder to define, something Sarah, in her breathless, trembling haze, could barely hold in her mind.

The crowd roared, bayed, screamed obscenities, clapped and stamped like a mob at the Colosseum. And yet, beneath the feral soundscape, there was a fracture in the air—an undercurrent of silence that was Amir's alone. His body stayed locked in hers, his chest pressed to her breastbone, his breath hot and ragged against her ear. He whispered, not for the room, not for the cameras, not for Musa or the Council or the Noticeboard—just for her.

"I'm going to breed you, make you a proper Muslim wife, make you submit," he growled, and for once, Sarah felt frightened, the words searing into her ear like a brand. For the first time all night, the challenge trembled on the knife-edge of spectacle and something else—something rawer, older, more terrifying. Her chest heaved, caught between fury and fear, between the narrative she had built and the narrative Amir was trying to seize for himself.

But before the weight of his body could cement itself into myth, there was a blur of movement.

Musa.

"Get the fuck off her, bruv!"

The words cracked through the feverish studio like a whip, and then Musa was there, striding forward with his usual swagger but eyes alight with something far hotter, far sharper than banter. The crowd parted instinctively, the lads who'd been laughing and chanting now holding their breath, sensing that the spectacle had shifted into a theatre none of them had rehearsed for.

Musa's hand shot out, grabbing Amir by the shoulder and yanking him back with the same force you'd use to tear a curtain off its rail. Amir staggered, his cock slipping from Sarah with a wet sound that seemed indecently loud in the sudden hush. The crowd gasped as though someone had ripped the script from their hands mid-performance.

Sarah sat up, chest heaving, face flushed scarlet with exhaustion and humiliation, her thighs slick with the mingled traces of dozens of men—and now Amir. She looked both undone and incandescent, like a priestess mid-sacrifice whose ritual had been interrupted.

Musa squared up to Amir, his grin gone, his jaw clenched. For once, he wasn't performing.

"You don't get to *own* her, fam," Musa hissed, voice pitched low but carrying, slicing through the babble.

This was her challenge. Her rules. Her legend. You don't get to twist that into some backwards sermon about wives and breeding. You think you're bigger than the game? You're not. You're just another dick in the line. I only told you that in Arabic to loosen you up, not treat her like the fucking spoils of jihad."

The words cracked through the fevered haze of sweat and cum like a fist through glass. The room, which had been baying like wolves seconds before, suddenly teetered on the edge of silence again, eyes darting between Musa and Amir like punters waiting for the next round of a boxing match. Even the camera seemed to hum with tension, its little red light blinking like a heartbeat in the corner of the studio.

"You said, Musa," Aisha intervened with a sudden sharpness that cut through the air, the kind of tone that made even the most loutish lad instinctively straighten up. Nobody had noticed her at first, slipping in with a small group of the Council girls, her hijab wrapped tight, eyes flashing with the fire of someone who'd been watching long enough to know that silence was a kind of consent. "Bial'iidafat 'iilaa dhalika, fahi eahiratun, wanahn naelam 'ana aleahirat mufidat liqadibina aljihadii. Ariha kayf yasheur alrajul almuslim alhaqiqiu biqadibiha fi thuqub tilk aleahirat al'iinjiliziati. That translates to Besides, she is a whore, and we all know whores are useful for our jihad cocks. Let her feel what a real Muslim man's dick feels like in her English slut holes.'"

The words cracked through the studio like a whip, like a dropped plate smashing into silence. Gasps, nervous laughter, a couple of jeers that died in throats. The way she said it—measured, clear, each syllable stripped of shame—was not just a translation. It was an indictment. It was a mirror turned towards Musa, who suddenly looked less the swaggering rogue and more like a schoolboy caught nicking chocolate bars from the Co-op.

Sarah's chest heaved as she blinked at Aisha. The world tilted, swimming between exhaustion, ecstasy, and the sudden bite of clarity. Her cheek still stung from Amir's slap; her thighs were sticky from a marathon that had blurred into a fever dream; her body trembled with the aftershocks of being used, fucked, worshipped, judged. But here, at this knife-edge moment, it wasn't the crowd of 180 lads, or the Noticeboard, or even her OnlyFans subscribers she was aware of—it was Aisha, standing like a blade of cold steel in the haze.

The room shifted. Laughter faltered, bravado withered. For the first time that night, the spectacle felt like it was collapsing in on itself, teetering between carnival and tribunal.

Musa sneered, trying to recover ground. "Bruv, come on. You know I was joking. These man know me, yeah? It's banter." He spread his arms, grin too wide, teeth too white. "You think I'm out here on some ISIS ting? Nah fam. I was winding him up."

****

CHAPTER 12 – You've Got Cum On Your Face...

Saturday 9th November 2024

"So, ladies," Maria Kovacs said, walking into the Rose Petal, as it was Ladies Night, a night where all the male students were banished (officially, at least) and the Rose Petal's doors were guarded by a burly man who had a face that could breach several ASBOs and a body that looked like a brick wall covered in faded tattoos. The bouncer—universally known as Trevor, though no one was quite sure that was his actual name—barely glanced at Maria as she slipped in, her ID already memorised from a hundred messy nights. The street outside was cold and puddled with half-frozen November rain, the city centre busier than usual for a Friday, but inside the Rose Petal was a feverish womb of heat, perfume, cheap prosecco and pulsing, bouncing bass. There was no other club like it in Manchester, and on Ladies Night, the place throbbed with an entirely different energy: feral, permissive, feminine, unrepentantly chaotic.

She stopped in the entrance, letting the sensory onslaught of pink LEDs, sweaty bodies and pounding 00s dance anthems wash over her. Maria was dressed for war: black mesh top, scarlet bralette, micro skirt and boots tall enough to be classed as a hazard. Her hair was up in a high, fraying ponytail, streaked with last night's glitter. She checked her phone, saw her group chat blowing up, then flicked it onto silent and made for the bar.

The Rose Petal's Ladies Night was infamous. It wasn't just a ban on boys; it was a rite of passage, an evening where, for one night only, the performative competition of the ballet studio, the silent cruelties of the practice room, the endless backbiting and gossip and sexual power play—all of it could, in theory, be set aside. In reality, it rarely worked that way, but it was the only time most Red Rose girls allowed themselves even the pretence of solidarity.

As soon as she walked into the bar, she saw Darya Ivanova eating out Ella Forbes with the gusto of someone who hadn't eaten in a week. Ella was spread like a starfish across a sticky velvet booth, her dress hiked up around her waist and her eyes rolled back in delight, one hand tangled in Darya's cropped hair, the other fist gripping a bottle of cheap pink cava like a trophy. Around them, girls howled, cheered, filmed, or simply carried on with their drinks as if this was entirely normal—which, for the Rose Petal on a Ladies Night, it almost was. If there were rules, they were written on toilet paper and dissolved in prosecco.

Maria rolled her eyes, but with a smirk—this was, after all, exactly why she'd bothered to show up. There was something tribal about the chaos, the sense of the pack let off the leash. She squeezed between tables littered with lipstick-smeared glasses, bodies pressed thigh to thigh and spilling secrets with abandon. The air tasted of perfume and sweat and a strange freedom.

She noticed Sarah in the corner, drinking, not even taking part in the orgy, just sitting quietly with a bottle of Lidl rosé clutched between her thighs, legs splayed, hair wild and skin still flushed in patches where she had, the previous day, spent been fucked into legend. Sarah looked like a castaway who had been rescued by pirates only to be thrown into the sea again, hair frizzy and tangled, face streaked with the ghosts of smeared makeup and the faint, tell-tale abrasions of the night before. Her hands trembled just a little as she drank, her eyes flicking between the bodies gyrating on the dancefloor and the more intimate scenes at the booths. For once, no one bothered her, though more than a few phones were aimed in her direction, surreptitiously or not.

Maria snaked her way over, sliding into the booth across from Sarah, tossing her phone on the sticky table with a heavy sigh. "You look like you've been put through a tumble dryer, babe."

Sarah didn't immediately reply, just took another swig of warm rosé, then finally turned her gaze to Maria. "It's that thing with Amir. How he grabbed the script and wrote his own ending. You know, I thought he was going to rape me."

Maria flinched. For a moment the throbbing background of the Rose Petal seemed to fade, the music retreating behind a strange, humming silence. The word was so stark, so clinical, it landed like a dropped glass between them. She glanced at Sarah—really looked this time. The bravado, the cultivated recklessness, even the ragged glory of last night was gone, replaced by a watchfulness that Maria had only ever seen on girls who'd come up hard or come undone.

Maria was the kind of girl who could drink a rugby boy under the table and then climb him like a tree, but the shadow in Sarah's eyes was older, sharper than any

Saturday morning hangover. She forced herself not to recoil, not to say something trite or, worse, nothing at all.

"And then when Aisha told us what Musa said and how he tried to play it off with the 'it's just banter' and 'you think I'm out here on some ISIS ting' lines. Honestly, I'm fucking tired, Maria. Tired in a way no sleep or shower or fresh set of knickers is going to fix." Sarah's voice was low, thick with the kind of rawness that could only come from someone who had laid herself bare for more than just an audience.

Maria, whose own heart had always been armoured in acid wit and bravado, felt that edge dull for a moment. She reached across the sticky table, rested her hand over Sarah's trembling fingers, the two of them shielded from the world by the pulsing bass, the stink of cheap prosecco, the screeches and giggles of their classmates gone feral.

"You're still here, though," Maria said softly, "and so am I. That counts for something." She squeezed Sarah's hand. "You could've let it break you. You didn't."

"I don't get why Amir did it though. He's always been the only sane male Muslim student, yet he went full fucking Old Testament on me," Sarah muttered, shaking her head as if the memory itself was a splinter working its way out of her skull. "Like, do you reckon he really hated me, or was it about the lads? Or was he just… I dunno. Showing off?" She reached for her drink, missing the glass by an inch, then smirked at herself and tried again. "Or do you think what Musa said to him was the reason he went full Jihadi John on me?"

Maria didn't answer straight away. She looked at her friend—because that was what Sarah was, after everything, even now—and let the throb of the bass and the shrieks of laughter around them fill the silence for a beat. Beyond the sticky table and the glowing phone screens, Darya was still eating Ella out, now with an almost competitive intensity, as though the outcome mattered to some invisible scorekeeper. On the dancefloor, girls in sequins and platform trainers stomped and whirled, bodies slick with sweat, mascara streaking as they screamed along to a remix of "Toxic".

"Maybe it wasn't about you at all," Maria said finally. "Maybe it was about proving he wasn't just another dick in the queue. Maybe it was about… I dunno, staking his own flag in the carnage. Boys are weird like that. Men are even worse."

Sarah huffed a mirthless laugh, pressing her knuckles into her eye sockets. "Do you think he's going to tell everyone he converted me? Like I'm another notch on his prayer mat?"

Maria snorted, shaking her head, "He can try, but you're not a convert, Sarah. You're a fucking comet. Whatever you do, it scorches. They can chase your tail for a thousand years and still be talking about it in the drama toilets."

Sarah tried to laugh, but it came out flat and exhausted, barely more than a rush of air between her lips. She stared at her chipped nail polish, the half-empty bottle of Lidl rosé glinting a wan, dusty pink between her knees. "It doesn't feel like I scorched anything. I feel like I got ground down. Like there's bits of me on the floor back in that fucking studio. And everyone's just going to walk right over them Monday on their way to ballet or whatever. Like it's just confetti from the world's shittest parade."

Maria studied Sarah for a moment, feeling the full weight of what wasn't being said in the space between them. Outside, the city was slicked with rain and the threat of another endless northern winter, but in here, under the pink haze of LEDs and the rising cackle of half-feral Red Rose women, there was a kind of warmth—a rough, battered, imperfect sort, but warmth all the same.

She squeezed Sarah's hand tighter, not letting go. "That's not how confetti works," she said quietly, voice thick with the dregs of her Hungarian accent, "Confetti makes everything a bit more sparkly, even when it gets everywhere. Maybe you're just… everywhere now, yeah? Inescapable. Part of the place." She tried for a smile, an echo of the bravado she wore like chainmail. "You're Red Rose legend, babe. There's power in that, even if it doesn't feel like it at four a.m. when you're sobbing in the bogs."

Sarah let out a small, bitter snort of laughter, her hand shaking in Maria's. "There's always some girl sobbing in the bogs at four a.m. at Red Rose. This week it was just my turn, that's all."

A roar went up from the far end of the club—someone had done a round of shots and now they were dancing on a table, four girls screaming out the chorus to "Dirrty" by Christina Aguilera, one of them yanking off her shirt and twirling it like a victory flag. In another booth, Darya finally surfaced from between Ella's legs, face smeared and shining, and accepted a drink handed to her by a giggling third-year whose mascara had migrated somewhere up near her eyebrows.

Maria watched them, watched the celebration and the chaos and the mutual devouring, and felt something in her chest unclench, just a little. "We all get our turns, I think," she said, dragging her gaze back to Sarah. "At Red Rose, the only thing that really changes is who's crying and who's dancing on the fucking tables."

Sarah managed a half-smile. "What happens if you're doing both?"

Maria laughed, properly this time, loud enough to draw glances from a cluster of music students at the bar. "Then you're finally doing it right."

They sat in silence for a moment, the beat of the music thumping through the banquette, the fug of sweat and perfume settling over them like a shroud. Maria sipped her own drink—tequila and Fanta, a Red Rose abomination—and glanced at her phone. The group chat was still blowing up: blurry photos from the night before, memes about Sarah's "record-breaking" performance, at least three new OnlyFans subscription links, and a video of Darya leading a conga line of topless girls through the corridor outside the toilets.

"I can't believe we're not banned from this place," Maria mused, mostly to herself.

Sarah tilted her head, blinking blearily at the club around them. "It's because Trevor used to be as barman at a brothel in Nevada for a few years, so he's seen everything. Last week he caught someone giving a blowjob behind the DJ booth and just offered them a wet wipe and told them to move along. Only place in Manchester where the staff are more traumatised than the clientele." Sarah's lips twisted, the old gallows humour fighting through the fatigue. "I reckon he's secretly proud. Or maybe just numb."

Maria grinned, glancing towards the door where Trevor— tattoos, bulldog jaw, indeterminate age—leaned against the wall, arms folded, eyes scanning the crowd with the bored, unflinching gaze of someone who'd once found a dead badger in the men's and simply shrugged. "We're his retirement entertainment. He probably goes home and tells his grandkids stories. 'Back in my day, girls didn't shag 180 blokes for an Instagram reel—did it for the love of the game.'"

They both laughed, the sound cracking something open between them, letting in the possibility that maybe, just maybe, the trauma could be carried lightly, if only for an evening.

"Anyway, babes, how about you eat me out, and make me the queen of the bogs for a change?" Sarah's voice, low and rough-edged, was only half a joke. Her eyes lingered on Maria, not with the hunger of seduction, but with the bone-deep desperation of someone who wanted to be seen, wanted to feel, if only for a few moments, that she was more than a rumour or a headline. Maria didn't answer straight away. She finished her drink in a single swallow, wiped her mouth with the back of her hand, and slid out from the booth.

"Come on then," she said, nodding towards the corridor that led to the toilets, that sacred, infamous liminal space at the Rose Petal where more had been confessed, confessed, and performed than on any stage in the Academy itself.

Sarah stumbled after her, bottle clutched in one hand, the other gripping Maria's wrist. As they pushed past the knots of laughing, drunken girls, Maria felt the eyes that followed them—jealous, admiring, predatory, bored. At Red Rose, privacy was a myth, but solidarity, at least on Ladies Night, had its own protective forcefield. The door to the toilets was flung open, the sharp, cleansing scent of industrial disinfectant mingling with perfume and old gin. Two first-years were giggling over the sink, taking selfies in the cracked mirror, one of them fixing a glittery pastie that had worked loose from her nipple.

Maria guided Sarah into the nearest stall, barely wide enough for both of them. The ancient lock clicked shut. Maria perched herself on the cistern, lips quirking in a half-smile. "Alright, you get to cry, but you don't get to wallow. This is Ladies Night. We reclaim the bogs. That's the fucking rule."

Sarah let out a shaky laugh, slumping back against the door, her legs trembling. For a moment, neither of them moved, the space between them thick with possibility— grief, lust, camaraderie, defiance. Maria reached out, gently brushed a stray strand of hair from Sarah's cheek, her fingers lingering a second longer than necessary. "Do you want me to?"

Sarah nodded, once, fiercely. "I want to feel like I'm in my own body again. Not just a rumour."

Maria knelt, pulling Sarah's knees apart, hands strong and steady. She pressed a kiss to the inside of Sarah's thigh, tasting sweat, salt, and the ghosts of a hundred nights spent navigating the bloody, glorious minefield that was Red Rose womanhood. She worked slowly, methodically, her lips and tongue drawing shuddering breaths and then sharp cries from Sarah, whose hands fisted in Maria's hair, not pulling, but anchoring herself to something real.

From the other side of the door came the usual cacophony: laughter, the shriek of a hand dryer, the thump of a phone dropped onto tiles, someone belting out the chorus to "Since U Been Gone" with the raggedness of heartbreak. Maria blocked it all out, her focus narrowing to the taste and heat and slow, building pulse of Sarah's pleasure. When Sarah finally came, it was silent, breath held, eyes squeezed shut—no spectacle, just release.

For a few minutes, they stayed like that, Maria's head in Sarah's lap, Sarah's fingers stroking Maria's hair, both of them breathing in tandem. Eventually, Sarah let out a soft snort. "Well. That's one way to get back at the bastards."

Maria looked up, lips quirking. "Best revenge is living, babe. And fucking. Sometimes both at once."

They left the stall together, stepping into the chaos of the bathroom—another trio of girls were now giggling by the sinks, one of them in the process of washing cum from her face, the other two hyping her up as if she'd just won a scholarship. Sarah caught Maria's eye in the mirror, and they both burst out laughing.

They made their way back to the bar, arms around each other's shoulders, a new kind of bond forged in the crucible of piss, tears, and ten quid rosé. The dancefloor was even more frenetic now, a blur of writhing bodies, hands thrown in the air, hair flying, cheeks flushed. On the raised stage, Darya and Ella were holding court, re-enacting their earlier performance with even greater theatricality, to a rowdy, cheering crowd.

Tammy Knight was perched on a table, rolling cigarettes for a huddle of drama students, her eyes red-rimmed and feral. Nearby, Aisha Al-Siyabiya was arguing animatedly with Lucy Grand about whether you could actually get chlamydia from a microphone, both of them punctuating their points with wild gesticulations and sips from stolen bottles. The air was thick with sweat, smoke, and a kind of giddy, post-traumatic euphoria.

Maria and Sarah squeezed into a booth, pulling in close to Darya, who greeted them with a grin, her face still shining, hair wild, dress rumpled. "Fucking hell, I love Ladies Night," she declared, swigging from a can of Red Stripe. "Best night of the year. No boys, no rules, no boundaries."

Sarah, a little steadier now, managed a crooked smile. "No boundaries is how I got into this fucking mess in the first place."

Darya shrugged, pressing a sticky kiss to Sarah's cheek. "Boundaries are for the weak. Or for the Monday morning tutorial."

They laughed, the sound rising and falling with the music, swept up in the wild current of the club. For a while, time lost its grip, everything collapsing into a blur of dancing, drinking, and confessions shouted over the pounding bass. Maria found herself pulled onto the dancefloor, hips grinding against Darya's, Sarah and Ella spinning in a circle of their own invention, arms flung around each other, faces flushed with sweat and freedom.

It was as if the trauma of the previous night, the constant, grinding pressure of the Academy and the unspoken threat of violence and humiliation, had, for one night, been burned away by the sheer, incandescent energy of collective, chaotic womanhood. Girls danced with wild abandon, grinding against each other, forming and dissolving groups, kissing, laughing, crying, and sometimes all three at once. The floor was a sea of limbs and sequins and unwashed hair, and for the first time in a long time, Maria felt almost—almost—at home.

In the smoking area, they found Tammy mid-rant about the canon of queer literature, waving a half-smoked rollie like a conductor's baton. "You think this is chaos?" she shouted, gesturing at the packed dancefloor, "You should've seen Red Rose during the 2012 Olympics. Half the choir pregnant, two violinists ran off to Glastonbury, and the head of music was found shagging a percussionist in the cleaner's cupboard. This—" she waved her hand again, "—this is civilisation, babes."

Maria knew that Tammy was lying to the First Years who she knew hadn't had sex yet, as the orgies hadn't started until after the pandemic, that the University had been basically shut down from 2020 to 2022, but she let the legend stand. That was part of it, wasn't it? The mythmaking, the oral history passed down in bar toilets and smoking shelters, growing in bravado and debauchery with each retelling. If Red Rose had a culture, it was one of self-invention—whoever shouted loudest, or fucked most outrageously, wrote the story.

Outside, the city smudged itself across steamed windows—rain streaked neon, buses sighing by in the cold. But inside the Rose Petal, it was pure, uncut now. Maria flicked the end of her cigarette into a puddle by the fire door, then turned back to the others, lips curling in a half-drunken smile.

"Alright, Darya, your turn for truth or dare," Maria said, balancing a can of Red Bull precariously on the rail.

Darya, whose accent seemed to thicken when she was tipsy, flashed a wolfish grin. "Truth, then. I have nothing to hide."

Tammy, never one to waste an opportunity, leaned in, her voice pitched just loud enough to cut through the clatter of taxis outside. "Alright, Ivanova. Who was the best lay at Red Rose, and don't say Justin because everyone says Justin."

Darya considered it, head tilted, the hint of mischief glittering in her eyes. "You want scandal or sincerity?" she asked, licking a smear of gloss from her lip.

"Both, obviously," said Ella, slumped against the door, her tights laddered and heels in her hand.

Darya took a sip, then, without theatrics, just the quiet weight of honesty, said, "It was Maria. She fucked me during lockdown in the ballet crypt. No music, no witnesses. Just us, and the ghost of every ambition we ever had. It was the first time I felt like someone saw me, not the legend, not the Russian, not the girl who needed to be taught. Just… me." She finished her drink in a single swallow, and wiped her mouth with the back of her hand, daring anyone to make a joke of it. For a heartbeat, nobody did. Maria, whose tongue was always quick to weaponize, found herself silent, the memory rippling through her like a chord struck in a hollow room. Even Sarah, who never missed a chance to laugh at sentiment, only gave a soft, knowing nod.

Tammy arched an eyebrow, lips twitching with something dangerously close to respect. "Didn't know you were soft, Ivanova."

Darya shrugged. "It's not softness. It's just… if you never tell the truth, you start believing your own bullshit. And that's how you end up crying in the bogs at four a.m. Or marrying a man from Oldham."

A ripple of laughter washed through them, the tension easing. For a few minutes, conversation spun away into safer waters: the latest drama from the Technical Theatre lot ("Mario shagged Irene in the lighting booth again and blew the main circuit"), who'd been kicked off the Noticeboard app for revenge porn, and which First Year had accidentally submitted a video of herself pissing in the costume store as her self-tape for Chekhov.

The Rose Petal's air grew hotter and heavier, the edge of midnight softening faces and smudging eyeliner, drinks replenished as if by magic. Darya and Ella vanished to the toilets for a round two; Maria found herself pressed between Sarah and Aisha, who had returned from her argument with Lucy brimming with the righteous fury of someone whose dissertation on "Postcolonial Performance as Self-Reclamation" had become a meme.

"You lot," Aisha announced, "are absolute legends. I mean it. I've spent all week arguing with men who think the word 'liberation' means 'permission to DM you dick pics.' We run this fucking school, and don't let the boys, or the old white men in tweed, tell you otherwise." She slammed her empty glass on the table, her Omani accent slicing through the noise like a conductor's baton.

Maria laughed, tipping her head back, feeling the throb of the music pulse through her spine, and shouted, "Aisha, you say that every Ladies Night and then spend all term dating white boys who think Rupi Kaur is radical."

Aisha rolled her eyes but grinned, tipping her glass in Maria's direction. "Babes, it's called anthropological research. Besides, some of us are trying to diversify the gene pool. I'm singlehandedly saving Manchester from becoming a monoculture of white men with anxiety and a Spotify playlist called 'Sad Vibes for Overthinkers'."

Even Sarah, who just an hour before had seemed too fragile to stand, let out a snorting giggle. "You're singlehandedly giving the GUM clinic fresh data, is what you're doing."

Aisha flipped her hair and leaned in close, eyes sparkling, "Better a fresh case study than another student show about trauma performed on IKEA furniture."

At that, the whole booth erupted. Maria clutched at her side, her laughter dissolving into tears. Aisha, cheeks flushed, pressed her forehead to Maria's. "We're chaos, babe. We're the reason Trevor prays every time there's a full moon."

Darya returned, a half-dissolved lipstick print smeared along her jaw and a look of wild, hungry triumph in her eyes. "It's a warzone in there. Girls are giving out orgasms like freshers' wristbands. Saw Lucy Grand deepthroating a cucumber. She's going vegan, apparently."

Aisha snorted, nearly choking on her drink. "Is she fuck. She's just trying to get on Bake Off. Saw her making profiteroles in the microwave last week."

Sarah, who had finally reclaimed her own body in the chaos of the bathroom, reached for the bottle of Lidl rosé and poured what was left into everyone's glasses. "To us," she declared. "To being chaos. To surviving, and then some."

They clinked plastic glasses, the sticky, sweet wine spilling over their hands. Maria felt a strange, liquid pride warm her throat. This was the real curriculum at Red Rose: not what happened onstage, or even in the classroom, but this—the bruised, battered, brilliant survival of a group of women determined to leave a mark, even if it was only in lipstick on a club bathroom mirror.

A beat dropped, and the crowd surged onto the dancefloor for a mass karaoke of "Since U Been Gone", a loose, joyfully tuneless scream of voices. Maria was hauled up, pressed between Darya and Sarah, their bodies slick with sweat, hair wild, voices raw. The floor vibrated with hundreds of stamping boots. Maria lost track of who was grinding on her, who was kissing whom, who was shouting lyrics into her ear. All that mattered was the pulse and the noise and the wild, exhausted joy.

Aisha grabbed her hand, spinning her in a drunken waltz that collapsed into giggles. "Did you ever think this would be your life?" she gasped.

Maria could barely breathe, the sweat and heat and emotion choking her chest. "I didn't think I'd survive first year, let alone third," she yelled back, her voice ragged but light, "but look at me now—Queen of the Cum-Splattered Bogs, High Priestess of Lidl Rosé, and Empress of Surviving By Accident."

Aisha whooped, spinning Maria again until she nearly collided with Tammy, who was mid-lecture to a pair of first-years about why Samuel Beckett would have loved TikTok. The two girls collapsed against each other, laughing, their feet tangled in sticky prosecco, their faces streaked with sweat and the remnants of their earlier makeup. The air was thick with the smell of cheap perfume, hair spray, spilled cider, and the unique, acrid tang of ambition and exhaustion found nowhere but among women who have spent their week performing, competing, and clawing for space in an institution that loved their talent but feared their power.

As the DJ segued into a mashup of Madonna and Dua Lipa, Maria realised she was crying—big, messy, ridiculous tears that streaked her glitter and made her nose run. She pressed her face into Darya's shoulder, the Russian girl's hand cool and steady at her back.

"Oi, Maria, are you alright?" Darya asked, her voice slurred but full of an unfamiliar tenderness.

"Yeah, I'm just…" Maria shrugged, her lips twisted in a grimace that wanted to be a smile. "I don't know. Happy, I think. Or just really, really drunk. Maybe both. And my feet hurt. Fucking boots."

Darya grinned and lifted her own bare foot for inspection, the sole black with spilled drinks and nightclub filth. "We are filthy, glorious messes. If only my mother could see me now—she would say I should have done economics."

Maria barked out a laugh. "If my mum could see me now, she'd try to have the place exorcised." She wiped her eyes, still smiling. "But you know what? I wouldn't trade any of this. Not for all the clean feet and undamaged tights in the world."

They were interrupted by a roar from the crowd near the bar—Ella was attempting to pole dance on a structural column, cheered on by a dozen whooping women. One of the first-years, a girl with a nose ring and a faint Northern Irish accent, climbed up after her, only to slide right down and land, howling with laughter, in a pile of limbs and spilled cocktails. Darya, never one to resist chaos, dashed over to join, dragging Maria in her wake.

Maria felt herself swept into the melee, pulled along by Darya's strong hand and the collective, irresistible current of Red Rose's finest. The dancefloor was now half-nightclub, half-battlefield, bodies pressing together in wild, joyful abandon, the air humid and thick, lights strobing pink and purple as the DJ lost any sense of subtlety and dropped a 2008 Basshunter banger. The floor shook with every stomp, every shriek of laughter, every heavy boot or delicate heel hammering out its own desperate claim on the night.

She barely had time to process before she was sandwiched between Darya and Ella, arms thrown around each other's shoulders, spinning, shrieking, gasping for breath. Around them, first years whirled in giddy constellations, cheeks slick with sweat and highlighter, some still fresh enough to be shocked by what they saw, others already surrendered to the wild current that made every Friday night at the Rose Petal legendary.

A bottle was pressed into Maria's hand—vodka, straight, burning and bright, and she took a swig, feeling it cut through the fug of rosé and Fanta, burning away the last vestiges of self-consciousness. This was what survival looked like at Red Rose: bodies and voices and the knowledge that, for tonight at least, nothing could touch them. The trauma of the studio, the cruelty of the Noticeboard, the whispers in the common room—all of it was swept away in the bright, loud, vulgar flood of solidarity and excess.

Later—minutes or hours, she couldn't have said—she found herself outside, crouched in the alley behind the Rose Petal, the cold air a slap of reality after the fever of the club. Darya was next to her, both of them crouched against the wall, sharing a cigarette. Above, the rain hissed against the neon-lit windows, pooling in the cracks of the broken pavement.

"Do you ever wonder," Darya said suddenly, her voice quiet, almost lost in the drip and hiss of rain, "what we're doing? All of this? The club, the sex, the fighting… sometimes it feels like we're all just trying to fill a hole that nothing can actually fill."

Maria exhaled, watching her breath curl away. "Yeah. But at least we're doing it together. That's got to count for something."

****

CHAPTER 13 – The Notice Which Changed Everything...
Monday 11th November 2024

The physical noticeboard at Red Rose had gained an avid following by the time Monday morning rolled around, and it wasn't just the usual suspects—the flyers for ballet recitals, the slightly passive-aggressive 'Please return borrowed pointe shoes' notes, or the pencilled scribbles advertising lifts to and from the station. This morning, the crowd was different. Girls who never normally loitered in the foyer before first period were clustered around, coffee cups clutched like talismans, craning to see through the crush. There was a low hum of chatter, more tense than gossipy, as if everyone sensed something was about to shift.

Maria arrived in the middle of it, her heels clicking against the marble tiles. She caught snippets of conversation: "Is it for all of us?" "No, it can't be—surely not that." "They wouldn't dare." A couple of first-years, still flushed from their dormitory dash, scurried away whispering to each other.

Darya, already stationed at the edge of the huddle like a queen surveying her court, caught Maria's eye and crooked a finger for her to come over. "You'll want to see this," she murmured, stepping aside so Maria could edge forward. The paper at the centre of the fuss was official Red Rose stationery—crest embossed in gold, typed in the sort of clipped formalities usually reserved for examination schedules or disciplinary summonses.

NOTICE TO ALL STUDENTS: CLOSURE OF NOTICEBOARD APP

Maria didn't have to read more than the headline before she felt the shift in the air.

The closure of the Noticeboard App might not sound earth-shattering to an outsider, but here—inside Red Rose's marbled, gilded, reputation-obsessed ecosystem— it was a seismic tremor. The digital noticeboard, with its anonymous posting function, had long been more than an administrative tool. It was a confessional, a rumour mill, a late-night dumping ground for grievances, hook-up stories, and scandal-laced accusations dressed as "community information." It was where grudges became public entertainment and inside jokes became weapons.

But it was also where, in the unspoken rules of Red Rose life, reputations could be cemented—or annihilated— without anyone ever having to say a word aloud.

The notice was short, clinical, and final.

"Effective immediately, the Red Rose Noticeboard App will cease operation. All communications of an academic, social, or extra-curricular nature must be conducted via approved channels. The use of unauthorised digital noticeboards is a breach of the Student Conduct Code.

Furthermore, all historical posts on the Noticeboard App are to be archived and permanently deleted from university servers by the end of the week. Any screenshots or recordings shared on social media or stored privately are considered subject to privacy laws and may constitute a violation of the Acceptable Use Agreement.

Maria stepped back, momentarily stunned. She blinked as though re-reading would somehow soften the finality of it. But the words didn't change. Around her, a ripple of anxious noise swept through the gathered students. Someone hissed "They're fucking deleting it?" in disbelief.

Another muttered, "This isn't just a shutdown. It's a purge."

"You ok, babe?" Justin asked, coming behind her, his tone more cautious than usual, his palm hovering near her hip as if testing the air before touching her.

Maria didn't answer straight away. She just stared at the printed notice, her eyes scanning and rescanning the sharp, clinical letters as if repetition might dull the sting. She could feel the tremor that ran through the crowd, that collective recognition of loss that was half panic, half nostalgia. Around her, conversations collided like waves.

"They can't just delete it—what about the archive?"

"It's probably the lawyers, innit? Someone must've sued."

"They've wanted to kill it for ages. Remember that livestream last week? Someone must've snitched."

Maria could feel Justin's erection poking against her body through his jeans and her skirt, but for once, the electric charge between them was dulled by something heavier. The Noticeboard wasn't just a scandal sheet or a digital toilet wall; it had been the pulse of their entire culture—an accidental oral history, a rolling archive of lust, bravado, humiliation, and survival. Its absence felt like someone had ripped the roof off the building and let the November drizzle pour into their souls.

Darya let out a short, sharp laugh—bitter, not amused. "They think if they delete the app, they can delete what we did? How little they know us." She said it loudly enough that the surrounding students, even those she despised, turned to listen. Aisha appeared at Maria's shoulder, clutching a coffee and a banana she'd probably stolen from the staff room. Her eyes were wide, but her mouth was set. "It's not about deleting, it's about control," she said, voice flat. "They're scared. Not of the sex, not really—of us talking about it. Of not being able to decide what matters."

Justin looked from one to the other, his usual irreverence faded into something like wariness. "They'll try to clamp down on everything now. Next it'll be hall checks, guest lists, monitoring the WhatsApp groups…" He trailed off. For once, the wildness in his eyes was edged with uncertainty.

A slow, angry murmur was building in the crowd. Maria looked around: all the old factions were there—ballet dancers with their hair up and faces sharp, drama students still smudged from last night's stage makeup, music students in ripped jeans and threadbare jumpers, techies lurking near the walls, all of them thrown together by the gravity of the news. It was the first time Maria could remember seeing so many of them united by anything other than desire or disaster.

She felt the urge to say something—anything—to anchor herself, but the words wouldn't form. The Noticeboard had been the way they all spoke, even when their mouths stayed silent; without it, she felt almost tongue-tied. Darya, of course, had no such hesitation.

"It doesn't matter," she announced, slicing the air with her hand. "They can delete the app, but they can't delete us. They can't make us invisible." A few people snorted, but more nodded. Even the first-years, huddling at the edges, looked reassured by her defiance.

"We ought to go out on strike, get the NUS involved," someone muttered from the back—a music student with blue hair and a broken wrist from a drunken fall during Saturday's Ladies Night. She was only half-joking, but the notion sent a ripple through the crowd, a mix of anxious giggles and genuine consideration. Red Rose had never been a place where protest meant banners and chanting; here, rebellion wore glitter and fishnets, and strikes looked more like mass walkouts to the park, or a mid-afternoon orgy staged in the quad just to prove a point.

But now, as the silence threatened to thicken into despair, Maria became aware of a subtle but significant shift. This wasn't just grief for an app—it was grief for the end of a certain kind of freedom, a kind of belonging, even a kind of power.

The first class of the day—Advanced Ballet—was muted. Miss Yelena, somehow returned from her mysterious sick leave, stalked the studio with her hawk's gaze even sharper than usual. Word of the Noticeboard's demise had already reached her, and she wasted no time addressing it.

"You think you are clever, yes?" she said, her English still fractured by her Siberian vowels. "Posting videos, making fools of yourselves. Now they delete your app. I say, good riddance." Her voice was laced with triumph and derision. "Maybe now you focus on real art. Not… this TikTok, this porno you call ballet."

"Oh, fuck off, you witch," someone muttered—too quietly for Yelena to pinpoint, but loud enough to ripple a wave of suppressed sniggers down the line of dancers. Maria didn't bother hiding her smirk. Yelena's arrival, as always, was less a beginning than a weather front, all pressure and electricity, the promise of storms to come.

"Line up!" Yelena barked, clapping her hands with the staccato impatience of a conductor who'd had enough of tuning. "No more distractions. You want to be remembered, you do it on stage, not on silly app."

As it was the Third years, the ones who, like Maria, were on the third and final year of their degree studies, she knew that they were expected to absorb the blow and keep moving—ballet had always demanded that, at Red Rose or anywhere. Maria slid into line next to Justin, muscle memory guiding her feet into fifth even as her mind spun with questions: How many videos, photos, notes, secrets would disappear by week's end? What happened to everything she'd uploaded—every drunken selfie, every performance post, every comment she'd ever written, bold or biting, name attached or not?

"You, Kovacs," Yelena said, looking at Maria with a glint of something cold in her eyes—triumph, disappointment, or perhaps a twisted sort of pride. "Are you still with us, or did you leave your brain on this app they deleted?" She pronounced 'app' as if it were a venereal disease.

Maria's lips twitched. She felt Justin's gaze flick over her, supportive but wary, as if he expected her to go up in flames or melt through the floor at any moment. She shook her head, more in bemusement than deference, and settled deeper into her stance. "Still here, Miss," she replied, steady as stone.

"Well, how come I have seen videos of you, when giving tutorials to the First Years, with your arse in the air and your tights around your ankles?" Yelena said, her voice ringing out, savage and precise as a bell. There was a gasp—a sharp collective intake of breath, not just from the First Years scattered at the far end of the barre, but even from the old hands. Maria kept her face neutral, the flush rising in her cheeks contained by sheer will, refusing to give Yelena or the room the satisfaction of seeing her squirm.

She could feel, rather than see, Justin's body tense beside her. "It's a new teaching method, Miss," he murmured, sotto voce, and Maria nearly laughed at the wildness of it, the way irreverence, even now, rose to the surface like a bubble in boiling water. "Very twenty-first century. Experiential learning." His eyes were bright with mischief, but his tone was steady, a hand on her back in the storm.

Yelena's glare swept over them both, withering as a frost, but she chose to ignore the bait. "I see too much of this now. You think it's art because you perform? Is nothing private? No secret, no shame?" She shook her head. "One day, you will wish for secrets." The words hovered in the air, heavy as rainclouds. "When I was a young girl in the Soviet Union, we were taught that shame was your shield. Here, you throw it away like broken shoes." She drew herself up, slender and severe, her arms folded as if bracing herself against the entire modern world. "You, Kovacs, you will lead the adagio. Prove you can be remembered for your art, not your... performances." Her gaze was flinty, but there was something almost soft in it—a flicker of understanding that perhaps, in another time, she too might have found herself swept up in the electric rebellion of youth. "Before that, Hopwood, swap with Harrison. At least Kovacs won't sleep with your kind."

Maria knew what Yelena meant by "your kind" to Liam Hopwood, an openly gay male from Preston whose willingness to provoke was rivalled only by his ability to draw the sharpest barbs from the staff. For a moment, Maria's eyes met his in the mirror—a shared flicker of grim amusement. Red Rose's progressive façade was often threadbare, its old prejudices only half-concealed by rainbow lanyards and clumsy diversity policies. Liam, tall and reed-thin, gave a languid, two-fingered salute and slid down the barre to swap places with Justin, who rolled his eyes and mouthed "welcome to the show" before stepping away.

The music started—Prokofiev, the kind of thunderous adagio Yelena favoured when she wanted to test the mettle of her students. Maria moved as if her body belonged to someone else, muscle memory taking over even as her thoughts roared. The loss of the Noticeboard app felt like a door slamming shut, not only on the chaos and humiliation of public spectacle, but on the anarchic sense of solidarity that had thrummed through Red Rose's unofficial channels for years. Every glance, every suppressed giggle, every whispered joke in the studio seemed to echo with the knowledge that the old order was dissolving.

During one move, she could feel Liam's flaccid cock from behind, which, unlike Justin's, proved to her that he was never truly aroused by these choreographed provocations—not sexually, anyway. Liam's energy was always performative, his camp banter more shield than invitation. As they swept through the long, slow grand plié, he leaned forward so only Maria could hear: "Tell me this isn't the bleakest Monday since they banned smoking in the canteen." His breath was warm on her neck, his words absurdly at odds with the severity of the movement. "No more filth in the group chat, darling. What's a girl to do?"

Maria's lips twitched into a smile despite herself. The ritual of the barre—pliés, tendus, battements—became a kind of secular prayer, a way of anchoring herself in something real as the world outside the studio spun. But even as her body moved through the familiar shapes, her mind kept returning to the notice, to the loss of the app and all it represented.

She danced as if in a trance, the walls and faces around her flickering shadows, everything reduced to the swirl of muscle and will and the churning undercurrent of panic. She'd never realised how much of her sense of place had been tethered to something as ephemeral as a digital noticeboard—how thoroughly it had underwritten the unofficial life of the academy, holding all their secrets, bravado, lusts, and humiliations in a collective, shifting memory. To have it swept away, not by their own abandon but by an edict from above, felt like a violation far more intimate than any midnight dare or exhibitionist escapade. It was the first time Maria truly understood what it meant to lose a history.

And yet, the body did not forget. Adagio flowed into allegro, the music driving them forward. Yelena prowled, correcting postures with her stick—always the threat of a sharp tap to calf or wrist, a sudden barked critique. She was in her element, her gaze as ferocious as the November wind howling outside the frosted windows. But Maria noticed, through the sweat and the discipline, that the old woman seemed oddly subdued, as if the loss of the Noticeboard app had rattled even her, stripping away one more layer of the world she thought she understood.

When the class finally broke for water, Maria collapsed beside the battered barre, panting, her legs trembling more from emotion than exertion.

Justin's hand lingered on her rump, his fingers tracing idle circles through the thin fabric of her rehearsal skirt. "That bitch ought to be more careful," he muttered, voice low, the usual cocky undertone gone. "If she keeps throwing that kind of shade, she's going to end up on someone's hitlist."

Maria snorted, half out of breath, wiping sweat from her upper lip. "You think we've got the energy for hitlists? We can barely make it through pliés."

He leaned back against the wall, his T-shirt clinging to his chest. "Oh, we'll find the energy. Trust me. They think they can censor us? They've just thrown petrol on the fire."

She gave him a sideways look, uncertain whether to be impressed or exhausted by his perpetual appetite for chaos. Around them, the others were sprawled along the studio floor, gulping water, exchanging barbed jokes that didn't quite land. There was an unsettled mood in the air—too taut, too aware. Even Liam, usually unflappable, sat cross-legged, staring at his reflection in the mirror like someone trying to read their own obituary.

Maria wiped her forehead with the back of her hand, feeling the sticky residue of both sweat and anxiety. The cold fluorescent lights above made every drop shimmer on her brow, as if the moment itself had crystallised her nerves and fears for all to see. Around her, the studio buzzed with a nervous, unfamiliar quiet; conversations now had gaps in them, silences that felt loaded, as if everyone was waiting for something to break.

"You know we've got time for a quickie if you're up for it," Justin said with a grin, his hands reaching to Maria's breasts, and she could feel the pulsating in her nipples, but she gently brushed his hand aside, the tension thrumming between them no less electric for being denied. For once, Maria was not in the mood for a hasty, semi-public fuck behind a bolted studio door or between the dusty velvet drapes backstage. Something more profound was pressing in, demanding attention: the sensation of a moment passing, a chapter closing, something lost that could not be recovered with a simple orgasm or a scandalous anecdote. She pulled her knees to her chest, watching the beads of water roll down the battered glass bottle in her hand.

Justin didn't press the point. He studied her face with uncharacteristic patience, eyes flicking across her features as if searching for the blueprint to her inner life. "You alright, really?" he asked, voice pitched low for her alone. His thumb found the pulse point at her wrist, grounding her.

Maria hesitated. Around them, the studio's energy was changing, its bravado faded into quiet uncertainty. The loss of the Noticeboard app had been like a bomb blast, shattering the fragile, illicit bonds that held their community together. Already, she could see students pulling out their phones, thumbing through familiar screens, searching for the icon that would no longer open, that portal to mischief and myth now just dead pixels and empty memory.

"I feel like…" she began, then faltered. "Like someone's switched off the lights, but we're still in the same room. We just don't know who's standing next to us anymore."

Justin squeezed her hand, not squeezing so much as holding on—quiet, careful, as if he knew she might shatter or fly apart. "We're still here, though," he said, soft, eyes drifting around the studio at the scattered, wounded ranks of their friends and rivals. "They can't delete us, not really. They'll try, but they never really get it, do they?"

Maria shrugged. Her muscles felt thick and heavy, her mind full of shadows and echoes. "I keep thinking about all the stories that'll vanish. Not just the filth—the funny stuff, the bits we won't remember when we're forty. Half the time I only knew what was happening here because someone posted a meme about it."

Justin grinned, but the edge was brittle. "Reckon there's still a few screenshots on my phone, if the coppers don't come knocking."

Maria finally let herself laugh—a short, raw bark that startled them both. It felt like the first clean thing all morning, a burst of air in the stifling pressure. For a second, the fog of loss lifted and she saw her friend, her lover, for what he was: a boy as lost as the rest, bluffing through the blackout.

From the corner, Liam's voice cut in. "I give it two days before someone starts a Telegram group or an email newsletter. We're too feral to die off that quietly." He gave Maria a wink in the mirror, more tired than cheeky.

"Besides, you can't really delete a rumour, can you? It just gets bored and mutates."

That got a round of muted snorts, and even Yelena, hovering in the doorway with a cup of violently strong tea, did not bark them back to the barre. She watched them over the rim, eyes sharp with something not quite satisfaction. Maria wondered, not for the first time, if Yelena herself had once held a secret or two behind some Iron Curtain noticeboard, as eager for gossip and rebellion as any of them.

"Right, now I've got you all moaning like orphans—back to work," Yelena declared. The last of her rare benevolence evaporated, replaced by the familiar sting of command. She rapped her stick on the floor. "If you can move your tongues, you can move your legs. I want double frappés. Next week, I will be changing your pairings.... and going to single gender classes."

The room groaned collectively. Single-gender classes? It was the sort of archaic measure that Red Rose students mocked in WhatsApp groups—the kind of threat you assumed would fade away once the grown-ups tired of pretending to impose order. Maria watched the ripple pass through the class: girls glancing at each other in silent question, boys feigning bravado. Justin muttered something under his breath about "segregation for the 21st century," while Liam made a face and began ostentatiously stretching, one leg perched on the barre like a dancer from a risqué cabaret.

But no one argued. Not yet. Red Rose had always been a paradox: the freest place Maria had ever known, and also a place where freedom was constantly under siege—from above, from the outside world, sometimes even from their own exhaustion. Still, something was shifting now. The loss of the app, the threat of division, the sense that grown-ups were closing in on the secret garden. Maria saw it in every tight jaw, every sidelong look.

The rest of class passed in a blur of sweat and whispered threats of rebellion. Yelena drove them hard, harder than usual—demanding more turnout, sharper allegros, cleaner landings. But her own edges had dulled; when she barked, it was less with authority than desperation, as though she knew her hold on their world was slipping too. By the time the lesson ended, everyone was too sore to do more than limp towards their water bottles, collecting their things with the silence of soldiers after a failed campaign.

Maria and Justin walked out together, the November wind snatching the warmth from their bodies as soon as they passed through the double doors. The foyer was still thick with clusters of students, but the earlier tension had grown brittle, more fragile. Maria spotted Darya in a corner, hands jammed in her jacket pockets, eyes darting across the foyer like a trapped animal. She caught Maria's gaze and jerked her head, a silent invitation.

Aisha was already there, along with Sarah Smith—her hair, for once, pulled into a severe bun as though daring anyone to comment. Sarah's eyes were rimmed red; Maria wondered if she'd slept at all since that mess at the Petal and everything that followed.

They grouped together by the doors, an instinctive huddle against the chaos. Aisha was the first to break the silence, voice sharper than usual: "Well, that's it, then. Goodbye to filth, gossip and unsolicited dick pics."

Darya snorted, eyes still scanning for threats. "Oh, please. You think that's ever stopped anyone? The moment they try to lock it down, we just find another tunnel. They'll be crawling up their own arses trying to keep up." Her bravado, as ever, was both armour and invitation—a dare to the world not to break her.

"There's all sorts of platforms, from Discord to the old-fashioned flyers in the toilets," Darya was saying, her arms folded with the kind of restless energy that made Maria wonder how long she'd slept. "They can lock down their servers, but they can't lock down our mouths." She nodded to Aisha, who managed a wan grin, half pride and half defiance.

Sarah looked from one to the other, then down at her hands, fingers knotted tightly around the strap of her battered rucksack. "It's not just about the filth," she said quietly, her voice almost lost amid the foyer's low-level din. "It's about who gets to tell the stories now. Who decides what's remembered."

Maria let the words sink in. She felt the truth of them in her chest—tight and hot. The loss of the Noticeboard wasn't just the end of gossip and wild confessions, it was the erasure of a running archive, a collective, messy biography of everything they'd dared, feared, laughed at and survived. It was the loss of a mirror, however warped, that had let them see themselves and each other, unfiltered.

A sudden noise—someone slamming a locker, too hard—
made everyone jump. It was Tammy, still in last night's
eyeliner, eyes wild as she stalked past with a notebook
clutched to her chest, muttering, "Fuck them, fuck their
rules, we'll make our own history." She didn't stop, but
her words hung in the air, a kind of battle-cry for the
bruised and sleepless.

The girls fell into step together, drifting through the
corridors with the purposeful aimlessness of those
avoiding both lessons and authority. Justin peeled away to
join a knot of boys in the side hall—Maria caught his eye,
and he offered a small, crooked smile, as if to say he'd
catch up later. The academy's corridors, usually so alive
with laughter and movement, now felt heavier, echoing
with the aftershocks of the morning's revelation.

"I'm surprised Hardcastle has come off his political
campaigning and actually decided that Red Rose is his
actual day job," Darya said, voice dripping with scorn as
they passed a poster for the Chancellor's next "town hall,"
the sheet already covered in dick doodles and red biro
graffiti. "He'll probably announce the next disciplinary
policy in an opera. Maybe we'll get our suspension
notices sung by the bloody chorus."

Aisha smirked, nudging Darya in the ribs. "Don't give
them ideas. Last time he tried to 'connect with the youth'
he nearly put us all to sleep with his speech about '21st-
century digital citizenship.'" She mimed exaggerated air
quotes, lips twisting in disgust. "As if he's ever logged in
to anything more illicit than the alumni newsletter."

Sarah, still quiet, ran her fingers along the banister as they headed up the back stairs toward the unused practice rooms. "It's the erasing that gets to me," she said, voice soft but steady. "I was a legend, for a bit. Now—what? If no one remembers, did it happen at all?"

Maria paused, looking at her. "You're still a legend. The Noticeboard was just the echo chamber. You were always the main event."

Sarah's lips curled, a wan smile that was more gratitude than bravado. "Tell that to my OnlyFans," she said, and the others laughed—not kindly, not unkindly, but with the grim camaraderie of survivors. In the half-light of the stairwell, they felt both very old and very young, carrying the strange inheritance of Red Rose's lost mythology.

They found the largest of the practice rooms unlocked— a miracle in itself—and collapsed in a heap on the battered sofas under the windows. The view from here, across the city's rooftops, was as grey as their mood.

Maria dug her heels into the tatty carpet. "What do we do now?" she asked, not expecting an answer.

Aisha shrugged, peeling the sticker from her banana and sticking it to the wall beside the long-faded signatures of past students. "We adapt. We always do. The stories will keep. They just need new places to live."

"And we fuck," Sarah said, unzipping her jeans as, knowing that the staff would be most likely in their own dining room and so not able to police any orgies or and so not able to police any orgies or chaos during the brief lunch break, Sarah's words hung in the air—provocative, irreverent, and so completely in character that the tension shattered with an eruption of laughter. Maria got down on her knees as soon as Sarah's jeans had dropped to the knees, her laughter mingling with the tension that still thrummed beneath the skin of the group. She pressed her face into Sarah's exposed thigh, the scent of sweat and sleep and old tears rising off her like incense from an altar. Around them, the afternoon light broke through the city's drizzle, casting long bars across the faded carpet, the battered piano, the walls covered in graffiti and band posters from decades past.

Sarah leaned back on the sofa, arching her neck, her fingers raking through Maria's hair with a desperation that spoke of sleepless nights and the vertigo of having her legend erased with the tap of an administrator's finger. For a moment, Maria let herself forget everything—the edict, the loss, the yawning emptiness where their secret histories used to be. She pressed her tongue to the soft, warm skin at the join of Sarah's hip, tasting salt and the electricity of risk, and the others shifted restlessly around her, the room's collective pulse speeding.

"YOU, GIRL!" the voice of Hardcastle boomed down the corridor, carrying with it the authority of a headmaster, a judge, a man certain of his own importance and his own rightness. It was the sound of a world closing in—a door slamming somewhere outside the practice room, then footsteps, hurried, angry, echoing in the stairwell. The laughter snapped shut; even Sarah's body froze, one hand clutching at Maria's shoulder, her pulse hammering beneath Maria's cheek.

No one moved at first. For a heartbeat, it was only the rain and the breathing and the knowledge that they'd been heard. Aisha, quick as a cat, yanked up Sarah's jeans; Darya pulled Maria to her feet and spun her round so she landed, dazed, between them. The door, swollen with years of paint and damp, rattled on its hinges.

"Don't open it," Aisha mouthed, but the damage was already done. The shadow through the glass was broad-shouldered, a silhouette the whole school recognised.

"Open this door immediately," Hardcastle barked. "Or I will have campus security remove it."

For a moment, Darya almost looked like she might do it. She squared her shoulders, her chin up, her eyes challenging. But Maria caught her wrist. "Don't," she whispered. "They're just looking for a reason."

It was Sarah who broke the deadlock, pushing herself up from the sofa, every motion heavy with exhaustion and old, inextinguishable bravado. "Let him in," she said, her voice so calm it sounded almost bored.

Aisha shrugged, gestured to the others. "Fine. Let's all go down in flames together." She pulled the handle.

The door creaked open, revealing Rowan Hardcastle in all his self-important fury: his red face, his thick hands clutching a printout of the morning's notice. His suit was too tight, his tie askew; the drizzle had dampened the edges of his trousers and flecked his thinning hair. Behind him hovered a junior admin officer, nervous and pale.

Hardcastle's eyes swept the room, taking in the tangled girls, the defiant stares, the sofa and its rumpled cushions, the faint scent of sweat and sex and defiance that hung in the air.

"What do you think you're doing?" he demanded. "This is not a social club. This is not a brothel. And I will not tolerate any more of your—" He searched for the word, lips curling in disgust. "—antics. The Noticeboard app is gone. This behaviour ends now, or I will get the Disciplinary Committee to consider expulsion for all of you. Am I understood?" Hardcastle's voice cracked through the practice room, its timbre brimming with the manufactured outrage of a man used to getting his way. He paused, letting the weight of his threat hang in the musty air. Behind him, the young admin officer—Tom, if Maria remembered right—hovered with the flustered unease of someone who regretted every career choice that had brought him to this moment.

For a long, frozen moment, no one answered. The hush was thick with adrenaline and defiance. Rain battered the panes behind them, the city's November melancholy barely audible above the racing pulse in Maria's ears.

Aisha was the first to break the silence. She peeled herself from the battered sofa, squaring up to Hardcastle with an insolence honed by three years of surviving Red Rose's shifting tides. "We're on lunch break," she said, her tone so level it was almost polite. "There's no rule against sitting in here, is there?"

Hardcastle glared. "Don't play clever, Ms. Al-Siyabiya. I know exactly what goes on in these rooms. I've had complaints. I've seen the footage—yes, I have." He waved his printout like a priest banishing demons, veins standing out on his neck. "The Noticeboard was just the start. I will not have this Academy's name dragged through the mud because of a handful of undisciplined, exhibitionist—"

Sarah cut him off, voice rough with sleep and defiance. "You mean, because of us?" She raised an eyebrow, her lips set in a wry, bitter twist. "Go on, say it. Girls like us. Sluts, troublemakers, not the Red Rose image you want on your next fundraising flyer. We get it."

Hardcastle's mouth twitched, fury battling with calculation. Maria could see him wrestling with the urge to say something that would only make things worse. He glanced at the admin officer, as if for backup, but found none.

"You're all on notice," he said at last, the threat rolling out like a fog, heavy and indistinct. "This is not a warning. It is the end of tolerance. Any further infractions—any breach of conduct, sexual or otherwise—will be dealt with without mercy. I suggest you remember why you came here. To study. To create. Not to—" He hesitated, voice cracking on a note of real despair. "Not to destroy this place from the inside."

He turned on his heel, ushering Tom with him, the admin officer scurrying to keep pace. The door slammed in their wake, the sound echoing like a gunshot.

The room sat in stunned silence for a moment, the adrenaline settling into something close to disbelief.

Maria's heart hammered in her chest, the taste of fear and triumph tangled on her tongue. She looked at her friends: Darya's jaw set, Aisha's eyes narrowed, Sarah's cheeks flushed with angry defiance.

It was Darya who finally broke the silence, her Russian-accented English slicing through the tension. "He thinks he can scare us," she said. "Let him try."

Sarah let out a breath that was almost a laugh. "That's it, then. We're officially an outlaw band. A conspiracy of sluts and queers and rebels."

****

CHAPTER 14 – The Rebellion Starts...

"Fucking wankers," Irene said, as she and Mario were ushered out of the stage door by a pair of harried security guards, the kind who looked too young and too badly paid to be dealing with a crowd of furious art students on a damp Manchester afternoon. The guards wore the glazed expressions of men who'd long since abandoned the hope of understanding why a group of twenty-somethings were shouting about "creative freedom" and "artistic censorship" outside an arts academy.

Rain spat against the cracked paving slabs. The air stank faintly of chip grease and damp velvet. Irene pulled her denim jacket tighter around her, its sleeves frayed from years of handling hot cables and heavy rigs. Mario, unbothered as ever, was puffing on an e-cigarette and looking entirely too pleased with himself.

"Cheer up, amore," he said, smoke curling around his grin. "We are not arrested. That's already victory."

"Not yet," Irene muttered. She glanced back towards the heavy doors. Inside, she could hear the dull roar of voices, the clatter of footsteps, the growing swell of a protest that had started as a few angry mutters and was fast turning into something closer to a riot rehearsal.

The Red Rose Academy had been teetering on the edge all day. Ever since the Chancellor's grand announcement — the "new era of discipline and respectability" — the place had been simmering. The students were used to chaos being sanctioned, even celebrated; now, with every new rule and restriction, the rebellion was finding sharper edges. The Noticeboard app had been shut down, public sex in studios banned, the Drama students threatened with expulsions for "moral violations." It was as if someone had flipped the world on its head and forgotten to warn the inhabitants.

The corridor lights inside Red Rose flickered like dying embers, and the muffled chaos carried out onto the damp courtyard where Irene and Mario stood. She could hear the chants starting already — low, rhythmic, gathering strength. It wasn't the usual kind of noise you got from a bunch of performing arts students — not drunken laughter or impromptu rehearsals of Les Mis numbers — but something raw, angry, electric. The kind of energy that made the air taste metallic.

Mario blew a slow stream of vapour towards the wet sky and glanced sideways at her. "You think they'll really do it?"

"Do what?"

He smirked. "Occupy the theatre. You've seen them, sì? Half the Drama lot have been talking about it since lunch. They say it's 'symbolic resistance'."

"Symbolic my arse," Irene muttered. "They just want somewhere warm to smoke and wank without getting told off."

Irene said, though a smile twitched at the corner of her mouth.

"Peters, Kempsey, get out of the control room now," Marcin Kaczmarek, the technician who controlled the booth and the rest of the technical side of Red Rose's theatres. Irene looked at Mario with a sigh as it seemed, to her, that two of the Third Years, Thomas Peters and Rose Kempsey, were obviously breaching the rules again. Both were sprawled in the tech booth with headphones askew, his trousers round his ankles, holding Rose close, his hands on her breasts, drilling her with the same quiet, insistent focus with which he usually programmed lighting cues. Rose had her eyes half-shut, biting her lip in an effort to stifle a giggle, and neither looked the slightest bit repentant as Marcin glared at them.

"Don't... fuck... stop... Tom..." Rose said, and Irene had to suppress a laugh, biting the inside of her cheek. Mario's eyes widened in mock admiration. Marcin, arms folded and patience frayed to a thread, gave them a glare that could have stopped a moving tram.

"Look, the Chancellor's orders are to be followed, whether you're on stage or backstage or shagging in the bloody fly tower," Marcin snapped, voice echoing over the tangled cables and battered mixing desks. "If I have to report another incident of... whatever this is, you'll be on the train to Huddersfield by teatime, and don't think I'm joking."

Rose, a pixie-faced girl with the poise of someone who'd once dreamt of the Royal Ballet but ended up wiring DMX for fringe musicals, disentangled herself, smoothing her skirt with a look of faintly theatrical dignity. Thomas, his hair sticking up at impossible angles, just grinned. "Can't sack us both, sir. There'd be nobody left to run the sound for Oklahoma."

"Try me," Marcin replied, but there was a resigned humour in it. This, after all, was Red Rose — a place where carnality and competence existed in perpetual, mutually assured distraction.

Irene and Mario slipped away, rain stinging their faces as they ducked under the battered marquee at the edge of the courtyard. The sense of mounting unrest was everywhere now, a charge in the air. You could feel it: in the way people moved, in the furtive glances, the burst of whispered planning. The crowd was thickening, a clot of students in battered puffa jackets and leotards and lurid jumpers — dancers with neat hair, actors in eyeliner, musicians in fingerless gloves, techies in all-black.

The drizzle thickened, flattening the pale afternoon light across the courtyard, while every gutter overflowed with old leaves and someone's forgotten glitter. The Red Rose Academy looked less like a citadel of the arts and more like an abandoned music hall under siege. At the edge of the concrete, Irene ducked under the cracked canvas marquee, shivering as water tracked down her neck. She watched as a fresh knot of students — drama, dance, music, tech, some who never usually mingled — pressed towards the theatre's glass foyer. No one was running, but the crowd was urgent, moving with the momentum of people who've just been told the doors to their sanctuary might be locked forever.

Inside, in the main atrium, the air was a hot stew of breath, coffee, sweat, and adrenaline. Flyers advertising everything from lost tap shoes to indie improv nights had been torn down or vandalised overnight — some in protest, some for sport. In their place, sheets of A4 paper had been Sellotaped up in mad, haphazard layers: slogans in Sharpie, cartoons of the Chancellor with horns and clown hair, a giant cock drawn in gold paint above the sign for 'Wellness Wednesdays'. At the centre of it all, a battered upright piano sat half-on, half-off its wheels, as though someone had tried to start a singalong and lost the will halfway through.

Suddenly Irene's phone pinged, a WhatsApp message from Tammy Knight.

Tammy Knight: *We're setting up a WhatsApp Group to replace the Noticeboard, so we can share our filth and manifestos. Add everyone you trust. If you see campus security, do NOT mention this chat.*

The rain was falling harder now, splattering the old stone steps of Red Rose Academy and turning the quad into a shallow lake of rainbowed oil and cigarette ends. Irene Walsh lingered under the leaky canvas marquee, the kind that had once shielded late-night jazz bands and now dripped cold water down the back of her neck. She could hear the restlessness inside, the way noise was growing not as a performance but as protest: voices overlapping, a kind of fever in the air. This wasn't just posturing, she thought. It was a tremor, real as muscle, shaking the bones of the building.

Mario stood close, hands jammed deep into the pockets of his battered jeans, smoke swirling from his e-cigarette as if trying to trace letters in the air. "Do you think we should go back inside?"

Irene hesitated, the sense of being watched prickling her skin, though all she could see was rain and the strange, migratory flock of students outside. "If we go back in, we're not coming out again till something gives," she said, voice pitched low. "You know that, right?"

Mario's grin was sharp. "What's the worst that can happen? Expulsion? Deportation? Both make good stories at parties."

She rolled her eyes. "I'm not getting thrown out for shagging in the sound booth, mate. Not when we could get thrown out for doing something that actually matters."

As if conjured by the words, the crowd surged again, someone shoving past with a battered cello case, a trace of incense smoke trailing in their wake. It was a little after four, the light already sloping into dusk, and the usual, lazy atmosphere of the theatre foyer had become something harder, charged. Students clustered near the front desk, others leaned against the windows, talking in urgent, quick bursts, heads close, eyes bright with the thrill of having nothing left to lose.

Inside, the main staircase was half-blocked by a growing knot of dancers and techies, their bags slung carelessly under the stairs. Marcin was there too, bickering with two of the security guards and waving a sheaf of timetables. His face was red, but not with anger; Irene recognised the look, somewhere between exhaustion and pride. The staff were as divided as the students, and she could see Marcin's loyalty warring with his contractual obligations.

She nudged Mario. "Come on. If we're going down, we might as well do it dry." Together they slipped through the double doors, avoiding the noticeboard (now stripped of its digital twin, the paper versions already thick with fresh slogans) and ducked into the edge of the main crowd.

Inside, it was all motion: someone strummed a battered guitar near the windows, a group of dancers limbered up by the lifts, and every so often a burst of song or laughter cut through the underlying tension. It wasn't a performance, not yet—more like the long, vibrating silence before the overture.

Maria Kovacs was there, perched on a radiator beneath a mural of Red Rose alumni, eyes sharp, lips pressed into a line that made her seem older than her years. She was surrounded by a clutch of younger ballet students, all of them watching the foyer as if waiting for the first punch. Maria caught Irene's eye and beckoned her over.

"Thought you'd scarpered," Maria said, voice pitched low.

Irene shook her head. "Only out the stage door. You know me: never miss a party."

"Party, she says." Maria's smile was wry. "The last time I saw this many drama students in one place, someone set fire to the piano."

"Party, she says." Maria's smile was wry. "The last time I saw this many drama students in one place, someone set fire to the piano."

Irene snorted, slinging her battered rucksack off one shoulder and letting it drop to the ground. "That was only because Justin tried to show off his fire-eating and someone swapped the kerosene for gin. I'll take a riot over spontaneous combustion, any day."

Maria's lips twitched—half a smile, half the residue of three sleepless nights and too much instant coffee. Around them, the foyer was an engine of unrest: pockets of students forming, breaking, reforming, like clouds scudding across a turbulent sky. On the stairs, someone—Tammy Knight, by the reckless hair and mismatched socks—stood addressing a cluster of students, her notebook brandished like a revolutionary's manifesto.

"Listen up, you wankers!" Tammy called, voice ringing out across the marbled hall. "We're not leaving. Not until they back off, not until they give us back the app, and not until Hardcastle personally apologises for being a repressive knob." A cheer—loud, not quite sincere—rose from the crowd, and someone in the back lobbed a stress ball at the portrait of the Chancellor, sending it askew.

"Typical," Mario murmured, sidling up beside Irene. "British revolution—comes with snacks and interpretive dance."

But the energy was shifting, turning sharper, more serious. On the edge of the crowd, Darya Ivanova leaned against the vending machine, arms folded, ballet bun bristling with angry pins. She was flanked by Ella Forbes and Aisha Al-Siyabiya—Red Rose's unofficial queens of chaos—each with a coffee in one hand and their phones clutched in the other, thumbs working furiously.

"Any word from the outside?" Maria asked, tilting her head towards the trio.

Darya looked up, face pale but set. "They've locked the south doors and put security on the fire exits. I just got a message—Haris and Bilal tried to leave and were stopped. If we go out, we're not getting back in."

Aisha, her fringe glued to her forehead by sweat and Manchester rain, rolled her eyes. "Someone tell Hardcastle it's not 1984. If he wants to keep us in, he'll have to barricade the fucking windows. And he'll need to send in the army if he wants to stop what's coming next."

"Or the cast of Oklahoma," Ella deadpanned, her voice cool. "Which, knowing this place, is about the same thing."

Maria let her gaze sweep across the foyer. If you'd grown up at Red Rose, this was what you recognised: not just the chaos, but the choreography beneath it, the way every outbreak of anarchy moved in time with a deeper, half-spoken rhythm. The revolution—if that was what it was—looked more like an overstuffed green room than a political action, but Maria felt the adrenaline in her veins all the same. The stakes, she knew, were as real as any opening night.

Tammy was still holding forth, her voice high and defiant. "We need to make ourselves un-ignorable. That's the only thing that works here. They want us quiet and split up, and we're not playing along. If you're scared, if you're knackered, good. If you're angry, that's even better." She brandished her notebook again, as though daring anyone to argue. "We'll lock down the theatre. No one in, no one out. If you want out, go now, because we're in this until we win."

No one moved. The crowd, if anything, pressed closer, eyes gleaming, some with mischief, some with something closer to panic, but all unwilling to break ranks now.

At the back, a group of techies had already started hauling flats and flightcases to block off the side doors. The noise of shifting scenery—wood scraping tile, the clatter of metal—echoed up the marble, drowned only by the chime of someone's phone as WhatsApp notifications multiplied like mice. Irene heard her own phone ping again, this time with a photo: the music department's entire percussion section had taken up residence by the main stairwell, looking ready to defend it with a wall of timpani and a snare drum.

"I told you it'd go off," Mario said, mouth twitching in a grin. He looked almost at home amid the chaos, the low thrum of open rebellion turning his usual insouciance into something more like pride. "Now we just need the drama lot to barricade themselves into the green room and start broadcasting interpretive protest pieces. You know— 'Stravinsky and the Art of Non-Compliance'."

"Oh, piss off, Mario," Irene shot back, but she couldn't help but smile. This was Red Rose at its best and worst:

wild, stubborn, dangerous, a family even in its own destruction.

The foyer had never felt so alive or so on edge, the usual lazy warmth of battered radiators and leftover croissants replaced by a prickling sense of anticipation. Every few seconds, another group pushed in from the rain-soaked courtyard, shaking out their hair, muttering about security, scoping out the mood. Irene's phone vibrated so often it was just a low, constant pulse in her hand—memes, warnings, rumours, and half a dozen invitations to join new WhatsApp groups with names like *"Red Rose Resistance"*, *"Not Another Strike Chat"*, and the slightly less subtle *"Wankers United"*.

Across the marble, the crowd thickened: dancers with ice packs and espresso shots, actors in costume and street clothes and every in-between, techies lugging battered flight cases and arguing over whether the barricade needed more sandbags or just an old skip. There were music students balancing guitars, saxophone cases and the kind of reckless bravado you only saw when an institution's future was truly under threat. Some had barely slept, the smudges of eyeliner and mascara evidence of last night's chaos at the Petal or one of the unofficial afters.

Above it all, the Red Rose coat of arms—peeling, half-defaced by a sticker reading *"Queer as Folk 4eva"*—looked down with a mixture of stern disappointment and backhanded approval. You could almost feel the ghosts of alumni lurking in the high corners: the misfits, the stars, the ones who'd made it and the ones who'd been quietly hustled out the back door for "bringing the school into disrepute".

The protest's epicentre was the battered old grand piano, now covered in an explosion of paper: student union leaflets, impromptu manifestos, a hastily scribbled *"If You're Reading This You're Part of the Rebellion"* in fat green marker.

The battered old grand piano, its varnish scratched and its lid warped by decades of bad weather and worse rehearsal tempers, had become the command centre of the rebellion. Pinned and taped to its sides were torn flyers, rage-scrawled petitions, and a few lewd sketches in lipstick—part protest banner, part living archive. Beside it, the stack of battered timps and a converted drinks trolley stood ready to serve as both barricade and snack bar, stocked with bags of crisps, cans of Red Bull, and a suspiciously home-baked tray of hash brownies someone claimed to have made for "morale".

The foyer's marble was already slick with the drizzle tracked in by boots and trainers, the air thick with the scents of old leather, deodorant, wet wool, and defiance. People had given up trying to tidy their appearance: ballet buns drooped, false lashes hung at odd angles, faces gleamed with sweat or smeared makeup. Here and there, students—dancers mostly—stretched on the cold floor, their conversation flowing around them, feet flexing, bodies wound tight as springs.

The mood was sharp, volatile: laughter rang too loud, voices trembled with adrenaline. The protest was a living thing, restless and borderless. Some students drifted up and down the main stairs, peering at the windows for signs of security, while others scrawled fresh slogans—*"FUCK CENSORSHIP", "RED ROSE RESISTS", "NO ART WITHOUT CHAOS"*—across the glass in dry-erase marker. Near the fire doors, a knot of second-years were trying to jimmy the alarm so it would sound only if a staff lanyard passed by, not a student, using a stolen library card and the sort of ingenuity only drama techs could muster.

Irene looked at Mario with a conspiratorial smile, both of them soaking in the ragged beauty of it all. She'd never seen the place quite like this—not during strikes, not even after wild show nights or the post-Edinburgh Fringe returns when half the students came back hoarse and hungover. This was something else: a campus in full mutiny, united not just by sex or mischief or the shambolic chaos of art school life, but by a genuine, shared sense of threat.

A commotion by the doors drew their attention—a security guard in a high-vis jacket, trying and failing to reason with a knot of dance students. They formed a living wall: broad-shouldered, elegant, completely unmoved by authority. Irene caught sight of Lucy Grand at the centre, her pink hair a beacon. "No one leaves, no one enters unless you can do a proper développé," Lucy was saying, balancing on one leg with a dancer's insouciance, daring the guard to challenge her technique.

Mario leaned closer, dropping his voice. "Do you reckon this is what Paris felt like before the barricades went up?"

"Paris? You mean, with fewer baguettes and more vapes?" Irene muttered, but her heart thudded with the possibility. The sense of something larger than their ordinary chaos—that they might, just this once, outlast the grown-ups and their edicts—sent a current through her veins. She looked about: students huddled in corners, plotting, a clutch of actors hunched over a laptop, composing what looked suspiciously like a formal press release, dancers stretching but never relaxing, music students tuning instruments with showy deliberation. Even the techies were out in force, duct tape in hand and a wild glint in their eyes.

The protest at Red Rose Academy grew with the subtle inevitability of a weather front rolling over the city: first a few cold drops, then a gathering sense of pressure, until the downpour broke. By late afternoon, what had started as splinters of defiance in forgotten practice rooms and backstage corridors had gathered into a mass—riotous, kinetic, unstoppable. The students, for once, were united not by a production or a party, but by a creeping sense of trespass: something precious had been stolen, and in its absence was left only adrenaline and rage.

Outside, the wind drove the drizzle sideways, slapping against the great glass doors of the main foyer and turning the quad into a patchwork of puddles and drowned cigarette butts. Irene Walsh hovered by the entrance, her eyes scanning the crowd. Every surface shimmered with nervous energy: boots squeaked on the marble; someone had left a trail of wet footprints across the floor. The air buzzed with competing soundtracks—dancers' playlists leaking from tinny speakers, a guitarist in the corner picking out the chords to "Creep", techies arguing in

Polish, a group of first-years videoing everything on their phones with the manic intensity of those who suspect their youth is being filmed for posterity.

Inside, the assembly had become a living organism. The barricades at the doors had grown more elaborate: flight cases, piano benches, music stands zip-tied together, a cello wedged at a strategic angle as if daring anyone to use it as a battering ram. Above it all, a sign read, in thick black Sharpie *THIS IS OUR SHOW NOW*.

Irene moved through it, greeted by nods and shrugs and the occasional squeezed shoulder. The hierarchy of Red Rose—so strict in class, so ritualised in the studio—was dissolving into something new. The ballet dancers had stopped stretching and were sitting cross-legged beside the drama kids; the techies, usually locked in their own world of QLab files and solder burns, were teaching a handful of music students how to loop extension cables across the main entrance. Somewhere in the middle, Tammy Knight and Maria Kovacs were holding an impromptu meeting over a battered clipboard and a pack of supermarket croissants.

"I say we broadcast it," Tammy was saying, her voice pitched to carry above the clatter. "Everything. Livestream it all. Make them see us—make them know we're not just troublemakers, we're the fucking heart of this place."

Maria frowned, tracing a finger through the condensation on the window. "And if they cut the Wi-Fi?"

"Then we hotspot. Someone's bound to have a data plan. Or we start a podcast. Or write it in bloody chalk on the pavements. But we do not go quiet."

Around them, the rest of the group was working fast. Darya Ivanova was orchestrating the moving of set flats like she was rehearsing for the barricades in *Les Mis*. "That one, there—yes, Justin, I know it's heavy, stop whinging, you'll live. Tammy, get me more tape. No, the good tape."

The foyer's acoustics lent the students' efforts a cathedral-like resonance, every scrape of a set flat or clang of a drum riser ringing out like some secular liturgy. The crowd's mood was swelling, their energy twisting between righteous anger and absurdity.

Darya was in her element, issuing commands with the clipped authority of someone who'd survived not only Russian ballet masters but the institutional bureaucracy of three different drama schools. "If you're not helping, you're in the way!" she called, her accent slicing through the muddle of accents and dialects, her dark eyes daring anyone to challenge her authority. Justin, lumbering beneath the weight of a battered rostra section, rolled his eyes but obeyed without further protest.

Maria's voice was lower, more measured as she directed a trio of younger girls—first-years, trembling with excitement and terror—to cable-tie music stands across the bottom of the main staircase. "Make it tight," she murmured, "and don't let the hinges show. If security come with crowbars, make them work for it."

Nearby, Ella Forbes was upending a box of props—plastic swords, a feather boa, half a dozen battered rubber chickens—onto a table. "If this gets on the news, I want to be the first one interviewed in a latex chicken mask," she declared, waggling the limp rubber beak at a passing group of dance boys.

At the rear of the foyer, by the vending machines, a knot of drama lads huddled in whispered conference. Marnie, her hoodie sodden and her mascara running, emerged from their midst with a glint in her eye. "We've got a plan," she announced to anyone who'd listen. "If admin call the police, we'll all claim to be in an immersive rehearsal of Animal Farm. Who's going to argue with method acting?"

A ripple of laughter followed, but not all were amused. At the edge of the foyer, one of the ballet boys—Freddie, tall and blond and much too posh for his own good—was pacing, phone pressed to his ear. "Mum, I'm not joking. They're actually locking us in. Yes, on purpose. No, I haven't taken anything—oh, for God's sake, just tell Dad I might be late for dinner."

Maria caught his eye, shaking her head. "You're not calling your solicitor, are you, Freddie?"

He managed a weak smile. "Might as well. At least then Mum can tell her friends her son was a political prisoner."

Maria snorted. "You'd last five minutes in Strangeways. Stick to pliés."

There was a rumble by the doors. Security, bolstered by a pair of admin staff in ill-fitting suits, made another tentative approach. The nearest barricade—a flight case topped with three chairs and a papier-mâché horse's head—did not budge. From behind it, Lucy Grand called, "Password?"

The admin, flustered, glanced at his clipboard. "We're… we're just here to check the fire exits."

"Password!" came the chorus again, louder, the barricade defenders shaking their snacks in mock threat.

Irene had to chuckle at the chaos that was spilling in every direction, all logic unravelled in a tide of wit, bravado and nervous delight. There was something properly theatrical about it—the sense of an audience, even without cameras rolling. The protest had become an event, and the students, natural-born performers, rose to the occasion with every ounce of their irreverence.

Lucy, ever the joker, called again: "Password! No password, no passage. And if you try to crawl through the window, I hope you're double-jointed."

One of the admin staff, looking soaked and defeated, tried a conciliatory tone. "Come on, Lucy. Let's not make this any more difficult than it needs to be. Chancellor's orders."

Lucy didn't miss a beat. "Chancellor's orders are to take up ballet and mind his own bloody business. What's the password?"

At this, the cluster of dance students behind her broke into a brief, defiant round of applause, laughter ricocheting across the foyer. The admin pair retreated, conferring in urgent whispers, as if a mutiny of dancers and techies was too much for their morning briefing to cover.

Near the centre, a nervous hum ran through the crowd—a tremor of uncertainty. Irene noticed it, the way bodies bunched closer, eyes flicked over shoulders, the usual Red Rose confidence edged with doubt. There was always the chance that the adults would escalate: call the police, lock the doors for real, cut the power. The what-if of real consequences circled the barricade like a stray dog.

It was Maria who broke the mood, climbing onto the grand piano with the elegance of a born rebel. Her trainers left a print in the dust; she raised her voice, high and clear, slicing through the babble.

"Oi! Eyes up, all of you!"

They looked. The crowd, nearly two hundred strong now, fell quiet in a heartbeat—Red Rose students knew when the drama was about to get real.

Maria steadied herself on the piano's warped lid, surveyed the motley crowd, and, for a split second, let them see how tired she was—cheekbones sharp, hair mussed, the stains of old eyeliner ghosting her eyes. Then she grinned.

"I know we're all pissed off. I know some of you want to leg it and some of you want to set fire to the Chancellor's toupee. But if we're going to do this—if we're going to make a stand—then we do it together, and we do it clever."

There was a rumble of assent. Tammy, arms crossed, gave a quick, sharp nod. "Tell them, Kovacs."

Maria swept a hand at the makeshift barricades. "This isn't just about the Noticeboard. It's about them trying to tell us who we are, what stories we're allowed to tell. About making us small, and quiet, and fucking ashamed. If they want us quiet, they can work for it. If they want us gone, they'll have to drag us out one by one."

A ripple of laughter. One of the first-years shouted, "Over my dead body!" A drama boy at the back, more inspired than sober, bellowed, "Vive la révolution!" and got a shove for his trouble.

Maria steadied herself, her voice growing soft. "Some of you are scared. That's all right. You should be. I'm shitting it, honestly. But I'd rather be scared together than sit at home pretending this place means nothing. We make Red Rose what it is. Not the bloody Chancellor, not the parents or the sponsors. Us."

She hopped down, landing lightly, her face set. "So, if you're in, you're in. No running to admin, no filming people for the 'gram without asking. We look after each other. That's how we win."

****

CHAPTER 15 – I Predict A Riot...
Monday 11th November 2024

"You see that, Ash?" Marnie Taylor said to Ashley Ketchum, her voice raised over the rising din that pulsed through the theatre lobby. It was just gone five o'clock, the amber streetlights outside blinking through the drizzle and the blue-black Manchester dusk crowding the windows, but inside Red Rose it felt like the start of some pagan midnight festival. The foyer had never been so full, not even after opening night or during the infamous 2022 Freshers' Strip Revue. Bodies pressed shoulder to shoulder, a patchwork of stage paint, torn fishnets, threadbare jumpers, black ballet tights, battered DM boots, and more makeup than a drag brunch.

Ashley looked out the window to see blue lights and vans pulling up outside the academy gates, tyres splashing through oily puddles, white POLICE letters smeared by the rain. Their eyes widened—not in fear, not exactly, but with the adrenalized rush that comes just before something explodes.

"Bloody hell. They've actually called the police," Ashley breathed, voice pitched low enough to hide the tremor, but loud enough for Marnie and those nearest to hear.

The word spread through the lobby before anyone needed to shout it. "Police are here!" someone called from the top of the stairs. "Police outside!" It became a chant, half panic, half gleeful, echoing off the high concrete and timber vaulting. Some of the first years looked uncertain—excited, maybe—but the third years, the ones who'd been through a dozen scandals already, just squared their shoulders and moved a little closer together. If this was going to be a showdown, then at least they were going to face it as a cast.

Ashley's phone buzzed in their hand, a WhatsApp notification from a group called Red Rose Survivors:

Lucy Grand: *They're lining up outside the back entrance too. No one in or out, it's like a fucking prison.*

Justin Harrison: *Got snacks. And condoms. Not that I think we'll need the latter unless the riot cops are fit.*

Marnie grinned, mouth twisted. "He's got a point. Coppers are only human."

Suddenly the sound of cymbals from a drum set and a guitar brought Ashley back to the present. Someone— inevitably one of the music students—had dragged an amp and a half-smashed drum kit out from the jazz studio and was already bashing out a riotous, arrhythmic version of "I Predict A Riot". The crowd, packed into the foyer, took it as their cue. There were catcalls, whoops, someone screamed the chorus, and for a heartbeat the air felt light, almost festive. Even the threat outside couldn't completely smother the old Red Rose habit of turning every crisis into a show.

Ashley looked at Marnie, eyebrows raised. "If we end up in the Manchester Evening News, I'm not letting them use that photo of me from last year's Cabaret."

Marnie, in her patched denim jacket and scuffed DMs, snorted. "If I get nicked, I want them to spell my name right. And none of that 'unidentified female, believed to be student' bollocks."

"Watching the people get lairy," the sound of one of the Music students—Tomás, by the wildness of his chords and the way he thrashed his fringe—roared out across the marble floor, half-singing, half-shouting the lines as if each syllable could conjure a spell.

"...is not very pretty, I tell thee!"

The foyer exploded, everyone yelling the chorus in glorious, off-key unison. "I predict a riot! I predict a riot!"

It was the most Red Rose thing Ashley could imagine— barely controlled chaos, a protest on the edge of pantomime, bodies bouncing in time, even the ones who'd never had the guts to audition for the main stage joining in. Laughter mingled with nerves, every face split with the wild, slightly manic grin of someone who knows the rules have changed but hasn't yet learned how to be afraid.

The music crashed, the cymbals rattling off the stone, and for a moment it almost felt like an afterparty, not a stand-off.

But then the reality pressed in again. Through the streaked glass, blue and red lights flashed, drawing long, trembling reflections across the crowd. Police radios crackled on the other side of the doors, voices sharp with the clipped vowels of Greater Manchester, a chill riding the back of every syllable.

At the edge of the crowd, Tammy Knight elbowed her way through, clutching her ever-present battered notebook. "Oi, Ash, Marnie!" she called, breathless. "They're blocking the main doors. Someone said they've brought shields. Shields, like it's fucking Waterloo Road and not a load of pissed drama students."

Ashley's lips curled. "Let them try and make us leave. They'll have to drag half the dance cohort out by their hair extensions."

A voice piped up from somewhere behind the grand piano—Sarah Smith, mascara smudged, lips pursed around a battered vape. "If anyone's getting arrested, it should be the staff for running this place like a circus. And I want my mugshot on a t-shirt, thanks."

The sound of laughter rippled through the mass, as if everyone recognised how fragile this bravado was—how little it would take for the tension to snap one way or the other. Out in the rain, police in high-vis and dark fleeces fanned out by the gates, radios crackling, the bounce of torchlight making jittery shadows on the soaking stone. A cheer went up as someone in the crowd inside—nobody ever saw who—pressed their arse cheeks to the glass doors, leaving a pair of fogged, wet prints for the world to see.

Ashley felt the adrenaline fizzing, skittering beneath the skin like a second pulse. The last time the police had turned up en masse at Red Rose, it had been to break up an end-of-term afterparty that had spilled out onto the quad; half the music faculty had ended up in the canal and three drama students had gone viral for attempting to "negotiate" with the officers via interpretive dance. But this was different. This was official, sanctioned, a line being drawn between them and everything they'd been allowed—encouraged—to get away with for three wild years.

Tammy shoved her notebook under Ashley's nose, scrawled pages dense with notes, half-legible, lines bleeding together in the poor foyer light. "We need a plan. If they come in, we do a sit-in. Stage left, all the way to the Green Room. Techies are already locking off the lighting gallery, so no one can fuck about with the mains. Dancers hold the stairs, drama students make noise, music lot keep the vibe up. I'll livestream as much as I can. We get them on camera and all over socials—'Manchester police break up peaceful protest at Red Rose Academy', that sort of thing."

Marnie nodded, chin lifted, eyes narrowed. "And if they drag anyone out, we film that too. No lone wolves. No quiet disappearances. We're not letting them pick us off, not this time."

The police outside were multiplying, dark shapes moving through drizzle and blue lights as the rain hammered down, pooling in oily slicks on the cracked Manchester paving. Inside, Red Rose Academy felt as though it were breathing—rising and falling with each new shout, every chanted refrain, the swell and crush of students pressing closer, united more by adrenaline and outrage than by any plan. The marble foyer was a tapestry of battered rucksacks, posters peeling off the walls, and bodies vibrating with the dangerous, exhilarating possibility of real trouble.

Ashley tried to count the officers visible through the glass doors—eight, ten, maybe more lurking behind the shadow of the vans. The nearest police were conferring with a knot of senior staff in raincoats, the Chancellor red-faced and gesticulating, flanked by administrators who looked as if they desperately wished they worked at a quieter institution. Ashley's hands trembled around their phone, not quite from fear—though the threat was real enough—but from that same old Red Rose energy: the knowledge that everything was about to tip over, and that for once, they had a say in which way it landed.

Someone was playing guitar again—Tomás, sleeves shoved up, curls stuck to his forehead, leading a ragged chorus through the Arctic Monkeys and Kaiser Chiefs, anything with a beat and a refrain everyone knew. It was messy, gloriously off-key, but the sound became a kind of armour, a declaration: we are still here, and you will hear us.

Marnie, pressed close to Ashley's side, her own jacket soaked at the cuffs, lifted her phone overhead, filming the crowd. All around them, students linked arms, shifting nervously, some joking, some pale, all alert.

Suddenly an alert came up on Ashley's phone, a Instagram Live notification, one of the pages he followed called The Disruptors, a group of Team GB Olympic athletes notorious for their scandalous social media presence and fearless, sometimes reckless, activism. The screen flooded with hearts and laughing emojis as a pixelated image of Freddie Gethin—rower, irrepressible agent of chaos—leaned into his camera. His backdrop, it seemed, was outside of Red Rose, with Rory Sloan, his partner in crime, right next to him.

Freddie's face was lit with the wild glee of a man who'd grown up baiting security at Henley, his voice cutting through the white noise of the crowd behind him. "Alright, Red Rose! They told us art wasn't a contact sport—looks like you lot are proving them wrong. We're outside, got your backs. Who wants us to handcuff ourselves to the Chancellor's Jag?" He was already moving, swinging the camera round to show a sea of police jackets, the wet glimmer of headlights on rain-slicked tarmac, and Rory Sloan, already shirtless and grinning, waving a banner that read, in messy black paint, *Solidarity With Red Rose! No Art, No Future*.

The Instagram Live chat went wild—hearts, fire emojis, a flurry of "do it!" and "oi oi, Sloan, keep your kit on!" Marnie and Ashley found themselves laughing, for a moment, at the pure ridiculousness of it—Team GB athletes, notorious even by Olympic Village standards, now throwing their lot in with a bunch of underfed, over-caffeinated drama students in a soaked corner of Manchester.

The moment didn't last. The crowd at the doors shifted; a hush ran down the foyer like static. At the far end, the glass doors juddered, then opened inward under the heavy hands of two police officers. They were followed by a senior admin in a Red Rose lanyard—Tom, junior admin, cheeks flushed, clutching a clipboard and trying to look authoritative. His eyes darted, first to the police, then to the mass of students, and finally to the camera phones pointing his way.

A sudden silence fell. Even the music stuttered, dying out as Tom stepped forward, raising his clipboard like a shield. "Alright, everyone. Please—if I can just—please listen. The police are here to ensure everyone's safety. No one wants trouble. We need you to disperse and leave the premises. This protest is now considered an unauthorised gathering. There are serious consequences for staying—please, let's not escalate this."

He looked, Ashley thought, exactly like a man who regretted every career decision he'd ever made.

Someone in the crowd booed. A ripple of jeers swept through the students, some sincere, others theatrical. Sarah Smith cupped her hands around her mouth and bellowed, "Go on, Tom! Sing us a song if you want us to move!" That drew laughter, a shriek of applause, a flash of mobile lights as more people started to film. The police, unsmiling, fanned out behind Tom, batons still sheathed but hands resting on their belts. It was a show of strength, carefully choreographed.

Tammy slipped forward, phone in one hand, her battered notebook in the other. "If we leave, it's to go to the BBC, Tom. How's that for escalation?" Her voice rang out, clear and sure, and for a moment she was all the newsreader she'd once dreamt of being.

Tom wavered, clipboard shaking slightly. "Please. The Chancellor's orders—this is for your safety. There will be disciplinary hearings—"

"We'll all go down together, then!" called Justin from the back, raising a bottle of Lucozade like a trophy. "Red

Rose doesn't rat on its own!" Someone started chanting—"No app, no peace!"—and within seconds the lobby was a sea of sound, arms raised, banners flashing. Even the dancers, usually reserved for end-of-term carnage, were on their feet, moving with the strange, synchronised grace that came from years of shared discipline.

A throb of feet echoed on the stone floor, defiant and unified. Marnie squeezed Ashley's hand, her palm clammy with nerves, but her voice clear: "Stay together. If they start dragging people out, we sit down. Everyone sits. Don't give them gaps." Around them, the crowd tightened, a shoal of bodies pulling in for warmth and solidarity, every phone camera raised.

From outside, the shouting of Freddie Gethin filtered through—muffled by rain and glass, but clear enough to add fuel to the charge inside. "Red Rose, don't let the bastards win!" he roared, the Olympian's voice cutting through the chaos. "Solidarity! No art, no future!" The words rebounded, first as a trickle, then a wave. Suddenly the chant took root—"No art, no future! No art, no future!"—until it was as though the building itself was roaring.

Ashley knew that everything—every rumour, every wild night, every forbidden performance—had been leading here, to this moment when the students refused to play by someone else's script. The air in the foyer felt alive, electrically charged, every breath syncing to the rhythm of feet stamping, banners waving, the thunder of voices raised not for spectacle, but for each other.

Outside, the police gathered at the entrance, hoods drawn, radios hissing with clipped updates. The senior officer, a woman in her forties with the sort of no-nonsense jawline that brooked no insubordination, strode forward, boots echoing off the marble steps. Her eyes, narrowed beneath her cap, scanned the row of students pressed against the inside of the glass. She leaned into Tom, the admin, who blanched, clipboard wilting in his grip.

For a moment, time stretched. Rain hammered the windows, the only sound inside the low, urgent chant: "No art, no future!" It built, rolling up from the bellies of a hundred students who had lost their digital voice but found something rawer, more powerful in its place.

Ashley felt a hand grip theirs—Marnie's, knuckles white, resolve clear. Around them, faces were tense, some pale with real fear, others flushed with defiance or the delirium of being finally, indisputably seen. Even the first-years, so often sidelined in the social hierarchy of Red Rose, now stood front and centre, arms linked, heads high.

The officer rapped on the glass, mouth moving in words they couldn't hear, but the meaning was unmistakable. The doors shuddered. The crowd pressed tighter, unwilling to be split. From the back, someone banged a drum, the sound ragged but rallying, and another voice took up the refrain, echoing through the thick air.

Before anyone could say anything, Rowan McIntosh, a Glaswegian Drama student with a heavy Scots accent, stood up. "You can take our app, but you'll nevvvveeerrrr take our freeedommmm."

Ashley had to chuckle at the Braveheart energy, the whole crowd erupting into a fresh wave of laughter and applause, the tension momentarily breaking as the iconic line bounced off the cracked plaster and bare brick of the old theatre foyer. Even the nearest police officer, visible through the glass, allowed herself a brief, weary smile.

Ashley steadied his breathing, trying to focus not just on the swirl of faces and bodies but on the feeling beneath it—the pulse of something ancient, tribal, the sense of the Academy as more than walls and rules but a gathering place for the unruly, the odd, the unapologetically alive. The foyer thrummed with chants and the whine of the battered guitar, the air heavy with deodorant, hairspray, cold sweat, and, somewhere near the door, the sharp tang of chips smuggled in from the chippy up the road.

Outside, rain thickened, beating so hard against the glass that the police lights dissolved into streaks of blue and red, as if the building itself was bleeding protest into the street. The senior officer—a woman with cropped hair and eyes like polished slate—leaned in to Tom, lips moving in terse instructions, then stepped forward, rapping on the glass. She gestured for the doors to be opened.

Inside, the students only pressed closer together, their resolve a living, breathing barrier. Someone—a dance lad with his shirt off and a tie knotted round his brow—raised his arms and shouted, "They'll have to carry us out one by one!" The cry was taken up in flashes, bodies shifting, voices layering and rising.

On the wide, paint-chipped stairs, the dancers linked arms in a line, backs straight, chins up, as if bracing for the world's most perilous audition. Down on the marble, the drama students—Marnie, Ashley, Rowan, Tammy, and more—wove between knots of music students and techies, checking in, swapping news, passing bottles of water and emergency snacks. The younger first years clustered in a nervous huddle, eyes darting from the doors to the third years as if by watching they might learn how not to be afraid.

Marnie, wiping rain from her glasses, turned to Ashley. "We need a statement—something for the cameras, for Insta, for everyone outside. We can't just be a noise. We need to say what we're fighting for."

Tammy overheard and nodded, flipping open her battered notebook, biro poised. "Who wants to speak? We go live, right now, not after the police have their say. This is our story, not theirs."

There was a pause. In the crowd, Maria Kovacs stepped forward, her leotard streaked with biro and her hair in a wild knot. "We do it together. It's not just about apps or shagging or 'conduct'. It's about who we are. If they can silence us here, where's left? They want a catalogue, a prospectus—perfect, polished, dead. We're the real Academy. We don't disappear because someone flicks a switch."

Ashley, trembling but steady, took the phone from Tammy. "Livestream's up. Go."

They spoke, voice echoing in the hush. "This is Red Rose Academy. We're not leaving. We're not scared. We're students, artists, dancers, techs, musicians, queer, straight, broke, brilliant, here because we believe this place can be more than the rules. They can close apps, ban group chats, threaten us with police, but they can't delete who we are. We're not ashamed, we're not going to be made invisible, and if they want us out, they'll have to face us—not just as students but as a family."

The response was a roar, more than applause—foot-stomps, whistles, a collective animal sound that filled the foyer and rolled up through the atrium to the studios above. Outside, police flinched at the volume. Inside, students laughed and shouted, "Yes, Ash!" "You tell 'em!" "Red Rose forever!"

The music crashed up again—Tomás and a couple of brass students improvising over the chanting, making noise not just for the joy of it but to stake a claim: this was their territory. On the edge of the crowd, Lucy Grand and Aisha were livestreaming, narrating events to a swelling online audience. Comments pinged in, hearts and fire emojis pouring over the screen, the outside world leaning in for a taste of the chaos.

Near the doors, the admin officer Tom hesitated, eyes flicking between the police and the students, knowing he'd already lost any real authority. The police moved as a unit—two at the doors, more behind, ready to force a passage if given the order. But still they waited, a visible tension in their ranks; nobody wanted to be the first to drag a crying teenager out in front of the nation's cameras.

Sarah Smith, vaping furiously, sidled up to the line of dancers and hissed, "If they try to move you, just go limp.

Don't fight, don't argue. They want footage of us kicking off—don't give them what they want."

Darya, at her side, nodded, expression grim. "Solidarity. No one leaves alone."

Marnie and Ashley squeezed through to where Rowan and Justin were rallying the music students. "Keep playing," Marnie whispered. "Make them work for every second of quiet."

Justin flashed a grin. "You lot ever seen Les Mis? The bit at the barricade? I always wanted to play Enjolras."

"Shut up and sing," Ashley muttered, grinning despite the adrenaline gnawing at his stomach.

"Make us worthy, make us proud!" The tune rose from somewhere by the pit, thin and defiant, and others caught it, layering in harmonies and spoken lines, some sweet, some ragged. For a moment it was as though Red Rose itself was singing—a battered, bruised choir sending up a hymn of defiance to the rain-lashed city outside.

A pulse ran through the foyer, everyone shifting, linking arms, standing taller. Even those who'd come out of curiosity—foundation-year musicians, technical theatre students in blackout hoodies—felt themselves woven into the crowd. Here and there, faces flickered with panic, but the prevailing mood was stubborn solidarity, something that belonged to them and only them. A cluster of third-year ballet girls formed a defensive huddle by the stairs, eyeing the police through the glass, whispering reassurances to the trembling first years in their midst.

"We'll try to fit in with the crowd, but we are Red Rose," the assembled students sang, the refrain picked up raggedly at first, then stronger, swelling as more voices joined in—united in their chaos, stubbornness, and need to matter in a world suddenly set against them. The foyer became an echo chamber, not just for noise, but for years' worth of myth, humiliation, late-night courage, and wild, untidy love for the place they refused to see made dull and safe.

The song, the Theme to St Trinian's, echoed off the rafters, wild and jarring and heartfelt in equal measure. The St Trinian's theme—half joke, half anthem—rolled over the crowd, a hymn for delinquents and visionaries alike, and by the time they hit the chorus ("And if they complain, we'll do it all again, Defenders of anarchy..."), even some of the police could be seen shifting awkwardly, a few mouthing the words from the safety of the rain-spattered steps.

The chaos inside Red Rose Academy's foyer had taken on a strange, feral beauty. What had begun as nervous posturing—quick jokes, phone screens lifted in hopeful bravado—had now bloomed into a living, breathing tapestry of resistance. In the gloom and gold glow of the evening, banners appeared as if by magic, torn from the backs of drama classroom noticeboards and painted on with whatever had come to hand, be it lipstick, theatre blood, the stubby ends of highlighters. *"No Art, No Future." "We Are Red Rose." "Censorship is Death."* One in neon orange simply read, *"You Can't Expel Us All"*.

The students packed the marble lobby so tightly that the air itself seemed heavy with heat and adrenaline. At the epicentre, Ashley felt the mass of bodies thrumming—a pulsing, living force with a single stubborn heartbeat. Arms were looped around waists and shoulders; nervous hands clasped tight. Sweat, perfume, the acrid tang of spilled vodka and cheap deodorant mixed with the scent of Manchester drizzle that seeped in every time someone cracked a window. At the far side, Marnie was leading a group of foundation-year dancers in a half-serious, half-mocking "warmup" routine, their pliés and leaps threading movement through the static defiance.

"Look, they're still just standing there." Ashley's voice had become low, threadbare. The police outside had not advanced, but the weight of their presence pressed in on all sides. The blue strobes turned every face in the glass into a pale, flickering ghost.

"We have to hold," Marnie whispered back, her eyes fixed on the doors as if sheer willpower could keep the constables at bay. "That's all it is, Ash. Just hold."

Near the centre of the crowd, Tammy had transformed her battered notebook into a command centre. With quick, decisive strokes, she scribbled down the names of anyone willing to go on camera, coordinated a handover for the makeshift livestream—Lucy Grand's cracked iPhone and a borrowed power bank—and started up a rota for toilet runs and supplies. She'd somehow convinced two music tech students to set up a portable amp at the corner of the foyer, and now sound spilled out in waves: first the "St Trinian's" theme, then "God Save the Queen", then a mash-up of Madonna's "Like a Prayer" and a snatch of grime from a second-year composer with green hair and the air of a sleep-deprived fox.

Outside, the police had begun to form a cordon, their reflective jackets pooling the streetlights into gold and acid green. Senior staff flanked the main entrance, Hardcastle with his jaw set, a knot of admin officers nervously clutching sheaves of paper, security guards shifting from foot to foot. Across the city, on a hundred phone screens, Instagram Live feeds and WhatsApp status updates pulsed—each one a window into the riot brewing at the battered heart of Manchester's art scene.

Sarah, standing on a bench near the grand staircase, took a long, theatrical drag on her battered vape and let the vapour curl around her smile. "First one to get a selfie with a copper gets a bottle of Prosecco from my locker," she declared. A burst of laughter, wild and sharp, ricocheted across the crowd. For a moment the tension shimmered—dangerous, defiant, exhilarating.

Down by the doors, the standoff intensified. Police radios crackled, echoing through the glass. The senior officer, her face pale and set, conferred with Tom, the junior admin, whose clipboard now hung limp at his side. Tom's attempts at authority were drowned out by the students' chant—"No art, no future! No art, no future!"—each repetition gaining strength, the edges roughening into something close to a battle cry.

Ashley squeezed Marnie's hand, the two of them pressed shoulder-to-shoulder. "This is bigger than us, isn't it?" Ashley murmured, half to herself, half to Marnie and anyone else within reach. "It's not just about Red Rose anymore."

"No," Marnie said. "But it's us that have to start it."

A wave of movement swept through the foyer as word spread that the side fire exits had been chained shut. Irene, hair wild, ducked under a streamer of bunting and announced, "Security's locked down Studio Three, but the techies are already on it. If they cut the power, we'll just run the PA off battery packs. There's a stash of torches in the props cupboard and Marcin's got the keys to every electrical cupboard in the building."

Someone nearby—a wiry dance lad with glitter on his cheekbones—grinned, "If they try to smoke us out, we'll just start the end-of-term cabaret now. Anyone fancy a spontaneous strip number?"

The rain had turned the city into a haze of sodium glare and puddle-rippled streets, but inside the Red Rose foyer the heat was rising. The old building, usually so grand and aloof, now pulsed with a dense humidity born of sweat, anxiety, hairspray, and wet coats. It was the kind of pressure that made your skin fizz and your heart kick against your ribs. Somewhere between the battered posters and the echoing marble, the students had become more than a crowd: they were a single organism, twitching with anticipation, wild with adrenaline.

The arrival of the police outside lent the whole spectacle a twisted sense of legitimacy. For years, Red Rose had been a rumour, a punchline, a whispered legend on Manchester group chats—"That's where all the weirdos go," "Did you hear about their graduation party?" Now, as blue lights smeared the glass and officialdom bristled on the steps, it felt as though the world beyond had finally decided to take them seriously, if only to shut them down.

In the press of bodies, Ashley felt his pulse thumping in their ears. Every breath was thick with deodorant and nerves; every passing hand a potential comfort or warning. Marnie, beside them, craned to catch sight of the doors, her jaw set in a way that dared anyone to break the line. "We stick together," she repeated under her breath, more mantra than reassurance. "Nobody gets left behind."

The rain had turned the city into a haze of sodium glare and puddle-rippled streets, but inside the Red Rose foyer the heat was rising. The old building, usually so grand and aloof, now pulsed with a dense humidity born of sweat, anxiety, hairspray, and wet coats. It was the kind of pressure that made your skin fizz and your heart kick against your ribs. Somewhere between the battered posters and the echoing marble, the students had become more than a crowd: they were a single organism, twitching with anticipation, wild with adrenaline.

The arrival of the police outside lent the whole spectacle a twisted sense of legitimacy. For years, Red Rose had been a rumour, a punchline, a whispered legend on Manchester group chats—"That's where all the weirdos go," "Did you hear about their graduation party?" Now, as blue lights smeared the glass and officialdom bristled on the steps, it felt as though the world beyond had finally decided to take them seriously, if only to shut them down.

In the press of bodies, Ashley felt his pulse thumping in his ears. Every breath was thick with deodorant and nerves; every passing hand a potential comfort or warning. Marnie, beside them, craned to catch sight of the doors, her jaw set in a way that dared anyone to break the line. "We stick together," she repeated under her breath, more mantra than reassurance. "Nobody gets left behind."

****

CHAPTER 16 – Consequences of the Curtain Call...
Friday 15th November 2024

Expulsion. That was the final word Maria Kovacs heard from the mouth of Chancellor Hardcastle.

It was the end of the week, four long days since the riot, yet the fallout still clung to every corridor, every noticeboard, every silence in the battered old building. The word itself seemed to echo, lingering in the air of the Chancellor's office like the aftertaste of burnt toast—bitter, acrid, impossible to swallow.

The room, always over-warm, was oppressive with the low hum of cheap radiators and the scent of dust, toner, and that peculiar tang of old academic wool. Maria, coat still buttoned to her chin, stood tall in front of Hardcastle's desk. She wanted to look like she could leave at any second—untouchable, even as the ground shifted beneath her feet.

Hardcastle's eyes never quite met hers, always drifting to the window behind him, where Manchester's November drizzle traced slow, mournful rivers down the glass. "You must understand the gravity of this," he intoned, as if reading from a script he'd written for himself in an easier decade. "The press, the funding bodies, the Board... There's no way to paper over what you've done."

Maria's lips curled into a brittle smile. "If I'm the problem, at least it means you can stop pretending the place is perfect."

Hardcastle's mouth twitched. For a moment, she saw something behind his mask—fatigue, maybe even regret—but it vanished. "This is about consequences, Miss Kovacs. There are lines that cannot be crossed."

She wanted to laugh, but there was too much at stake. Instead, she folded her arms, willing her chin not to wobble. "There are lines you never noticed until we drew them in permanent marker."

He pressed on, brisk, efficient, almost relieved. "Your actions were visible, public, indefensible. You'll have until the end of today to clear your possessions. Security will be informed. There will be no appeals."

And then he looked away, already lost to another crisis, another name, another email. Maria turned and left, feeling each footstep sharpen as it echoed down the corridor—each one a punctuation mark at the end of something she could not yet name.

Outside the office, the world felt oddly muted. Rain beat a steady tattoo on the windows, softening the edges of the view. The admin block was always cold, always slightly damp, and Maria's boots squeaked against the worn blue carpet. She thought for a moment of running—bolting down the corridor, up the stairs, out onto the roof to shout her fury into the wind—but dignity was all she had left, and she would not give Hardcastle the satisfaction.

At the far end of the hall stood Mrs Cartwright, Red Rose's longest-serving administrator and, in some ways, its quiet conscience. She waited with a battered cardboard box and a look of quiet apology that stung far more than Hardcastle's scolding.

"Maria, love," she began, voice soft as lint, "he says I've got to escort you back. But I'll give you a bit of dignity—nobody needs an audience for this." She hesitated, lowering her voice. "It's not fair, but nothing's ever fair in this place, is it?"

Maria managed a half-smile. "I've survived worse than a cardboard box and a farewell tour. I'm just glad it's you and not one of the rent-a-cops."

Mrs Cartwright gave her a look full of secret understanding. "It won't be the same without you lot. None of this new crop's got your spark."

For a moment, Maria wanted to collapse into her arms, to cry and rage and demand to know what it had all been for. But she just nodded, hefted the box, and walked out—down the main stairs, past the laminated posters advertising Christmas panto auditions and a "wellbeing drop-in" that nobody ever attended.

She passed the foyer, now emptied of last week's chaos, its banners neatly folded and tucked away, as if hiding the evidence would erase the memory. The only traces left were the faint scuffs on the marble, a scrawled "NO ART NO FUTURE" in biro on the edge of the reception desk, and a ghostly echo in the hush.

Two first-year music students glanced up as she walked by, their conversation dying mid-whisper. She caught a snippet—"That's her, Maria Kovacs…"—before they dropped their gaze, suddenly fascinated by the amp cable they were untangling. Maria gave them a nod, part warning, part solidarity.

The corridors seemed to stretch and twist, warped by the tension of the week. She made her way through the warren of practice rooms and empty common spaces, passing a window where rain streaked the glass in grey waterfalls. The main quad outside was deserted save for a few stray crisp packets and a sodden copy of the *Guardian* that someone had abandoned on a bench. The theatre loomed at the far end, dark and silent, like a ship run aground in the drizzle.

At the entrance to the dancers' wing, Maria paused. The door to Studio 2 was propped open, letting out a sliver of heat and the faint, syncopated thud of a rehearsal playlist. For a moment, she considered walking on by—leaving quietly, with only Mrs Cartwright for company—but something pulled her inside.

The studio was foggy with condensation, the mirrors beaded with sweat and breath. Darya Ivanova was at the barre, her body angled in a stretch that betrayed the week's exhaustion and her own stubbornness. Her bun was half-collapsed, eyes rimmed in smudged mascara. Aisha, by the window, sat cross-legged, head bent over her phone, headphones looped round her neck, black kohl smudged at the corners of her eyes.

Darya looked up first, catching sight of the box in Maria's hands. She let go of the barre and strode across the room, her embrace fierce and unsparing, arms tight as wire around Maria's shoulders. Aisha, slower to move but no less certain, crossed the space and wrapped both girls up in her arms.

"So it's done?" Aisha asked, voice dull with fatigue.

Maria nodded, her own voice tight. "End of today. Apparently I'm poison."

Darya's lips twisted into a half-smile, all teeth and defiance. "If you're poison, we're all toxic. They'd have to clear out the whole school."

"Maybe they will," Maria muttered. "Make an example of us. A warning for the new intake."

"Are you scared?" Darya asked, forehead pressed to Maria's, her accent thickened by exhaustion.

"Not scared. Angry." Maria bit her lip, jaw set, forcing her eyes not to water.

Aisha patted the box, lips quirking. "You're not packing your room alone. If you start crying, someone's got to film it for the archives."

That was enough to make Maria snort, the sudden flare of laughter breaking the tension. The three of them walked together, out into the corridor and down the echoing halls toward the dorms.

The building, normally alive with the sounds of music and chatter, felt subdued. Doors were closed. The usual click and stomp of tap shoes, the stutter of scales from practice rooms, the bursts of laughter from the canteen—all had faded to a hush, as if the school itself were holding its breath.

318

They passed Tammy Knight sitting cross-legged on a window ledge, battered notebook open, phone propped on her knee. She was mid-text, but looked up as the group passed. "They got you too, then?" she asked, her tone brittle, eyes red.

Maria nodded. "How many?"

Tammy shrugged. "Ashley. Justin. Sarah, maybe. They're calling people in one by one, classic divide and conquer. Marnie's locked herself in the costume cupboard with a bottle of Echo Falls and says she won't come out until she's guaranteed immunity."

Darya rolled her eyes. "She'll suffocate in there before she gives up."

Aisha grinned. "She'd haunt the theatre for eternity, make a proper ghost of herself."

The banter felt forced, but it helped. They moved as a small knot, passing others in ones and twos—some offering quick hugs, others ducking their heads and slipping away, not wanting to be seen. Shame and solidarity mingled in every glance.

Maria's room was at the end of the third-floor corridor, above the quad. As she unlocked the door, the familiar scent of cheap hairspray, vanilla body mist and old rehearsal sweat greeted her. Her desk was littered with sheet music, overdue library books, and an ever-growing pile of unpaid canteen tabs.

She set the box on her bed. For a moment, she just stood there, letting the weight of it all settle into her bones.

Darya moved to the window, pulling back the curtain. "Looks like rain's never going to stop."

Aisha flopped onto the bed, immediately picking up a battered Red Rose hoodie and folding it, running her fingers over the embroidered logo, meticulous even in her irreverence, folded each garment with care that was almost ceremonial. "You want this for nostalgia or bonfire fuel?" she asked, holding the hoodie up.

Maria managed a wry grin. "Both. If I burn it, I'll just end up crying in the garden like last summer's leavers." The box was hardly big enough for the odds and ends she'd accumulated. She glanced at the stack of dog-eared sheet music—scraps from nearly every production since her first year. A lyric from a half-remembered show flickered at the edge of her mind, some nonsense about "never saying goodbye"—how she'd once mocked the sentiment as hopelessly twee. Now she wanted to pin it on the wall and scream at it until it meant something.

Darya, quick with her hands and quicker with her judgements, started collecting Maria's scattered possessions. She found an old pair of ballet slippers stuffed behind the radiator, battered beyond recognition. "Still can't believe you wore these for that Carmen rehearsal," she said, half to herself. "The elastic's held together by hope and cheap hairspray."

"That's what they'll write on my gravestone," Maria replied, fighting the urge to sit down and never get up again. "She persisted. By hope, and the fumes from Sally's spray bottle."

Aisha, unamused by sentiment, was rooting through the pile of books. "Are you taking *all* of these out or returning them to the library like a model citizen?" She dangled a battered volume of Lorca plays by the spine, one corner dog-eared to mark a scene about burning down the house.

Maria laughed despite herself. "If they're desperate, let them fine me. I'm not about to make the librarians work overtime for Hardcastle's moral crusade." She stopped, caught by the realisation that she was already talking as if she'd left.

There was a strange numbness to the afternoon. The corridors, usually echoing with the thrumming, irrepressible pulse of student life, had been muffled by a collective anxiety. Every door she passed on her way up to the dorms had been closed; every glance, even from the most boisterous of first years, was fleeting, apologetic, and edged with dread. There was a sense of being watched—not by authority, but by history. The knowledge that after this week, nothing would be the same.

"I'm all out of faith, this is how I feel, I'm cold and I am shamed, lying naked on the floor..." the radio in the room, which Maria had left on all week in the hope that music might drown out anxiety, was now crooning Natalie Imbruglia's "Torn"—the lyrics achingly, comically on the nose. Maria let the chorus wash over her, at once cliché and heartbreak. Darya, who never missed a cue, picked up the battered remote and flicked the volume down to a murmur.

Maria sat on the edge of her bed, the battered cardboard box between her knees, her fingers absently tracing the battered logo on its side. The hum of the radiators seemed to fade behind the slow, heavy drumming of rain on the windowpane. Her world, usually so saturated with colour and noise, was muted to shades of grey and the low, ghostly echoes of memory. She watched as Darya methodically emptied her wardrobe, plucking costumes and leotards from hangers with a briskness that barely concealed her trembling hands.

Aisha moved through the room in her own orbit, scooping up Maria's collection of sheet music, postcards, and yellowed programmes from old Red Rose productions. She paused occasionally to read a scribbled note on a prop script, or to flick through photos—group shots from the first-year showcase, backstage selfies, candid captures from drunken afterparties, arms thrown around each other in triumphant, sweaty camaraderie.

Maria took each object from her friends and packed them in silence, turning over trinkets as if seeing them for the first time. A cracked compact mirror, covered in rhinestones and dried mascara. The faded ticket stub from a Royal Exchange show, scavenged during her first week. The *"No Art, No Future"* badge, still streaked with face paint from the riot. Each relic was a metronome marking time in a world now out of sync.

She ran her hands along the bookshelf, plucking out battered plays—Chekhov, Churchill, Kane, Lorca—each annotated in the margins with cryptic, obscene, or simply exhausted notes. She hesitated at the spine of *Three Sisters*, finger hovering over the page marked with a post-it: "*MOSCOW OR BUST.*" Darya saw the pause and squeezed her shoulder, silent but fierce.

Aisha, never one to shy from the unsentimental, grinned. "If you take all this with you, it'll weigh more than you do." But even she was gentler than usual, folding Maria's favourite rehearsal hoodie and slipping it into the box with a care she'd never show her own belongings.

Maria's gaze lingered on the Polaroid tacked above her bed: the three of them, arms looped round each other's shoulders, paint and glitter streaking their faces, grinning like bandits after the spring cabaret. She peeled it from the wall and tucked it into the front pocket of her jacket, the gesture a talisman against what came next.

"You know Marnie's already gone?" Aisha said with a sigh. "Her sister, Jess, was here while you were with Hardcastle."

Maria did not cry. The impulse came and went in waves, crashing against her pride and the prickly sense of unreality that had wrapped itself around her since Hardcastle's verdict. Expulsion: it sounded final, dramatic, almost glamorous—until you realised it meant cardboard boxes, damp stairwells, and saying goodbye to a world that, for three wild, wasted, dazzling years, had been the centre of your universe.

Darya moved with an energy that betrayed her nerves, snatching Maria's costumes from hooks, folding leggings and threadbare dance socks with more care than she'd ever shown her own clothes. She was muttering half in Russian, half in English—a running commentary on the unfairness of it all, the stupidity of Red Rose management, and the idiocy of first years who "wouldn't know real risk if it bit them on the arse." Every so often she'd pause, fists clenched, as if she wanted to hurl something at the wall, then quietly slip another memento into the box instead.

Aisha, pragmatic as always, took charge of the books and scripts. She was ruthless—old show notes, last year's call sheets, doodles from "Cabaret" rehearsals, all went into the recycling with a surgeon's calm. But she handled the treasures—the battered prompt book from "Three Sisters," a postcard signed by every cast member of "Sweeney Todd," the theatre keys Maria had forgotten to return after a late-night tech—like sacred relics, wrapping them in old tights for protection.

Maria, meanwhile, floated between the two, clutching objects as if each were the last link to a world she hadn't finished with yet. She hesitated over everything: the mug scrawled with "Kiss Me, I'm Choreography," the rose quartz heart from last Valentine's, a set of enamel pins shaped like pointe shoes, the faded script from her first ever Red Rose audition, pages now heavy with scrawled notes and in-jokes from an era when she was still just "the new girl with the dodgy Salford accent."

The rhythm of packing, the banter, the pauses for memory and mockery, settled around them like a ritual. Outside, rain hammered against the window. The quad, visible between the streaming rivulets, was empty, every sodden flagstone bearing silent witness to the drama that had exploded there less than a week before.

The pace of the afternoon slowed to a crawl. There was something faintly sacramental in the way Maria, Darya, and Aisha worked—each item handled like a talisman, every corner of the cramped room invested with memory and sweat and stories only they would understand.

Somewhere down the hall, a piano faltered through the opening bars of "Your Song"—one of the jazz students, Maria guessed, always prone to mournful Elton John covers when things got tense. The music bled faintly through the wall, lending the moment a cinematic edge Maria would have mocked if it didn't so perfectly fit her mood.

Aisha, half-buried in the pile by the desk, surfaced with a stack of scripts, some tied with fraying ribbons, others loose and bristling with post-it notes and doodles.

"You keeping this one?" she asked, waving a coffee-stained copy of *Angels in America*, its spine cracked, corners softened by years of anxious flipping.

Maria hesitated, then nodded. "That one's seen more tears than the GUM clinic waiting room."

Darya snorted. "That's not hard, considering the Tuesday queue."

Even Maria managed a laugh, brittle but real.

She turned to the wardrobe next, rifling through hangers heavy with costumes: a thrift-shop tuxedo from the infamous gender-bent *Hamlet*; a patchwork catsuit hand-stitched for last spring's devised piece about Manchester nightlife; a dress still faintly scented with rosewater and stage blood from a "modern" *Macbeth* that had nearly got the lot of them banned from the city council's youth showcase.

Maria ran her hand along the sleeve, feeling the tackiness of fake blood dried into the weave, and remembered the rush of standing centre stage, heart hammering, eyes locked with the audience. She wondered—would she ever feel that again?

Darya, reading her thoughts, said softly, "You will. You're too bloody stubborn not to. You know they'll regret this. Red Rose is nothing without people like you."

Maria shrugged. "They'll fill the place with new faces. Give them another scandal in six months."

Aisha dealt a new hand. "Doesn't matter. We'll still be us. You'll still be you."

A silence, softer this time.

"Promise me we won't lose touch," Maria said. "Not now."

Darya grinned. "You'll be sick of me by Christmas. I'm crashing on your sofa for New Year."

Aisha smirked. "Don't threaten me with a good time."

They laughed, and for the first time since the Chancellor's office, Maria felt the knot in her chest loosen.

The packing took on the rhythm of a funeral—slower, more methodical, the jokes trailing off until silence pooled around them. Outside, the corridor felt haunted:

every few minutes, someone would creep past, pausing just long enough to register the open door and the shambles within, then hurry away, as if Maria's fate might be contagious.

Occasionally, a familiar face appeared—a first-year dancer Maria had once helped with an audition piece, a third-year music student who'd once kissed her in the stairwell during Freshers' Week, a foundation drama girl whose name she'd never known but who always smiled in the canteen. Each lingered for a moment in the doorway, muttered a quick "good luck" or "we'll miss you," and vanished. Some brought gifts—half a pack of Silk Cut, a plastic tiara rescued from last year's panto, a bag of Sainsbury's Jelly Babies, the packet torn open and already half-empty. One by one, Maria's last days at Red Rose became a parade of tiny offerings—half comfort, half apology.

The only ones who truly lingered were her friends. Darya and Aisha worked with an unspoken urgency, determined to make the leaving as bearable as possible, though Maria could see the cracks forming behind their bravado. Tammy drifted in for a while, reading a draft of her latest "manifesto" aloud in a sardonic monotone until the room dissolved in snorts and groans. Even Justin sloped in, arms folded, his battered trainers leaving faint muddy prints on the carpet.

He said nothing at first, just picked at a loose thread on Maria's suitcase, his brow furrowed. Then, voice raw and unsteady, he blurted, "They're saying I'm next. For… you know. Instigating, they said. Organising." He shrugged, a gesture that tried to be casual but failed. "I told them to fuck off, obviously."

Maria put a hand on his arm. "Don't let them grind you down. They need someone to blame—it's easier than fixing anything."

He gave a hollow laugh. "They can try. I'll make them work for it." He lingered by the door for a while, eyes fixed on the window, before slipping out with a muttered, "You know my flat is fully owned, not one of Red Roses, so… if you want to join me there and we can stay together, considering we're dating… on/off dating that is…"

Maria had to chuckle at Justin's sheepish bravado. "I mean—just saying. I've got a sofa, at least. Two, if you count the one in the kitchen." He rubbed the back of his neck, eyes darting to Darya, then to Aisha, as if searching for permission or forgiveness or some way out of his own embarrassment.

Maria, for her part, found the moment oddly grounding. "Is this your pitch, Harrison? 'Get expelled, come live in my questionable student flat, limited heating but excellent Wi-Fi, guaranteed mice'?"

He grinned—properly, finally, like himself for the first time all afternoon. "You forgot: fridge full of Sainsbury's reduced section and at least four unfinished bottles of Echo Falls."

Darya scoffed. "Sounds like a fucking paradise compared to the halls."

The laughter, once released, was infectious. Even Aisha allowed herself a rare giggle. For a flicker of a moment, the room felt like itself again—crowded, ridiculous, more alive than it had any right to be.

****

Books by Thomas Brant

Broadcasting Boundaries

BROADCASTING BOUNDARIES
BROADCASTING CHAOS
BROADCASTING DISRUPTION

Fallen

IRELAND IS DOWN

PanEuro

STICK AND LIPSTICK
SPRINTER OF THE SKIES

The Manic Collective Candidate

THE MANIC COLLECTIVE CANDIDATE

The Wirral Gal

IN SPEKE
NOW A MAM

Other Shared Universe Novels

THE BROOKES BABES
THE DAY THE QUEEN DIED
VIXEN
RED ROSE ACADEMY